Counterspell:
the Second Law

Volume 2 of the Counterspell Chronicle

Robert C.A. Goff
and
Micah M.A. Goff

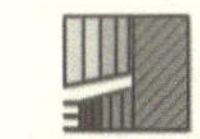

Dreamsplice
Christiansburg, Virginia

This book is a work of fiction. The wording for the excommunication narrative within the story was, sadly, inspired by the actual excommunication document, the *Herem*, directed at the philosopher, Spinoza, by his own community in Amsterdam on July 27, 1656. (The *Herem* was translated from the original Ladino Spanish and published by Dan Levin in his biography, *Spinoza: the Young Thinker who Destroyed the Past*, Weybright and Talley, New York, 1970, pp 262-3.) Appendix 1 is adapted from Wilder, R.L: *The Axiomatic Method* (in Newman, J.R. (ed.): *The World of Mathematics*, Simon and Schuster, New York, 1956, pp 1647-67.)

Counterspell: the Second Law

Dreamsplice
3462 Dairy Road
Christiansburg, VA 24073

www.dreamsplice.com/books

ISBN-13: 978-0-9761559-1-1
ISBN-10: 0-9761559-1-5
Library of Congress Control Number: 2019901918
First Edition: May 2019

For Donald Edwin Goff, who sparked a flame, leaving me with a lifelong love of books.

RCAG

This book is dedicated to someone who will never read it. Thank you for your inspiration, Terry.

MMAG

The Counterspell Chronicle:
Counterspell: Guardian of the Ruins
Counterspell: The Second Law
Counterspell: Age of Fools (upcoming)

also from the world of Counterspell:
Ternaria: Legacy of a Careless Age

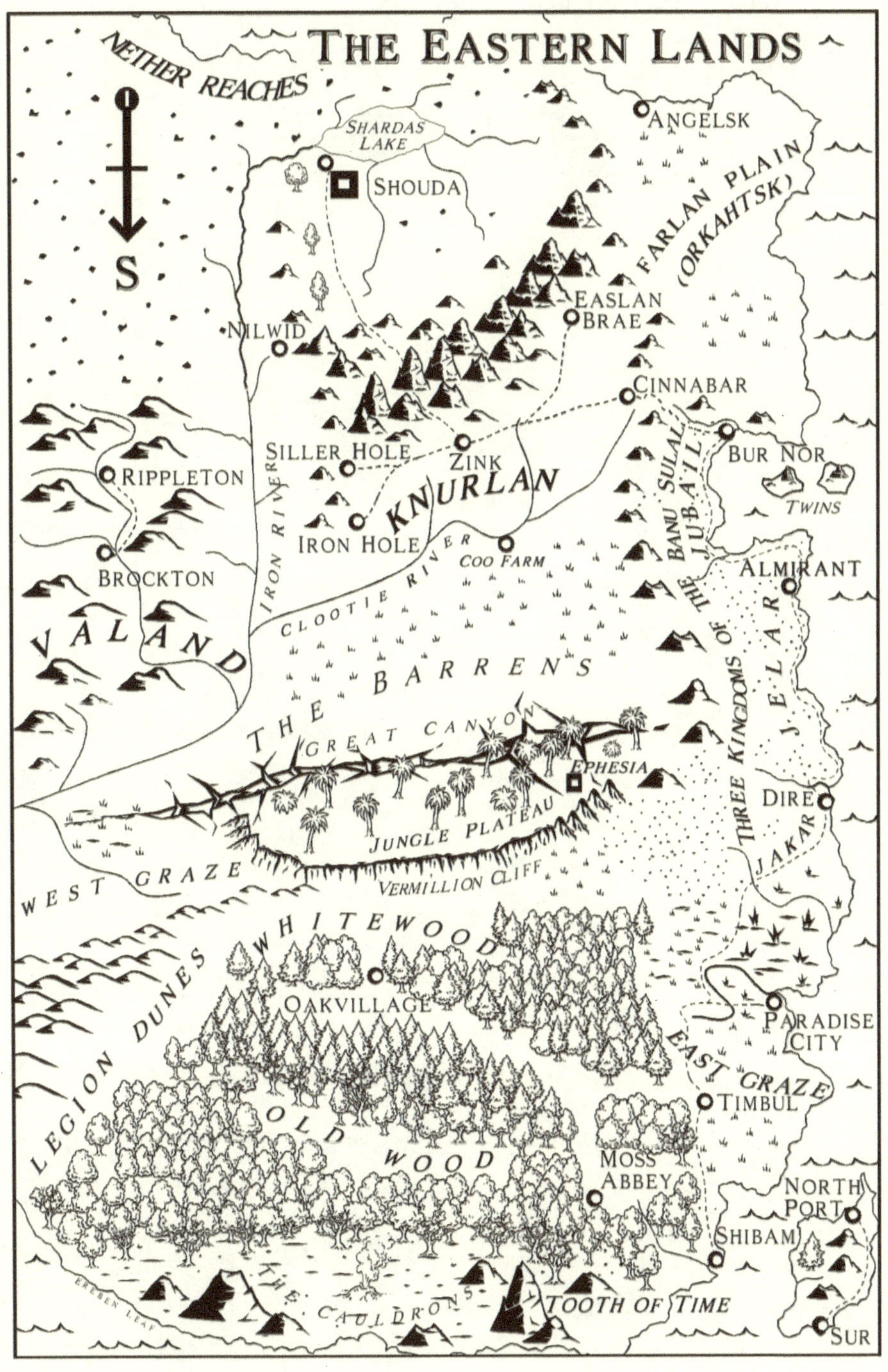
THE EASTERN LANDS
NETHER REACHES
S
SHARDAS LAKE
SHOUDA
ANGELSK
FARLAN PLAIN (ORKAHTSK)
EASLAN BRAE
NILWID
CINNABAR
SILLER HOLE
ZINK
BUR NOR
TWINS
RIPPLETON
KNURLAN
IRON RIVER
BANU SULAL
THE JUBA'IL
IRON HOLE
COO FARM
BROCKTON
ALMIRANT
CLOOTIE RIVER
VALAND
THE BARRENS
THREE KINGDOMS OF
JELAR
GREAT CANYON
EPHESIA
DIRE
JUNGLE PLATEAU
JAKAR
WEST GRAZE
VERMILLION CLIFF
WHITEWOOD
LEGION DUNES
OAKVILLAGE
PARADISE CITY
EAST GRAZE
TIMBUL
OLD WOOD
MOSS ABBEY
NORTH PORT
SHIBAM
THE CAULDRONS
TOOTH OF TIME
SUR

In less than half a year, The Redeemer and his disciples rose from obscurity to near absolute control of the eastern lands. Centuries of peaceful relations among the races of man were swept away in the reign of religious terror which ensued.

Ereben Leaf: Chronicle of the Counterspell

"The priests appear to be heaping branches around each of them," Minkar Jarad observed.

Ereben Leaf closed his eyes at the thought of what he was about to witness. He had heard rumors that heretics were being burned alive, but he had not expected the well armed Dwarfs of Zink to allow such a thing without a fight. He looked down into the market square again. His view from the earthen wall of the city made it difficult to recognize the thirty Dwarfs tied to posts. One, he thought, was the Baillie of Zink. Several others seemed to wear the uniform of the Baillie's guards.

"Is there nothing we can do?" Minkar asked. The words of the brown Shouda warrior were filled with sadness.

"No more than all of them," Ereben answered, indicating the hundreds of Dwarfs standing about the market square in cowed silence. "If the Baillie had fought the Knights instead of trying to appease them, this wouldn't be happening." The Knights of the Redeemer, Ereben had decided, were nothing more than opportunistic thugs. They surely would have avoided the walled city if there had been any chance of a battle.

"May Elloh forgive me," Minkar whispered, "for not lifting my spear against this."

The great mounds of twigs were set afire. Frightful screams rose from the market square. Ereben could not watch. He turned his backside to the wall and skidded down the long, grassy embankment, then up over the outer wall of the dry moat.

Barrow stood waiting at the bottom. "We hed better move oursels away from the city," the Dwarf said. Barrow leaned on the handle of his great, golden battle-ax as he watched Minkar follow Ereben down from the earthen wall.

"It's true," Ereben said to the Dwarf. "They burned them all alive."

"Aye, lad," Barrow replied, "I was telt as much by a farmer escapin' tae the norlan brae. I couldna find the courage tae climb the wall and watch. He said that the Baillie was one o' those tae be burnt, the poor bastard."

"I think I saw him there," Ereben continued, "and some of his guards."

As Minkar reached the base of the wall, he ran toward them, urgently waving an arm. "I believe one of the knights has seen me. Four of them are climbing the inside of the wall in this direction."

They ran to the cover of the heather mounds, then wove their way along a game trail to the gully where Jasper waited with the kelpies and two Dwarf ponies. Ereben had decided it would be safer if they were seen on natural appearing mounts rather than the giant birds. Four ponies would have been ideal, but Dwarf ponies were so small that Ereben's feet dragged the ground. For Minkar, keeping his knees off the ground would have been difficult. At least full size horses had become a more common sight in Knurlan since the Knights of the Redeemer had gained the upper hand. Although the kelpies, Dantel and Kehlibar, were sometimes difficult to control, in their current form as horses, they appeared to be natural so long as they were not coaxed to sprout their wings and lift into the air.

"What did you find out?" Jasper asked.

"It's true," Ereben answered. "They're burning heretics."

"It'll be us they burn, if we stand around tradin' stories." The Dwarf climbed onto his pony and tied his ax to the rear of the saddle.

Ereben hoisted himself onto the broad shoulders of Kehlibar. As Jasper mounted the other pony with the aid of his carved wooden staff, it was plain from the expression on his face that the boy would have preferred to ride "his" kelpie, Dantel. Minkar, for his part, was not happy riding a river demon, but had agreed to it with the understanding that the arrangement was temporary. They headed south at a deliberately innocent pace. Ereben hoped that they appeared as simple travelers, even though Minkar's dark brown skin, pointed ears and extraordinary height raised eyebrows wherever they went, especially here, in the Dwarf land of Knurlan.

Gentle ripples on the Clootie River cast sparkles of late day sun into Phaena's eyes. Her golden hair danced in the breeze of early summer. Ereben longed to reach out and touch her cheek, kiss her lips. But she had built a wall about herself. She seemed to desire his company, but not his affection. Since the death of her infamous father, Lord Corban, High Protector of Dragomin, she had been transformed from heiress of privilege to loathsome criminal. She still expressed confusion about her father's aims and his posthumous disgrace. Now, all Ereben could offer was his steadfast love. He was grateful to the dragons for sparing him the responsibility for Corban's death.

"Where did the dragons go?" Phaena asked.

"Some people say they flew north, to the Nether Reaches," Ereben answered, "but I don't think anybody knows for sure."

"Do you think they'll come back?"

He knew they would, eventually. "I hope not. Yarnish is trying to find out what's happening with them." The tinker, Yarnish Blen, had left them two weeks earlier for Valand. Barrow had suggested the trip, since Blen was not known to the priests of the True Faith, and most of Corban's Protectors, those few that had survived the recent spate of burnings, were in hiding and not likely to cause Blen any problems. "Barrow says that it might not be safe here for much longer. He's heard that Crotus is nearly beside himself over not being able to find us."

"I'd like to go somewhere else," she said. "Living on a cow farm in the middle of nowhere gets pretty boring."

"But nowhere is about the only place we can hide. The priests and those Knights of the Redeemer are crawling all over the cities and towns. Where else could we go?" He didn't care what Phaena's answer would be, transfixed as he was by the subtle, pouting movements of her lips.

"Oh, Ereben. Anywhere else. The mountains or the forests or the sea coast. Just somewhere with something to look at besides grass and cows. Somewhere that we could fly without worrying about priests and religion."

"I don't know too many places where a bird five yards high wouldn't cause a little curiosity." A scent of wildflowers wafted from Phaena's hair, distracting his logic. "Or winged horses."

Phaena smiled. He loved to see her smile. It reminded him of the days so long ago when their lives were predictable and peaceful. Since the death of his family at the hands of the Protectors, everything had become more complex, more dangerous. Just surviving required concerted planning and constant vigilance.

Minkar Jarad's five year old son, Bahsa, wandered toward them from Liddie Burn's mound house. The handsome Shouda boy seemed to grow taller by the week. Since witnessing his mother's death in the Shouda massacre, he had not spoken. Bahsa seated himself in the space between Ereben and Phaena, and leaned his head against Phaena's shoulder. She stroked his tight, black hair and kissed him on the forehead, playfully pinching the points of his ears. Ereben considered how normal the dark brown skin of the Shouda seemed to him now. Before his flight from Rippleton and beyond the borders of Valand, he had never even heard of people with brown skin.

"You are so handsome," Phaena said to the boy, "and you're getting so tall. In another year, you'll be taller than Jasper."

Bahsa smiled and took her hand. When he looked at Ereben, his smile seemed to reveal a satisfaction at being able to hold the hand that Ereben could not hold. Ereben found the boy's manner and behavior much more engaging than he would have expected from a five year old. He remembered Minkar's endless stories about Bahsa filling the arduous journey through the Broken Mountains.

"Did you do your letters?" Phaena asked the boy. Phaena had been teaching him to read and write.

Bahsa squirmed a bit, then shook his head.

"You have to have them done before dinner, or no sweet bun for you."

The boy's demeanor assumed one of consummate hardship, as he stood and headed back to the house. Ereben found it hard to understand why Bahsa would not talk. He listened well, and expressed his thoughts well without words. It seemed as though it would be a simple thing for him to just talk. But he didn't. Minkar had tried all sorts of incentives and tricks to get him to say even one word, but to no avail.

"Ereben," Phaena asked, "when are you going to do that spell thing with the dagger?"

"Pretty soon, I think."

"Do you really believe your grandfather is in there? I mean alive?"

"Yes."

"That's all so strange."

"It's... It's strange and scary. The ice leopard that came out of it looked different than before."

"What do you mean?"

"It was old and feeble, like Grandfather. And its fur was all white and brittle, like Grandfather's hair. The leopard's eyes were tired and kind of cloudy. And... it had no tail."

"Ereben! You mean your grandfather might have a tail?"

"I don't know. But I'm pretty sure he'll be different. I'm not sure that bringing him out is the right thing to do."

"And you're going to do it anyway? Maybe he wanted to go into the dagger and stay there."

"When he went into the dagger, it caused something like a fire ball. I saw a burned body, but it was someone else. That means that somebody else was there. It was probably one of the Protectors trying to steal both of the daggers—Grandfather's and mine. So I think Grandfather went into the dagger to escape, and to keep them from getting both daggers. It seems like he would want to come back out."

"I hope you're right, Ereben Leaf."

At dawn, Ereben sat alone in the misty paddock beside Liddie's mound house. He had stacked three large sacks of potatoes on the ground two yards away from where he sat. The blade of his dagger stood embedded in the upper sack. In his left hand, he held munu, the praying hands mushroom, which would supply the power for the spell. The potatoes, he hoped, would channel the counterspell. Ereben's right hand gripped Hobart's dagger to focus the casting of the evocation.

Both hands trembled at the thought of what he was about to do. If he failed, then his grandfather, Chrysanthus, Guardian of the Ruins, would be lost forever. If he succeeded, his grandfather might emerge with unspeakable deformities. But Chrysanthus must have learned more about the dragons than either Hobart or Ailantha knew. Hobart was now merged with the rock of the great canyon, and Ailantha was probably dead. And his own inadequate understanding of all of this left him with no choice but to try to release his grandfather from imprisonment within the forged layers of steel.

"Oh, Grandpa, I hope I'm doing the right thing."

"Are you going to do it now?" The sound of Jasper's voice startled him.

"Yes."

"Why so early?" As usual, the eleven-year-old's sandy brown hair stood out in several directions above his dirt smudged face. He carried his carved wooden staff, attempting to twirl it in one hand the way Minkar twirled a Shouda spear. "Nobody's up yet." The staff fell. Jasper retrieved it with a forlorn sigh.

"I couldn't sleep last night," Ereben answered, "so I decided to do it now." He had hoped to be alone. That thought seemed so silly when he considered the tens of thousands of priests and Protectors surrounding him the last time he had tried, during the Battle of the Black Pyramid.

"Can I watch?"

"Well... I suppose so."

"Is your grandfather real old?"

"He was when he went into the dagger."

"Does he like kids?"

"If you're going to watch, you'll have to be quiet."

"Sorry."

Ereben took a deep breath and silently reviewed the details of the evocation. Ailantha had spent only that one night teaching it to him, but he had turned it over in his mind a dozen times a day for the past five months. He knew what she had taught him, but he was not certain that it was the correct evocation for what he needed to do. The scant discussion on evocations he was able to decipher from his paltry library of magic only added to his uncertainty. While he continued to have difficulty translating the ancient Shadae, in which many of the materials were written, he was convinced that they dealt with other, unrelated subjects. He had to admit to himself that one of his motivations for releasing Chrysanthus was that he felt incompetent. *I'm the last Guardian of the Ruins, and I don't know any magic!*

"How long does it take," Jasper whispered. "Sorry." Jasper placed his fingers over his lips.

Ereben returned his attention to the dagger perched atop the sacks of potatoes. An unsettling thought crossed his mind. *What if Grandpa doesn't recognize me? What if he's changed so much that he attacks me?* He laid Hobart's dagger on the ground and drew the third dagger from his belt, the dagger Corban had used to kill the ice leopard. Hobart had said that three of the daggers placed in a certain arrangement would create a field of power. It was just such an arrangement which had opened the portal in the face of the black pyramid. Ereben envisioned the distances between the daggers when they had been inserted into the slots of the portal. *About two yards.* He stabbed the third dagger into the dirt on the far side of Jasper, then seated himself again, equidistant from the two daggers. When he lifted Hobart's dagger again, he sensed a thrumming of power within it. Waving the dagger slowly through the air, he was able to feel a point of consonance, a point at which the three daggers seemed to be attuned. The handles of all three daggers glowed softly. His heart raced. He knew that he was tampering with powers which he did not understand—powers that could change the attunement of nature, that could consume him in an instant.

"Ereben?" Jasper whispered

"Shhh."

"Ereben," Jasper persisted, "look at my staff."

Without moving Hobart's dagger, Ereben turned his head toward Jasper. The munu, the praying hands mushroom Jasper had carved at the head of his staff so many months ago glowed a soft red, pulsing subtly with the palpable thrum of the power field. Its carved menagerie, which spiraled from one end of the staff to the other, seemed alive. The animals and birds and fish remained in their assigned places, but each of them moved a head or legs or fins. Jasper held it by the smoothly carved grip above its center. The boy's hand trembled. His eyes stared wildly. As the red glow of the carved mushroom extended down the staff toward his hand, he released it, allowing the staff to tip into the triangle marked out by the three daggers. The head of the staff came to rest at the center of the triangle. By then, the entire wooden staff glowed red. Jasper sat immobile.

Ereben sensed power and control resonating within his body. It did not flow from the munu gripped within his left hand. It echoed in harmonious play with all that surrounded him. His vision grasped a gossamer connectedness that reached from dagger to dagger and from within himself to all things. His ears heard the melodies which played from fair to foul and back again. The odors of growth and decay swirled about one another as opposite poles of the same message. Sour and bitter, sweet and salt extended as dimensions of a solitary sensation. In an instant, he understood that all things were connected—that the daggers and potatoes and the earth itself were all expressions of the same substance. Everything was connected by resonant strands to everything else. He recalled his journey within the rock of the great canyon. He knew the weave of matter through time. Tendrils of each connection reached into the past and into the future. It was those connections, those relationships that he wished to alter. With their dependencies and paths now visible, Ereben understood what he must change and what he must not change. He stepped his mind through the evocation of releasing, confident that he would succeed.

Within the triangle of daggers, a mist of matter began to condense. As it grew more solid and opaque, the sacks of potatoes sagged. Ereben's dagger descended toward the ground as the sacks collapsed. When the figure within the triangle had become completely substantial, Ereben moved Hobart's dagger beyond the point of attunement. The field of power subsided.

Jasper gasped. In front of them stood a man without clothing. His skin was covered in short white fur, stippled with ghostly spots. About his head flowed white hair and a full white beard. Little white tufts rose from the tops of slightly pointed ears. He blinked. A feline quality about his green eyes revealed confusion and caution. Massive muscles rippled beneath the surface of his chest and arms. From each finger grew a dark, metallic claw. Ereben's eyes followed sleek, powerful legs to fur covered feet. Most remarkable of all was a leopard tail swishing nervously behind.

Ereben looked at the unmistakable face of this leopard-man. "Grandpa?" He asked, tentatively.

The man opened his mouth as if to speak. White leopard's teeth glistened in the light of dawn.

ஒ

Friendship is a jewel claimed by many but deserved by few.

Ereben Leaf: Chronicle of the Counterspell

The leopard man raised his clawed hands and flexed his fingers, examining his claws with apparent curiosity. Each muscle of his forearms rippled independently with the movement of each finger. His massive chest expanded with a great breath. He returned his attention to Ereben and Jasper, staring at each of them with expressionless eyes. After a long, silent moment, he turned and took up the dagger which lay on the empty potato sack. Ereben knew that the displacement of that dagger would prevent him from reestablishing a field of power. The leopard man then lifted Jasper's staff from the ground and held it out to Jasper. Jasper stared with wonder.

"I think he wants you to take it," Ereben said softly.

"Thank you," Jasper whispered, as he accepted his staff.

The leopard man held up Ereben's dagger and flicked one claw in the tiny notch at the base of its blade. He turned the dagger and offered its handle.

Ereben took the dagger. "It is you, Grandpa."

Chrysanthus reached out and touched Ereben's cheek with the back of a clawed hand. Ereben's first impulse was to throw his arms around his grandfather, but he hesitated at the sight of the fur-covered, unclothed body. Chrysanthus looked down at himself. He turned away, retrieved the third dagger, then made four slits into one of the empty potato sacks, converting it to a crude tunic. After pulling it over his head, Chrysanthus' muscular body was covered from shoulder to knees. He crouched on his haunches and looked about at the cloudless sky and the grassy plains surrounding Liddie Burn's cow farm. As he shuffled his furry feet to balance himself, metallic claws extended and retracted.

Jasper leaned toward Chrysanthus. "Can you talk?"

Chrysanthus stared at the boy for a moment, then lifted a twig from the ground. Grasping it with both hands, he snapped it in two and tossed the pieces in opposite directions.

"It's broken? I don't think he can talk, Ereben."

"I know."

"Do you think he can understand us?"

"Yes." Ereben was lost in a storm of emotion. He felt so happy to see his grandfather, but was smitten by the result of this act of magic. He wanted to tell Chrysanthus all the things that had happened since he last saw him, but somehow he knew that Chrysanthus was already aware of everything that occurred in the presence of the dagger that had imprisoned him. *Is there a way to put him back to normal?* He knew the answer. For Chrysanthus now, this was normal. It was the attunement of nature that had changed. His grandfather was now stable within that attunement.

Ereben looked at his own dagger. Its translucent stone handle was green once again. What had been green stippling while Chrysanthus was within the dagger had now changed to white stipples. Lamination lines within the steel of the blade were less distorted than before. At the contact between the blade and the guard, a soft crusty material had accumulated.

"You greet the sun early," Minkar Jarad called from the mound house. Minkar's approach to Ereben slowed noticeably as Chrysanthus stood from his crouch. The nearer Minkar came, the wider his eyes grew. He placed a hand on Ereben's shoulder. "What has the will of Elloh brought us?"

Chrysanthus extended his arms with the palms of his clawed hands held upward. He bowed deeply. After some hesitation, Minkar responded to the Shouda bow.

"Minkar," Ereben said, "this is Chrysanthus... my grandfather."

"He can't talk," Jasper added. "He's sort of like Bahsa."

Minkar looked at Ereben and back to Chrysanthus, apparently uncertain of the danger of the present circumstance. Chrysanthus grasped his jute tunic and tugged at it.

"You want some clothes?" Jasper asked.

Chrysanthus motioned to Jasper with one hand, then pulled at the lower edge of the jute. His leopard tail swished into view.

"Liddie can make you some clothes," Jasper offered.

"Grandpa," Ereben said, "I didn't know what else to do. I didn't think you wanted to stay inside the dagger. But after I saw the leopard, I knew that you would be... changed."

Chrysanthus motioned toward the mound house, then encouraged them toward the door.

"Liddie and Barrow will sure be surprised," Jasper said as they entered.

Barrow sat before the hearth. When he looked up, a smile spread across his face. "I see ye've got yersel in quite the fix, auld friend." He stood and threw his arms about Chrysanthus. Barrow examined one of Chrysanthus' clawed hands. "Ye're nae as handsome as ye were," he said, shaking his head, "but ye appear tae be a tiny, wee bit stronger." The Dwarf stared up into Chrysanthus' face. "Wha's the matter? Cat got yer tongue?"

"He can't talk," Jasper explained.

Barrow looked up again with a sorrowful expression. "There must be a way tae fix it."

Chrysanthus shrugged.

"Gae ootside if ye want tae jabber at this hour," Liddie called from the sleeping chamber.

"Liddie, sweet," Barrow replied, "Come oot an' greet an auld friend."

As Liddie Burn emerged from the chamber wearing a rumpled sleeping gown, she gasped in surprise. "Chrysanthus?"

Chrysanthus grasped his tail in one hand and sheepishly held it out for Liddie to see.

"If young Jasper is right," Barrow said, "he hes nae way tae speak."

"And he wants some clothes," Jasper added.

"Is that so?" Liddie asked with a smile, raising her eyebrows. "What else might ye be hidin' aneath my potato sack, aside that fancy tail?"

"Liddie Burn!" Barrow muttered.

Four days Ereben had avoided Liddie while she labored irritably over suitable clothing for Chrysanthus. Her supply of fabric was sufficient for one garment of Dwarf size. Since she was not about to sacrifice her own clothes, she sent Barrow to the town of Ironhole for a bolt of gray wool. While Zink was half as far away, Barrow was less likely to be recognized at Ironhole. In the meantime, she had created a pair of thin leather breaches. Today, she had caught Ereben sneaking away to the river. He was the closest in size to Chrysanthus, so was recruited to model the breaches while Liddie stitched in the bottom. At least she allowed him to stand outdoors while she worked.

"I wad be dressed like the quaen o' Dwarfs with all the wool that goes intae one simple robe for yer granfather," Liddie complained. "Bring yer leg oot farther. Aye, right there."

"I'm sure he'll feel better once its done," Ereben said.

"I suppose I kinna blame Chrysanthus for bein' sae tall," she continued. "But it wad be a tiny, wee bit more practical if he were smaller."

"Liddie, does Phaena ever talk about what she wants to do?"

"Keep yer leg still. Sometime. She's carryin' a heavy pain about her father an' all."

"Do you think she'll ever be...the same again? You know, like when we were talking about getting married."

"None o' us is e'er the same from one day tae the next. Once a time is gone, it be gone fer good. That's not tae say there will ne'er be good time again. It'll be different time that are good. Stop yer twitchin'."

"But it's been so long, and she still spends most of her time off by herself, or with Jasper and Bahsa."

"Ah, when yer young, six month seems like a lang time. When yer aulder, six month will go by as quick as a cauld caup o' barley-brie."

He realized that he knew the truth of Liddie's words. He had been old—very old. When he had been rock, he had savored the insignificance of the passage of time. In six months of fretting over the little urgencies that filled each day, he had almost forgotten what it is like to be a rock. Ereben caught sight of Barrow approaching from across the Clootie River. "Here comes your wool."

"Easy tae say. Liddie's the blastit fool what hes tae sew it all thegither. There, now go in an' tak it off, then bring it back oot."

Ereben looked about in all directions. The others had managed to disappear before Liddie had awakened this morning. He waved to Barrow, who moved across the shallow water on his Dwarf pony.

When Ereben returned from the mound house, Barrow was dismounting from his pony. He seemed concerned. The bearded Dwarf strode over to Liddie and handed her a bolt of gray wool.

"How much did I pay?" Barrow volunteered. "A siller an' two coppers. Aye, it wes too much. Now, we've important things tae discuss."

"Aren't we the grumpy one," Liddie said.

"We've got a problem, Liddie. Ereben, ye need tae hear it too. As I wes about tae leave Ironhole, a boy handet me a note." Barrow pulled a rumpled square of heavy vellum from his belt and passed it to Ereben.

THEY ARE HOLDING YARNISH BLEN HERE IN THE TOWER.

HOLNICK FIRTH, A FRIEND

"Who is Holnick Firth?" Ereben asked.

"The name is new tae me," Barrow answered. "But I know that Yarnish wes tae go through Ironhole on his way tae Valand."

"What should we do?" Ereben asked. He still experienced some difficulty in thinking of Yarnish Blen as a friend, after years of hating the man.

"Minkar wad definitely stand oot in Ironhole. That leaves the two o' us. We'll go the morn, at first light. Maybees we can find this Holnick Firth. If no', then we go tae the wooden tower thae Knights o' the Redeemer built when they took o'er the town. Ye know, they set up a wooden palisade completely around the bailiwick and a tower on the motte. Ye've got tae pass the guards now jes tae get intae the town."

"Like the wall around Zink?"

"Nae. That wes built durin' the Dwarf war, nirly eighty year ago. All the fuss with the guards at Zink wes just from the Baillie puttin' on airs. This motte an' palisade business at Ironhole is for serious defense. I fear they're plannin' on swoopin' through the whole country an' takin' control."

"How do we get Yarnish out, once we get in?"

"Ah, I huvna figurt that oot yet."

"Yer bolt o' fabric, Barrow love," Liddie interrupted, "is perfect."

Barrow looked at Liddie in amazement. "Truly?"

"An' worth twice what ye paid for it."

"Liddie Burn," Barrow said, wrapping his arms about her, "ye're sech a devil."

Ereben and Barrow stood outside the gate of the wooden palisade of Ironhole. They had made the two day journey from

Liddie's farm on foot rather than chance bringing one of the kelpies to the town. Since Liddie had attached three frogs to the front of Ereben's ice leopard cape, he was able to fasten it, completely hiding his golden breastplate, as well as the dagger at his hip. Barrow carried only a wood cudgel hidden beneath his blanket cape.

Rather than Dwarfs guarding the gate of this Dwarfish town, full-size Valanders stood guard. They wore their hair cropped short. Hair in the back had been shaved bare up to the tops of their ears. Brass rings covered their black leather tunics. Each of the three guards milling about the gate carried a pike.

"Jes walk through as if ye dinna care what's guardin' the gate," Barrow said softly.

"What is your business in Ironhole?" the tallest of the guards asked. He looked curiously at Ereben.

"Aye, ainly fer a place tae kick aff these buits an' lay back fer the nicht," Barrow said in as thick a Knurlish dialect as Ereben had ever heard. "The morn, we'll tak oursels tae the market an' plenish our stock."

"What did he say?" the tall guard asked one of the others.

"I think they're looking for the inn," the other said.

"Are you carrying any weapons?" the tall guard asked.

"Nae," Barrow answered. "Are ye warkin' fer the Redeemer Knights?"

"We're just protecting the people here."

"Mighty good pay, I'll bet."

"Your friend needs to open his cape, so we can check him for weapons."

"Dae as he say, lad," Barrow said to Ereben. "Ye men are no' afraid o' catchin' the scabies, I hope. The healer rubt him doon with balm an' telt him tae co'er it up with the cape tae remead his weepin' flesh."

The guards looked at one another. "Go on through."

Barrow and Ereben passed the gate and headed into the business quarter of the bailiwick, merging quickly into the crowd.

Ereben had imagined Ironhole would be similar to Zink, with its paved streets, well built houses and bustling market filled with only Dwarfs. Instead, he found himself pressed among scores of ill-bathed workers, both tall and Dwarf, who looked about cautiously in all directions as they hurried to their unknown destinations. They seemed to eye Ereben with particular suspicion as they passed. Absently, he wondered if there might be a water shortage to account for the sweaty, rotted smells assaulting his senses. He stepped carefully along the rutted dirt street to avoid slippery smudges of crushed garbage and animal dung. Shabby wooden buildings displayed pendant signs indicating the nature of the shops within.

"Where do we go now?" he asked.

"Tae the Goat's Teat, Ironhole's finest." In response to Ereben's puzzlement, Barrow added, "Goat's Teat Drinkerie."

"Is that an inn?"

"Aye, lad. An' nae one will ask a question in a place like that."

Ereben followed Barrow. Looking toward the western edge of town, he noticed a tower about ten yards high, built of newly cut lumber, rising above the older buildings. Through an alley, he glimpsed the low earthen mound upon which the tower stood, just inside the palisade. *That's where they're keeping Blen.* The tower was still barely in view when Barrow turned and entered a doorway beneath the peeling placard of a goat's teat. A blast of stench emanating from within reminded Ereben of the foul cell in which the Baillie of Zink had imprisoned him, and in which he had finally found "a stump called Whittig Trench." He now followed that same Whittig Trench into the dimly lit Drinkerie.

The two dozen patrons of the Goat's Teat all appeared to be Dwarfs. If Ereben stood out in the paltry light filtering through the shuttered windows, it was not apparent on their sodden faces. Compared to these mumbling patrons, the myriad insects skittering about the floor showed more signs of life, as they avoided the fall of Ereben's boots. He joined Barrow at an empty table.

A hugely fat Dwarf girl with a crooked left eye lumbered toward their table. "Wha' will ye drink?" she blurted, wiping the splintery table top with a filthy rag.

"Yer finest barley-brei," Barrow cheerfully replied.

She rolled her eyes. Her face otherwise remained frozen in an expressionless stupor. "Wha' else?"

"Water is all I need," Ereben answered.

The fat girl's face came to life, as she assumed the hauteur of one who has been unjustly slandered. "We will gie ye nae water here. We hae a reputation tae uphold!"

"Water in Ironhole will give ye a week o' the runnin' regrets," Barrow explained. "An' it reeks with iron an' sulfur. Not a good choice."

The "running regrets" seemed to describe the last year of his life, but Ereben understood. "Do you have any fruit wine?" he ventured.

"If tha's wha' suits ye," she said impatiently.

"Anither favor, sweet," Barrow interjected. "We huv need o' somebody tae deliver a message fer us."

She nodded silently as she plodded back to the kitchen.

"It doesn't seem very safe around here," Ereben whispered. There was something inhospitable and disquieting about the entire town. The way people looked about, at least those who were not too drunk, spoke of unrest and distrust. Maybe it was the burning of heretics. Or the occupation by foreign troops. He wasn't sure.

"Aye. We surrendert safety when we left Liddie's coo farm."

The fat girl returned with their beverages. Trundling behind her was a slovenly, dull-faced Dwarf boy of about ten. "Fray will tak yer message. Two coppers for yer drinks, an' anither for Fray." She dropped the proffered coins into her bodice, then left Fray standing expectantly.

"Lad," Barrow began, "have ye heard o' someone by the name Holnick Firth?"

Fray shook his head.

"Well," Barrow continued, "ask aroun' an' find him. If ye can, then say that his friend awaits him at the Goat's Teat." When Fray's facial expression revealed no hint of comprehension, Barrow slowly repeated his instructions then sent Fray on his errand.

"Ironhole's finest," Ereben reminded his friend. He sipped his fruit wine. It curled his tongue like spoiled cider. "Is the food any better?"

"Worse."

They waited nearly an hour with no sign of Fray, so Ereben gave in to his hunger and ordered some stew. Since there was nothing else on the menu, Barrow ordered stew as well. To Ereben's surprise, the promptly served stew was a thick, delicious mixture of hot beef and vegetables, and served up in generous bowls. The accompanying stale biscuits reminded Ereben of the hard parmak baked by Jasper's mother the day she was killed in Nilwid by Lord Corban's Protector and his oversize ravens. The ravens seemed to have vanished since Corban's defeat. He had seen one giant vulture in the sky over Knurlan, but it bore no rider.

Silence swept over the patrons of the Goat's Teat. When Ereben looked up from his nearly empty bowl of stew, it was into the pointing finger of Fray. Behind him stood a richly uniformed officer of the Guard. Barrow spun around on his chair. Ereben's eyes followed. Eight armed guards took up positions around them.

The face of a zealot is either an honest expression of ignorance or an elaborate mask of deceit.

Ereben Leaf: Chronicle of the Counterspell

Ereben realized immediately that there would be no escape. Pounding filled his ears as a vision of heretics consumed in flames clouded his mind. The guards held pikes at the ready, awaiting only the word of their officer.

"Stan' aside, ye randie fools!" The fat Dwarf woman with the crooked eye shoved her way through the circle of guards. Her posture bristled with defiance. "Yon fugies huvna paid for thir vittles." Before the officer was able to speak, she thrust her finger in his direction. "Afore yer sodgers drag 'em off tae the tower, I want six coppers." She stabbed the finger repeatedly into the palm of her other hand.

Fray, the young messenger, cringed at her tirade and quickly slipped beyond the ring of men.

The officer sighed. "Ma'am..."

"Ye may be the maister o' these dogs," she shrieked, gesturing at the guards, "bu' I'm the laird o' this drinkerie!" Both hands perched on her corpulent hips, her raised chin and fiery eyes daring the officer to challenge her authority.

"Get her out of here," the officer said impatiently.

The nearest guard lowered his pike threateningly.

"Dinna point tha' at me, young man!" she responded, brushing aside the pike with one stubby arm. "An' don't ye be glowerin' at me. I'll nae be swickt oot o' my coppers! Two bowls o' stew are nae giftie frae the quean. They pay, then ye can trade yer licks and skaith each ither 'till ye're aa' chitterin i' yer buits!"

I'm already chittering in my boots. Ereben wished he could draw the dagger he had so carefully concealed beneath his ice leopard cape.

Barrow smiled broadly, raising both hands. "If ye might allow me." He reached beneath his blanket cape.

Ereben understood instantly. "I should pay my share." He fumbled with the frogs of his cape, finally unbuttoning them.

The expression of relief on the face of the officer faded quickly. "Take them!" he shouted.

At the sight of Barrow's wooden cudgel, the woman screamed and collapsed into a heap, covering her head with both arms. One powerful swing of Barrow's arm drove the cudgel into the head of the nearest guard, dropping him like a felled beast and showering blood across the room.

In a smooth sweep, Ereben brought his dagger from its sheath into the chest of one guard, withdrew it and slashed the forearm of another. Ereben pivoted the wounded guard into the path of an approaching pike. By then, Barrow, with his free hand, had lifted their wooden table as a shield, which he used to shove three more guards into the scattering crowd of patrons, where they tumbled over one another in a maelstrom of boots and barlie-brei. Ereben took up a discarded pike and launched it, like a Shouda spear, into yet another guard.

Ereben fled out the front door, propelled by fear. He turned in time to see Barrow stop in the doorway, parry the thrust of a pike, then toss a silver coin to the laird of the Goat's Teat Drinkerie.

They turned away from the wooden tower looming over the far side of the town and sprinted into the dirt alleyways behind the Goat's Teat, working their way toward the eastern palisade of Ironhole. Wooden pickets, three yards high, brought them to a halt.

"How do we get over this?" Ereben asked, panting to catch his breath.

"Use yer magic... tae open the wall," Barrow gasped.

"I don't know how to do that!"

"Ye hed better learn quick, lad."

Ereben's mind spun. He had no munu mushroom to power magic. He knew no spell for such a situation.

"Here they come." Barrow stood beside him, rolling the handle of his cudgel in one hand.

On an impulse, Ereben plunged the point of his dagger into the dirt beside the palisade, holding it with both hands. He focused his thoughts on spreading, separating, opening, while he stared intensely at the wooden pickets. Cold swept from the dagger's handle up his forearms. He forced it back, toward the dirt. *Spread. Separate. Open. Spread...*

Footsteps rushed toward them.

He closed his eyes. *Spread. Separate. Open. Now!*

Power surged upward from the dagger. He cast the power back upon itself. In a terrific fountain of dust and dirt, the ground opened beneath him. He fell a short distance, landed painfully, then was struck from behind by the full weight of Barrow dropping on top of him. They both scrambled to their feet, coughing. In the dim, dust-filled light, Ereben saw a tunnel extending in opposite directions.

"The mines!" Barrow exclaimed. "Ye've drapt us intae the tunnel o' the iron mines." He pointed in the direction which would pass beneath the palisade.

As they ran into the darkness, Ereben could hear from behind the clamor of guards jumping into the tunnel to pursue them. They ran in darkness for a short distance, stumbling over each other once. They rounded a curve. Ahead, maybe forty yards, Ereben saw the light of an oil lantern. They hurried toward it. Halfway to the lantern, Ereben spotted a darkened side-tunnel. He turned into it, immediately colliding with a Dwarf hidden in the shadows. Before they could fall, Barrow again slammed into Ereben's back, toppling all three of them to the ground.

"Guards are chasin' us," Barrow whispered to the barely visible Dwarf.

After a moment of silence, a gruff whisper replied, "Fallow me."

As quietly as possible, Ereben and Barrow followed the stranger as he hurriedly guided them through a maze of interconnecting tunnels. For nearly a quarter hour they moved silently along the darkened tunnels, sometimes descending, sometimes climbing, past vertical shafts and horizontal intersections, leaving behind the sounds of their pursuers. The final ascent was bathed in dusty beams of light. Breathless, Ereben and the two Dwarfs stepped out onto sun-drenched heather mounds.

"Thank you, friend." Ereben grasped the miner's thickly calloused hand.

"Aye," the Dwarf replied. "Any wha' thwarts thae knights hes earned my help, nae doubt."

As soon as the sun had set and the clear sky darkened, Ereben and Barrow approached the picket wall at a point where the tower stood closest.

"I don't see any guards from here," Ereben said, peeking through a thin gap between the pickets, "but I can't see the entrance to the tower. There's nobody up on the wall back here."

"Tha' wed be either a stroke o' fortune," Barrow replied in a hoarse whisper, "or a trap. Climb up my shoulders, lad, an' see what ye can see."

Ereben climbed up Barrow's broad back and massive shoulders. Now standing against the wall, Ereben still came short of the top. "I think I can reach the top if I jump."

"Careful o' the flinders," Barrow warned.

"Flinders?"

"Splinters, lad, splinters."

Crouching a little, and then leaping upward, arms extended, Ereben planted his hands around the top of one post. He pulled himself up enough to allow his eyes to inspect the guard scaffold along the interior of the wall, and the area of ground this side of the tower. It was clear. Without consulting Barrow, Ereben lifted himself over the wall. Now among the barrels and bails of stores beneath the scaffold, he located a suitable length of rope, ascended the scaffold using the ladder placed there for the guards, and assisted Barrow over.

Once below the scaffold, and well hidden by the shadows, Barrow studied the movement of distant guards. "We wait. If a guard ne'er patrols tae the end o' the baillie here, then this is a trap."

They rested in the shadows a quarter hour. Finally, a somewhat inebriated guard carefully stumbled his way to the end of the scaffold, then retraced his steps. So far as Ereben could determine, only a single guard stood outside the entrance door to the tower.

"How do we get past that guard?" Ereben asked.

Without answering, Barrow stood and casually walked to the tower entrance. The guard, picking his teeth with the point of a small twig, glanced contemptuously at the lone Dwarf. Barrow smiled, nodded politely, then swung the cudgel from behind his back into the guard's head, dropping him to a motionless heap. Barrow then hefted the guard over his shoulder. He walked back to Ereben and plopped the burden among the shadows beneath the scaffold.

"That's how."

The two intruders opened the tower door and entered a storeroom, illuminated by a single candle. The tower, at its base, appeared to be about eight yards across. Its thick, wooden walls were interrupted by vertical slots to enable defenders with bows to fire arrows. Each slot was crossed midway with a narrow, horizontal slot. A steep wooden stairway descended from the plank flooring into a dimly lit room below. A second steep, wooden stair ascended to a darkened floor. Barrow pointed upward.

They silently climbed to the darkened room. As Ereben's eyes adjusted to the darkness, he noted that a wall closed off the half of the room that faced away from the baillie wall outside the tower. At its center, a closed door, locked on Ereben's side by a sliding bolt, bore a tiny square window. The remainder of the exterior wall was slotted like the room below. From there, a ladder ascended to yet another darkened floor. If this was a trap, Ereben thought, the locked room might contain half a dozen guards. He peeked through its tiny window, but could see only darkness.

Ereben pointed questioningly toward the cell door. Barrow merely shrugged in response. With his dagger drawn, Ereben slid the latch and gently pushed the door inward. An acrid whiff of stale sweat startled him. Two dark figures slumped against the outer wall, apparently sleeping. "Blen," he whispered. "Blen." One figure stirred. "Yarnish Blen?" The awakened figure kicked the sleeping one.

"What?" the other mumbled.

"Yarnish Blen?" Ereben asked again.

"Ereben Leaf," the second figure whispered.

They exchanged hasty and greetings. Blen's cell mate was introduced as Root, a young Dwarf.

"Let's get out of here before we're caught," Ereben advised.

"A door in the cellar," Root said, "gaes oot tae the iron mine tunnel. Ye would'na have tae gae oot the front o' the motte."

"Are ye certain?" Barrow asked.

"Quite certain," Root replied, thumping his chest. "I built it."

"Then, let's use it," Ereben whispered enthusiastically.

Down they went, tiptoeing like cats. As they descended to the cellar, Ereben halted at the site of a man sitting at a small, candlelit desk, intently writing. The man faced away from them. He was clothed in a deep brown monk's robe, with its generous cowl covering his head.

"It's alright," Blen whispered. "He's a monk from Moss Abbey. He may want to go with us."

Ereben was stunned by what he saw on the shelves and tables of the cellar. Books and scrolls were stacked everywhere. He could clearly see, on open parchments, writing in the ancient Shadae script. Scattered about were a few red, translucent stones, like the ones he had acquired from the meager belongings of Hobart, the Guardian of the Ruins who existed now only within the rock of the Great Canyon. There were gold and silver articles of various shapes. Beside the monk's writings stood an odd, bowl-like construction of gray metal rods outlining a five-sided figure at its base, and walls composed of rods which outlined more five-sided figures. "This is a library of magic," Ereben exclaimed in a strained whisper.

The monk turned to look at them, then returned to his studies. Root moved to the western wall of the cellar, then rocked his head backwards with a great sigh.

"We huv got a wee problem."

"What wee problem?" Barrow asked.

"Thae sodgers hae sealt my tunnel."

"That we have done," came a crisp Valish voice from behind them.

Ereben spun around to see a soldier, an officer by the complex markings of his uniform, leaning down the stairs.

"No need to raise a fuss," the officer said mildly. "I have twenty men with me. So, I'm afraid your burgling is over for the night. My name is Holnick Firth, and you are now my guests."

"Aye," Barrow replied, "a friend."

Firth turned to a guard who descended behind him. "Be sure to get the dagger and cuirass from our red-haired guest, and leave those items down here."

Ereben watched a mound of golden sun peek above the eastern baillie wall of Ironhole. The soft touch of its warmth spread over his face. His hands were tied behind him, around a post. To his right, Barrow stood tied at a similar post about one yard away. Yarnish Blen, the man who had been the object of his hatred for so many years, stood stoically at his stake to the left. Root was tied likewise to the left of Blen. Piles of split wood surrounded them. Guards directed several Dwarf women in heaping dry twigs on and around the woodpiles.

He thought of Phaena. Beautiful Phaena. He would never know her tender touch again. He had tried to be patient with her. He had waited for her to emerge from her wall of pain. He had learned to view time like a rock. Now, he would live out the remaining moments of his life without her. He remembered the scent of her hair, but his nostrils were now filled with the foul stench of Ironhole's dung-covered, muddy streets. He looked at Barrow, whose irascible self-confidence had been replaced by the slack introspection of failure and resignation. Root, scarcely older than Ereben, wept silently as he trembled. Ereben's fear was swallowed by his longing for Phaena. Two soldiers now approached with guttering torches.

The method by which a fool seeks to prove his protective ability is to clamor for the wars that endanger everything he loves.

Gumushtigin: The Arts of Warfare

Jasper winced, trying to free his left ear from Liddie Burn's powerful grip.

"Ow! I don't need a bath!"

"I'll have nae swine livin' at my coo farm, young man!" She tugged him toward the bank of the Clootie River. "Ye can bathe yersel in private, or I'll strip ye bare mysel and scrub ye with a bristle."

"I don't have to listen to you," Jasper insisted.

With one hand holding to Jasper's ear like a snapping turtle, Liddie untied his shirt with the other.

"Alright. Ow! Alright."

Her fiery eyes stared him down, then she released his ear. "An' wash yer smelly clothes the while. I'll send Bahsa oot with a tunic tae wear in thir place." She headed back toward the mound house. "Dinna forget yer crusty hair," Liddie called over her shoulder.

Jasper waited until Liddie Burn had gone back into the house. He removed his new leather boots, then jumped into the chill water, clothes and all. He gasped at the shock of cold. Rubbing his arms and legs warmed them slightly and, as a bonus, removed some dirt. He plunged his head under the surface and washed his hair and face. As an afterthought, he washed behind his ears and the back of his neck. Once he got started, he ended up washing himself from head to toe. Since he was not about to undress, he accomplished this by reaching inside his clothing or pulling up the legs of his trousers. He looked up to see Bahsa holding a brown tunic.

"What are you looking at?" Jasper snapped. He resented Bahsa's privileged status. Bahsa did little work and, since he never spoke, was offered everything and denied nothing. Everybody felt sorry for Bahsa because his mother died. Jasper seethed at the recollection that his own parents as well as his brother were killed. *Nobody remembers that. I'm just a slave here.* "Come on in. It feels good."

Bahsa shook his head and stepped away.

"Don't be such a girl." When the younger boy took on an offended expression, Jasper splashed water at him. Bahsa whined loudly and ran toward the house.

This was the part Jasper hated most about bathing—having to sit in wet clothing while it dried. He smoothed his hair with his hands, and climbed onto a large rock. There he could dry in the sun while practicing his aim by skipping flat stones down the river.

A half hour later, with his clothes still damp, Jasper pulled on his boots and returned to the mound house. Liddie Burn stood in the entryway, her hands on her solid hips. Jasper walked up to her and waited for her to move so he could enter. Liddie inspected him, checking his fingernails and behind his ears.

"That's good lad." She placed her hands on Jasper's shoulders and looked up into his eyes. "Ye're becomin' a young man now, Jasper. When ye grow aulder, yer sweat grows stronger. If ye fail tae bathe, it gets rancid. That's just the way it is. An it's a wee bit easier if ye tak off yer clothes." She pinched his cheek, then slapped it affectionately and allowed him to enter.

Inside, Jasper entered the simple chamber he shared with Ereben, Minkar and Bahsa. Only the Shouda boy was there. Ereben had gone with Barrow two days before. Minkar and Chrysanthus had left before sunrise today, taking Titus and Krey with him. Jasper ignored Bahsa and began to put on his travel gear.

He slipped into his stiff, oversize chain shirt, and strapped on his knife, Rat Slayer. Bahsa watched with a forlorn silence.

"I'm just going out hunting—if I can find Dantel." He put on his golden helmet and looked about the clutter for his carved staff.

Bahsa slowly put on his golden chain hood, keeping his eyes fixed on Jasper. He found his matching dagger, Bat Slayer, and tried unsuccessfully to fasten the belt clasp. He watched as Jasper took up the carved staff and his cloak of silver wolf fur.

"Alright. If Liddie says you can go, then you can go." Jasper fastened Bahsa's knife belt and handed him Hobart's alderwood staff.

As the two boys stepped out of the chamber, Phaena set down a broom. "Where do you think you two are going? There's work to do."

Liddie rushed into the mound house with panic in her eyes. "Those Redeemer Knights are crossin' the river. About six on horse."

"What should we do?" Phaena asked.

"Phaena, dear, climb oop intae the lum and hide yersel." Liddie pointed to the chimney above the cold hearth. "Lads, set yersels on the groun' and dunna come oot o' the house." She took up her iron flail and tucked it part way into the back of her leather trousers. "Ye dae what I say!" she whispered harshly, then strode confidently out of the house, her right hand on the flail.

"What could they want?" Phaena asked.

"I don't know," Jasper replied. "Nobody is supposed to know we're here."

The three of them stood in the shadows of the entry, where they could watch. Seven Knights, wearing black quilted coats, stitched with brass rings, approached on horses.

They rode up to Liddie. One dismounted. Four of them moved beyond Jasper's view.

"You have a Valish girl here," the dismounted Knight said. "Where is she?"

"I raise coos here, not Valish girls."

"We know she is here. Turn her over, and we'll leave."

"Ye're mistaken, honorable knight."

The man on foot drew a short sword and motioned to the others, who carried pikes.

"She's armed!" a voice called.

In a single, fluid movement, Liddie Burn swung her flail, striking the Knight on the side of his jaw. With a crack of bone, the Knight fell to the ground.

Bahsa rushed from the house to Liddie's side. Jasper swallowed hard and ran out after him. One of the mounted guards lowered his pike to impale the Dwarf woman, but a twirl of her flail yanked the pike out of the Knight's hand. A second swing destroyed the man's knee, and a third crushed the top of his leather helmet as he fell. Blood pumped from his head in gouts.

Jasper was grabbed from behind, trapping both his arms and his carved staff by his side. His attacker screamed and released him. To Jasper's astonishment, the wolf figure carved on his staff showed fresh blood on its teeth. The man held a bloody hand over the left side of his neck. Jasper quickly drew Rat Slayer and stabbed him in the thigh.

"I've got her," another man shouted. "Let's go." He held Phaena by twisting her arm behind her.

"Not 'till this stump wench is dead."

A broad shadow swept over them. The great peregrine falcon, Pelegri, dove at the Knights. Talons snatched a rider from his fleeing horse. Pelegri lifted the screaming man high into the air, then released him.

A pikeman lunged at Liddie. He froze in mid stride as Bahsa struck a glancing blow at his hip with his alderwood staff.

When Liddie's flail impacted the man's chest, his entire body shattered like blown glass.

The Knight holding Phaena hoisted her onto the back of the one horse still bearing its rider. "Go," he shouted, while mounting his own horse. The other horses galloped away in panic. These two surviving Knights fled toward the river, with Phaena thrashing and shouting from behind a rider, but unable to free herself.

Jasper called Pelegri to land, hoping to fly ahead of the riders and stop them. He climbed up onto the great bird and lifted off.

When the horsemen reached the bank of the river, both horses reared and turned back. A long, reptilian neck extended from the water, its elongated head snapping a challenge with dozens of brown, hooked teeth. Swirls of blue and indigo illuminated its scaled skin. With blurring speed, the creature tore an arm from the rider holding Phaena. Both he and Phaena fell to the ground. The beast climbed out of the water, showing its clawed legs and long, serrated tail.

Phaena, screaming in terror, scrambled away from the bleeding man who had been holding her moments before. As Phaena ran toward the mound house, the beast bit off a knee of her former captor. The monster fed carelessly, leaving body parts scattered about. Then it crawled forward to feed on the other fallen Knights, starting with those not yet dead.

Jasper considered following the one Knight who succeeded in crossing the river, but decided against it. *They already know we're here.* He circled back to the mound house, confident that the beast was one of the kelpies.

A second beast crept up from the river and began to eat the pikes and swords lying on the ground. Metal parts seemed to go down as easily as the wooden shafts.

Phaena, Liddie and Bahsa had run into the house and now stood cautiously in the doorway.

When all the weapons had been devoured, and all the bodies reduced to small pieces, the two beasts nuzzled one another, then shimmered into the forms of horses, a white mare and an amber stallion.

"Ye dinna have tae mak a drama of it," Liddie scolded the kelpies. She walked to the river and washed the blood and flesh from her iron flail. Phaena accompanied her and washed blood from her own arms and face.

"Maybe I should fly to Ironhole and let them know what's happened." Jasper felt a vague sense of vulnerability with all the men gone, though he had acquired a new degree of respect for Liddie Burn.

Phaena turned to him, still scrubbing her hands. "We need you here."

"Why?"

"What if more Knights come?" she said.

Jasper savored the suggestion that his martial skills might be in demand. "You're right."

Pelegri lifted into the air and flew rapidly to the North. Jasper called after the great bird. Then he saw a dragon, so high above that he could barely identify it. The dragon flew over from the South.

"Look at that!" Jasper gasped.

"What?" Phaena asked, following Jasper's gaze. "Huh!" A strange expression came over Phaena's face as she followed the course of the dragon passing high above them.

"Knights, beasts, and now a dragon," Liddie moaned. "We're not havin' a very promisin' day."

Phaena looked at Jasper, then at Liddie. Though her thoughts appeared to be focused somewhere far from the farm. "Liddie," she said, almost in a whisper, "that dragon...I felt...something..." "Do you think we should stay here?"

"I would rather not abandon the coos, but I think we better find a safer spot for a while."

"Where would we go?" Jasper asked.

"The Barrens are nae place tae be in the summer."

"That's south," Jasper clarified in response to Phaena's puzzled expression.

"Well, we can't go toward Zink or Ironhole," Phaena added. "We'd just run into more Knights."

"Tha' only leaves somewhere in the Easlan." Liddie scratched her elbow. "We can fallow the Clootie as far as the mountains, then go oop tae Cinnabar."

"We should wait for everybody else to come back," Jasper suggested, "or at least 'till Pelegri gets back."

As they walked to the mound house, Phaena suggested leaving a note. "That way they'll know where we've gone."

"That's dumb," Jasper observed. "Then the Knights'll know too."

"Our men will need tae pit thir heads thegither and figure oot that Cinnabar is the only place tae go."

"Are you sure?" Phaena asked.

"Nae, but I'd be afeared tae leave a message."

After agreeing that Ereben and Barrow would have no trouble guessing where they had gone, they gathered some belongings and climbed onto the two kelpies. Liddie took the stallion, Kehlibar, with Phaena seated behind her. Jasper, as always, rode his mare, Dantel. He hoisted Bahsa up behind him.

Starting off at a walk, then quickly shifting Dantel into a canter, Jasper expected her to sprout her wings and lift into the air. Instead, both Dantel and Kehlibar stubbornly held to the ground, keeping close to the south bank of the Clootie River.

"She won't fly," Jasper shouted to Liddie.

"Maybees they know I'd prefer not tae fly."

Although their kelpie horses refused to fly, they maintained a prodigious pace, not stopping or even slowing until brought to a halt in late afternoon. Despite their exertion, Dantel and Kehlibar did not break a sweat. And, as Jasper had noted many times before, their demon bodies gave off no warmth.

Jasper took them south from the riverbank far enough to locate some dense brush that would hide their camp for the night. But the kelpies, once unloaded, would not stay at the camp. Ignoring Jasper's instructions to remain, Dantel and Kehlibar returned to the river and melted into the water.

"They're acting really strange," Jasper observed.

"Will they come back in the morning?" Phaena asked.

"I don't know. Bahsa, lets get some firewood."

"I never trustet thae kelpies," Liddie grumbled.

The kelpies had not returned in the morning. Jasper felt a certain degree of injury that his own kelpie, Dantel, would abandon him. Of course, there was no way for Jasper to understand the thoughts of a kelpie, but for them to have left him and his companions, especially now, seemed unlike them. In the past, the demon creatures had always seemed to respond to Jasper's endangerment. Now it was as though that no longer mattered to them.

Walking east along the Clootie, they passed the fork, where the clear Eascloot, discharging directly from the foothills to the east, joined with the murky Wescloot, which drained the Easlan basin of Knurlan, to form the Clootie River.

"If we fallow the Eascloot," Liddie said, huffing under the burden of her pack, "we kinna cross the mountains. Only oop by Cinnabar can ye go through. A road winds oop above the city tae Cinnabar Pass."

"Do we want to leave Knurlan?" Phaena asked. "I thought we were just going to hide until Ereben and Barrow returned."

"Aye," Liddie answered. "But if those Redeemer Knights find us first, we'll be trapt if we need tae go farther."

"Well," Jasper offered, "lets just cross the river and go see what's in Cinnabar. The last I heard, the Knights were nowhere near there."

Liddie Burn frowned. "Cinnabar has a reputation."

"What kind of reputation?" Phaena asked.

"The streets are filt with thieves an' whores an' wastrels. Brothels set on e'ery corner, with nae but drinkeries in between."

"It sounds like a good place to hide," Jasper suggested. He had heard fascinating rumors of brothels, but had never actually seen one.

"A good place tae have yer throat slasht."

"Maybe Jasper's right," Phaena said. "I'll bet everybody minds their own business."

Liddie sighed. "I suppose ye might be right. But if we go tae Cinnabar, ye mind what I say. I'll nae tolerate argey-bargeys o'er what I tell ye tae do. That is understoot, Miss Phaena?"

"Yes ma'am."

"Maister Jasper?"

"Yes ma'am." Jasper could hardly conceal his delight.

"Maister Bahsa?"

Bahsa simply smiled.

Finding a well-used ford, they crossed the Eascloot just above its confluence with the Clootie, and traveled north along the east bank of the Wescloot, continuing for three days, meeting no other travelers along the way. Nights were spent away from the river, in whatever brush or copse of trees they could find. The Easlan plains stretched away as undulating grasslands in all directions, punctuated here and there by small stands of stunted trees and occasional rocky outcroppings. Days were hot and dry. Nights were cooler. Each morning a fine dew left everything damp until the summer sun had time to toast it dry again.

As they traveled, they usually walked in silence. Jasper seldom commented on the thoughts drifting through his mind. When he did, Liddie usually cut him short. She seemed to grow more irritable the farther they traveled from her coo farm.

"Twenty year I've raist yonder coos. Now I've left the entire herd fer bandits an' wolfs."

"They'll be alright," Phaena reassured her.

"Aye, mixt intae the stew pots o' thief gangs."

At mid-day, they approached a wooden kingpost bridge, where the Zink-Cinnabar road crosses the Wescloot. From several hundred yards away, Jasper could see a sparse, but continual movement of people, animals and occasional wagons passing in both directions. He went ahead alone to reconnoiter.

"It's mostly Dwarfs," he informed his companions on his return.

"Any sodgers?" Liddie asked.

"I don't think so. I saw a Valish couple—a man and a woman."

"The form o' us four mak a recognizable group. We separate," Liddie decided. "Bahsa comes with me. Jasper, ye an' Phaena walk about a hundert yard ahind, but keep us in yer sight."

"I don't think we should split up," Phaena whined.

"Those rascals'll be searchin' fer four."

Liddie and Bahsa moved onto the road, heading toward Cinnabar. Jasper followed with Phaena a hundred yards behind. Between himself and Liddie, Jasper noted a group of five Dwarf men, all on foot, and a Dwarf woman riding alone on a pony. Immediately behind him was a wagon filled with kegs and driven by two Dwarf men. As far as he could see in either direction, there were no full-size horses.

Unlike most of the long roads Jasper had seen in Knurlan, the Cinnabar road was blessed with primitive, though inviting inns spaced about a day's journey apart. Their first night, they stopped at an inn built as a large Valish barn—an exotic sight in Knurlan. The ground level was split in half lengthwise, part enclosed as a single, long sleeping chamber, part open, facing the river and set with tables and benches, and served by an open hearth kitchen. From within the enclosed section, a ladder ascended to an upper level, which was one large chamber where each guest staked out a patch of floor on which to sleep. A privy stood twenty yards to the East.

Liddie surreptitiously passed a few coppers to Jasper, so he and Phaena could pay for their lodging and supper. Jasper passed them to Phaena. The innkeeper, a neatly dressed Dwarf in his twenties smiled broadly as he inspected Phaena.

"Would ye care fer a private chammer, miss?"

"My brother and I will just take a spot upstairs," she answered, also with a smile.

The innkeeper examined Jasper disappointedly. "Thae travelers get a mite grabby oop there, if ye know what I mean."

"We'll be fine." Phaena brushed road dust from her travel cloak with a delicate flicking movement of her fingernails. "My brother is very protective, though his temper does seem short at times."

Jasper casually drew back his silver wolf cloak, exposing Rat Slayer in its sheath. He tapped his thumb nervously on its milky red pommel stone.

"Aye," the innkeeper responded. "Two coppers with vittles, drink extra. Ye pay the morn."

As Jasper and Phaena ate their stew of pork, potato and parsnip, Jasper could not help but notice that most of the two dozen other guests, all the men at least, were staring openly at Phaena. He had always seen her as beautiful, but had never seen others regard her with such unmistakable lust. He became conscious of his proximity to her on the bench. Maybe, he thought, they were just staring at her golden hair. He glanced at her tousled locks, which softly brushed his ear when she turned her head. His self-consciousness grew.

When they had finished eating, Phaena placed her delicate hand on Jasper's, and whispered, "Would you come with me to the privy?"

"What?"

"I don't feel comfortable going out there alone."

"But...I..." He could feel blood rushing to his cheeks.

"Please?"

He nodded. As they rose and walked from the tables, Jasper felt many eyes following them. He wrapped his wolf cloak about him and followed Phaena to the privy.

After Phaena had entered the privy and latched the plank door behind her, Jasper stood guard, feeling both silly and important. Although most guests went about their own business, two Dwarf men seated under the eave of the barn seemed to be amused by Jasper's distress. They spoke in low tones, laughed, elbowed one another and grinned toward Jasper. Between the soft rustle of clothing coming from within the privy, and the snickers and laughter of the guests, Jasper felt entirely out of place.

When they returned to the tables beneath the barn, they took seats near Liddie and Bahsa, though not alongside them. An elderly man, a Valish traveler in tattered formal attire, sat on the bench across the table from Jasper.

"Going to Cinnabar, Miss?" the old man asked Phaena. His beige doublet was shy a button, and the cuffs of his linen shirt were frayed to a fuzz around both bony wrists.

"Yes," she replied. "My brother and I are planning to buy some rugs for my father's shop."

"Cinnabar is a good place for rugs, if you have a taste for the small, colorful, knotted wool rugs of the Banu Sulal. We don't see many in Rippleton, because of the slave trade."

"What do you mean?" Phaena asked.

"The Banu Sulal are slavers. The knotted rugs are all made by slaves, mostly children that the Banu Sulal capture or purchase. Not too many folks in Rippleton are fond of the thought of buying a rug made by enslaved children." He looked at Phaena with a slight glint of recognition. "Where did you say you were from?"

"Brockton," she answered.

"Ah. Never spent much time there. You know, it's remarkable, but you remind me of a young woman who used to live in Rippleton. You look very much like the daughter of Lord

Corban, the High Protector of Dragomin." The latter part he whispered uncomfortably, his eyes darting about the room.

"I don't think I know him," Phaena said. Beneath the table, Jasper could see her fingers twisting a fold of her cloak.

"Well, he's dead now. No one knows what happened to the poor girl. Last anyone heard, she was held prisoner in his tower. After he got killed, they never found her. The Knights of the Redeemer are offering a reward for the girl. Twenty gold. I don't know why." The man's eyes moved between Phaena and Jasper. "I guess if she's smart, she's a long way from here."

"Or maybe she's dead too," Jasper interjected.

The old man's gaze held on Jasper. "I've heard that the slavers have been catching children around Cinnabar. You best not wander out alone in Cinnabar."

"What do they do with them?" Jasper asked.

"I understand that the youngest are put to work in shops and on the rug looms. The older ones, like your age, they raise as warriors to do the bidding of the kings. Once they make you a warrior, you remain in their army until you die in battle...or in old age. Not too many of those, I suspect."

"They have more than one king?" Phaena asked

"There are three kingdoms of the Banu Sulal. Each one has a king. King Kalish is the high king. I don't know who the other ones are. Not too many folks from Valand, or Knurlan for that matter, actually go into the Three Kingdoms. Merchants do their business with them in Cinnabar. That way they don't have to worry about the slavers or the Orcs."

"Orcs?" Jasper asked.

"Oh yes. North of the Three Kingdoms, the Farlan Plain swarms with Orcs. They're not human. They have lizard eyes and fangs. Their skin is yellow."

"Do they take slaves too?" Jasper had never heard of Orcs.

"No. They eat them." The old man's eyebrows raised.

Jasper smirked. He remembered the stories he had heard about Shadows, who lived in trees and ate children who wandered too far from Nilwid. What he and Ereben had found were the Shouda, and they definitely did not eat children.

The old man winked at Phaena.

Jasper could not decide if the old man had indeed recognized Phaena and was cryptically warning her, or if he believed Phaena's feeble ruse. Either way, his information was disturbing. When the man had moved on to chat with other travelers, Jasper caught a frown on Liddie Burn's face. He guessed that she had heard most of the conversation. But speaking to her would foil their attempt at appearing to be strangers.

Jasper preceded Phaena up the ladder to the darkened upper chamber, redolent with road dust and sweat. Scant moonlight sifting through the shuttered window revealed a dozen or more silhouettes of slumbering bodies scattered across the floor. Jasper chose a bare spot against the wall, above which he located two pegs for hanging their packs. Stretching out on the floor beside the wall, he wrapped his wolf cloak about him and folded its hood into a pillow. Phaena set out her bedroll beside him.

"Good night," she whispered.

"Night," he replied.

Susurrations and soft snores merged into a hypnotic drone. Jasper gratefully relinquished the tensions of stealth, subterfuge and the stares of strangers. The days of unaccustomed travel melted away to a nearly dreamless sleep.

Jasper awakened to a smothered whimpering. Confused, he momentarily studied the thrashing silhouette beside him. As his mind cleared, he resolved the dark image of someone struggling with Phaena. The assailant held one hand over Phaena's mouth, the other hand tugged at her clothing.

Phaena's hands flailed at the hand covering her mouth. Jasper drew Rat Slayer and pressed its point against the assailant's torso. With a gasp, the figure lurched away, looked toward the faint light reflecting from the blade, then turned and scrambled into the darkness. Footsteps stumbled, eliciting a curse from a recumbent guest. A sonorous tapping of ladder rungs ended in silence.

"Are you alright?" Jasper asked Phaena.

Between muffled sobs, she whispered, "Yes. I'm fine."

"Let's trade places."

Without a reply, Phaena moved her bedroll against the wall.

"I shouldn't have gone to sleep," Jasper mumbled, mostly to himself.

Phaena reached out in the darkness, kissed him on the cheek and enfolded him in her petite arms. "You were awake when I needed help," she sniffed.

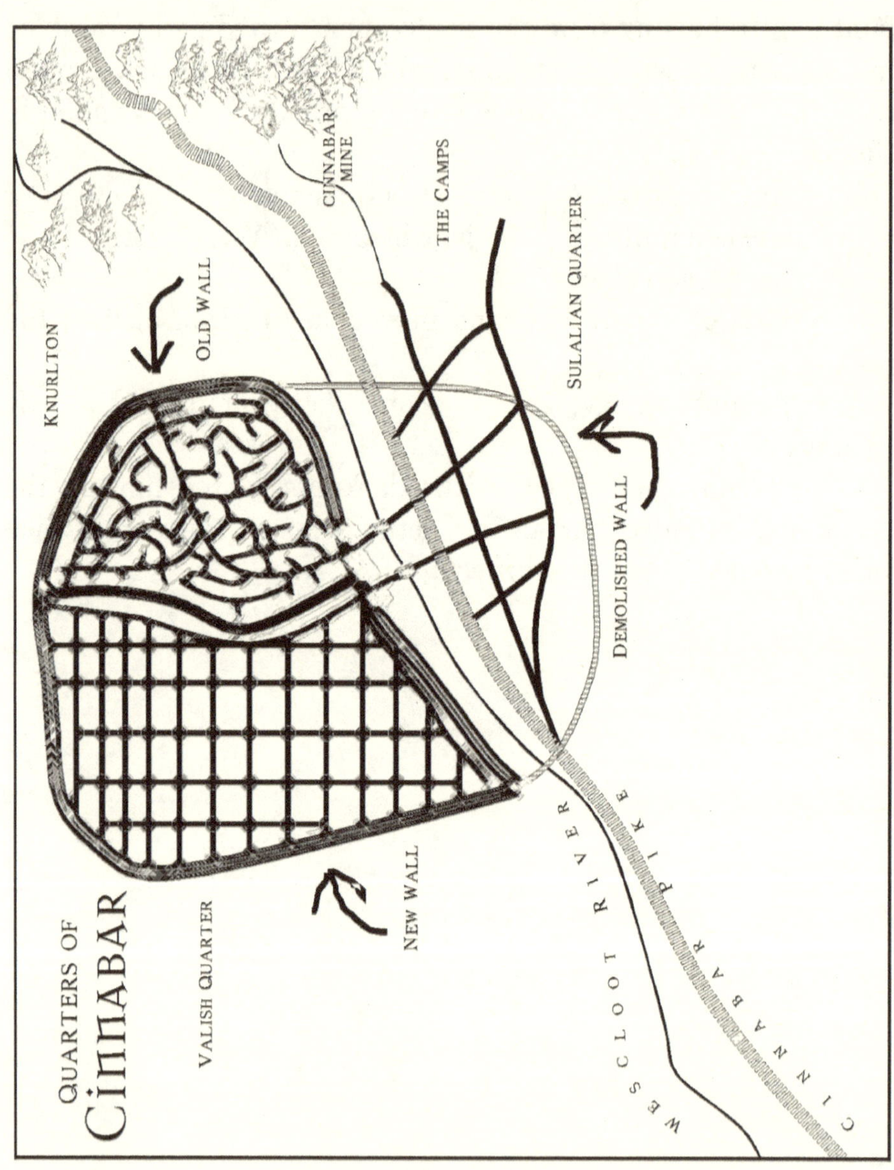
QUARTERS OF
CINNABAR
VALISH QUARTER
NEW WALL
KNURLTON
OLD WALL
CINNABAR MINE
THE CAMPS
SULALIAN QUARTER
DEMOLISHED WALL
WESCLOOT RIVER
CINNABAR PIKE

***

The practice of slavery requires that the slaveholder assign a characteristic by which he may identify those eligible for enslavement and by which he himself may be seen as ineligible.

Gumushtigin: History of Sulalia

"Well, ye see, Cinnabar has four quarter." Finny Burnewin, thirteen year old son of the proprietor of Mither's Corner, explained the odd arrangement of the town of Cinnabar to Jasper. Mither's Corner was by all accounts the cleanest and safest inn to be found here. The choice of where to stay had, of course, been Liddie's. And since Mither Burnewin was a Dwarf, and sister, no less, to the Baillie of Cinnabar, Liddie had decided to depend on Mither Burnewin's discretion for their safety. "The brothels," Finny continued, "are all in the Valish Quarter. All those slavers pretend that brothels are evil. So none can be found in the Sulalian Quarter. Ye see, slavers have tae trouble thirsels tae sneak o'er tae the Valish brothels whilst nae body's lookin'."

"What part of town are we in?" Jasper asked. Talking privately with someone near his own age was something he hadn't realized he missed, until he met Finny.

"Why, the Knurlish Quarter. But all the folk what live here call it Knurlton." It was mid-afternoon. The tables were empty and the dining area deserted. Jasper and Finny were seated on tables, their feet on the benches. "Then ye've got the camps. That's what they call the tents o' the miners. It's nae actually inside the town, but just east, aside the cinnabar mine."

A Dwarf girl, about Finny's age entered the room. She was attractive, and like Finny, stood a little more than half Jasper's height. Her light green gown reached to the floor. Taking a seat beside Finny, she fended off a kiss while waiting to be introduced.

"Yer so thick," she grumbled. "Who's yer friend?"

"That's Jasper. He's stayin' here." Finny tried to kiss her again. "What?"

The girl sighed and knocked her knuckles on the top of Finny's head. "My name is Opal Houlet." She held out a hand to Jasper. "Though it seems Finny Burnewin has forgot it."

"Oh," Finny mumbled.

Opal grasped Finny's head in her hands and kissed him on the lips for a long enough time for Jasper to feel awkward. He hopped down to the floor and turned to leave.

"Well, when do ye want yer tour?" Finny asked.

"I've got nothing else to do," Jasper replied.

"Want tae come alang?" Finny asked his girlfriend.

"Where ye goin'?"

"Over tae the Valish Quarter."

"Mum don't allow me tae go there."

"It'll only be a couple o' hours."

"I better stay."

Finny kissed her again. "Will ye come back later?"

"Maybees."

Finny led Jasper out into the narrow, cobbled streets that wound among the ancient, multi-storied houses of Knurlton, which, Finny explained, was the original walled city of Cinnabar. Now, its thick walls and threatening bastions only faced out to the newer quarters of the city to the West and South. Only two gates breached the walls of Knurlton. The main gate opened to the South and immediately crossed the narrow course of the Wescloot River, which separated Knurlton from the Sulalian Quarter, and a seldom used sally port that passed into the northern corner of the Valish Quarter. Finny chose the closer, main gate. On the south side of the bridge, the exotic spires and domes of the Sulalian Quarter spread southward from Cinnabar Pike, on which Jasper and his companions had reached the city the previous day. The pike continued on up the mountains to the East, eventually leading to the Three Kingdoms of Sulalia.

Following the pike westward, they crossed the river again on the first of three bridges that led into the Valish Quarter, and passed the New Wall, a much less ambitious structure which surrounded the Valish Quarter. The gates of the New Wall could no longer be closed, since its wooden doors had apparently rotted in disuse quite some time ago.

In stark contrast to the seemingly aimless meandering of Knurlton's narrow streets, the broad, straight avenues of the Valish Quarter left Jasper with more of a sense of direction. Here the streets formed a flagstone grid running north-south and east-west. Looking north or west at any intersection, Jasper could see the New Wall blocking the ends of the streets, and the Old Wall to the East. They passed tidy shops of every sort. One sold, to Jasper's amazement, nothing but books. There were jewelers, clothiers, hat shops and grocers.

"That street is mostly brothels," Finny pointed out to the left.

"Can we go see?" Jasper asked.

"Well, sure. An' if ye have some money, ye can even go inside."

Jasper felt the silver coin he had stitched into the waist of his trousers. It was the coin he had carried with him since he had left Nilwid so long ago. They turned down the street. On either side, women stood in the doorways. The women seemed to be of various races, though he saw no Shouda woman. Some blew them kisses, others spread the tops of their blouses or hiked their skirts at passing men. Most, though not all, ignored Jasper and Finny.

"Have you ever gone inside?" Jasper asked.

"I got my own girl. I have nae need tae pay a painted leddie."

"What do you have to do?"

"Ha ha! Yer nae ready tae find oot, it ye dunna know." Finny took Jasper's sleeve and turned him around.

"I know," Jasper protested. "I meant how do you figure out what to pay?" He allowed himself to be led back up the street.

"There's a bakery where we can get a piece of pie fer free." Finny turned north.

"They just give it away?"

"Well, Mum buys thir desserts fer the inn, so whenever I come by, the baker gives me a pick o' somethin'."

As they passed an inn, three Valish men exited into the street.

"We've got to check two more," one man said.

"I don't think she'd be foolish enough to hide in the slavers' quarter," a second replied, "so that leaves the stump side of town."

"How could she hide there?" the third asked.

Jasper followed Finny into a bakery. The aromas were intoxicating, but his mind was on the three Valish men. "We have to get back to your place."

"Well, alright, but let's get some pie first."

"No. I mean right now."

"What's wrong?"

"I can't tell you, but I've got to talk to Liddie in a hurry."

"This was nae much o' seein' the sights."

"They're in danger."

"Ye could just say so." He led Jasper out the door and farther up the street. "We can tak the north port intae Knurlton."

Along the way back to Mither's Corner, Jasper decided that he had to trust Finny with at least some of his secret. He explained that Phaena was in danger, and that men from Valand were searching for her.

"Now tell me again exactly what they said." Liddie had yet to be convinced of the need to worry.

"Liddie," Jasper shouted in exasperation, "there are only two gates out of Knurlton."

"The lad has a point," Rosie Burnewin said. "Best tae be safe. Finny can show ye a fine hidey spot oop in the hills."

"I suppose yer right," Liddie conceded. "Gather oop yer things children. Meet at the back gate."

"Finny," his mother said, "Avoid takin' the Pike oot o' town. Slip through the slaver side, and go oot the top o' the Camps."

Jasper helped Bahsa collect his belongings from the room they shared, then joined Liddie, Phaena and Finny Burnewin by the back gate of Mither's Corner. From there, they followed a circuitous route to the main gate of Knurlton. While Finny stood watch on the bridge, they walked, one at a time, over the bridge, across the pike and into the Sulalian Quarters.

They passed rug merchants, spice vendors and booths selling brass wares, fabrics, vegetables and worked iron. One shop displayed daggers and curved swords.

"That one," Finny whispered to Jasper, "sells khash. Ye smoke it an' yer mind goes funny fer a while."

Sulalians stared at them with close-set, dark eyes beneath colorful fabric turbans. All wore full beards. Jasper saw no women, only men. From their expressions, few outsiders passed through their markets.

"This doesn't look very safe here," Jasper whispered back, as they moved quickly along the street.

"Ye're fine when ye're with me," Finny explained. "They know me. And they know I'm the Baillie's nephew."

They passed a line of stone rubble, which Finny explained used to be part of the New Wall. Apparently, over the years, the wall surrounding the Sulalian Quarter had been used as a ready supply of stones for new construction.

"All these shacks and tents are used by the miners." Finny pointed to the shanty town that occupied the relatively flat ground between the eastern edge of Cinnabar and the mountains rising a mile farther east. "We'll cut through the Camps and tak tae the Pike oop above."

The Camps, like the brothels, seemed to be peopled by all races, though workers of both genders and all ages worked the cinnabar mine. Their faces were pale and ulcerated, their expressions vacant. Their hands seemed blistered and festering. None spoke to one another. All moved silently in response to the foremen, whose whips were superfluous and tied out of the way.

Finny pointed out a group of workers emerging from a mine opening in the side of the hill, each worker pulling off a mask and hungrily breathing the fresh air. "Ye see, well, they wear pig bladders o'er thir heads tae keep from breathin' the poison air o' the cinnabar. But they never live very long, once they start workin' the mine."

"Why do they do it?" Jasper asked.

"All those workers are slaves," Finny replied. "Even the wee lads."

Jasper noted that every one of them wore an iron or brass band on the upper arm. Even children that looked to be as young as three years wore a band.

Near the continuation of the Pike stood large cages, most filled with people. The cages were locked and guarded by fierce looking Sulalians, each armed with several weapons. Finny steered them well clear of these.

"Are those slave pens?" Phaena asked.

"Aye," Finny answered. "Those what don't go tae the mine are taken o'er the mountain intae the Three Kingdoms tae be sold."

Once on the Cinnabar Pike, they climbed eastward. This stretch of the road carried almost no traffic. Near dusk, Finny took them north of the road and into a steep valley that formed the source of the Wescloot River. Near a spring that seemed to pour directly from a rock face, they found the entrance to a cave.

"I call it Burnewin Cave," Finny announced. "Few folk know about it. With supplies, ye can live here quite a while. I keep a pine torch by the entry."

"We can nae very well live here more than a few day," Liddie said.

"That might be long enough for them to stop looking for us." Phaena always seemed to find a brighter side to any situation. "Finny, maybe you could come back up and let us know when they leave town."

"I can do that. But I'll stay oop here the night. The way back is tricky in the dark."

Jasper sparked the torch to life, and wandered into the cave. Its roof arched five yards above him. The floor was generally level, with a stone fire ring near the entrance and stacks of firewood nearby. A fat lizard the size of his foot scooted deeper into the cave. Jasper followed it into a side cave, which turned out to be a blind alcove.

The soft sound of movement deep in the alcove drew his attention. Behind a yard-high stone, he detected a crouching shape, pressed against the wall. He stepped back, startled at first, but quickly realized that it was a young girl, her eyes wide with terror.

"Hello," he said. "What are you doing here?" The girl remained silent. "Hey everybody," he called, "there's a little girl in here." He noticed an iron band on her tiny arm. Her face looked odd, broad with puffy, slanting eyes. She wore a pointed wool hat.

Finny was first to reach Jasper. "Well, that's a first time. She's a runaway slave."

When Liddie Burn reached them, she pulled the two boys out of the way by their ears. "Ye boneheads, ye're scarin' her wits oot. Come along dear." She held out a hand. "We'll help ye find yer Mum and yer Papa. Liddie'll tak care o' ye."

As the frightened girl reached out to Liddie, her hand was seen clearly to have only three long fingers and a thumb. Jasper then saw that her feet each had only four long toes.

"What's yer name, sweetie?" Liddie asked. "What does yer Mum call ye?"

"Yava," she said in a tiny voice.

"Come with Liddie, Yava. Ye must be starvin'." They walked toward the cave entrance. "How long have ye been oop here?" The girl shrugged. "Have ye run away from those slavers?" She nodded.

In the fading daylight, Jasper started a fire, while Phaena prepared some of the sausage and biscuits that Rosie Burnewin had provided them.

"It's nae a good idea tae anger yonder slavers," Finny pointed out.

"Yon slavers," Liddie huffed, "are nae goin' tae tak back this wee lass, and that's all there is tae that. Where do ye live sweetie? Do ye know the name o' the town or city where ye live?"

Yava offered no answers. When the food was ready, she consumed it in silence. Jasper noted that her teeth were also odd. Instead of four flat teeth in the center, she had two flat teeth surrounded by dog teeth.

"Did you see her teeth?" Jasper whispered to Finny. "And her fingers and toes?"

"She might be an Orc," Finny whispered in reply.

Jasper remembered the conversations with the old Valish man in a wayside inn. He had said that Orcs have yellow skin, lizard eyes and fangs. In the dim light he couldn't tell much about her skin, but the rest seemed to fit. "They're from across the mountains?"

"That's what they say."

"Liddie," Jasper said, "Finny thinks she might be from across the mountains. She might be an Orc."

Phaena turned to Jasper to say something, but instead turned to examine Yava more closely. Turning back to Jasper she raised both eyebrows. "Well."

Liddie took a dab of water and washed Yava's face. "I never set much credence in tales about Orcs, but the proof's right here. O'er the mountains, ye say?"

"Yes," Jasper replied, "north of the Three Kingdoms somewhere."

"What's oop there, Finny, past the mountains?"

"I dunna know, ma'am."

"Yava, sweetie, ye'll stay with us 'till we find a way tae get ye back home." Liddie shook her head. "Just look at this crowd. Two Valanders, two Dwarfs, a Shouda and an Orc. The gods must be amused." She plunked a fingertip on Yava's flat little nose. "Dae ye know yer papa's name, Yava? Yer papa?"

"Kozhdu."

"If ye're seein' Finny along his way this fine morn, dip yersel in the water afore ye return." Liddie stared directly at Jasper, offering no hope of miscommunication.

"But the water is like ice," Jasper retorted.

"Nae bath, nae food."

"Well, Jasper, I have just the spot." Finny tugged on Jasper's sleeve. "The creek widens over black rock. It's much warmer." He pulled Jasper's head down and whispered, "Me and Opal go in there in our all thegithers, if ye know what I mean." His eyebrows bounced.

"Yes ma'am," Jasper answered. He glanced down at his gear, deciding to take along Rat Slayer, but leaving the rest.

Bahsa strode up to Jasper with a pleading look on his face.

"You'll have to take a bath too," Jasper pointed out, expecting this requirement to change Bahsa's mind.

Bahsa removed his chain hood and knife belt and, along with his alderwood staff, handed them to Liddie.

"Keep yer eye on him," Liddie reminded Jasper.

"Yes ma'am." Jasper turned from the cave, its mouth still deep in the morning shadows of the mountains rising to their east, and followed Finny down into the stony ravine that entrained the robust flow of spring water.

The act of walking away from Bahsa, knowing that the boy wanted to accompany them, struck a buried recollection of having frequently acted in the same way with his younger brother in Nilwid. That, he reflected, was before his life had been overturned by the Protectors and their vicious beasts. But Bahsa could not plead with him to wait. He pictured his brother's face, but the name was blank. He stopped, and called over his shoulder, "Hurry up, Bahsa." The more he pressed his mind to remember his brother's name, the deeper it fled into the recesses of an unreachable past.

Once Bahsa had shuffled down into the ravine, Jasper continued on toward Finny. "I told Liddie I'd watch him," he shrugged. Finny rolled his eyes.

After a short stretch of scrambling over and around boulders and rocky shelves, they reached a spot where the creek spread out over a purplish-black layer of stone, spilled over a smooth, twenty-yard slope and into a second, lower pool.

"That slide hes nae bumps nor rigs tae scaithe yer bare bum, if ye care tae tak the ride." Finny skipped over the narrow neck of creek above the upper pond. "I wish ye the finest, Jasper." He climbed the ridge to the south of the creek and vanished.

Without prompting, Bahsa stripped naked and waded into the upper pond, wrapping his long, thin arms about his shoulders. When he reached the slope at the far end, he turned and looked inquisitively at Jasper.

"I don't care if you go down it." After feeling the water with his hand, then verifying that none of the others had followed them into the ravine, Jasper reluctantly proceeded to disrobe. He looked up to see Bahsa seat himself on the slope, then slide out of sight.

Jasper waded into the water. The soles of his feet could sense the warmth of the underlying black rock, smooth as the wood floor of his bed chamber in Nilwid. "Willen! His name was Willen." Tears welled in his eyes. He threw himself into the shallow expanse of water and glided toward the slope at its far end. Raising himself just enough to look over, he verified that Bahsa had made it safely into the lower pool and now seemed to be enjoying an unsuccessful effort at trying to crawl back up the slippery green slope. Jasper swam back toward his clothes.

Finny stood at the upper end of the pool, motioning silently for Jasper to hurry and to be quiet. Swallowing his embarrassment, Jasper stood and walked briskly through the water toward his friend.

"Slavers," the Dwarf boy whispered, pointing downstream. "They're close."

Jasper turned to go for Bahsa, but a hand on his elbow restrained him. Finny pointed to Jasper's clothing heaped alongside the pond.

"We can have a look this way without bein' seen," Finny whispered, pointing up the southern slope of the ravine.

After throwing on his clothes and boots, Jasper followed Finny up the side of the ravine, strapping Rat Slayer to his hip as he went. A dozen yards later, they were squatting beneath a copse of gnarled junipers that leaned out over the ravine, offering a clear view of the lower pond and the creek downstream.

Bahsa made no sound as a bronze-skinned man in baggy trousers and a cloth-wrapped head grabbed him from behind. Finny slapped his hand over Jasper's mouth, and drew his face against Jasper's ear.

"They'll tak us both if they find us here." He swiveled Jasper's head toward five other men, all in slavers' garb and each wearing several weapons, ascending along the stream bed. "They ne'er come oop this way." His breath smelled of sausage. "Must be searchin' fer that runaway wee yellow lass. We need tae go back an' warn the ithers." He slowly released Jasper's head.

Jasper followed Finny back to the creek and up the ravine to the cave. "Liddie," Jasper whispered, when he was close enough to be heard, "Slavers, six of them, are coming up here. They caught Bahsa."

Liddie Burn stood expressionless for a moment, then motioned for everyone to gather all their belongings.

"What about Bahsa?" Phaena asked in a desperate whisper.

"We all wad be kilt!" Liddie replied. A look of anguish flashed across her face, replaced almost instantly by determination. "Finny, show us a way tae the road. We'll fallow them back tae Cinnabar an' see if yer uncle can get the boy freed. Quick now!"

Finny led them north, through the scrub, to a trail that ascended a short way, then traversed south, well above the entrance of Burnewin Cave. Liddie carried little Yava against her hip as she walked. Phaena and Jasper brought up the rear.

From the height, Jasper could see five slavers arrive at the entrance to the cave. He approached Liddie. "One of them must have gone back with Bahsa."

"That is plain tae see."

He knew she blamed him. He wanted to explain what had happened. That he had intended to rescue Bahsa. *What difference does it make now?* Again he thought of Willen. *I'm never where I need to be.* As they moved farther south, they caught one last glimpse of the slavers, now heading back down the drainage.

An hour later, they reached the Cinnabar Road. To their left it wound upward toward the pass into the Three Kingdoms of the Banu Sulal. To their right, the road descended in ever lazier switchbacks trending westward toward Cinnabar. No travelers could be seen in either direction.

“I wed doubt ye want tae tak that wee lass back tae the slavers,” Finny observed.

“And I don’t want to go back there,” Phaena added. “Not so soon, anyway.”

“I’ve got an idea,” Jasper said to Liddie. “There are way too many slavers for us to fight. You and Finny together won’t draw any attention, and you could go to see his uncle. I can take Phaena and the...Yava...up the road and find a place to make camp.”

Liddie Burn frowned as she looked at each member of their company. “I suppose we won’t find any ither help here abouts. We’ll do as Jasper said.” She lowered Yava to the road. “Yava, sweet, you go with Phaena. Go on.” She shook a pointed finger at Jasper. “Watch them.”

“Yes ma’am.” Jasper placed his palm on the pommel of Rat Slayer and felt the milky red stone of the handle. “I’ll find a place where we can watch the road.”

Without further discussion, Liddie headed down the road at a brisk pace, with Finny racing to catch up. Soon they vanished around a bend.

“They had Bahsa before I knew they were even there,” Jasper said to Phaena.

“They’ll get him back,” she said without much conviction. She held out her right hand. “Let’s go, Yava.”

Jasper walked to Phaena’s right, with Yava between them as they headed up the steep, winding road. “I was going to try and stop them, but Finny wouldn’t let me.” Yava reached up and grasped Jasper’s left hand. “He said we’d all be captured.”

After a quarter hour of walking, they reached a point where the road, supported on a solid stone arch, dodged into and out of a creek drainage. Jasper could hear the rush of water over rocks. “We can camp on that spot above the creek...” He pointed to a level area about thirty yards from the road. “...and look down to watch the road.”

“That’s good,” Phaena agreed. “And there’s water.”

"If we can find a way to get up there," Jasper added. He saw no easy way to get down from the road and over to the slope that led up to his selected spot.

Before they had left the road, the winded voice of Liddie Burn interrupted them. "Slavers are right ahind me! Head for the pass." Liddie ran faster than Jasper could imagine a Dwarf of her age running.

When she reached them, Phaena picked up Yava and they all sped up the winding road toward the pass. Jasper guessed that it was at least another mile away.

"How many are there?" he asked.

"All the whole lot o' them," Liddie grunted. "Fifty, maybees. Horses and wagons. They have Bahsa in a cage on one o' the wagons."

"Where's Finny?" Phaena asked.

"I sent him back to his mum. When those slavers...stop fer the night..." She gulped several breaths of air as she ran. "...then we find a way...tae break Bahsa oot o' the cage."

As they climbed the steepening switchbacks, the air grew cooler. Now at each outer curve, they could see the slaver caravan below them, growing nearer at each sighting. The slopes were so steep above and below the road, that Jasper found no route to safely take them off the road and into the treeless terrain.

Up ahead, the pass came into view. Shouting rose from the switchback below. Looking down, Jasper clearly saw men pointing at them. "They've seen Yava!" Three mounted slavers pulled their horses in front of the caravan and increased their speed.

At the crest of the pass, with the pounding of hooves close behind, Jasper stopped. Ahead of them stood dozens of bowmen on horses, blocking the road. Behind them, the pursuers halted as the remainder of the caravan climbed toward them.

Liddie, still gasping from the run, took Yava from Phaena and held the little girl close with one arm, while defiantly drawing her iron flail in the other. Jasper drew his golden helmet onto his head and unsheathed Rat Slayer.

Common rock, upon which we build our hopes and lead our lives, serves as a universal conduit for those who attune themselves to its nature.

Ereben Leaf: Chronicle of the Counterspell

From his perch amid the piles of kindling, Ereben watched as the fat proprietor of the Goat's Teat Inn shoved her way to the front of the silent crowd. Her one good eye was fixed intently on Barrow.

"Thae scoundrels are mine!" she shouted at the nearest man with a torch. "The Goat's Teat is a wreck on thir account." She lifted a stubby arm toward the torch. "Allow me, yer honor," she said effusively to the soldier.

Apparently pleased to find an eager volunteer among the populace, the flattered soldier proffered his torch and motioned for the other torch bearer to follow the lead of the hateful Dwarf girl.

She turned to the sullen crowd. "Let this serve fer a lesson tae thae tha' thinks tae break oop the Goat's Teat."

As the girl's speech continued to ramble, Ereben felt that she was intentionally stalling. There was some movement beyond the crowd, by the town gate. An exceptionally tall gate guard turned a dark brown face toward Ereben.

"Get on with it!" shouted the soldier beside the Laird of the Goat's Teat.

"Aye," she acknowledged, turning from the crowd. "Aah!" she wailed, dropping the torch. "Tha' burned my hand." She laboriously bent at the waist and cautiously grasped the bottom end of the torch. With even greater effort, she raised her corpulence erect.

"Give that to me," the impatient guard demanded.

"Aye, yer honor." She reluctantly held out the torch to him, but with another cry of pain, dropped it again.

The soldier, now irate, motioned to his partner to light the twigs surrounding the captives. "Do it!" As his partner tossed a torch onto the kindling in front of Root, the unfortunate young Dwarf screamed in horror. The first soldier bent and retrieved his own torch, but as he stood, an arm reached around his neck from behind. A single metallic claw stroked beneath his chin.

Chrysanthus, in a full-length, hooded robe, lowered the gurgling soldier to the ground. With a grimace of his fanged maw, Chrysanthus halted the second soldier in his tracks. From behind the now frightened onlookers, a mass of Firth's pikemen began to surge toward the center. Chrysanthus dropped his hooded cape to the ground, leaving him clothed in only his leather trousers. Every muscle of his bulging, fur covered chest rippled as he held both massive arms extended. His metallic claws reflected the morning sun as the leopard-man bellowed a shattering roar, his shifting cat eyes defiant.

The crowd, in unbridled panic, stampeded away from Chrysanthus in every direction, bowling over many pikemen, and delaying others.

Yarnish Blen, somehow freed from his bonds, cut the ropes that held Ereben. "To the gate," Blen shouted above the chaos.

Ereben looked toward the agonized screams of Root, Blen's young Dwarfish cellmate. Flames lapped at his chest. He was lost. A massive hand grasped Ereben's arm and yanked him toward the gate. Guards were now striking down any who stood in their way. Ereben stopped at a fallen pike and launched it into his opponents. Barrow and Blen battled their way to the gate, kept open by the flashing, twirling spear of the only Shouda Observer, Minkar Jarad.

A mass of guards, under the commanding shouts of Holnick Firth, formed into a solid phalanx and started at a jog toward the escaping prisoners. Within five yards of colliding with the vastly more numerous mass of terrified townspeople, the phalanx collapsed and dispersed in chaos. Two gigantic birds descended, disemboweling any soldier within reach. The white and ghostly gray gyre falcon, Titus, streaked back and forth through the fleeing guards. Krey, with the smooth silence of a gray owl, swooped again and again, catching one guard each pass, then lifting high to drop the screaming victim to his death.

As Ereben fled through the gate, he caught a glimpse of a furred figure in leather trousers, far back within the town, leap from the ground and over the three-yard-high picket wall in a single fluid movement, a gray cloak clasped in one hand.

With Minkar seated behind him, Ereben urged Titus into the air. Soon they caught up with Krey, carrying Barrow and Blen. Ironhole fell away in the distance, and with it the column of smoke from the unfortunate Dwarf who perished at the stake.

"They still have my dagger and my breastplate," Ereben called over his back.

His Shouda friend gripped his shoulder and spoke into his ear. "It is certain that one of us, perhaps all of us, would have perished had we attempted to reclaim those things which are rightfully yours."

The wind in Ereben's face gradually calmed his racing heart. Undulating hills and plains of Knurlan passed far below as they flew toward the morning sun. He closed his eyes against the glare and imagined Phaena running up to him as he dismounts. *Yes.* Soon he would reach Liddie's cow farm.

"So far as I can tell," Blen was saying to the group standing before Liddie Burn's mound house, "there are bits and pieces of about a half dozen Knights of the Redeemer. Hoof prints seem to lead away in all directions."

"Liddie's iron flail is gone," Barrow mentioned.

"Such a weapon," Minkar suggested, "might be taken away by a captor, but young Jasper's carved staff is nowhere to be found, and my son's alderwood staff is also missing."

"There is no way to really know if they escaped," Blen sighed, "or were carried away."

The great peregrine, Pelegri, circled once above, then descended, bearing Chrysanthus on its shoulders. A wild look in the leopard-man's eyes stifled any greetings. He glanced briefly at the torn bodies scattered about, sniffed the air in all directions, then inspected the confusion of hoof prints. The others repeated their discoveries to him, but no one was confident that Chrysanthus could fully comprehend their words or logic.

At length, Chrysanthus stopped near the river, somewhat east of the mound house. He stood erect, arms folded, and turned toward his companions.

"I think Grandpa has found something," Ereben mumbled. He had not spoken since arriving at the farm. His heart was crushed at the first sight of a recent battle as they landed. He wandered toward Chrysanthus. The others had paid no attention.

When he reached Chrysanthus, the leopard-man simply turned his head upstream, then looked again at Ereben.

"Someone went that way?" Ereben noted hoof prints leading eastward, along the river. "But who was it?"

Chrysanthus crouched and picked at the hoof prints with a metallic claw. He tipped his head to one side, then stood and stamped his bare foot into the soft dirt twice. His gaze leveled on Ereben.

"I don't understand, Grandpa." Chrysanthus' penetrating eyes caused Ereben to look down at his own feet. *How can I ever know what he's trying to say?* Ereben's eyes drifted to the two footprints his grandfather had made. One print was with claws extended, the other without. "They went this way," he called excitedly to the others.

"Grandpa noticed it," Ereben explained, once the group had assembled. "The horses of the Knights are shod with iron. These prints are not. They must be from Dantel and Kehlibar." He knew that the kelpies possessed hooves only when they chose to.

"Why huvna they used thir wings?" Barrow asked.

"I don't know."

"And," Blen added, "did all of them escape?"

"We must learn the truth of it," Minkar Jarad insisted. "Since we have arrived from the West, we must explore the remaining possibilities. I will go north upon the back of Krey."

"Aye," Barrow agreed "and I tae the Easlan with Pelegri."

"Someone should stay around here," Ereben added, "in case they are able to return."

"I'll do that," Yarnish Blen volunteered, "and try to find out what Firth has been planning to do with all those magic contraptions."

"Then Grandpa and I will search to the South on Titus." Ereben thought he heard a faint, deep purring sound.

They gathered supplies and traded farewells. Each had lost someone he loved, and each departed with determined expressions tempered by a pall of uncertainty. First Minkar lifted to the North on Krey, then Barrow to the East on Pelegri. Finally, Ereben and Chrysanthus climbed upon the great gyre falcon, Titus, and urged him up toward scuttering white clouds to the South.

Ereben had become accustomed to wearing his golden breastplate when he traveled. At least, he thought of it as his—one of the many pieces of golden armor belonging to the Chamberlain of the library of ancient Ephesia. Now it was gone, as was his dagger—made by his own hands. He carried Hobart's dagger in his sheath, and wore the striking, ice leopard cape presented to him by Minkar. Chrysanthus, with his gray, hooded robe that Liddie had made for him, carried his own dagger. The leopard-man steadied himself with only his clawed feet.

The Great Canyon came into view, appearing from their cloud height as an enormous crack across the surface of Knurlan. Chrysanthus grasped Ereben's arm, then extended his own arm toward the canyon below.

Ereben was learning to read his grandfather's signs. They were not language and not mime. Instead, they were more like notions—substantial and almost never without significance. Although Chrysanthus seemed to understand Ereben's words with little difficulty, expressing his thoughts to Ereben appeared to require a great deal of effort from his part-leopard mind. Given Chrysanthus' inability to speak, Ereben wondered how his grandfather had succeeded in calling Pelegri to ferry him from Ironhole back to Liddie Burn's cow farm following their escape from Holnick Firth.

They began a long, spiral descent toward the bottom of the Great Canyon. The level of the river was nearly a mile below the rim. With any luck, he thought, Brother Eretz Mor and Sister Zaratha would still be watching the bridge over the Death River. In the past, they had been able to communicate with Ereben's enlarged birds, not to mention the rocks. Perhaps they could understand Chrysanthus' thoughts.

"Well," Sister Zaratha chuckled, "Isn't that interesting." She examined the metallic claws of Chrysanthus' right hand. "You know, I've seen a lot of...blended things, but this is a new one for me," said the tiny woman, dressed in her usual purple robe with a sickle tucked beneath its cinch. "Brother Eretz Mor, see if you can get some refreshments for our guests." Standing only as high as Chrysanthus' waist, she continued her inspection.

"Yes, yes," he replied. Brother Eretz Mor, as tiny as Sister Zaratha, hurried back to the shack they shared, nestled by the river bridge at the bottom of the Great Canyon. His brown robe hid the movement of his feet, creating the impression that he simply glided over the dark stone.

"He seems to understand what we say...," Ereben explained.

"Of course he does," Sister Zaratha interrupted.

"...but he doesn't speak."

"Hmmm. I can see that. Yes. Very unusual. Well, not really unusual by itself, you know." She scratched her forehead. "He...you," she corrected herself, tugging at Chrysanthus robe, "hear what we say, just as a man would. But you put together what you want to tell us the way an animal would, you know. That's hard, dear, isn't it?"

Chrysanthus opened his fanged mouth as if to speak, but instead, placed his hand gently atop Sister Zaratha's head.

"Come," Brother Eretz Mor signaled with a flapping hand. "Come have a drink. Come."

Sister Zaratha cocked her head. "Titus, you'll have to drink from the river. You can't fit in the house, you know."

Titus blinked, then looked dubiously at the silt-laden river rushing by.

"Oh, don't be so fussy," she scolded. "It's perfectly good water. Just don't fall in."

The hot, dry air of the canyon was somehow excluded from the interior of the shack. Ereben stepped into the coolness, uttering a soft, "Aah."

At a stone table, Brother Eretz Mor had set out four ceramic cups of chilled water. In the center of the table was a plate heaped with small, thin strips of crispy smoked fish and wedges of sweet citron. A finger-size bowl of salt rested nearby.

Ereben explained events since his last visit to the canyon floor, when he had been dropped into the abyss by a giant vulture. Sister Zaratha and Brother Eretz Mor seemed to be aware of all but the most recent happenings.

"What puzzles me," Ereben continued, "is the collection of magic books and scrolls and tools that Firth held in the cellar of the tower in Ironhole."

"Yes, that is worrisome," Brother Eretz Mor interjected. "Yes."

"It's no surprise that it's a large collection," Sister Zaratha pointed out, "since we know that the Knights of the Redeemer sent a large party to pillage the ruins of ancient Ephesia."

"When?" Ereben asked. He had explored only a small part of the overgrown ruins.

"Oh, a few weeks ago," she replied. "But the tough question is why. Those folks run about the countryside burning up people for having anything to do with magic. Then they set up their own library. It sure is confusing."

"Very confusing," Brother Eretz Mor added.

"Not only that," she continued, "they're sweeping south into Whitewood, in search of something. What exactly they're looking for, I don't know."

Sister Zaratha's brow furrowed. She gazed silently at Chrysanthus and then said, "Red rock? They're looking for red rock? Red rock. Huh! Chrysanthus thinks that's what they're looking for."

"What does that mean?" Ereben asked.

"Red rock. Strong red rock." Sister Zaratha stared intently at Chrysanthus. "This is not very easy. Do you mean strong like a ruby, or powerful like a sarcite? Well! How about that. He thinks they're searching for sarcite."

"You lost me," Ereben sighed.

"There are a number of kinds of stone that have special attunements," she explained. "Me and Brother Eretz Mor are familiar with stone, if you hadn't noticed. Now, the green handle of your dagger...that's jadeite. It's extremely rare—found only on the island of Malagaro. I think you've noticed that it has some rather special properties."

"Yes, it has," Ereben admitted. He had never considered the nature of the stone handle.

"Well, another special stone, called sarcite, is red. Actually it's kind of milky red. Anyway, it's found only in one place, far to the South."

"Where is that?"

"From what I understand—and I'm not at all sure it's true—it's in mines in the side of an extinct volcano. They're called the Warded Mines. Many hundreds of years ago, I'm told, the mines were sealed with magic by a Troll conjurer, to keep people from getting in. That's if it's true at all." She scratched her forehead. "It's really not far from our home in the Dunes, but the location of this volcano is in such a nasty place that I don't know of anyone alive who has actually seen it."

"Where are these dunes?" Ereben asked.

"Oh, the Legion Dunes," she replied. "It's where all of our folks come from. It's south west of here."

"Are all of you...your folks...your size?" he asked delicately.

"If you're wanting to know if were a race of midgets," she smirked, "don't be bashful. Just come right out and ask."

"I wouldn't have put it quite that way," Ereben clarified.

"Well I would," she said with a smile. "We are a race of midgets. It's just that we call ourselves Gnomes. It sounds more...descriptive."

"Other people sometimes call us Rock Gnomes," Brother Eretz Mor added on his own. "Nobody does rocks like we do." He smiled, apparently proud to have made a contribution to the conversation.

Ereben remembered his own passage within the rock of the Great Canyon, and what it is like to be a rock. Only by biting down on the bitter Nagel radish had he been able to escape the peaceful seduction of stone.

"Are you still with us, Ereben?" Sister Zaratha interrupted.

"Yes." Ereben shook himself from his reverie. "So, what do you suppose the Knights are planning to do with sarcite? It seems like they would want to destroy it, if it can be used for magic."

"But it sounds to me like Holnick Firth may be interested in its possible uses." Sister Zaratha drummed all ten fingers on the stone table. "He must have figured out its value when he raided the ruins of Ephesia. I really doubt, though, that he could read that Shadae script."

"There was that monk in the cellar of the tower," Ereben said softly, almost to himself. "Blen...Yarnish Blen, said he was a monk from Moss Abbey, but I don't know where that is?"

Sister Zaratha's eyebrows perked up. "That's beyond the forests of Whitewood, in the heart of Oldwood. The legend is that the monks of Moss Abbey dedicate themselves to holding back the chaos unleashed on the world many generations ago. My own impression is that they're just another cloistered religious cult."

Chrysanthus belched, attracting the notice of the others seated about him. He smiled in reply to their glances. The plate in the center of the stone table was empty. Chrysanthus licked the steel claws of his right thumb and index finger.

"Are you pleased with where the discussion has gone?" Sister Zaratha asked the leopard-man.

"I think, where the food has gone," Brother Eretz Mor mumbled irritably, as he rose to refill the plate.

To the surprise of the others, Chrysanthus walked directly to the blank stone face of the boulder that enclosed the magical artifacts and books which Ereben had placed there after his visit to Ephesia. Without the slightest sound or motion from Chrysanthus, the stone opened its four compartments to reveal the stash.

"I've never been able to do that," Sister Zaratha commented.

Chrysanthus reached in, lifted a blue leather-bound tome and opened it eagerly. He stared at the open page with intensity and visible effort. Then tears welled up in his eyes. He gently closed the book and replaced it.

Ereben took up the same book, turning to its title page. He read it aloud. "The Chaos of Ternaria, by Chrysanthus of the Eighty-fourth Generation" Ereben threw his arms around his grandfather and wept with him. "I'm sorry, Grandpa," he whispered.

For a few moments they grieved for Chrysanthus' lost literacy. The leopard-man turned back to the stash and extracted two items, which he handed to Ereben. The first item Ereben recognized as the drawing he had salvaged from his grandfather's burned home. Titus had nested in it beneath the floorboard, back when Titus was still Chrysanthus' pet mouse. Back before Ereben had fled from Rippleton. It was the drawing of a strange ax. Hobart had mended its fragments, rips and tears the night before his own death. It was the ax depicted in Ailantha's tapestry—the ax used to fight a golden dragon.

"Is this important, Grandpa?"

Chrysanthus replied with the vague semblance of a shrug.

"At least I can try to read it."

The second item was the flat, wooden box that contained what Hobart had called The Glaive of Brenden. Ereben lifted its hinged lid and stroked the polished steel surface of the glaive. Like four rounded ax blades, their razor edges at the perimeter, their backs joined to form a glistening disk, the glaive displayed four concentric rows of glyphs. Ereben found that he now could understand several of the words. "Evocation, invocation, summoning," he read aloud. "Brother Eretz Mor made a rubbing of it onto parchment," Ereben stated with an inquiring expression. He hadn't wanted to carry the weight of the steel original in his pack.

Chrysanthus grasped the box in one hand, then carefully lifted the glaive, holding it by the deep notches between the blades. He rotated his hand to reveal similar glyphs on the reverse side of the glaive. The few words Ereben could recognize appeared to be in the same sequence, but written on different blades than their counterparts on the obverse. Chrysanthus replaced the glaive, closed the lid, then sunk his steel claws into the box, leaving five deep gashes in the wood.

Ereben, Sister Zaratha and Brother Eretz Mor looked at one another. The Sister shook her head. "I don't know what you're trying to say, Chrysanthus." She frowned.

Chrysanthus replaced the box within one of the stone vaults. Without an audible or visible signal, the boulder closed its surface.

"How did the Knights get to Ephesia?" Ereben asked. "The Protectors could fly there on giant vultures, but the Knights of the Redeemer ride horses."

"They passed here," she replied, "crossing the bridge—twenty on horseback. I expected them to die in their attempt to find the route to the rim, but they must have had a map."

"Did you speak with them?"

"No. We hid from them," she said bluntly.

"We don't guard the bridge," Brother Eretz Mor clarified. "We only maintain it and watch it. That's what we do."

"And only four of them came back through the canyon," she added, "So, the others are probably still looking around the ruins."

Circling several hundred yards above the ancient ruins of Ephesia, Ereben could hardly believe what lay revealed. During his last visit, with Hobart, he had entered a single, jungle-covered mound which turned out to be the library. Now, five major buildings were exposed, completely cleared of the jungle canopy. Each building was roughly the same immense size, each in the shape of a pointed mound composed of white stone steps, each step the height of a man. The five buildings formed a gigantic, five-sided figure, a pentagon. As they descended, Ereben could make out what appeared to be a five-sided socket at the apex of each building. Most of the sockets, about a half-yard across, were empty. In the socket of the nearest building was a fragment of milky red stone. He remembered the five-sided figures composed of metallic rods in the cellar of the tower in Ironhole. *Pentagons*. And here, a giant pentagon of enormous buildings. Each building, at some time in the ancient past, apparently mounted a column of sarcite at its apex. The green jadeite of the Guardian's daggers could be attuned as a field of power using three daggers to form a triangle.

Ereben saw movement at the edge of the cleared area. Tethered horses were apparently becoming restive at the approach of the great gyre falcon. Their riders, he assumed, were inside the buildings. He directed Titus upward and to the South. Just outside the entry to one of the buildings, two men stood, looking up at him. As Ereben continued south, he had no way of knowing what Chrysanthus, seated behind him, had seen or thought.

Late in the afternoon, the southern boundary of the jungle plateau came into view. A narrow margin of scrub vegetation extended beyond the lush jungle, and fell away in a broken cliff. Grassland continued a thousand yards below the cliff. Ereben brought Titus down at the top of the cliff. He and Chrysanthus dismounted and stretched their joints, made stiff by the long flight.

Standing at the verge, Ereben looked for any route down the vast, escarpment of purple stone, but saw none. In the southerly breeze, the air was drier and no longer scented with the humid decay of jungle. He did see ant-like movements at the base of the cliff. The scores of people far below, moved about randomly, as though at a village, but he saw no structures or tents. Chrysanthus grasped his shoulder and pulled him away from the edge and crouched him to the ground.

Startled, Ereben turned to his grandfather, whose gaze was fixed to the South. He looked into the broad expanse of blue. There, on the horizon, a tiny twinkle slowly grew, until he recognized the unmistakable silhouette of a dragon, sparkling gold in the late sun. Ever so slowly, the dragon grew larger and descended directly for the unseen community at the base of the cliff immediately below Ereben.

Ereben crawled to the edge. At the dragon's approach, the tiny people below stopped their movement. *Run!* He held his breath, waiting for them to recognize their danger. He heard no screams as they finally fled. What he did hear was a hissing roar shortly after a spray of flame blossomed from the mouth of the dragon. It dove toward the base of the cliff, then circled around to attack again. Five times the dragon circled and dove, spewing fire on each approach. Then it spiraled upward on the thermal which rose from the cliff heated by sun and fire.

From behind Ereben, Titus flapped his great white and gray wings and rose into the sky. As the dragon turned and climbed to pursue the gyre falcon, Titus climbed and vanished to the North. Clearing the rim of the cliff, the clawed feet of the dragon passed within a yard of Ereben. The dragon abruptly circled over Ereben, focusing his eyes briefly on him with what seemed like recognition. It returned its gaze toward the North, where Titus had fled. With a violent flapping of its leathery wings, the dragon sped in pursuit.

ꕤ

A simple and predictable act of self-defense may enrage a more powerful adversary.

Ereben Leaf: Chronicle of the Counterspell

A volley of arrows arced over Jasper and his companions, embedding into the torsos of three mounted, Sulalian slavers. Others struck their horses. The three slavers crumpled to the ground, twitching and crying out, while their injured horses fled in panic, down the road toward Cinnabar. Jasper held his blade, Rat Slayer, but didn't know which side was more dangerous—the mounted archers in front of him, or the slavers behind him.

The Banu Sulal caravan, amid shouts, gesticulations and obvious chaos, attempted to reverse direction on the narrow mountain road. Five mounted Sulalian swordsmen passed through the retreating mob, their brightly colored robes flowing behind them, and blocked the road, to guard their retreating caravan. Despite a distance of a hundred yards separating them from the mounted archers, another volley of arrows passed high into the air. Before the arrows could reach their mark, the Sulalian guard turned their mounts and galloped back to the caravan.

Jasper studied the mounted archers who had driven off the slavers. Unlike the slavers, these men wore armor—slats of painted wood, in fitted panels, protecting shoulders, torso, hips and thighs. Each man's armor displayed a single dominant color, but a color unique among his comrades. Atop their heads rested a simple, peaked gray hat that flared widely above the ears. These opponents, he knew, were not the decorated thugs of the Redeemers, or the impulsive slavers. He faced a mounted phalanx of skilled, disciplined warriors.

One of their members, wearing deep red armor, above gray, woolen trousers that tucked into high leather boots, tied his bow beside the quiver on his saddle and dismounted, while the others maintained their positions, an arrow nocked in every bow. The man in red approached Jasper and his companions at a casual pace. At his hip, a remarkably long and narrow, gently curved, black scabbard promised a fearsome sword. He stopped just out of range of Liddie Burn's iron flail.

Liddie offered only a defiant grimace, her flail held ready at her shoulder. Yava peeked from behind Liddie's generous hip.

At this distance, the man in red revealed a young, weathered face that reflected years of sun and wind—a yellowish, broad face, with pointed ears and slanted, puffy eyes.

"Papa!" Yava shouted, tearing herself from Liddie's grip. As she raced forward, the red-armored man lowered himself to one knee and wrapped his arms about her. They spoke softly to one another in an unfamiliar language. While she spoke, Yava pointed at Jasper, then at Liddie and Phaena.

Yava's father rose to his feet, and led the little girl to his horse. After placing her into the saddle, a subtle motion of his hand caused all the bowmen to lower their bows. He again approached Liddie, this time ignoring her flail. "Kozhdu owes debt to you. Now, Banu Sulal enemy to you. Where you will go?"

Kozhdu smelled of earth and horse sweat and faintly of rancid milk. Although his demeanor remained severe, a kindness sparkled through.

Liddie lowered her flail. "Yon slavers took a young Shouda lad from us." She raised a thumb over her shoulder, indicating the mountain road up which she had run, and down which the slavers had just retreated. "We'll have tae wait an' fallow them."

Kozhdu frowned. "Nye. Very bad plan. You are brave, but they kill you all." He stroked his finger across his throat.

"We can't leave him with the slavers!" Jasper interjected.

"Kuyuk," Kozhdu stated, as he turned from Liddie and walked back toward his men, "take all weapons. They come with us to Orkahtsk."

"Da."

On foot, Jasper, Liddie, and Phaena were led by the horsemen through the mountain passes to the north. The three captives traveled without their weapons, but Jasper had been allowed to keep his helmet. Their mounted captors left them unbound, not even taking the time to inspect their packs, but kept a close watch over them. Travel through a narrow pass required only one day to come to the northeastern slope of a mountain range that curved from the northwest to the southeast. Jasper recognized that he would have never found this pass on his own. The skyline had revealed no dip, until they were already within the serpentine trail that crossed the ridge.

Snow-capped peaks gave way to a vast open plain. Grass, entirely devoid of even an occasional tree, blanketed the land to the horizon, with a chain of blue peaks trailing away northward to his left. Just below the nearest undulations of the foothills, gentle smoke of several fires rose from what appeared to be an encampment. Since their capture, the three of them had been kept separated, and unable to speak with one another. As they approached the encampment, Jasper saw spacious, circular tents, arranged in a broad half-circle. Every tent was as large as any of the houses back in Nilwid, and was covered in a coarse fabric, nearly white in color. Each appeared to have a well-built wooden door, painted red. Wood chimes clicked and clonked in the gusty breeze. Dozens of sheep wandered about, grazing lazily on the knee-high grass. From the cooking fires, ribbons of smoke streamed eastward, and dissipated high above. The small clusters of women who tended the fires stopped what they had been doing, to watch while the three strangers entered the camp.

The breeze also carried the scent of roasted mutton. A crisp disk of sun settled toward the high, western ridge.

Jasper, Phaena, and Liddie were brought together, led into the clearing within the arc of tents, and left under the watch of one of their captors, near a large fire in the center of the camp.

"What do you think they want with us?" Jasper whispered to Liddie.

"They maybees believe we wer' a part o' takin' tha' wee lass," Liddie replied. "Yava will put truth tae the situation."

Jasper heard a clamor among the grazing sheep in the distance. The flock drew closer together, then moved toward the camp. Among the sheep, a man rose to his feet. On his right arm stood an eagle nearly half the man's height. A quick flick removed a piece of fabric from the eagle's head. Immediately, the bird lifted into the air, flew a short arc, then descended with shocking speed toward a spot on the ground just beyond the flock. The eagle's handler remained standing, until his eagle returned with a dead fox in its talons.

A man came out of the door of a central tent, and walked over to the group. "Come with me. Leader will speak with you." He led them back to the same tent, and gestured for them to enter its framed, red door, though he remained outside.

The air inside felt thick and warm. A tall, brown clay stove burned at the center, its smoke channeled cleanly within a cylindrical clay chimney that exited through a hole in the center of the tent's domed top. Wooden lattice work and wood spars supported it all.

To Jasper's relief, "Leader" was the red-armored man whom they had met at their first encounter—Yava's papa. Now dressed in trousers and robes, he sprawled atop a mound of pillows on the far side, about eight paces away. The clacking of wooden chimes outside continued in fits and pauses. Liddie, Phaena, and Jasper remained standing before the stove.

"These are really big tents," Jasper said, pivoting his head to examine the expanse of the felt walls, most hidden by brightly figured carpets that hung throughout. Some sections of the tent were partitioned by more hanging carpets suspended by rods.

"Ger. Ger," Kozhdu corrected. "It is called ger. What are your names?"

"I am Jasper. Jasper of Nilwid. This is Liddie Burn, and this," pointing to Phaena, "is Ph... Freya... of... Brockton." He swallowed hard, hoping he hadn't let slip Phaena's identity.

"I am Kozhdu, leader of this camp. Yava tell me what happen. How you find her, give food, and help her flee Banu Sulal. I have thanks for what you do."

"Nae thanks required," Liddie said. "I wad do the same fer any wee lass. Tha' be only proper."

From the side of a carpet partition, the face of a young woman came into view. Beneath her, Yava peeked out as well. Kozhdu smiled indulgently at his daughter, then waved them away with his hand.

Kozhdu nodded his head toward Liddie. "Tonight we eat in celebrate of Yava return. Day grows late. Stay, eat or leave. You to choose. You all guest with us."

Jasper offered a half-bow. The three of them left the ger and walked to the central fire. Their weapons were returned to them, but one of the men accompanied them wherever they went.

Music twanged from a high-pitched, pear shaped instrument with three long strings on its neck, in duet with a haunting flute sound made by a man holding an assemblage of wooden tubes, each note deftly blown from a different tube. There was food enough for all of Nilwid to feast for a year. About seventy people, men, women and children of all ages emerged from their gers, and gathered around the central fire, helping themselves to chunks of spit-roasted mutton.

"What do we do now?" Jasper asked Liddie, through a mouthful of roasted meat.

"Find Bahsa. Maister Kozhdu maybees could help. She rose, and headed in the direction of Kozhdu. She abruptly turned back. "Jasper, you an' Miss Phaena stay put." She raised a finger, then emphatically lowered it to point to where they were seated.

Liddie walked around to the opposite side of the fire, to where Kozhdu was seated on the ground, his legs crossed.

Phaena clicked her teeth. "You don't have to make a pig of yourself, Jasper."

Jasper glanced at the grease dripping from his fingers. One by one, he licked them clean, then wiped his chin with his sleeve.

Phaena shook her head. They were seated on the ground close enough to the fire to feel the heat. As the celebration continued, some people danced; others engaged in loud, unintelligible debates.

Liddie returned. "Kozhdu say he will help with findin' Bahsa. He say we must travel to a place called Gotagrazh. There, a man called Gota Bopu, or somethin' o' the like, will know how to find him."

"When do we leave," Phaena asked.

"We leave the morn, right early. Kozhdu will send alang a few men fer our safety, an' provide us with horses. I suggest we all get some rest."

The group bunked together in a ger, along with the family of its owner. Jasper drifted into sleep with the soft clacking of the wind chimes.

The sun offered no warmth, though enough light for them to see. They had left the small encampment several hours earlier, traveling on horseback to the north-west, skirting the eastern slope of the high range of mountains. Kozhdu had decided to come with them, bringing along four other Orkahti men. Chigu was tall and broad, one of the biggest Orkahti men Jasper had seen. He hadn't spoken a word since morning. Kuyuk, Jasper recognized from the previous day. It was Kuyuk who had eventually accepted Liddie's flail, and eventually returned their weapons to them. Since Kuyuk had returned Rat Slayer to Jasper this morning, he found himself repeatedly touching its sheath, just to reassure him that it was there.

Two of the men rode to the rear. Badai kept an eagle perched on his right shoulder, to supplement their food during the journey. Much of the time, a blue cloth remained wrapped about its eyes. "It keeps her calm," Badai had said. Beside Badai rode Od, the youngest of the Orkahti men in the group. His principal charge seemed to be tending all the horses.

They reached Gotagrazh mid-way through the day. It consisted entirely of a large temple that appeared to grow out of a steep slope. Its granite walls blended seamlessly into the mountain, making it appear from a distance as a natural part of the terrain. Badai and Od remained outside with all the horses, while the others headed in.

From inside the open, wooden doors of the gate, a long, granite staircase led ahead, directly to the top of the temple. Jasper guessed it was hundreds of steps—too many to count.

Kozhdu led the way, reaching the top winded. He paused for a moment, and walked through an intricately carved, double doorway. Jasper stopped to catch his breath, and inspect the carvings, while Phaena and Liddie followed Kozhdu through the door. Before entering, Jasper looked back at the enormous stairway they would have to descend, once they were done here.

The doorway opened into a vaulted central room. Their course, from the outer wall, all the way to this room had been devoid of guards or other people. This one, central room was huge, and also empty of people. To Jasper's eyes, Gotagrazh appeared to be deserted.

Centered at the far end of the room, a dozen granite steps rose to a small platform, surrounded with dark, dusty curtains in back and along both sides. Seated toward the rear, an ancient Orkahti man, cloaked in a wine-red, woolen robe, slowly lifted his cowled head. His face and limbs were emaciated, but his dark eyes seemed bright and alert.

"Gota Bopu, forgive us. We seek wisdom and guidance," Kozhdu uttered softly, bowing low.

"Kozhdu, my old friend, please come closer."

"Wise One, these people return my daughter to me. They are friends. I wish to repay this debt. They seek locations."

Gota Bopu cast a glance in the direction of the others gathered at the bottom of the stairs. "Come closer," he said, motioning with a frail hand. His voice carried softly and clearly in the granite room.

As Jasper, Liddie, and Phaena approached the shriveled old man, Jasper's staff burst into life. Its carved creatures jostled and shrieked. The High Priest quickly reached toward a head-sized sphere of intricately linked rods, which rested on a small table to his right. He opened one of its many sides. Immediately, Jasper's staff resumed its usual quiescence. Jasper descended the steps and held out his staff to Chigu.

"Can you hold this for me?" Reluctantly, Chigu accepted the misbehaved staff from Jasper, who then bounded back up the steps to rejoin the others.

"Kozhdu is my friend," the old man said. "He has helped me many times. If he says you need my help, I will do what I can. However, I require a gift from those I help. This gift must be an item treasured by you. All that I can provide you in exchange for a gift is the location and movement of any one person or thing."

Jasper approached first. "Gota Bopu," Jasper said, tearing the stitching of his waist, "I offer you this silver coin." It was the coin he had taken from his house after the death of his parents.

"Who or what do you wish to find," the old man asked.

Jasper looked at the sphere-like object next to the Gota Bopu. It was hollow, and made from many thin rods formed into five-sided figures, assembled into the shape of a ball. "I seek the location of a friend of ours, Bahsa Jarad. He is only six years old. A Shouda."

The old man closed the side of the sphere, and held his right hand on it, while his left hand slipped into a cloth pouch that hung from his shoulder. His open eyes seemed to lose focus, and the expression on his face grew distant. Several moments passed before the old man jerked his hand away from the hollow sphere. He paused, head bowed, then turned to Jasper.

"Your young friend travels south. His body rocks, as though on a ship. His hands are bound." Gota Bopu bowed his head in silence.

Jasper waited for more information. He had given a silver for this—his only silver. Once he realized that there would be no more, he stepped back, disappointed, and looked at Phaena.

Phaena reached over to Jasper, and placed a delicate finger on the milky red pommel stone of Jasper's Rat Slayer. "May I borrow this, Jasper?"

"What for?" he asked.

She gathered her long, flowing locks of golden hair in her free hand, and raised her eyebrows. Jasper understood.

"Ye may regret that, child," Liddie said to her, sadness in her voice.

"My hair is something I treasure, perhaps more than I should."

Jasper lifted Rat Slayer from its sheath, and solemnly passed it to her.

Phaena walked to the shriveled man, Jasper's sword pointed towards the floor. "Gota Bopu, I do not have much. The only thing I can offer you, I do give with regret." With that, she gathered her hair once again, and cut it all just beneath her ears. The blade sliced silently. She handed the lock to the priest, bowing.

"I wish to find someone I care for. His name is Ereben Leaf."

Gota Bopu put the golden lock of hair into his lap alongside Jasper's silver coin. One hand caressed the sphere to his right, while his other hand once again slid into the cloth pouch. His mind seemed to journey elsewhere. The old man sat as lifeless as the granite walls around him. After a moment, he spoke.

"Ereben Leaf travels south. All around are ancient oaks. Along side him is a strange beast. This beast does not attack, rather it seems companionable." The old priest bowed his head.

Phaena returned Rat Slayer to Jasper. "Thank you," she said.

Finally, Liddie approached the High Priest of Dwalune. "Maister Bopu, all that I have with me that I truly value, ye maybees dunna want. I offer ye breast stays, made o' the finest bone and linen." She untied them under her shirt and handed them to the man.

"I wish to find a man call't Barrow, Whittig Trench, a Dwarf," Liddie said.

Once again, the seeker's hand strayed to the strange, spherical object to his right, while his other hand reached into his pouch, causing him again to drift into a trance. "Barrow is traveling east. There are great wings on either side. They are not his. A great bird carries him."

"I thank you Gota Bopu," Kozhdu said softly. "We travel to Angelsk," he informed them, "to north. From Angelsk, we take ship to slave coast and look for Bahsa."

"I sense danger in your going to Angelsk," the old seeker volunteered, a worried wrinkle in his brow.

"Be there nae ither option?" Liddie asked. "We must find the lad."

"Ships go from Angelsk," Kozhdu stated.

All bowed once more, and descended the steps. Jasper retrieved his carved staff from Chigu, then they rejoined Badai and Od outside the gate. Departing Gotagrazh, they headed northeast across the barren, Farlan Plain of Orkahtsk.

More than a day before they reached it, Jasper discerned the silhouette of the Orkahti port of Angelsk, resting on the northern horizon, across the flat, windswept terrain. The nearer they came to it, the smaller the town seemed to become.

Several two-story buildings, constructed of large pebble stonework, were surrounded by smaller, single-level houses of similar stonework. The taller buildings appeared to be inns, each marked by a long, pointed banner of a different color. They all dismounted, allowing Badai and Od to take the horses to graze outside the town.

As Kozhdu led them to an inn with a yellow banner, Jasper looked toward the bay and its docks. A half-dozen ships of two and three masts stood at anchor, their sails furled. Interspersed, were smaller boats and simple barcs. Dozens of people loaded, unloaded and transported bales and barrels about the area. Between the docks and the Yellow Inn, Jasper noted scores of small wooden shacks, some at the water's edge, most lining either side of narrow streets paved with crushed seashells.

Inside the Yellow Inn, as Jasper decided to call it, the ground level consisted only of a large room filled with sleeping pallets, in orderly rows across the floor. Kozhdu led them up narrow stairs to the second floor. Tables and benches, mostly empty, were arranged with half of them beneath a roofed portion, the others in the sunshine, overlooking the docks and the ocean beyond.

Kozhdu selected a table in the sun. Phaena and Jasper sat on the same bench, while Kuyuk and Chigu sat across. Liddie had insisted on inspecting the smokey kitchen, which was located within the covered section.

When Liddie returned from the kitchen, and had seated herself beside Kuyuk, she announced, "Our food should be right alang," Liddie said.

"What is it?" Jasper asked.

"Wee little tarts of flesh." In response to Phaena's look of alarm, she added, "Small, baked pies o' lamb." She turned to Jasper. "Efterin ye eat, ye can tak more o' them tae the men watchin' all the horses. An' one for thir pet bird."

As they gobbled their tarts of flesh, two apiece, Kozhdu raised the issue of identifying a ship that might carry them south. An Orkahti man seated beside their table shouted frantically, pointing at the sky to the south. All eyes turned upward to see the immense body of a winged serpent soar overhead. The beast turned about in a broad arc of sky, then flew lower, coming directly at them. Jasper knew that it was a dragon. It was surely one of the seven released from beneath the black pyramid of Shouda by the now dead, Corban, High Protector of Dragomin—Phaena's father.

Kozhdu pulled from his waist a thin chain mounted with a small iron ball at either end, and twirled it over his head. As the dragon approached, Kozhdu released. The chain struck one of the horns above its face, wrapped around once, then spun one of its iron balls into the beast's eye.

Fire burst from its mouth, aimed at the eatery. Chigu grabbed the dumbstruck man who had first alerted them of the dragon's approach, and dove with him beneath a table. Jasper and the others in his party fled to the corner of the open area, hiding behind fallen benches. The brief blast of dragon fire scorched most of the wood, but was not sufficient to ignite any of it. The dragon vanished to the northwest as quickly as it had come.

The man Chigu had saved from the fire rose to his feet, looked about, then turned to Chigu. He simply stared, then sat onto a charred bench, among curls of light smoke.

Chigu placed his hand on the shoulder of the befuddled man. "It is gone now." He bent, and looked into the man's eyes. "I am Chigu."

"I would have been burnt," he said, his voice trembling. "Thank you, Chigu." He breathed deeply. "I am Kipik, First Mate of the Kiriati. If I can repay the debt, simply name it."

"You can help us," Kozhdu interrupted. "We need a ship to carry us south."

"I will take you to the Master of the Kiriati, Muldu," said Kipik.

The Kiriati was a ship of two masts, each rigged with a single, fan-shaped sail of leather, and crewed by twelve Orkahti men, in addition to its First Mate and Master. Below deck was a large cargo hold, crew quarters, and a small cabin each for the Master, Muldu, and his First Mate, Kipik. It was slender—seven yard beam and thirty length.

Muldu seemed irritable. Jasper suspected that the man had not stood on land in a long time.

Jasper, with Liddie and Phaena, followed the Master below deck to the Mate's cabin.

"You three will sleep in Kipik's quarters. Kipik and the three men with you will take crew quarters."

Badai and Od had headed back home, taking all the horses with them. Kozhdu had reluctantly decided there was no other way.

They had sailed east, skirting the northern coast of Orkahtsk for several days, and now headed south along its eastern coast. Although seas had been fairly smooth, that changed when they rounded the point into the eastern sea. A constant chop and intermittent waves kept the Kiriati continuously heaving and rolling.

Liddie leaned over the rail to vomit. "This blastit boat swayin' about..."

"My stomach is not so good either," Jasper said.

An unusual wave washed over the deck. A monstrous serpent head and long, amber-colored body broke the water just beyond the rail, quickly rising to the height of the main mast. Water poured down its glistening, amber scales. The deck hands yelled as they went for weapons or any tool near to hand.

Fishing spears and arrows sailed towards the creature. Most of the arrows glanced away, but a few of the spears embedded into its thick, serpentine body. It thrashed in response, snapping the foremast in half, and sweeping the leather foresail into the water. It then struck the foredeck with its teeth, tearing away a portion of the rail. The enraged serpent arched its head, and struck at the deck once more, snatching one of the crewmen in its maw. It twisted to the opposite direction, then sank back beneath the surface.

Muldu stood in the mid-deck, searching his eyes over the crew. "Who did it take?" he softly asked his First Mate.

"Narvim is gone," Kipik replied. "It took Narvim."

Jasper hesitantly walked to where the missing crewman had been standing. Splintered wood surrounded tooth marks, each as wide as Jasper's arm, scraped into the wood decking.

Kipik ordered the diminished crew to return the Kiriati to its original course. He eyed Kozhdu and his two men with suspicion. "Strange beasts follow you." He went forward to assist the Master in inspecting the ship's damage.

After several hours of fighting to maintain its course south, across a strong westerly breeze, the ship's Master spotted the body of a man in the water ahead. Using gaffs, they hauled it up onto the deck. Only now, Jasper saw fear in Muldu's eyes.

The crew backed away from the supine body. "He is still alive," one of them gasped. "He sank under water...back there."

"Why are they afraid of him?" Phaena asked no one in particular.

Muldu approached her, and muttered, "It is Narvim. Yet all saw him taken by the serpent. Will one of you..." He glanced at Liddie Burn. "...will one of you tend him below?"

Liddie slowly turned her pallid face to Phaena.

"I will watch him," Phaena offered, her eyes scanning beyond Muldu to the body of Narvim on the deck.

"Take him to Kipik's cabin," he ordered the crew.

As the sun approached the rim of mountains to the west, Liddie leaned against the rail. With a pained smile, she shook her head at the crewman holding out a steaming bowl of dark chowder.

"I'll take it!" Jasper said.

"Jasper will tak it tae Phaena," Liddie added, pointing below.

Kozhdu nodded in agreement. "Da."

"Yes ma'am." Jasper accepted the bowl, and headed down the hatch ladder. As he opened the door to Kipik's cabin, Narvim rose from a pallet, fastening his clothing. Behind him, on the pallet, lay Phaena, her eyes wide, her face bruised, and her clothing torn.

"Liddie!" Jasper screamed. He leaped onto Narvim, pounding the man's head repeatedly with his fist. Narvim shrugged him off. Jasper jumped on him again. Narvim again threw Jasper to the deck, then turned around into Liddie's fist to his face. Narvim crumpled to the deck, and did not move.

All of the crew had been gathered on deck, to watch as Narvim was bound, face up and naked, to a hatch cover propped against the rail.

"All of you are seamen," Muldu fumed. "There are rules you can break, and there are rules you will not break. This man forced himself on a woman. On my ship! He abandoned decency." Muldu's hand went to his hip, then raised a small knife. The blade curved like a scythe, ending in a sharp point. He approached a terrified Narvim, reached down to Narvim's genitals with one hand, and yanked the knife with the other. Narvim screamed in short gasps.

Muldu cast two bloody globs into the sea. At the spot they struck the surface of the water, a winged horse emerged from a froth of red, lifted into the air, and flew off toward the western sun.

Jasper slowly raised his hand to his mouth. *A kelpie! An amber kelpie stallion? Kehlibar?*

The bleeding Narvim, now whimpering in a staccato of agony, broke free of his bindings. He turned wild eyes toward Jasper. Before anyone could reach him, Narvim launched himself over the rail, and into the water. He disappeared beneath the chop.

As the crippled Kiriati ran before a northerly wind, it rounded a hilly spit of scrub-covered rock to reveal twin mountains, each rising as a dark spike from the sea. These mountain islands were surrounded by scarcely anything that Jasper could recognize as beach. Densely forested crags leaped skyward, only to lose their summits within roiling masses of dazzling, white cloud.

"We stop here," Muldu informed them, indicating the nearest of the ominous islands. "We repair the Kiriati, then we go. We will stay only a short time. This is a dangerous place. There," he pointed to the mainland, "Bur Nor, is worse. The Banu Sulal. Here, it is only Dryads. The Dryads may not be happy we stop."

They hauled the Kiriati's bow as far onto the narrow, rock-strewn beach as the combined strength of the crew and the three horsemen could manage, and made camp in the only flat spot they could find. Two driftwood fires were started for supper, one for the sailors and one for the six passengers.

"Save three long pieces of driftwood, to repair the mast," Muldu cautioned. "We cannot cut the wood of the Dryads."

"Liddie," Jasper asked, as he poked at their small fire with a pointed shaft of gray flotsam, "what are Dryads?" His thoughts were still on the ghastly punishment that he had witnessed, and on what had happened to Phaena. *Was it Kehlibar?*

Phaena sat silently, between Jasper and Liddie, staring at the dancing flames. She had not spoken since her encounter with Narvim.

Liddie glanced at the buttressed trunks of the nearest trees, then up to their canopy of broad, deeply incised leaves undulating in the off-shore breeze. "Who, or what." She returned to her task of picking weevils from four fist-size biscuits.

Kozhdu, Chigu and Kuyuk, sitting across from Liddie, turned their eyes to the canopy of waving leaves, then to one another. Kozhdu shrugged his shoulders, but his hand brushed the long scabbard of his sword.

Leaves rustled above them in the forest. Jasper picked up his carved staff, while checking to make sure he could feel his sword, Rat Slayer, at his hip. Out of the trees walked three willowy, bear-breasted women, their skin as pale as milk. One carried a filmy, white garment over her arm.

The crewmen turned to Muldu. "Dryads," the Master whispered.

The women walked directly to Phaena. Without protest or resistance from Phaena, they lifted her to her feet, and then removed all of her clothing. One Dryad caringly draped her in a white, gossamer cape.

Jasper sensed a rush of warmth in his cheeks and ears. *They're so beautiful.* In the fading light, Jasper could see that their hair, which reached down their backs to their waists, and partly covered their breasts, was actually comprised of delicate boughs of myrtle, bearing small, green leaves—some boughs with tiny white blossoms, others with blue-black berries. The boughs seemed to grow right out of their scalps.

He had never seen the petite figure of Phaena naked. Her small breasts gazed back at him with dark round eyes.

Liddie slapped him across the face. "I'll nae huv ye starin', young man."

ꕥ

The connection of each thing to all things may allow a sleeping dream to occasionally inform more reliably than a waking experience.

Ereben Leaf: Chronicle of the Counterspell

Jasper poked at the fire with a long, slender piece of drift wood. He couldn't tear his mind away from the vision of Dryads, barely clothed, whisking Phaena into the dense foliage. Days had passed since then, but Jasper remembered it as though it had just happened. The Dryads had seemed keenly interested in Phaena's well-being. He remembered myrtle growing out from their heads. Are *they half plant? They seemed to know...something happened to her.* The wind gusted softly, blowing ashes on Jasper's leg. He brushed them off.

By the water, Kipik supervised the crew of the Kiriati in mending the broken foremast as best they could, and in rigging the only spare, leather sail to it. Chigu assisted them, while Kuyuk sat with Kozhdu and Muldu, discussing their plans.

Liddie walked to the fire and selected a comfortable rock on which to sit. She seemed to know as little as he did about the women from the forest. She handed Jasper a bowl of oyster stew, and kept one for herself. He devoured it in silence.

"Why doesn't Phaena come back? Do you think she's alright?" Jasper asked, as he cleaned his empty bowl in the sand of the narrow beach.

"I dunna think they mean harm," Liddie said, savoring her bowl of oyster stew more slowly.

"What's taking so long?"

"When she feels ready, maybees." Liddie spoke to the fire, her mind obviously on something else. "Maister Kozhdu say the ship be ready to take to sea soon. We leave the morn for Bur Nor."

"What about Phaena?" Jasper asked. "We can't leave her here."

"Phaena seems tae be taken care of. Bahsa may be chained on some dread slaver ship, headed tae be sold into filthy hands. We'll come back here. We leave the morn." With that, Liddie rose, and stomped over to a place in the sand, away from the fires, and sat, looking out across the sea to the west.

The tone of Liddie's voice left Jasper with a nagging discomfort. *I was guarding Bahsa.*

Muldu, the horsemen, and the crew of the Kiriati spaced themselves around several fires, now that the repairs had been completed. Most of them were already asleep. Jasper left his perch on a rock and curled up alone next to the fire. Jasper's eyes wandered to the trees swaying gently at the edge of the wood. They spoke to him in whispers. He could almost understand what they were trying to say.

Jasper sat up with a start. The Kiriati was nowhere in sight. Standing, he turned toward the trees. They seemed closer. A dark shape darted out from the forest. Jasper turned to run, but fell face down in the coarse sand. He rolled over to see a dark shape standing over him. Jasper yelled as loud as he could, but what came out was softer than a whisper. He tried again.

The dark shape seemed human. Its arms and legs were stocky and rough, with gnarled joints. Twigs grew out of its head. Its eyes glowed a dull white, pulling at Jasper. His heart raced. It leaned closer, scratching and grasping at Jasper's chest.

Jasper tried again to flee, but couldn't. It gripped Jasper tightly in its knobby fingers, and brought its face within inches of Jaspers' nose.

"Ssperrrrrrr," it called, its voice like dry leaves in a breeze. "Jssperrrrrr," it called again, shaking him violently.

Jasper let out a cry. The shaking continued.

"Get oop!" a familiar voice called. "The day awaits." A plump Dwarf woman came into focus.

He sat up, rubbed his eyes, and brushed sand off his face. His fire smoldered, the breeze stealing the fragile tendrils of smoke rising from it. Water lapped at the hull of the Kiriati. A crewman stood on the beach, beside the Kiriati's only small boat —a shallow, blunt-nosed dinghy.

"Everyone is already on board," Liddie continued. Time to move."

Jasper kicked sand over the coals of his fire, grabbed his belongings, and joined Liddie in boarding the dinghy. The crewman shoved off, hopped in, and used its stern sweep to propel them through the calm water, to the Kiriati. Liddie was first up the rope ladder, which had been thrown over the side. While Jasper waited for his turn, he cast a glance toward the line of trees into which Phaena and the Dryads had vanished. There was no sign of them. The dream of the previous evening was still fresh in his mind. Jasper felt exhausted...and his chest hurt. His right hand wandered to his chest, as he recalled the gnarled thing with glowing eyes, grasping at him. Jasper climbed the ladder.

The crewmen of the Kiriati raised the two, ribbed sails, secured them, and stowed gear from the encampment. The ship headed west, toward the Sulalian port city of Bur Nor, in the Kingdom of Jubail. The bay in which the coastal city nestled was broad. Dry hills to the north and south were visible in the distance. Jasper envisioned a giant mouth inviting him and his companions inside.

As they approached Bur Nor, distinct buildings rose above the western horizon. Many were topped with bulbous spires. Three docking areas spaced along the waterfront were filled with ships of every size and description. Scores of people loaded and unloaded cargo. Given its reputation, the city seemed rather small to Jasper. From his view at the Kiriati's bow, he counted twenty-one small structures, widely dispersed around fifteen larger buildings. The Kiriati veered toward the right shore about a mile from the docks. Jasper turned from the bow, crossed the recently damaged deck, and walked to the stern, where Liddie, Kozhdu and his fellow horsemen were engaged in a conversation with the ship's Master and First Mate, Muldu and Kipik.

"We anchor here," Muldu said to Jasper. "You two will have to go to Bur Nor alone. We must all stay." He swept both arms to encompass all the Orkahti men, horsemen and sailors alike.

"Why are we going alone," Jasper asked, confusion setting in.

"Orkahti not go into Bur Nor," Kohzdu said as though everyone knew. "Orkahti...Banu Sulal. Everybody hating everybody."

"You will take the dinghy to port," Muldu said, pointing at the small boat hanging off the stern quarter. "We will wait aboard the Kiriati."

Chigu placed his huge hands on the shoulders of Liddie and Jasper. "Learn where nearest slave...mmm...market. Then you come back soon."

"Da?" Kozhdu nodded his head toward them, apparently awaiting a sign of agreement.

Jasper glanced at the stone-faced Dwarf. Liddie nodded. "Will it be safe?" he asked.

Kozhdu answered, "Da, nye," and lowered his head.

The small dinghy was lowered into the water. The sea was clear and shallow enough for Jasper to see a sandy bottom through calm, crystal green ripples. Small shadows in the water flitted about, evading larger shapes. The dinghy bumped lazily against the hull of the Kiriati.

Liddie and Jasper climbed awkwardly down the ladder and into the dinghy. Larger fish moved beneath. They seemed to not notice two people in the little craft, bringing to Jasper's mind the garfish of the Iron River.

Liddie took a seat near the bow, while Jasper slowly propelled them toward the dock. It became easier for him as the rhythm and response of the stern sweep became more intuitive. Jasper steered the dinghy beneath the northernmost dock, and up onto the sand. The two of them, heaving and grunting, pulled the boat out of the water far enough to tie it.

Liddie stood with her hands on her hips, staring up at the activity on the dock. "We want to learn where we can buy oursels a young boy." She turned to Jasper. "Do your best at lookin' like my servant"

"Yes, ma'am." He smiled to himself, wondering how that differed from his usual interactions with Liddie over the past, many months.

They left the dinghy, walked around the pilings, and up onto the dock. Scores of men moved to and from the anchored ships, carrying bundles, pulling small wagons, or rolling wooden casks. Most were clearly laborers; some no doubt slaves. Their garb ranged from long gowns to shirt and trousers, but all appeared to be of limited means.

Liddie walked up to the nearest man who seemed better dressed, was engaged in no obvious task, and wore a deeply curved dagger at the center of his waist. "Where might we purchase a boy?"

The man seemed surprised, but said nothing. When Liddie repeated her question, he frowned, then pointed toward the city. Liddie thanked him, then headed toward the unpainted, wooden buildings that were nearest to the docks.

Jasper caught up with her. "I don't think he understood anything you said."

"Maybees."

At a large building, a man in a long, dark tan robe stood by its wide doorway, watching as laborers entered with their burdens, and exited without them, heading again toward the docks. Liddie approached him.

"Slave," she said, grasping a hand around her upper arm. "Where...to...buy...slave?" she loudly asked, with exaggerated gesticulations.

"If I am not mistaken," he replied, with only the slightest Sulalic accent, "you are inquiring about the location of a slave market."

"Tha' would be correct. Where might we purchase a boy?"

"There is no slave market in Bur Nor. The closest would be in Almirant." He pointed a bejeweled hand toward the south. The next is in..." He paused. "...four days."

The Kiriati left Bur Nor, making a straight line for the twin islands, and dropped anchor near the closest one. Muldu made it very clear that they were not to make camp on the isle. A small group was to land and try to locate Phaena. Kozhdu, Chigu and Kuyuk would go ashore, along with Jasper and Liddie.

The dinghy was lowered into the dark water, making contact with a dull splash. No one spoke. The tension of being back on the Dryad island kept Jasper alert. The Kiriati had anchored fairly close to the beach they had used the previous nights. Jasper heard the now familiar sound of the under side of the small craft scraping up onto the coarse sand of the beach. Thoughts of his dream came crawling back. He sighed.

The sun peeked over the canopy of trees. Sunlight splintered into a thousand thin beams. Jasper squinted to see the edge of the forest, where it met the sand, nearly ten yards away.

He looked down at the nearby sand. "Where are the camp fires we used?" His eyes scanned the entire beach and then back again. "This is the same beach, isn't it?" he asked no one in particular.

"Same beach," Kozhdu replied. His fingertips drummed lightly against the long, curved scabbard at his hip.

"Unnatural." Liddie placed one fist onto her hip, near the handle of her flail. Her other hand went to her brow, to block the glare of sunlight.

Kozhdu, Kuyuk and Chigu stepped towards the tree line. Liddie and Jasper followed. Rustling in the undergrowth announced the emergence of Phaena from the trees. She wore a long, hooded cloak. Two Dryads followed her.

"Bless her heart," Liddie said.

Phaena turned her head toward Liddie. With a nod of acknowledgment, her eyes seemed to smile. She likewise nodded toward Kozhdu and his horsemen. Then she walked directly up to Jasper. "Will you help us tonight?" Her soft voice and direct gaze felt both inviting and ominous. "We need you."

Despite our knowledge of the Dryads, and experiences with them, their motives and abilities remain a mystery, even to one who has studied them with great interest.

Ereben Leaf: Chronicle of the Counterspell

Jasper glanced at his companions. He saw only puzzlement on their faces.

"We came here to bring you along, Phaena dear," Liddie said. "Almirant holds the slave market. Bahsa may be lost forever, in only four days."

Phaena still held her gaze on Jasper. "There will be a celebration tonight, a feast in honor of Apelloh. You would accompany us to the summit of Mt. Parnoth in the traditional way. This will help me to heal. It's important for you to be there."

Jasper nodded.

"We will come for you at dusk."

"We must be goin'. Time grows shorter for Bahsa the longer we wait." There was resignation in Liddie's voice.

"Thank you, Jasper," Phaena whispered.

The three women turned, and walked back into the forest.

Jasper watched as his companions climbed into the dinghy, and returned to the Kiriati.

As Jasper wandered the beach alone, daylight began to fade. The sun settled on the western horizon, above the port of Bur Nor, which Jasper had visited that morning. His stomach reminded him that supper should be approaching. Phaena would return for him shortly. *A feast!* He headed back to the landing beach to wait.

Darkness seeped over the island, shadowing Jasper's vision. Underbrush and then smaller branches from the trees waved at him. A wind caressed everything, stronger than it had been since their first arrival on The Twins.

Two Dryads emerged from the green. The pair of slender, nearly naked women stopped ten paces away from Jasper. "Are you prepared, Jasper of Nilwid," one of the Dryads asked.

"I guess I am."

"The ritual requires a youth, not of our people to accompany us up Mt. Parnoth. This person must carry our blessing gifts, for we can not. We ask this of you, Jasper. What is your answer."

"Are they heavy?" He again noticed thin sprays of myrtle emerging directly from their scalps. "Alright."

"We are pleased to hear this. We will return you safe. Come with us, now." Both Dryads turned and walked into the forest.

The lightly-worn trail wound gently up the mountain. He followed the Dryads for over an hour, barely able to keep up with them. Broad-leafed trees allowed some moonlight to filter down to the ground. Most of them were massive in girth, each distinctive and humbling. Jasper felt small, walking beneath them. Hefty roots meandered across the path, requiring him to concentrate on where he placed each step.

The trail reached a small, stone pavilion. Both Dryads stopped. One of them raised her head, and sang a soothing melody. The other soon joined a harmony below it. The entrancing music soothed Jasper's fatigue, and heightened his anticipation of the celebration.

"We wait here for the rest."

In the dappled moonlight, Jasper noticed stone benches surrounding the circular pavilion. It appeared to be covered above by a dark fabric, suspended from six stone pillars around the periphery. Jasper sat on the cool stone of one of the benches.

Dryads began to emerge from the surrounding forest. They made almost no sound as they approached. There were dozens of them, perhaps a hundred, each clad in a similar garb of greens and browns. Some of them took seats on the benches, while others stood about in silent groups. There were no children among them, but they seemed to range in age from young to quite ancient. Even the oldest of them walked upright and confidently in the near darkness. Phaena appeared, leading a white goat by a rope, and joined the group. She still wore her hooded cloak.

"Jasper, I am glad you came. The ceremony is of great importance for me to become whole. The mountain calls to us." As she spoke, Phaena removed her cloak, folded it neatly, and placed it on one of the outer benches. She was completely naked.

Jasper gasped, and could not avert his eyes.

He turned away, embarrassed, but found himself looking at her again. His face felt flushed. *Ereben has no idea what's happening*. He stood, numbed and detached, as in a dream. All of the Dryads, young and old alike, removed their clothing, and placed it onto the stone benches.

"You too," Phaena said calmly.

Jasper's mind blurred. It had not occurred to him. He was surrounded by naked Dryads, standing patiently, waiting. Jasper drew in a deep breath, blew it out slowly, then removed all of his clothing.

Phaena handed him a small bundle wrapped loosely in dark fabric, and the rope that was tied about the goat's neck. The bundle was fairly light.

Jasper, with his bundle and his goat, was ushered to the front of a long procession of Dryads. The trail felt rough on his bare feet, and rockier, as it snaked up the increasingly steep slope.

Now the path was brightly lit by a full moon, making obstacles easy to see. The canopy of the trees became open directly over the trail. The procession reached a circular bald, near the top of Mt. Parnoth, ringed with towering trees. In the bald, grew nothing but a broad patch of dense moss, that appeared mostly blue-green in the moonlight. In the middle of the bald stood a small rock outcrop, almost the size of Jasper. As he came closer to it, he noticed that the top was shaped like a shallow water basin. Dark stains had collected and dried at the margins of the bowl shape. Next to the outcrop was a fire pit, wreathed with fist-sized stones. Jasper noticed for the first time that some of the Dryads carried bundles of driftwood.

Two of the Dryads set about building a small fire in the pit. Once it was burning, all but Jasper formed a circle around it, and waited.

Jasper felt uncertain as to what he was expected do. Looking at the circle of Dryads, the moss, the goat, and the altar, he stood there as naked as he had come to think of the rock outcrop, with its stone bowl. Finally, several Dryads lifted their heads toward the full moon, which was in full view.

"It is time," an older one said, even though the rest of them seemed to already know. "We must begin."

An unsettling silence crept over the moss floor of the bald. Nothing, not birds nor animals nor insects, could be heard. There was no breeze. Jasper felt uneasy. His ears rang from the absence of sound. The circle of Dryads, with Phaena, rotated around the fire. They then began to chant loudly, their individual voices combining into one single voice. At every pause, Phaena responded.

Jasper could not understand a word. They spoke a language he had never heard before. It soothed his ears and his mind. He began to relax, adjusting the bundle he still carried to a more comfortable position. After several minutes, the circle reversed direction and began the chant again. Jasper shared in the serenity of the Dryads. He felt comforted.

The chant faded as a large, metal chalice was handed around the circle. Each in turn, drank deeply from it.

Everyone now looked at Jasper. He shifted the bundle nervously.

"Jasper, place the package in the gleaning bowl, and open it," a voice said from the circle around the fire. He walked to the rocky basin, and placed the small bundle in the smoothed, rock bowl, and opened it. It contained several small packets of dried herbs, ivy leaves, an egg, and a small curl of what looked like blonde hair. He stepped back, still guiding the goat by its rope.

One Dryad approached the gleaning bowl, still holding the chalice, and spoke unintelligible words. Then she drank from the chalice and poured some of it over the items in the stone basin. She ate the egg, and ignited the rest of the items with an ember from the fire. The chalice was passed around again. The fire in the bowl went out, leaving a curl of smoke.

"Jasper, bring the goat."

He walked back to the basin with the goat, and handed the rope to Phaena. The goat sniffed at the charred herbs, but made no effort to flee.

He knew what was going to happen. The Dryads were going to sacrifice the goat to their god, Apelloh. All of the Dryads and Phaena gathered around the rock. Jasper backed away to the edge of the bald.

An old Dryad bashed the goat's head with a pointed rock, causing the goat to immediately collapse. A knife slit its throat, and the pumping blood was collected into the chalice. All of them chanted a short phrase in unison.

To his horror, the unconscious goat, still alive and pumping blood, was hacked apart—ripped into pieces. The Dryads and Phaena lapsed into a wild rage and feasted on the torn bits of bleeding goat flesh, consuming all but the skin, horns and bones. Even its eyeless skull was crushed, and the brain consumed.

Jasper turned toward the path, and fled down Mt. Parnoth.

No man can be entrusted with the fate of mankind. The temptations are too great and the power too corrupting.

Phaena Cervona: Legacy of Man

Phaena watched as a group of seven young children sang and played a game of dancing in a circle, each child passing beneath the joined arms of two others, who formed a bridge. When a stanza of the song would end, the bridge dropped onto the circle, trapping one child who then replaced one of the two members of the bridge. Each time the bridge dropped, all the children screamed with glee and laughter. This unbridled joy flowed into her spirit, just as the comfort of the sun-warmed limestone bench seeped into her body.

Drusa, a seemingly fragile Dryad, whose height barely exceeded that of Phaena, had rowed her across the water and surf last night in a narrow boat made of waxed fabric stretched over a worked iron frame. Phaena had been led into the low branches of an ancient tree, and provided a bower. Now Drusa sat beside her on the bench.

"Aube is the smaller island of the Twins," Drusa explained, "but you can't tell unless you stand on the summit of Mt. Vierge..." She pointed to the forested slopes rising abruptly beyond the meadow in which the children played. "...and look to see Parnoth still above you."

"What do you call this village?"

"Chaleur. Only Dryads raising children live here."

"And the men?" Phaena asked. "Where do they live?"

"No men live here. We seldom need them. If a Dryad needs a man with whom to mate, she takes him, and then allows him to go. Men who seek the wisdom of the oracle are granted safe passage. Most Dryads never mate, since few suitable men have the courage to land on these islands. A Dryad who does mate will bear a single child in her lifetime."

"But, the children." Phaena indicated the group playing in the meadow. "I see four boys. What happens when they grow older?"

"If they choose celibacy, then they may stay as priests of Apelloh and serve the oracle. Otherwise, they must leave The Twins when they reach maturity."

"That seems...sad."

"We love our sons as dearly as our daughters, but they have different destinies. Most sons choose to leave. All daughters choose to remain. If you should have a son, he will make his own choice in due time."

"But neither am I a Dryad, nor have I taken a mate." Phaena closed her eyes to drive away the violence she had experienced on the Kiriati.

Drusa turned to her and took her hand. "You are of Dryad blood. Of that there can be no question."

"I don't understand what that means." A coldness swelled in Phaena's breast as she sensed the truth in Drusa's words. How that could be true eluded her. She recalled how often in her childhood others had commented on her strong resemblance to her father, Lord Corban. They insisted she had his eyes and his mouth. And yet, he had imprisoned her so readily, so callously. "My parents were Valish."

"Your father was indeed Valish."

"My mother died when I was very young, but I've seen paintings of her. She bore no resemblance to a Dryad." She glanced at Drusa's pallid skin and strange, leafy hair.

Drusa squeezed her hand. "I believe you have too much of a burden already, for me to add to it a troubling tale."

"My father was Lord Corban," she blurted out. "I carry that discomfiture without shame, but with daily fear of its being recognized. I refuse to continue fearing who I am. I loved him and I miss him, despite his disgrace." She stood and pivoted back to Drusa. "You can tell me nothing that I can not bear." A rage filled her. "I've been led along as a cripple for too long. It's time for that to end." Tears filled her eyes. She swatted them away like carrion flies. "Tell me what you know of my parents."

Drusa looked back at her, as if weighing Phaena's strength and resolve. "If that is your wish." She observed the children as she spoke. "I was not witness to these events, but I have no reason to doubt their truth.

"At the time that I was a small child, about their age..." Drusa nodded toward the children. "...two young Valish men landed on the shores of Parnoth. They had no intention of seeking the wisdom of the oracle. Their behavior was haughty, but they were observed to be strong, handsome and intelligent. Two Dryads took them by force and mated with them. The men were then released. At their departure, I am told, they threatened to punish those who had humiliated them.

"Within a year, they returned by night on a rowing boat with fifteen companions. They did not land on Parnoth, but here on Aube. No outsider should have known to come here. For days, they hid, watching the two Dryads who had forced their will upon them. They discovered that each had given birth to a female infant. Eventually, they were able to identify the two trees to which these Dryads had been pledged, whereupon they set fire to them. Our people, still not aware of the presence of the men, ran out to save the trees, leaving the infants unattended. The men stole both infants, slaying one Dryad in the effort, and escaped to their rowing boat.

"These details were assembled later from the signs of their presence. Both trees were destroyed, so these two mothers died. No trace of the two infants had ever been found, until your arrival. We do not know which mother was yours. She was either Gerina Plessia or Dara Cervona."

Phaena gasped. "My mother's name was Dara. A sliver of truth." She swallowed the emotion. "And there is another Dryad in Valand."

"Perhaps. She may be alive, or she may be dead. You were both sucklings. It is amazing that either of you survived."

"You see," Phaena said with pride, "I bear it." Her thoughts swirled.

"Do you wish to bear the rest?"

"The rest?"

"There is more to tell you." Drusa lowered her eyes.

Phaena seated herself on the stone bench. "Tell me the rest."

"You carry a child in your womb."

Phaena sat silently. That she might be carrying a child had nagged at her consciousness, and been consistently dismissed. The sailor, or demon, had forced himself on her while she was tending to him. He had been hauled from the sea. She steadied her voice. "That is possible, but it is difficult to understand how you would know, since I do not know it myself."

"We are often blind to those things in ourselves that are obvious to others. And Dryads are well attuned to one another."

"If it is true, then my life has changed more than I could ever have imagined." She thought of Ereben Leaf. The image in her mind seemed like so young a lad—striking blue eyes hiding beneath such long, red lashes. His lip bore only the faintest red fuzz, and his chest was as pink and hairless as a cow's udder. He had not yet reached full manhood. The sharp scent of charcoal and steel had permeated his clothing from the smithy. She felt his absence acutely, but could not identify the feeling as love. The passion, she realized, had departed some time ago, without fanfare. *He is a good man. He loves me. He is the only one who loves me.*

"It is neither good nor bad, but it is true."

The stone road surface beneath Phaena's bare feet continued in a gentle curve up the southern face of Mt. Parnoth. Drusa walked beside her in the crisp breeze of mid-morning.

Parnoth's summit remained hidden beyond a disc of lumpy cloud. They passed ornate stone structures, each the size of a tiny house, on either side of the road. Most were nothing more than a square of columns supporting a simple roof, and enclosing a smaller, stone chamber. Some were circular with domed roofs.

"These are treasuries from various nations that often seek the wisdom of the oracle." Drusa indicated the little stone buildings. "Their offerings are kept safe, and separate from those of other nations."

"I have no offering," Phaena said aloud, as she continued walking upward.

"The oracle of Apelloh speaks through a Dryad. Dryads are a treasure in themselves."

Beyond the treasuries, and situated a short distance downhill from the course of the road, Phaena passed above a large, mostly enclosed stone building. Through its open windows she witnessed Dryads apparently wrestling with one another.

"That is the palaistra," Drusa said, "where we train to improve our skills. It also contains a running track and a pool of water in which to swim." On the opposite side of the road, a small pond caught the gentle spill from a waterfall of enormous height. Drusa guided Phaena to the pond. "We must bathe our faces and our feet here before we proceed to the temple."

At the pond, Phaena followed Drusa in splashing her face and rinsing her feet. On seeing Drusa drink water from her cupped hands, Phaena did so as well. The clear, cold water sparkled with minute bubbles and carried a slight taste of sulfur. She tipped her head and gazed toward the top of the cleft in the sheer cliff from which the waterfall emerged.

"We call the pillars at the top the Weeping Ones. They weep for the trees that have perished over the ages."

They proceeded up the road, now steeply zigzagging, to an irregularly shaped building. The stone road continued up the face of Mt. Parnoth, but Drusa turned from it and entered the angular temple.

"It is from here that the oracle of Apelloh speaks. Only men may approach the oracle with a question, and only through the auspices of a priest, but Dryads may enter directly and without a question. To the Dryads alone, the oracle speaks whatever should be spoken. A pythia will deliver Apelloh's message to you. You must not speak."

As they ascended two broad steps into the oracle's temple, Phaena smelled the subtlest scent of sweet perfume. A pale, elderly priest, dressed in a white gown that reached to the floor, bowed briefly to them, then stepped outside. The main chamber consisted of slender, milky columns surrounding a milky stone floor. Toward the far end, the floor dropped into an oddly angled pit about a yard deep and several yards across. In the center of the pit, a Dryad sat in a shallow basket perched upon a metal tripod. Her eyes drooped. Her head drifted from side to side. Drusa led Phaena to the edge of the pit, then departed.

Phaena stood at the verge of the pit in silence. The air was redolent with sweet perfume. Water could be heard trickling from somewhere within the pit. After standing in silence for a quarter hour, Phaena sat by the edge. The scent of perfume grew stronger.

"You must stand up," the pythia whispered.

Phaena rose to her feet, not certain if the pythia had delivered a message with deeper meaning. After standing a while longer, she considered the message complete and turned to leave.

"That which was divided must be joined," the pythia mumbled, "or all is lost."

Phaena turned back to the pythia, who seemed to ignore her presence and her actions.

"Strength hides within weakness." The pythia became more agitated, swaying her shoulders. Her droopy eyes closed completely. "Defeat travels the road of death; victory, no road at all."

Phaena repeated the pythia's statements within her mind, hoping to remember the exact words. She had no idea what they meant.

"Even the innocent bear evil." With that, the pythia slumped, her chin resting on her chest, her arms limp.

After a quarter hour of silence, and no sign of motion in the pythia, Phaena turned and walked to the entrance. Looking back, she saw only the immobile head of the pythia.

Phaena rejoined Drusa outside the temple. As they descended the stone road, Phaena repeated the words of the pythia to her host.

"We will seek their truth in council," Drusa said. "The oracle often speaks in riddles."

"The pythia's first statement is clearly valid in every possible interpretation," a middle-age Dryad said. She spoke to members of the council gathered in the palaistra. "Of course she must stand up, as we all must." The group of thirteen sat on the low perimeter steps that rose above the central floor. "In addition, it may simply have been the pythia's instruction to Phaena in order to prevent her from breathing the vapors of the cleft."

Phaena listened in silence. She had been instructed to repeat the words of the oracle. Now she was to remain silent as they considered their interpretation.

"Agreed," Aldebith Gai said. The ancient Dryad sat on a higher step than the others. As Prime Dryad, she controlled the meeting and all other decisions of importance, according to Drusa, who was not on the council and not present. Her voice seemed richer and carried farther than Phaena would have expected from so old a woman. "The second. 'That which was divided must be joined, or all is lost.'"

"People who have been estranged," one offered.

"A group of tribes or nations must unite," another suggested.

"Perhaps an important set of objects has been dispersed."

"Phaena must be rejoined to us," said the youngest member of the council.

Aldebith nodded. "This lost child must be pledged to a tree, of course, but the wording seems to refer to objects that have been divided, rather than people who have been divided. I lean toward objects." The Prime Dryad consulted her written notes. "The third statement. 'Strength hides within weakness.'"

"Phaena may carry a strength greater than one may suspect."

"A tiny creature may slay a much greater one."

"A small nation may conquer a larger one."

"That which appears weak may serve to hide its strength from its opponent."

"The Banu Sulal have a prophecy that a child shall lead them into battle."

Aldebith Gai raised both hands. "This is so much a truism that we will not resolve it. The fourth statement. 'Defeat travels the road of death; victory, no road at all.'" She held up a single finger. "Of all the statements, this is the clearest. We do not know the conflict to which it refers. It seems that the only choice that can be followed is one that will lead to chaos." She glanced at her notes again. "The final statement. 'Even the innocent bear evil.' Thoughts?"

"A child might unknowingly carry destruction in the form of a plague or a poison."

"An honest endeavor may lead to an undesired result."

"Children may carry weapons."

"An innocent beast may be used to kill."

"An innocent beast may carry an evil person."

The suggestions paused. Aldebith nodded. "There is another interpretation we might consider. An innocent woman may give birth to an evil child." She sighed. "The word, *even*, and the use of the plural, *bear* instead of *bears*, suggest a more categorical or group statement. That can not be resolved. We are done."

Hundreds of Dryads, the young and beautiful, as well as the aging and decrepit—some carrying infants, others holding the hand of a child—stood naked in a circle beneath the canopy of trees near the southeast foot of Mt. Vierge, on the island of Aube. As the western sky splashed an orange pink, the brilliant white disk of a full moon blossomed through the foliage to the east, beneath a cloudless sky.

At the center of this Dryad circle stood Phaena, before a thin, straight poplar tree of about her age. Beside her, Aldebith Gai, stoop-shouldered and withered, supported herself on a polished alderwood staff. In her right hand, Aldebith held a delicate truncheon topped by a tiny shard of obsidian.

"You will share the essence of your life with this one tree," the Prime Dryad stated in a firm voice, "and it with you." A soft, steady rhythm sounded from a tambour. "As it lives, so will you. As it dies, so you will die." In a figure the size of her frail hand, she inscribed the symbolic curves of a woman into the bark with the truncheon. She then turned to face the rising moon. The rhythm continued. After reaching its full brightness, the moon began to dim, taking on a jaundiced hue. In unison, all of those present chanted a single syllable that continued without end. Aldebith then faced Phaena. With a touch as gentle as a feather, the Prime Dryad inscribed the straight lines of a symbolic tree between Phaena's breasts. The voices droned on.

As Phaena looked down at her chest in the reddening twilight, fine dark lines appeared where Aldebith had marked her. *Blood.* The wound on the tree faintly glistened.

Aldebith then guided Phaena's arms to embrace the poplar. The ancient hands pressed on her back, forcing her bleeding skin to the bleeding bark. The tambour and the voices fell silent. "You are now one."

Phaena caressed the smooth bark. She tasted the salt of tears. A sense of life and growth and strength flowed into her from the tree. It enfolded her and washed over her in waves of warmth and chill. She gave her spirit willingly to the poplar—to herself. But the poplar resisted. She sensed a vague discord within her new, larger self. A stinging in her wounded skin caused her to jerk her body away from the tree—away from herself. The stinging intensified to a searing pain. Phaena pressed her hands to the burning mark on her skin and screamed.

Blinding light flashed with a colossal boom, causing every muscle in her body to contract, casting her to the ground several yards from the poplar. She gasped a breath in the ringing silence, then looked up to see one branch of the tree, her tree, crumble to the ground as a puff of smoking embers. In a wide circle about her, everyone seemed to be slowly lifting themselves from the forest duff. Beside her tree—herself, Aldebith Gai, Prime Dryad, lay motionless, her ancient eyes open to the faded moon.

∽∾

They did not know the secret of the way things are, nor did they understand the things of old, and they did not know what would come upon them. Without the secret of the way things are, they could not rescue themselves.
Anonymous Beddu Scroll

Minkar Jarad rubbed his eyes. *If I should fall asleep, Bahsa will be made an orphan.* Seated upright on the shoulders of Krey, his view below was mostly obstructed by the huge wings of the great gray owl. So he frequently found himself leaning against Krey's head in order to see beyond the leading edge of either wing. But this nearly-prone position made it far too easy for his mind to drift. That would be fatal. He had seen no sign of Bahsa or the others. He had flown low from Liddie Burn's cow farm north toward the city of Zink. Had they traveled in that direction, he would have seen them. Unless the Kelpies took to the air. Knowing that Jasper had visited Ailantha in the past, Minkar decided to check her home in the Broken Mountains below Punishment Pass.

Ailantha, a Guardian of the Ruins—the last of Chrysanthus' and Hobart's generation, had warned the Shouda Observer that his future would be painful. She was indeed a strange woman, he thought. Though blind, she saw deeply in all directions, and into a man's heart and spirit. She had appeared to be near death the last time Minkar had visited.

On arriving at Ailantha's ramshackle cabin, Minkar noted that the vegetable garden had been neglected, now choked with weeds as tall as his own considerable height. Her goat was gone. The cabin door stood ajar. He tapped his spear against the wall.

"Ailantha," he called out, "it is Minkar Jarad of the Shouda." He entered the cabin. Instead of the tidy interior of his previous visit, scattered debris and rodent droppings suggested that it had been abandoned for some time. The beautiful, knotted carpet was gone. *Most probably stolen.* Kitchenware and table ware were gone as well. He peered into her sleeping chamber. Nothing of value remained.

As Minkar exited the sleeping chamber, he noticed a torn tapestry on the wall. Its fabric was so aged and fragile that it fell apart with the slightest tension. It depicted a knight in golden armor battling a dragon with an oddly designed ax. The dragon's fire engulfed the knight.

Minkar's attention was drawn to the plate girdle about the knight's waist. On the hip, both in front and in back, it was decorated with a spot of green. He pulled aside his Shouda cape and studied the plate girdle he wore. It also bore green decorations. A small, translucent green stone was mounted at the hips, one in front and one in back of each hip—four in all.

He could not clearly remember the appearance of each of the pieces of the Chamberlain's armor, from the library of ancient Ephesia, but the tapestry matched them as well as he could recall. He wondered if the tapestry showed a style of armor, or if the ancient embroidery was of that specific suit of armor. He attempted to salvage the image of the knight, but it crumbled in his hand.

Minkar then wondered about Ailantha's dagger. If she had been a Guardian of the Ruins, then according to Hobart, she would have carried a dagger like that of Ereben. *What happens to the daggers when they die? Do they destroy them just before they die? How would they destroy such a thing?* He looked into the stone oven, then searched the cupboard. *Who buried her?*

Outside the cabin, he searched for a grave. There was not much level ground, since the cabin was perched on the side of a mountain. Twenty yards west on the narrow, fertile shelf that Ailantha had called home, Minkar located the grave. A flat, horizontal rock surface bore a relief carving of Ailantha in repose, her frail hands clasped in front. "May you rest in the arms of Elloh." He bowed toward the grave. When he rose, a startling question entered his mind. Who would have created this superb sculpture? The truth of it seeped in gradually. If she knew a spell to bring Chrysanthus out of a dagger, then she might well know a spell to send herself into stone. *She cast a spell to bury herself!* Minkar shook his head in wonderment at such a will.

He dropped to his knees and raised his arms to the sky. "I praise you, Elloh, Mufta of the Universe, who has given me the law and commanded me to follow it." With the formulaic words spoken, he now searched his mind for the right question. There was no right question. The mere asking of it would violate the very law for which he had just expressed his gratitude. With clenched teeth, his body began to tremble. He lowered his arms and wept. The image of his son filled his thoughts. That Bahsa was lost and that he himself knew of nowhere to look pierced his heart. He turned his tear stained face to the sky and begged. "Show me the secret of the way things are. Give me understanding of the things of old...that I may rescue my son."

When Minkar once again reached the cow farm of Liddie Burn, Yarnish Blen and Barrow were there. They each related their findings. Whittig Trench had found witnesses who identified the women and the boys. He had followed their trail to just past the town of Cinnabar, but then they seemed to have vanished. Yarnish Blen had seen a solitary dragon pass high overhead a half dozen times.

"I will go to find my son," Minkar said, finally.

"Ye may choose tae do that," Barrow replied, "and nae one could find blame with that choice. But I have a weenie request tae mak."

"Yes, my friend?"

"Those Redeemer Knights are swarmin' everywhere, and thir numbers continue tae grow. Maister Blen suggestet that we ask yer Mufta Gebir tae join us with some o' his sodgers from that city aneath the ground."

As Minkar was about to decline, Yarnish Blen interrupted. "Barrow is planning to continue searching for Bahsa and the others. Since it's not unusual for Dwarfs to cross over into the Three Kingdoms, he would have a better chance at getting information while passing unnoticed."

Minkar considered how even the Dwarfs, neighbors to the Shouda, responded with suspicion when he approached. As much as it pained him to acknowledge that Yarnish Blen was right, he saw the truth of it. "I will return to Shouda, if Elloh is willing."

Yarnish Blen planned to cross into Valand and raise a resistance there.

"It distresses me," Minkar said, "that there is no word of Ereben Leaf and his grandfather."

"He is a clever lad," Whittig Trench said, "and ye saw Chrysanthus tak care o' things in Ironhole."

"Yes," Minkar agreed, "but I still worry."

Minkar, atop Krey, descended steadily from the high peaks of the Broken Mountains. The pinnacles of Shouda glistened white around the periphery, as did the pyramids. Toward the center, some pinnacles were broken, others gone entirely. At the very center, a blackened wound was all that remained of the great Black Pyramid.

He landed near a guardhouse above the city. Jasper had described the labyrinth in great detail. Leaving Krey to fend for himself, Minkar entered the guardhouse, and descended to the dimly lit, musty corridor. He called out, "I come to speak with Otah Kadeef. I am Minkar Jarad."

An unfamiliar Shouda man approached from the end of the long corridor. After inspecting Minkar from a few yards away, the man extended his open hands and bowed, saying in a thick accent, “Minkar Jarad, welcome.” The man wore a loosely fitted, tan tunic, and carried no weapon.

Minkar returned the bow. It was good to be back among his people, even though they were strangers. He was led straight down the corridor, past an intersecting corridor, and into a room lit by a glowing green ceiling. Three other unfamiliar Shouda men sat expectantly at a table littered with tiny, illustrated tiles. The men dressed in tunics identical to that of his guide. They stood and exchanged bows with Minkar. He understood none of their words, nor apparently could they understand his.

His guide said something to the others, who expressed annoyance, indicating the empty chair at the table. The guide shrugged and waved them off. “I... name... Fadil Kaddum. Minkar Jarad... mmm... stay. I... look... Otah Kadeef.” He pointed to an empty bunk and a chair, then left the room.

Minkar looked about. Around the wall were six sleeping bunks, two of which were unused. On one wall was engraved what appeared to be a map of the labyrinth. On another wall were hung various articles of armor and a small collection of weapons, enough for the four men who seemed to reside here.

The three remaining men were engaged in animated discussion regarding the tiles on the table. Many tiles had been scattered face down in the center of the table, while others were aligned in neat rows along each of the four edges of the table. Some were face down, and others were face up, revealing their colorful illustrations.

Minkar seated himself across the room from the table and waited patiently. He was unaccustomed to being under the ground, and although his mood was colored by that thought, he was vaguely happy to be home. He noted a writing desk, complete with parchment and quills. Yes, he thought, this is all that remains of my home.

A half hour later, Fadil Kaddum returned with Otah Kadeef, Prince of the Shouda. They exchanged bows, then Otah

Kadeef took Minkar's hand and led him down the corridor a short distance.

"How have you been, my friend?" asked Otah Kadeef.

"I, myself am well, my prince, but my son has fled with Liddie Burn, Jasper of Nilwid and Phaena, daughter of Corban."

"Oh?"

He explained what had transpired, and what was being done. "I have come here at the request of our companions. They would have me implore the Mufta Gebir to send warriors to fight against the Knights of the Redeemer."

"These Knights of the Redeemer," Otah replied, "move about the land discouraging the practice of unclean and unholy acts, so I am told."

Minkar frowned. His companion had never accepted magic as a part of the truth of things. The Holy Tor said nothing of it, other than to warn of straying into the path of darkness at the peril of one's soul. "Indeed, they discourage those whom they wish to conquer. They murdered the Baillie of Zink, together with his guards."

"The Baillie was no friend to us."

"This is true, my Prince, but the Baillie practiced no magic. His only crime was to have cooperated with Lord Corban and the Protectors of Dragomin."

"Unbelievers all. It was Corban who destroyed our homes and our families."

"But these Knights harbor no greater respect for Elloh, blessed be His name." Minkar struggled to focus his argument. "If we say 'these are unholy; let them be destroyed. 'Those are unclean; let them also be destroyed.' who will be left to stand with us when the Knights turn their arrogant eyes upon the Shouda?"

"Do you no longer trust in the strength of Elloh?"

"If the strength of Elloh were the beginning and the end of it, we would carry no weapons. The world is changing, Otah

Kadeef. Ancient secrets have been revealed. You, yourself, rode across the sky upon a great dove."

"I can not listen to this, Minkar Jarad." Otah Kadeef raised one arm as if to ward off the truth. "Nor should you be speaking these words."

"Perhaps the Mufta Gebir would be willing to hear of the danger. Your father chose to assist Ereben Leaf, an outsider who shared none of our beliefs."

"That was before his entry into Lamblar."

Minkar had been told of the ancient Shouda people who had lived scores of generations in these warrens beneath the Pinnacles of Shouda, awaiting the return of the Mufta Gebir according to the prophecies of the Tor. "Do these people not accept his leadership?"

"They accept him as Mufta Gebir, but they are truly more devout in their service to Elloh than we had ever been. The Lamblari observe the Holy Tor to the perfection of the law, and these laws, our laws, constrain him more stringently than in our years of ignorance. He has changed. We all have changed. You also must change, and become a part of our Holy Community."

"Ignorance? The lives we lived before the Great Massacre? Those are the years of *ignorance?*"

"You do not yet understand, Minkar Jarad."

"I understand it to be a different kind of ignorance. Will you take me to him, my Prince?"

Otah Kadeef hesitated, a pained expression on his face. "I fear, Minkar Jarad, that your words may disturb the Council of Elders."

"What is this council?"

"The Council of Elders has ruled Lamblar all these generations, awaiting the return of the Mufta Gebir. As my father sits among them, they weigh all decisions in light of the Holy Tor."

"Then I will meet with him alone."

"That would not be possible."

"Is he held captive by these elders?" Minkar realized that his rhetoric verged on the unacceptable. This was his prince. "Forgive me, my Prince."

Otah Kadeef maintained his penetrating gaze into Minkar's eyes, though his expression softened almost imperceptibly. "You do not understand," he said softly.

"I will write him a letter to read in privacy."

"That may be unwise."

"Will you carry it to him?"

"These things, if written by your hand, may pose a grave danger to you."

"But will you carry it?"

"If I can not dissuade you from this, then I will carry it, my friend."

Drizzle drifted through the open window of the guard house. Its milky white stone walls and stone roof echoed the dull gray of the overcast sky. For two weeks Minkar Jarad had waited for a reply to his letter. For two weeks he had lived in the bunk-room of the subterranean maze, only occasionally coming up to the surface to refresh his sensibilities with a view of sky and mountains. Today the weather matched his mood. Although his letter had required two days in the writing, surely it could be read in a quarter hour.

He looked south to the gray smudge where the Broken Mountains should be. He thought of Bahsa, lost in the West. *Perhaps he has been found.* This useless waiting tortured him. Perhaps this effort to obtain the Mufta's aid was a foolish one. He considered giving up, returning South. Despite his months of longing to return home, his home was no longer his own. Not the people. Not the place. Gone were all the reminders, great and small, of his youth, his family, his life. Only the cold stone pinnacles and pyramids remained.

A loud, flapping swoosh overhead startled him. Minkar stepped out into the light drizzle. It could not have been Krey. The great owl flew with a surprising silence, despite its size. A golden dragon came into view, breaking below the overcast for only a brief moment, then disappearing once again into the murky sky, though it could be heard a while longer. Minkar now understood why Krey had not remained in the area. He had not seen the great gray owl since his arrival at Shouda City.

Minkar descended once again into the musty labyrinth. As he approached the bunk-room that had been the center of his life for the past two weeks, Fadil Kaddum, the guard who had first greeted him on his arrival at Shouda City, came out to meet him.

"Minkar Jarad, take up your things. You come down to Lamblar."

Minkar gathered his few belongings and followed Fadil Kaddum. Fadil had used every free moment with Minkar to improve his second language. Fadil had explained that the Mufta Gebir had ordered all the people of Lamblar to learn Shalish—the same language that Ereben Leaf called Valish. It was now taught in the Lamblari schools.

After walking a considerable distance down a dimly lit corridor, they turned left at an intersection and continued on. Minkar could see light at the far end which, when they reached it, he recognized as the dazzling subterranean plaza that Jasper had described so vividly. He knew that he was now below the great square of Shouda City. The pinnacles and pyramids appeared as round or square columns suffused with milky light.

They descended a stairway to a second layer of the great square. This layer carried a residual odor of offal, of an animal den, though the floor appeared to have been recently scrubbed. They moved to another stairway and continued descending into the earth, level after level.

Minkar was aware that he was merely a farmer, rather than a scholar. Nevertheless, he had spilled his thoughts and beliefs and fears into his letter to Ibrah Kadeef. It described the magic he had witnessed and the dangers that had been revealed to him. It implored the Mufta Gebir, for the sake of his own people, to assist in the struggle against the Knights of the Redeemer. Minkar knew that he was not a subtle man, nor one skilled at debating. He trusted in the truth of his simple words and an obvious response from a people sensitive to justice.

Minkar lost count of how many levels below the surface he had descended with Fadil Kaddum, before he noticed the change. He guessed a dozen or more. Now they were traversing one of these unusual levels. People moved about the corridors. They passed through a vegetable market, then a fish market and a meat market. He wondered where these things could have been procured so far beneath the surface. One stall displayed a variety of dried mushrooms and dried roots. Most surprising were three adjacent jewelers. They sold intricately crafted silver filigree for necklaces, ear baubles, clasps, brooches, candlesticks and buttons. The wares were not as surprising as the shelves and cabinets used for displaying them. Where he would have used a thin plank of wood, mounted in iron fittings, these strange Shouda of Lamblar used finely dressed slate, mounted in gold fittings.

As Minkar considered this, he began to see gold in every sort of utilitarian role. Still following Fadil Kaddum, he saw common bowls of gold, tableware of gold, shoe buckles of gold, even a dustpan made of gold. They passed beyond the market to an area that seemed to be family homes with doors opening to the corridor. The air here seemed fresh, with a gentle breeze. While some areas were lit with lamps or candles, a soft, creamy light radiated from the milky stone all about.

He was shown a door. "You stay here...inside," Fadil Kaddum said without emotion. "We call you when Mufta Gebir to see you."

Minkar turned the golden doorknob and entered the chamber. Within, he noted a bed, a small table with two chairs, simple house wares made mostly of gold, and a small mushroom garden in a darkened corner. The chamber was illuminated by light transmitted through the stone ceilings. Off to one end, a tiny adjoining room appeared to be a privy, separated from the main chamber by a loosely woven, red curtain. In the solitary cabinet, Minkar found squares of paper and a writing quill and ink well. The chamber was quite tidy, but did not seem to have been inhabited recently.

A soft rattling noise came from the golden doorknob. Minkar stepped to the door. The noise repeated. Minkar opened the door to find a handsome Shouda boy, perhaps in his mid teens, standing with a golden cylinder in his hands.

"For you...eat," the boy said with a smile.

"You may come in," Minkar replied.

The boy entered and placed the cylinder on the table. It was an odd assembly, about one hand wide and twice as tall, made up of four golden baskets, nested upon one another, held together with a bail that locked over the top. Pointing to the door, the boy said, "I get water." He reached around the doorpost and retrieved a bottle of liquid, which he placed on the table.

"I am called Minkar Jarad." Minkar bowed in the Shouda fashion.

"I am called Yassar Khayin," the boy replied, returning the bow. Yassar then disassembled the golden cylinder by sliding its bail off of a shallow detente in the lid. The top layer was a lid which contained a tiny compartment of salt. He unstacked the four baskets and arranged them on the table. One contained a light broth with slivers of green onion. Another held a small, round loaf of bread. The third appeared to be a cooked grain of some sort. The last held an aromatic mixture of steamed mushrooms in a thick, transparent sauce, seasoned with small berries, perhaps currants. "You eat," he said smiling. "I go. I come...tomorrow. You teach Shalish...me?"

"How long shall I be kept here?" Minkar asked. He had done nothing but wait since he had arrived at Shouda City and the labyrinthine warrens of Lamblar.

Yassar shook his head with incomprehension.

"How many days must I wait here?"

"Ah. Yassar not know." He moved to the door. "Silim," he said, then departed, closing the door behind him.

Minkar wondered if the door was locked. He turned the golden doorknob and drew the door inward. People passed by in both directions, paying him no notice. Across the corridor, a man sat on a tall stool. His impassive face studied Minkar. The unarmed man lifted one hand and rocked it from side to side. Minkar understood this to indicate that he was not supposed to leave his chamber. He nodded his head to the guard and closed the door.

Returning to the food, he sat at the table and sampled the fare. This was a significant improvement over the dry rations he had been provided in the guard's bunk room. He could only wonder why an outsider, practically a prisoner, should be served with gold. Even the spoon was of gold.

On the following day, and for many days thereafter, Yassar would come with his food, twice each day. Each such visit was longer than the last. Minkar taught Shalish to the eager lad. As the young man's comprehension improved, Minkar found himself relating stories of the world outside. Yassar asked for more and more details of the battles and stared wide-eyed at accounts of magical happenings. As always, Yassar had no idea as to the reason for Minkar's long delay in speaking with the Mufta Gebir.

One day, after several weeks of detention deep within the subterranean city, Yassar did not bring his meal. Instead, a gruff old man handed it to him at the door.

"Where is Yassar Khayin?"

The old man squinted his deep set eyes, emphasizing decades of wrinkles on his brown face. He clearly could not understand the words Minkar had spoken. The old man shrugged and departed.

For three days, it was the old man who brought his food. No one else came. Minkar surprised himself at how much he missed his conversations with Yassar. The discussions had made the day pass. More than that, he missed the companionship. He had come to look forward to Yassar's arrival. Now, loneliness seared his waking hours. And Bahsa. *Shall I ever find my son?*

The next morning, two men, armed with swords, came to the door. "You come," one of them instructed.

At last! Minkar's mind raced as he was escorted down the corridor. He would finally speak with Ibrah Kadeef. He turned over the various arguments he would present to the Mufta Gebir. He must convince him of the genuine danger in the world above. And, almost as important, he could soon return to search for his son.

They descended two more levels into the city. At this level, there were fewer columns and much brighter light. Great squares of milky stone in the ceiling radiated light as dazzling as the sun. Hundreds, perhaps thousands of Shouda stood around the perimeter, and fell silent as Minkar was escorted toward a massive, golden throne situated at the far end of the plaza. Golden steps supported square-faced, golden columns engraved with intricate designs. Embedded among the golden supports, a sculpted silver chair commanded the focus of the chamber. To the left of the throne, seven elderly men hunched on a bench, each wearing cowled, red robes that reached to the floor. To the right sat Otah Kadeef, his eyes downcast. About his neck, he wore finely crafted silver chains. To the right of the prince sat Menash, watching Minkar's approach. Upon the throne, Ibrah Kadeef, Mufta Gebir of the Shouda, leaned on one of the throne's sculpted silver arms. His purple robe bore a silver breastplate hung about his neck by a silver chain and decorated with seven jewels of various colors. Above the back of the throne rose a munu mushroom in silver. The Mufta Gebir looked upon Minkar with a bittersweet expression.

Minkar's two guards ushered him to a stool ten paces from the throne and indicated that he should sit. They remained standing behind him. Minkar, still standing, offered a formal Shouda bow to his Mufta Gebir. The Mufta only nodded in response. Shaken, Minkar seated himself.

A short, ferret of a man in a yellow robe stepped forward from the left. He spoke in the Lamblari language, ancient Shadae, which Minkar could not understand. Menash, still seated beside Otah Kadeef, translated.

"What is your name?"

"I am called Minkar Jarad. I have come to speak with..."

His words were cut short by a hostile shout from the man in yellow.

Menash raised his hand to the angry man and spoke softly, in words Minkar could not understand. "Minkar Jarad," he then said, "you must understand why you are here. You must answer only what you have been asked."

"My friend," Minkar replied, now puzzled and apprehensive, "I have only come to speak with the Mufta Gebir concerning a request for aid."

"Yes. We have read your writings. It is because of these writings and the words you have spoken that you are here."

Otah Kadeef then spoke sadly. "My friend, you are being tried for heresy. Anything that you say may be used by the Council of Elders in judging you."

Minkar stared at his prince in disbelief, until Otah Kadeef once again lowered his eyes. The Mufta Gebir sighed deeply, then indicated to the man in yellow, apparently his prosecutor, that he should continue.

For several hours, the prosecutor interrogated Minkar, while the audience remained standing. The Council of Elders, the seven aged Shouda in red robes, occasionally whispered among themselves with animated hand gestures.

"So you state that you have never attempted to teach others these unholy things?" Menash translated.

"As I have said many times, I have come only to request aid of the Mufta Gebir."

The prosecutor signaled to the rear of the plaza. Yassar Khayin came forward hesitantly. Minkar's teenage companion stood while the prosecutor spoke with him in Shadae. The boy's eyes appeared hollow, his wrists and ankles chafed and bruised. He appeared thinner. Over a quarter hour, Yassar answered the questions put to him, occasionally turning his defeated visage to look at Minkar. Minkar could understand none of it, other than several mentions of his own name, but the meaning was clear enough. When the boy retired, shoulders bent, Otah Kadeef shook his head.

Sitting alone in his chamber, Minkar pondered the trial of the previous day. His Mufta Gebir had never spoken to him. Ibrah Kadeef had aged since coming to Lamblar. He wondered how his friends could have abandoned him. Surely it was the will of these Lamblari strangers that had brought about the trial. He now awaited the judgment of the Council of Elders. They were not his elders—those had all died in the great massacre at the hands of the Protectors of Dragomin.

No one had brought food to him this morning. That mattered very little, since he had no appetite. But it did not bode well for what was to come.

He raised his arms toward the ceiling. "I praise you Elloh, Mufta of the universe, who has given me the law and commanded me to follow it. Lead me along the path of your will."

At mid-day, the same guards came for him, leading him once again to the plaza of the golden throne. The murmuring crowds were there again, as were the Council of Elders, Otah Kadeef and Menash. The throne, however, was empty. The silver munu mushroom above its back had been covered with a black fabric bag. The yellow clad prosecutor sat to the left of the Council.

Once Minkar had been seated, a member of the red-robed Council of Elders stood and approached him. Though conspicuously the youngest of the Council, he was nonetheless quite ancient. He held a scroll of paper which he unrolled with gnarled fingers. As he slowly read it in a rich bass, Menash Translated:

> *The Leaders of the High Council of the Shouda hereby declare to all of you that, having long had knowledge of the evil opinions and deeds of Minkar Jarad, they did try to bring him back to the path of righteousness by every means and promise. Unable to set him right and each day learning of the new and terrible heresies which he perpetrated and taught and the abominable acts he committed, they summoned trustworthy witnesses who spoke and gave their testimony in the presence of the said Minkar Jarad, by which he was convicted. When all this was examined in the presence of the Mufta Gebir, the High Council decided that the said Minkar Jarad should be accursed and exiled from the people of Shouda and the Holy Community of Lamblar, which they do by this Haram, the Haram that follows.*
>
> *By the judgment of the messengers of Elloh and the pronouncements of the devout, we accurse, exile, give to the demons and excommunicate Minkar Jarad, with the consent of Elloh, blessed be He, and all this Holy Community, before the Holy Tor and the one hundred forty four proscriptions included therein, with the anathema that Jurush brought down upon Ephesia, with the curses that Eljah pronounced to curse the crowds, and with every anathema*

written in the Law. Accursed be he day and night, sleeping and waking, in his goings out and his comings in. May Elloh never forgive him, may the fury of Elloh descend upon him henceforth, and may He curse him with all the curses written in the book of the Law. And Elloh shall wipe out his name from the Book of Life and Elloh shall separate him from the tribe of Shouda and shall damn him with all the curses of the firmament, written in the book of the Law. And you who cleave to Elloh your God, you shall live.

We give warning that no one must speak to him, nor write to him. None shall render him service, or remain under the same roof with him, or within a distance of four yards, and none shall read anything written by him.

Minkar was speechless, cut to the foundations of his beliefs. Would he never dwell in the arms of Elloh? Were his very prayers blasphemy?

The Elder rolled the scroll of paper, flattened it, then tore off one corner of the document. At that signal, the six remaining Elders stood with some effort, and turned to face away from Minkar. Otah Kadeef and Menash did the same. Then the mass of spectators turned to face the walls. Only the two guards had not turned away.

In the day since his eviction from Lamblar, Minkar had wandered along the hills surrounding Shouda City. He searched for any sign of Krey, for without the great Gray Owl, he would have to journey alone into the Broken Mountains, cross the Ledge of Leopards and traverse much of Knurlan, simply to reach the cow farm of Liddie Burn.

He now wandered along the stone path on the ridge west of Shouda. It was here, Jasper had said, that his wife had died during the massacre. As he walked, his eyes rose to the charred tops of the trees. Nearly all the trees were dead. Burned by the Protectors and the Priests. He had walked this path a thousand times, shaded by the canopy of trees. He had walked it in total darkness. Now, a mocking blue sky silhouetted the blackened branches.

Minkar's tear filled eyes returned to the path, but not in time to prevent him from tripping on a log lying across the stones. His shoulder and head crashed to the paving. For a moment, he lay there, wondering if all of creation was now turning its back on him. As the log moved beneath his ankles, a loud rustling of leaves and brush startled him. He rolled over. The log that had tripped him extended up the hill. His eyes traced its gold-scaled contour to an immense body. His heart pounding, Minkar Jarad tipped his recumbent head further to look into the melon-sized eyes of a horned and bearded dragon.

❧

When one dies, the living seek to assure that the spirit of the deceased passes-on to its proper destination. This effort is a testament to man's fear both of oblivion and of lingering, perhaps mischievous dead spirits.
Ereben Leaf: Chronicle of the Counterspell

Chrysanthus led, as they carefully felt their way down the thousand yard, vertical face of the vermilion cliff. Ereben had been unable to locate a route, but Chrysanthus exhibited an uncanny skill at finding a break here, a ledge there. Three hours of arduous descent had brought them about one third of the way down the stained limestone escarpment. Every step, every foothold and handhold moved them further down the precarious face.

They had watched from the rim through the evening and all that night, hoping for the return of Titus, but by morning, the great gyre falcon had not come back. Ereben feared the worst. Could Titus out-fly the dragon? He had no way of knowing. If the Knights of the Redeemer were seeking the Warded Mines, trying to acquire sarcite, then he and his grandfather must find a way to prevent it. To do that, he knew that they would have to locate the Warded Mines themselves. If today were any indication, the journey would be a long and difficult one.

By mid-afternoon, a primitive trail became evident. This sped their descent dramatically. Their movements were less exposed and less strenuous. They reached the bottom about a mile west of where they had begun that morning. Turning then to the East, they headed along the cliff base toward the site of the dragon's attack. Although he could see no tents or houses, Ereben could see the movement of people in the distance, close against the base of the cliff.

As Ereben and Chrysanthus approached the chaotic cluster of people, it became clear to Ereben that there had been deaths and injuries from the attack. Some people wandered about aimlessly. Others knelt weeping, to wrap charred bodies. A smell of burnt flesh hung in the dry air. Reaching nearly fifty yards up the face of the cliff were block-like houses set into the stone. Each level of square-windowed houses connected to those above and below by wooden ladders, some of which were charred and collapsed, others of which remained intact. Some of the burned ladders had been bypassed with crude rope.

All of the people were dressed in sleeveless tunics of a coarse, beige fabric sparsely decorated with tiny silver beads. All wore their straight black hair cut short, high above their bronzed shoulders. The men wore a band of twine across the forehead, dangling several silver beads in the back. The women wore no head bands.

A nearby group seemed to ignore the two outsiders, until one young man pointed to Chrysanthus and shouted to his companions. Several men drew stone knives as they forced the women and children behind them.

Ereben held both empty hands into the air and shouted, "We come as friends." He had no idea if they understood him.

The young man who had first roused them sheathed his knife and waved his companions back. "Other look like danger," he said cautiously to Ereben. His dark brown eyes studied Chrysanthus.

"He will not harm you."

"Have face like demon."

"He is my grandfather. He will not hurt you."

"Grandfather?"

"He is father of my father."

"Ah." The man approached Chrysanthus, keeping his hand on his sheathed knife. "Flying demon come last morning. Demon kill much people."

"Yes. We saw from the top of the cliff." Ereben pointed upward.

"You climb from top?" he asked incredulously.

"We started from the top this morning."

"Only best Kasazi know path."

"Chrysanthus, my grandfather, showed me the path. I am Ereben Leaf."

"I Pimaqua," he said without gesture. "I speak Valishi. Other Kasazi know little."

"Is there something that we can do to help?" Ereben gestured toward the weeping women who were dressing charred bodies in new clothing.

"I not know, Ereben Leaf." He rubbed his hairless cheek. "Demon burn much ladder. We work much time. Make path for Kasazi in home come down."

Ereben studied the ropes and charred ladders.

"Wise one, Utumqua, live in cave. Utumqua ladder burn. Utumqua not come down." Pimaqua pointed to the highest of the dwellings. "Utumqua much old. Kasazi not have wood. Kasazi not make new ladder. Kasazi go Whitewood. Get much big tree. Make new ladder."

Chrysanthus approached the cliff village and began to ascend the ladders and ropes. People along the way gave him a wide berth, but otherwise ignored him.

"What is the name of this place?" Ereben asked.

"Here Ciboney. People Kasazi tribe."

As Ereben and Pimaqua watched, Chrysanthus reached the highest level below the twenty yard, charred ladder that reached up to Utumqua's cave. The face of the cave appeared to be a house not unlike the others in the cliff village. The long ladder, now charred beyond use, leaned precariously to one side. The burned log had been alternately notched over its entire length. Now it threatened to crumble of its own weight. Using the steel claws on his hands and bare feet, Chrysanthus scaled directly up the stone and baked clay face of the structure. On reaching the open entry at the top level, the leopard-man crawled through and vanished.

Pimaqua turned to Ereben. "Grandfather much strange."

Ereben spread a small dollop of munu ointment on the burned forearm of a crying Kasazi child.

"Where Ereben Leaf home?"

A wave of caution swept over Ereben. "Valand. My grandfather and I are studying the sources of metals and stones. There are traders who offer great gifts for certain metals and stones." He felt foolish for having not prepared a credible explanation for who they were and where they were going.

Pimaqua drew his stone knife. "Pimaqua understand. Pimaqua go far. Get stone."

Ereben released the tension in his shoulders. Pimaqua was showing him the stone of the blade, rather than threatening him. He accepted the knife by its stag horn handle, and examined the glassy, black stone blade. Its finely undulating edge was as sharp as any blade Ereben had ever forged. He returned the knife with a nod.

"Silver," Pimaqua added, indicating one of the tiny silver beads stitched to his tunic. "Pimaqua learn Valishi from get silver."

Ereben extracted a small, milky red stone from a pouch and showed the sarcite to Pimaqua. "Do you know where to find this stone?"

Pimaqua turned the sarcite in his fingers, then held it up to the light. "Utumqua have fire stone." He gestured toward the top of the cliff village and returned the sarcite to Ereben.

Ereben worked with Pimaqua until sunset helping to carry the bodies of the dead Kasazi up to a burial cave a quarter mile east of the cliff village. Although most of the Kasazi people were wary of the stranger, they accepted his assistance in their somber task. More and more, they looked up to the top of the village.

"Kasazi want Utumqua," Pimaqua explained. "Utumqua send spirit dead Kasazi...Sipu...spirit place. Utumqua not send, spirit not go Sipu."

Late sun poured its warmth over vermilion striations on the cliff high above. Wrens, barely specks, dove and soared their acrobatics on the fading thermals. A murmur arose from the huddles of mourning Kasazi. Ereben followed their upturned faces to the opening of Utumqua's cave. Two figures emerged. One in Kasazi garb clung to the back of Chrysanthus. Moving cautiously down the sheer face of stone and baked mud, Chrysanthus descended. When the two reached the ledge upon which the long, charred ladder rested, Chrysanthus untied a rope about his waist. The Kasazi man then released his arms from Chrysanthus neck and patted him on the shoulder several times. With surprising vigor, the aged Kasazi man descended to the base of the village on the remaining ladders and makeshift ropes. Chrysanthus followed.

Hundreds of Kasazi gathered around Utumqua. The old man spoke for a moment, then patted his hand over Chrysanthus' left breast. Then each of the Kasazi present—men, women and older children—formed two lines and walked past Chrysanthus, patting him twice on the left breast.

"Utumqua say Chrysanthus old friend," Pimaqua explained. "Utumqua say Chrysanthus part man, part spirit. Utumqua say Chrysanthus help send dead...spirit place."

It had not occurred to Ereben that his grandfather might have traveled here in years past. He wondered if Chrysanthus already knew where to find the Warded Mines.

Utumqua then led the procession of Kasazi to the burial cave. At its entrance, the old man, whose attire differed from his fellow Kasazi only by the presence of a tiny sarcite bead in the center of his head band, chanted baleful tones. He then scooped a handful of dust from the cave entrance and cast it into the air. All the people chanted in reply. Utumqua then turned to Chrysanthus expectantly.

Ereben wondered what his grandfather would do. Surely Utumqua had discovered that Chrysanthus was unable to speak. Chrysanthus raised his arms, looked upward, and began to hum —a soothing, purring sort of hum. Utumqua joined in the hum. From high above, scores of cliff wrens plummeted toward them. As one great organism, they abruptly angled into the mouth of the burial cave. The Kasazi gasped in unison. Moments later, the wrens burst forth from the cave and streamed westward into the sunset, vanishing as the molten dome slipped from view.

"Does Utumqua know where we can find the red stone—the fire stone?" Ereben asked, pointing to his own forehead. They sat on the floor of a cliff home, eating baked squash and a thick paste of ground maize, flavored with mutton fat.

A stooped Kasazi woman served them silently. It appeared to Ereben that her hospitality had been requested since Utumqua's quarters were currently inaccessible. Pimaqua passed Ereben's question to the Wise One. "Utumqua not know." Their stooped-back host crackled a comment. "Woman say far." He continued to translate. "Woman say past Whitewood." The two spoke back and forth, then he said, "Pimaqua not understand. Woman say Ereben make...spirit body? ...demon body? ...demon house? ...spirit house? Pimaqua not understand."

The woman motioned with her hands as if holding a loaf of bread, then she waived her arm dismissively. She shuffled up to Ereben and leaned to his ear, her breath heavy and foul. "Go Mohani! No stay Mohani. Mohani bad." She returned to her duties as host.

"Mohani?" Ereben asked.

"Mohani people live Whitewood," Pimaqua answered. "Mohani say good talk. Mohani do other. Mohani bad people. Mohani kill Kasazi"

Ereben attempted to explain about the Knights of the Redeemer. In the end, he was not certain what of it they understood.

They set out from the cliff village of Ciboney shortly after dawn and headed south. All that Ereben could gather from the old woman's comments was that sarcite came from somewhere beyond Whitewood, and that the Mohani tribe, which inhabited Whitewood were not to be trusted. *If only Grandpa could talk....*

On foot, their travel seemed pitifully slow across the shadeless expanse of grassland. The hopeful sight of a village in the distance was seen, when closer, to be a small herd of scrawny, ox-like beasts with shaggy beards. On several other occasions, Ereben spotted two wild dogs that followed them at a safe distance. The only other animals he saw were rabbits nibbling on the greener patches of grass.

Their packs had been lashed to the harness on Titus, and were lost. The grief-stricken Kasazi had generously provided them with food and water containers, as well as two blankets, which they used as packs drawn diagonally across their backs.

The first evening, Ereben set up a slab of rock as a deadfall trap and baited it with a slice of squash—a technique he had learned from Jasper. In the morning, he checked the trap and found a rabbit, already dead. This he carried for their supper. Its scent seemed to encourage the dogs to follow a little closer.

Ereben skinned and cleaned the rabbit, and roasted it on a spit over a small fire. When it was only partially cooked, Chrysanthus lifted the spit from the fire, tore away half the flesh, and replaced the remainder over the fire. Ereben watched as his grandfather lustily consumed the partly raw meat, bones and all. Apparently, his grandfather's dietary preferences could be listed among his other changes.

When Ereben had eaten his own well-cooked share of rabbit, he tossed the bones into the darkness beyond the circle of light from the cooking fire. Before long, the silence was broken by the snarls of the two wild dogs fighting over the discarded bones. He considered how he once would have been concerned by such a sound so close to his camp at night, but after coming face to face with a dragon—seven dragons in fact—the dogs were hardly more than an amusement.

As the fire burned low, Ereben walked to the edge of the forest and rigged several snares, hoping to catch something for tomorrow's dinner. In the darkness and silence he felt the chill pang of loneliness. Phaena was so far away, possibly in danger. Looking up at the rising, nearly-full moon, he wondered if Phaena stood somewhere looking at that same moon. *Are you thinking of me? If you can hear my thoughts, please know that I love you. And miss you. You're so far away.* He closed his eyes and searched his awareness for any message from Phaena. Only his own hopes seemed to be there.

Ereben selected a distinct landmark on the far southern horizon, then climbed down the splayed branches of a pine tree. On the forest floor, his direction would be difficult to determine for that bulk of the day when the sun was farther from the horizon.

This forest, he noted, contained only young trees, the largest of which he could enclose within his arms. Most were pine that grew closely enough to one another so that their lower branches, those lost in the shade of the canopy, had dropped off. In cool air, redolent with the scent of pine, they stepped onto the silent needle duff, heading southward.

Here and there, barely protruding from the pine needle covering, wide stumps of once-great trees could be seen. Each stump that Ereben noticed had been cut with axes. He guessed that not so many years ago, perhaps thirty, an ancient forest had stood here. The trees beneath which they now walked had grown up after all the great trees had been cut down, over a short period of time. *Who could use so much wood?*

At mid-day, Ereben climbed a tree to find his bearings. In the distance, somewhat west of their course, a thread of dark smoke dissipated above the treetops. They could reach it by late afternoon.

"Grandpa," he said on returning to the forest floor, "I see smoke from a small fire about half a day away. I think we should head toward it. Maybe we can get directions."

Chrysanthus looked at him, but, of course, said nothing in reply. It reminded Ereben of talking to his pet cat when he was a boy. He closed his eyes and sighed, immediately feeling shame for having thought such a thing about his grandfather.

They continued on toward the smoke. Walking on the pine needle duff required a little more effort than walking across the hardpan of the grasslands, but its resilience was gentle on his feet and knees and back. *Like walking on pillows.*

As the afternoon wore on, the scent of pine smoke intensified, until they reached the edge of a large clearing–one that had recently been cut from the forest by ax. They crouched at the edge, but observed no movement. On a small rise near the center of the clearing, smoke emanated from a blackened mound. A shallow trough extended from the mound at a slight decline. Within the trough, black, viscous liquid flowed drip by drip into a wooden tub at its end. They moved closer.

The blackened mound and its trough had been formed of clay, now baked hard by the heat of smoldering wood within. *The Mohani make pitch from the pine trees.* He wondered what they could do with so much pitch. *A whole forest cut down for pitch.*

Ereben decided to stay for the night at the edge of the clearing, so that the smoke from his cooking fire might not attract attention. He once again set out snares, then built a small fire on which to cook three squirrels he had snared the previous night.

Chrysanthus looked back in the direction from which they had come, then walked off purposefully into the forest. A quarter hour later, Ereben heard a single yelp, then all fell silent. By the time the squirrel was cooked and Ereben had eaten his share, his grandfather had still not returned.

He walked cautiously in the direction Chrysanthus had gone. He was not so much concerned about his grandfather's well-being as just curious. After all, the heavily muscled leopard-man carried a score of deadly steel claws, not to mention his wondrous dagger, which, Ereben assumed, he carried for reasons other than defense. His boots stepped softly in the pine needle duff. The full moon hardly penetrated the dense canopy above. Ahead, he could barely make out the crouching silhouette of Chrysanthus. Though Ereben stood quietly, Chrysanthus turned his head toward him with a start and growled softly, threateningly.

"Grandpa?" he asked, his heart suddenly pounding. He stepped backwards and steadied himself on the corrugated trunk of a pine.

Chrysanthus huffed, then returned his attention to whatever was hidden by his crouching form.

He's eating something. Feeding on something! Ereben recalled the yelp. It seemed that his grandfather had killed a dog, and was now devouring it raw. A wave of disgust came over him. He turned and walked back toward the dim glow of his cooking fire. *Grandpa is changing.* If he had never drawn the ice leopard into the dagger, he thought, then his grandfather would not have become part animal. *But the claws.* Somehow Chrysanthus had acquired some of the nature of the dagger itself. *I don't know the spell!* For the first time, Ereben considered that fact. The dagger, on its own, had drawn the leopard within itself. Or perhaps he had merely willed it to go in. Or even stranger, Chrysanthus, from within the dagger, had willed it so.

Ereben wondered if his grandfather was changing from within, or if he was behaving differently as a result of the wilderness which surrounded them. *Will I change?* He lifted the remaining squirrel on its spit. His appetite had faded. Tearing the meat into thin strips, he placed it on rock near the fire, so that it would dry and keep for several days.

When Chrysanthus returned, Ereben lay awake beside the glowing embers. He did not know what to say. His grandfather showed no sign of blood on his hands or beard. His face appeared as impassive as ever. Chrysanthus returned his gaze for a moment, then curled himself on the ground to sleep. Ereben said nothing.

For five days, as they headed south, Chrysanthus encouraged Ereben to veer more and more to the West. Ereben assumed that if Chrysanthus had visited the Kasazi years earlier, he might also have traveled to Whitewood. Although they had come across two more pitch stills, they had yet to see the Mohani. They were finding ax-cut openings in the forest more frequently.

Now they approached the sounds of axes against tree trunks. When they entered the clearing, Chrysanthus walked behind Ereben and covered himself as well as he could with the gray, hooded cape that Liddie Burn had made for him. Some of the working men stopped what they were doing and watched the two approach. Others noted the strangers, but continued swinging iron ax blades against the trees.

"Hello," Ereben said, holding both open hands in the air.

"Peace," the man replied. He wore tanned leather trousers, but was bare-chested, as were the other workers. His light bronze skin was smudged with soot and tree sap.

In the center of the clearing stood three pointed clay ovens, about the height of a man. Heavy smoke seeped from a tiny hole in the top of each oven. Ereben guessed that they were making charcoal from the wood they cut. With his own training as a bladesmith, Ereben judged from the crudely forged ax heads that Mohani skills in metallurgy were primitive, but practical.

"We are hunting for red stones," Ereben explained, holding up one of his sarcites.

The charcoal maker took the stone to each of his dozen fellow workers. He returned it to Ereben. "None has seen such a stone." He looked about, then called out, "Moniku. Moniku, where have you gone?"

Shortly, a handsome boy of about eight bounded from the forest. "Yes, hopa?"

"This is my nephew," the man said to Ereben. "We call him Little Moniku."

"Moniku, take the men to see your father."

Moniku sighed, "Yes, hopa."

Ereben and Chrysanthus followed Little Moniku into the forest, moving west. Moniku moved confidently in his tanned leather trousers and embroidered leather shirt. His wavy brown hair, like that of the charcoal burners, was tied in a bunch on either side of his head. The Mohani, so far at least, all had green eyes.

"How far away is your father, Moniku?"

"He is in Oak," the boy replied, as if that answered the question.

"And how far is Oak?"

"Two hours."

"My name is Ereben."

"Oh." The boy continued his brisk pace on a distinct trail.

"Do you help the men make charcoal?" He knew that he did not, since his clothing bore no telltale smudges of charcoal.

"No." The boy wore a small knife at his hip, and carried a long, thin twig that he used to sweep away the occasional spider web that crossed the trail.

They emerged from the forest. Ahead lie fields of maize and beans beneath a lowering sky. In the distance Ereben saw the Mohani town of Oak. It was comprised of six long, curve-roofed, bark covered buildings, each over twenty yards long and seven yards wide. People moved about. Women sat outside the longhouses grinding maize with hand held stones against stone troughs. Two men were dressing a deerskin on a wooden frame. Oak, despite its name, was a treeless place. Ereben could not recall a single oak tree since entering the forest of Whitewood.

Moniku led them inside one of the long houses. Ereben could see that it was made of bent poles tied with twine. Herbs and vegetables hung from the interior of the roof. The air was filled with the mixed scents of sweat and smoke and dirty babies.

"Papa," Moniku called. A seated man looked up, putting down a metal knife he had been sharpening. "Hopa told me to bring these strangers to you."

The man stood taller than Ereben, his thick arms stretching the lacing of his leather sleeves. "Peace, strangers. I am Moniku. What brings you here?"

"I am Ereben Leaf. This is my grandfather, Chrysanthus. We come from Valand." He now understood why the boy was called Little Moniku.

"I have heard of it."

"We are looking for the source of these red stones." Ereben held up a sarcite from his pouch.

Big Moniku stepped backwards, eyeing the stone cautiously. "To the South. The witch men of Oldwood use them to taunt the spirits. You must take it outside the house." It was then that he took notice of Chrysanthus. "What is this?" he called out as Ereben and Chrysanthus stepped outside.

Turning around, Ereben saw Big Moniku's eyes widen as Chrysanthus removed his hood, exposing his pointed, fur-covered ears, and showed his teeth ever so subtly.

Ereben groaned. "Chrysanthus...is a spirit-man. He brings good hunting and fair weather."

That evening, a great fire was lit, and drums were played as the Mohani acknowledged the spirit-man in a wild dance amid shouts and cries and gyrations. Moniku had asked Ereben what offering would please Chrysanthus.

"Meat. Uncooked meat."

So they brought out a haunch of wild pig, still bloody. To the amazement of all, Chrysanthus removed his cloak and revealed his leopard tail swishing in the fire light. He roared into the overcast night. When Chrysanthus devoured the raw haunch of pig, the Mohani fell silent, moving slowly away from him. He tossed the stripped leg bone into the fire, then danced around the fire circle, imitating the dance he had just witnessed. The drums started up again. Dancers joined him.

A flash of lightning exploded from roiling clouds, striking directly into their frenzied gathering, causing all those present to leap in horror. Two women fell dead, the tips of their feet steaming. Others nearby were knocked to the ground.

Ereben found himself crouching near the fire. He stood cautiously. Chrysanthus held his ears and shook his head.

"It is an evil spirit!" Big Moniku shouted. "It has tricked us!" Others expressed their agreement. "We must save ourselves from his evil. We must drive it out!"

Men with iron-tipped spears began to emerge from the crowd. Soon, Ereben and Chrysanthus were running from Oak with Mohani men in pursuit. Rain now fell, gently at first, but strengthening minute by minute. By the time they had run a quarter mile, the storm had unleashed its full fury. Wind broke branches and uprooted whole trees. Rain blew horizontally in opaque sheets. But still the enraged Mohani pursued them through the night—through the storm.

ꕥ

The greatest of the ancient trees possess only one weapon with which to combat the ravages of time—a tiny seed which sends forth a delicate sapling.

Ereben Leaf: Chronicle of the Counterspell

All night they ran. Little by little, Ereben and Chrysanthus increased the distance that separated them from the Mohani. By day break, the storm had passed, leaving only gray and pink shreds of clouds in the East. Ereben could run no farther, so they walked and stumbled and continued southward. Chrysanthus grasped Ereben's arm and hurried him along. Looking back, Ereben saw the Mohani still coming.

The trees changed. The young pine forest had abruptly given way to ancient, massive oaks and poplars, alders and chestnuts, some of them ten yards in girth. Ereben turned to see the Mohani stop and gather at the edge of the pine forest.

"Stay away, devil spirit!" one of them shouted.

Realizing that they were no longer being chased, Ereben collapsed against a massive oak, sinking into a fork of moss covered roots. He watched until the Mohani finally departed, then lapsed into a fitful sleep, dreaming of running endlessly.

When he awakened, Ereben thought it was night, but the view northward into the pine forest revealed that it was late afternoon. The ancient forest canopy admitted only a hint of daylight. Everything that grew there was old beyond imagining. He saw no young plants, no saplings, no suggestion that anything new had sprouted from its ancient soil in many years. The very fragrance of this dark realm bespoke its age. Fallen trees sported huge fungus ears.

Chrysanthus handed him a puffball mushroom the size of a man's head.

"Thank you, Grandpa." Ereben became aware of how hungry he was. He carved off a chunk with his dagger and tasted it. A musty, slightly nutty flavor emerged from its smooth, friable flesh.

Three days they walked, guessing a southerly heading on a barely visible sunrise and sunset. During the day, the forest floor of Oldwood presented a maze of deep shadows and twisted roots. As they traveled, they searched for food, but found only the giant puffballs and other less palatable fungi. The occasional shrubs which should have borne berries were without fruit. Plants with edible tubers were nowhere to be found. Ereben had set snares each night and each morning found them empty. When Chrysanthus would stalk away some distance, apparently hunting, he would invariably return empty handed, making do with chunks of mushroom.

At night, Oldwood closed in about them like a tomb. Ereben heard no sounds. No insect or bird or animal broke the oppressive silence. The darkness was absolute. Chrysanthus' vision, however, seemed unaffected by the darkness. *Like a cat.*

Ereben had always prided himself in his ability to walk forest paths in darkness. His feet could sense the difference between the compacted earth beneath a path and the slight resilience of surrounding duff. Here in Oldwood, they had found no path. The only discernible difference was between earth and root.

They continued. Mid-morning they discovered a distinct path aligned roughly north to south. Ereben smiled at how civilized the rude path felt, after so many days of dead reckoning. He wallowed in the luxury of simply walking, without consideration of bearing or of obstacles hidden in the shadows. Although their pace accelerated, Ereben could not focus on a destination or a distance. Perhaps this path led them closer to the Warded Mines, perhaps not. Chrysanthus could not offer suggestions or cautions. The only indication Ereben could weigh was that his grandfather continued willingly along their mutual course.

On the trail ahead, a man waved to them. "Welcome," he called. As he approached, Ereben recognized the deep brown, cowled robe as similar to that worn by the monk in the cellar of the tower at Ironhole. Yarnish Blen had said he was a monk from Moss Abbey. "Welcome, pilgrims." The monk smiled broadly. "You are journeying to Moss Abbey?" The pallid face of the monk was gaunt, but lined with joviality.

"Yes," Ereben responded, since any place was better than endlessly wandering through Oldwood.

"I am Punalur. Maha Neruti is expecting you. His Holiness sent me to greet you."

"I am Ereben Leaf. This is my grandfather, Chrysanthus."

Punalur raised his eyebrows at Chrysanthus, then smiled again. "I am so pleased to meet you," he said to the leopard-man. "Maha Neruti has spoken of you, but His Holiness does not know that it is Chrysanthus who comes to Moss Abbey—and with his grandson!"

As they followed Punalur, Ereben related their experience with the Mohani, though he excluded some of the more controversial details. Knowing now that Chrysanthus had visited Moss Abbey in years past, Ereben did not wish to confound his grandfather's relationship with this Maha Neruti.

The ancient forest opened to a broad expanse of plowed fields which surrounded a walled compound of tall buildings, the tallest of which held a small bronze bell in its cupola. The fields were quite barren, a bizarre appearance for mid-summer. Nearer the wall, a vineyard hung lush with deep green foliage, but without fruit. An orchard to the West was likewise verdant but barren. Punalur led them through a wooden gate of sturdy, dark timbers. Inside the wall, vegetable gardens lay bare. Not even weeds grew there. Surrounding grass grew dense and green.

They entered the main building. Ereben immediately detected the aroma of freshly baked bread. Everywhere, white plastered walls were framed in massive, brown timbers, slightly roughed with skillful adze cuts. Stained wooden stairways rose in several directions. Punalur left them standing in a hallway while he passed into a doorway, closing the door behind him.

"You've been here before, Grandpa?"

Chrysanthus squeezed Ereben's shoulder.

The door opened. A tall, thin monk of considerable age stood before them. His cowl was pushed back, revealing a bald head rimmed with a fringe of short, kinky white fuzz. The scent of cedar wafted from his robe, which showed no distinguishing features that might indicate his rank or status. "Please come in." Ereben followed Chrysanthus into the small chamber. The old monk took Chrysanthus' hand in his own. "You have grown young, my friend, while I have grown old. But you have acquired some...new features." When Chrysanthus failed to respond, the monk frowned and continued. "What can I do for you?"

"He can't talk," Ereben interjected. "I am Ereben Leaf."

"I see. You are his grandson?"

"Yes."

"I have forgotten my manners. I am Neruti. I am Warden of the March. You must be exhausted from your ordeal. Punalur will show you quarters and give you directions to the dining hall. We will speak at length tomorrow."

"Chrysanthus was a young man then, and quite full of himself." Maha Neruti smiled at the leopard-man. "He once made a hen lay acorns instead of eggs."

"I've heard that," Ereben replied. He recalled Ailantha's recounting of it. Chrysanthus had caused a hen's egg to pass into an oak tree and had then called it out again. The egg eventually hatched into a hen that would lay only acorns. These acorns would germinate, but the sprout would produce only feathers instead of leaves, and so would die. Ereben elaborated none of this as he sat with the Warden of the March. His grandfather's leopard features were too poignant a reminder of that very same process—the counterspell.

"That is trivial enough to be amusing, but nature was distorted in far more troubling and dangerous ways in the distant past." Maha Neruti looked out the tiny window in his office. The walls on all sides held shelf upon shelf of books in various colors of leather bindings. "So tell me, Ereben, what purpose has brought you and your grandfather so far from home?"

"We are trying to prevent the Knights of the Redeemer from acquiring a red stone, called sarcite."

"Indeed?" Maha Neruti became more alert. "You are certain that the Knights are seeking that specific stone?"

"Well, fairly sure. I don't know what they intend to do with it, but Grandpa seems to think it's important. Do you know where it comes from? I've been told that a place called the Warded Mines is its only source."

Maha Neruti looked pained. He scratched the white fuzz at the side of his head. "This is not a subject I would normally discuss. But Chrysanthus knows the facts. If I may judge you by the dagger you carry, then he would have told you this himself, were he able to speak."

"In ancient times, the practice of magic was widespread and carelessly applied. Men—and women—pressed the limit of the unnatural things they could accomplish, without regard for the attunement of nature. That which defines life itself is an attunement of orderliness. The food we eat is used to feed that engine within each of us that drives back the chaos of the universe. When that engine fails, the body returns to chaos—the decay of death. Chaos is non-life. The continual striving toward orderliness is unique to life. It is the very core of this balance which the ancient practitioners of magic failed to regard. They ruptured bonds that can not be restored.

"Our order has striven for century after century to hold back that chaos. We work to keep that pestilence of disorder from spreading beyond its current bounds. To the North, the attunements of nature are relatively intact. To the South however, in Ternaria, the chaos is beyond repair. Oldwood is the march. It is the demarcation between the two."

"Where does sarcite come in?"

"We use the sarcite stones to power a Sphere of Order, a pentalphic sphere. It is this sphere which enables our brotherhood to adjust attunements—to drive back the chaos of nature. Day and night we attend the sphere, watching the compressions and attenuations of attunements, making subtle adjustments as best we can."

"But it's no longer working," Ereben added.

"You have taken note of our gardens and fields."

"I saw no fruit, no new plants."

"Regularly, we replenish those sarcites on the sphere which have been most consumed by our efforts. This year, at the winter solstice, the longhaulers of the Moss Faeries failed to return with fresh stones. By the springtime, our sphere began to lose its power. This season, no seeds have germinated; no plants have borne fruit. In all of Oldwood, no creatures have been seen to bear young. Although our granaries are full, we can not survive another year of such disastrous crop failure."

"Have you learned why the Moss Faeries stopped coming?"

"We have not. We are unable to go to Ternaria..."

A monk burst into the room. "Forgive me, Your Holiness..." He seemed startled to see strangers in the chamber. He began to tremble.

"What is it, Gujara? You may speak freely."

"The...the sphere. You must come quickly!"

Maha Neruti indicated with his hand that Ereben and Chrysanthus should accompany him. They rushed down the corridor and up the stairs to the level just below the cupola.

In a windowless room, lit only by a red glow at its center, five monks hovered about a metal structure. Steel rods, outlining pentagons, were linked together to form a sphere one yard across. At each apex, a small sarcite glowed red. Four monks knelt around it, eyes closed, each hand touching a stone. The fifth monk hung limply from two apices which did not glow. Chrysanthus grasped his head, screamed an agonized howl and fled from the room.

"Changiri's stones have faded," Gujara sobbed. "The sphere has consumed him."

As they watched, his flesh drained toward the sphere, leaving only a skeleton covered with shriveled skin. The dead monk clattered to the flagstone paving.

Ereben opened his small pouch and handed two sarcites to Maha Neruti, who accepted them with surprise. The Warden of the March rushed to the sphere and deftly snapped the new sarcites in place. They immediately began to glow. The sanctum brightened. He kept one hand on each stone, closed his eyes and assumed an expression of great effort. Maha Neruti released the sphere, then signaled to Gujara to take over the duty. Gujara bent down and briefly touched the head of the fallen monk, then joined the four who ministered to the glowing device.

One of the other monks at the sphere moaned as the stone in his right hand flickered and died. The monk's hand melded to the apex.

Without hesitating, Ereben withdrew Hobart's dagger from his sheath and touched its point to the hungry apex. It's translucent green handle began to glow. Cold swept into his hand and up his arm, clawing at his being, reaching for his heart. Rather than force it back, Ereben softened its hunger and allowed it to enter his being. It moved through him, searching, probing. He inserted his left hand into a small pouch and grasped its three remaining sarcites. Warmth radiated from the stones and into his heart. He watched within himself as, with each beat, his heart surged that warmth throughout his body, and out into the pentalphic sphere.

Gossamer connections joined his being to the nineteen remaining apex stones and to the five monks about the sphere. He saw their lives, their dreams, their victories and failures. He understood that they could see he knew what it is like to be a rock. They shared his love for Phaena. They combed leaves from Ailantha's gray hair with their hands. He knew the chaos about them, and the greater chaos to the South. He understood that Holnick Firth was attempting to create a pentalphic sphere. The past spread before him as a finely detailed painting of people and of things, of movement and impermanence. This past, all pasts, moved toward a maelstrom of indistinct chaos.

With his left hand, Ereben and the five monks lifted a single stone from the pouch and placed it, glowing, into the waiting apex of the sphere. Ereben Leaf, Guardian of the Ruins, released the stone and withdrew his dagger. As he did so, he fell to the floor. Darkness swallowed him.

"His changes have caused him to become, at least partly, a magical being." Maha Neruti explained. The Sphere of Order exerts a focus of power that must have been too much for him to bear in such proximity. He awaits you south of the Abbey."

"These are the last of the sarcites," Ereben said, handing the two remaining stones to the Warden of the March. We'll bring some back, once we find the Warded Mines."

"Should you find it, you will not be able to enter. Its entrance is guarded by a powerful ward that will not permit a human to enter."

"Then how do the Moss Faeries get to it?"

"They are not human. You will have to find Gelith and persuade him to assist you."

No trail headed south from Moss Abbey, other than the firmly packed, brown ribbon of earth—no more than a finger's breadth wide—that led from a tiny hatch at the rear of the main building southward to vanish into the edge of the forest. The monks were forbidden to step on this, known as the Faerie Path. So once again Ereben and Chrysanthus entered the sullen shadows of Oldwood Forest, judging south as best they could, this time veering toward the East to find Ternaria, home of the Moss Faeries. On the morning of the second day, the trees were noticeably smaller, though just as ancient. By mid-day, they walked through Dwarf trees, no taller than knee height, and gnarled shrubs, equally Dwarfed. This abruptly ended at a narrow limestone slab that stretched to the East and West.

On the other side, Ereben stood at the edge of a vast glade. Flowers of every color scented the air. Dozens of varieties of mushrooms sprouted between them. He picked two munu and placed them in his pouch. Above the flowers, an occasional thistle bobbed gently in the mid-day sun.

"Is this the way, Grandpa?"

Chrysanthus remained on the limestone and seated himself.

A buzzing sound caused Ereben to shoo a large bumblebee that approached too close. The bumblebee then descended toward the ground and repeatedly circled a patch of shaggy moss. The fat, black bumblebee bore a broad stripe of green fuzz across its abdomen. The bee flew up toward Ereben's face, causing him to pull his head back. It then returned to circling the moss. Twice more, the bumblebee repeated this, drawing Ereben's attention to the moss. It was then that he spotted a tiny figure, scarcely taller than his fingernail, struggling to free itself from a sticky substance which seemed to exude from the surface of the moss. As he stooped over, the bumblebee landed on the grass nearby.

The tiny, struggling figure called out in a high pitched, barely audible sound. He bent further, and recognized the shape of a human-like girl. She lay on her back, her arms and legs trapped in the sticky exudate.

"Can you help me out of this," the tiny voice said. "It burns."

A soft purring sound came from Chrysanthus, who sat watching from the limestone slab.

"Wait," Ereben said, looking about for a suitably tiny tool. Finally, with the points of two stiff blades of grass, he pried the tiny girl free and placed her on the ground.

"Do you have some water?" she asked in her tiny voice. "I need to wash this stuff off."

Ereben picked the blossom of a yellow flower and poured a small amount of water into it.

"Look the other way," she insisted.

He turned his head away. When he peeked a moment later, he saw that she had removed her clothes, and was sitting in the yellow flower, splashing the water about and washing her hair. He peeked once more to see her standing beside the flower washing her clothes.

"You're such a sneak!" She immediately covered herself with the wet clothing. "Now just turn around, and I'll tell you when I'm done. You sneak!"

"I'm sorry."

"The monks wouldn't have peeked. You're definitely not a monk."

"I won't peek."

"You better not."

"Are you a Moss Faerie?"

"That's very funny."

"What?"

"I'm a Faerie, as you can plainly see. Not yet! But I don't usually lie around on that nasty moss."

"So you're not a Moss Faerie?"

"Faerie! Just plain Faerie."

"Are there Moss Faeries around here?"

"Okay, you can turn around."

"Were looking for Gelith."

"Oh. He's in his castle."

"Can you take us there?"

"Not a chance!"

"Why not? It's important."

"Because your feet are so big. No telling what you would crunch between here and there."

Ereben began to understand. Everything here was so tiny that his footsteps would be catastrophic. "Wait here." Ereben carefully tiptoed over to Chrysanthus. "Grandpa, is there some way to be smaller, that is, some way that can be undone when we leave here?"

Chrysanthus reached over to Ereben and touched Hobart's dagger.

"I think I know how to make it happen, but the counterspell would be tricky."

Chrysanthus drummed his claws on the limestone slab.

"Of course!" He understood rock. He could adjust the attunement. But the reverse would require a large quantity of living matter from which to regain not only their body matter, but their life force as well. The rock would absorb it, but would not easily release it to reverse the process.

With munu in his left hand, Ereben drew his dagger and focused it. He touched the forged blade to the rock and explored familiar connections. The Path of the Horizon was not clear. He drew Chrysanthus' dagger, placed it in his grandfather's hand, then joined hands with him, so that they held the munu together between them. With both daggers touching the rock, he once again examined the connections of matter. Unexpectedly, he understood the hardships of life as a leopard high in the Broken Mountains. He sensed the biting cold, the blowing snow, and the companionship of the pride. He sensed that his grandfather now longed for that intimacy. Ereben made a subtle adjustment of a minor attunement, causing matter to flow, and with it, the essence of his life and that of his grandfather. Something was not right, something barely beyond his awareness. An imbalance. His vision blurred.

When he could once again focus his eyes, he sat with Chrysanthus at the edge of a limestone cliff. Their hands rested against gigantic, horizontal cylinders of translucent green stone. He had succeeded in shrinking himself and his grandfather, but their daggers had remained unchanged, and now loomed above them on the limestone slab like fallen monuments.

The wisdom of a child may conquer. Be slow to dismiss the waif who may lead you to victory.

Sulalian Proverb

As the Kiriati sailed farther south, the days grew warmer. The Kiriati herself, was old. Much of the wood of the deck and rails was worn smooth, polished by years of passing hands and shuffled feet. Some of the rigging and sails were new though. The Master's jury-rigged foremast, supporting its fan-shaped sail, seemed to stand as straight and sturdy as the older mainmast.

Jasper spent much of his time alone at the bow of the ship. If he leaned forward onto the juncture of rails at the prow, he could see nothing but the water and an occasional large fish keeping pace with the ship. The Kiriati would disappear, and there would be only himself, flying leisurely over the swells of the Great Eastern Sea. Jasper sensed that, although the northerly wind was favorable to their southward journey, once they had moved out of the broad bay of Bur Nor, warm ocean currents were pushing up from the south.

It was late in the day when Jasper caught sight of brilliant green lights sparkling on the distant coast to the west. The Kiriati veered toward it.

"Almirant."

The voice of Muldu, and a firm hand on his shoulder startled Jasper. "Is that where we are going?"

"Yes. Almirant is a great city – a great fortress. Almirant has never fallen in war. A thousand years."

"Have you been there before?"

"Two times, when I was young."

"What are those green lights?"

"You will see." Muldu turned away, spoke some commands to his First Mate, Kipik, who then barked them at the crew.

Liddie joined Jasper at the prow. "Kozhdu says he will nae come ashore with us."

As they approached Almirant from the warm sea, circular rooftops, glistening in glassy green tile, rose higher. The city rested on a cluster of hills, all encircled together by walls—three complete walls. The outer wall, built at the edge of the sea, stood taller than any wall Jasper had ever seen. Its construction was of finely dressed, white stone. Within it, the second wall was taller, and the third, innermost wall reached even higher. Stone towers divided the outer wall every 30 yards. Towers of the inner walls were spaced more closely, and were more numerous.

The harbor itself was enclosed by two arcs of coarsely dressed sea wall, a narrow entrance near the center. Within, hundreds of boats and larger ships rested at anchor. Muldu directed Kipik that the Kiriati should enter the harbor, but anchor just past the opening in the sea wall.

Once again, all the Orkahti men, horsemen and sailors alike, refused to disembark at a Sulalian city, especially Almirant, the capital of the Kingdom of Jelar, and largest city in all the Three Kingdoms–the seat of High King, Kalish ibn Sulal.

Liddie and Jasper wandered among hundreds of market stalls–some canopied, some exposed in the searing sun–spread densely over the paved, gentle slope that separated the outer wall from the second wall. The market sprawled in a circular band nearly a hundred yards across. Jasper guessed that they could easily waste half a day following these endless stalls of trinkets and foods and utensils all the way around the outside of the second wall. Liddie seemed to share that impression, and steered them toward the massive, open gates of the second wall.

A loud clang startled Jasper. High above, suspended from the upper tier of the gate, Jasper could see a bronze figure of a man. A large ball, attached to a swinging rod, had struck the bronze man. It was one of four such balls now dangling near the bronze man. He counted eight more balls still held well away from it.

"That marks the fourth hour," a nearby stranger volunteered.

Jasper turned to see a middle-aged, well groomed man. He was engaged in no obvious work. His tan robe allowed his right arm to remain uncovered. Blue silk pantaloons blossomed from beneath the bottom of the robe. A curve dagger with a jeweled handle rested within a sheath at his belly, and a simple small, white turban capped his closely cropped head.

"It keeps activities orderly. May I assist you in finding the goal of your search?"

Liddie drew herself to her proudest affect. "We huv need of a new house servant. Perhaps a boy." She smiled.

"The market for house servants is within this middle wall..." He gestured toward the towering, bronze-trimmed gate that had just sounded the fourth hour. "...to the north, near the innermost wall."

Jasper and Liddie thanked him simultaneously, then headed into the second ring of the city of Almirant.

The first obvious difference that Jasper noticed between the market area they had just explored and the much cleaner courtyard that filled this second public area was the heavy presence of armed, uniformed men. While some stood smartly in pairs, adjacent to doorways and gateways, others walked about in tidy rank and file units. Still others wandered throughout the area individually, atop sturdy horses. Each of them, mounted or on foot, carried one or more sharp weapons considerably more threatening than a dagger at the waist. Most sported a scimitar at the hip. Those who marched in small groups carried wooden pikes, each with a small, pointed banner near the steel point. All the pike banners within a single group matched in color, which differed from the colors of other marching groups.

Another striking feature was their stature. Every armed man appeared to be taller than most Sulalians. And they appeared to be from many races of man. Some showed the dark brown skin of the Shouda. Others the paleness of wild men he had been told about as a young boy, who came from the Nether Reaches. Still others appeared to be of Orkahti blood. Yet they were all conspicuously dressed in similar colors of turbans, robes and pantaloons. And all were extraordinarily tall.

As he and Liddie worked their way around scattered market stalls, all carefully canopied, offering impressively refined household items, such as large sculptures, beautifully decorated water vessels, and conspicuously expensive fabrics, Jasper found one stall particularly curious. Within the shade of its broad canopy were huge, stunning carpets of richly colored, finely detailed pile, depicting gardens and woodlands, or scenes of people engaged in trade or war. Carpets hung from the sides of the stall, covered the pavement, and rested in stacks. He had seen a carpet like these once before–partway up the mountain slopes above Zink, in the ramshackle home of the aging Ailantha, a Guardian of the Ruins. He had never seen such a large carpet for sale anywhere in Valand or Shouda or Zink or even in the Sulalian quarter of Cinnabar. *Ailantha must have visited Almirant.*

He thought about Ereben and his few other remaining friends, all of whom he might never see again. Wispy threads of meaning and counter-meaning, destiny and intrigue seemed to pervade everything and everybody. Phaena now was lost among the Dryads. While he felt the acute burden of locating and rescuing the captured Shouda boy, Bahsa, he sensed the shadow of a deeper calling, a more demanding weight that he should be carrying. But he had no idea what that might be for a boy of...

He could no longer remember his age. *Twelve? I think I'm twelve years. But I might be thirteen.* An uninvited thought of his mother brought moisture to his eyes.

"Liddie..."

"Have ye spotted Bahsa, lad?"

"No." He turned her shoulder, until she faced a unit of tall troops marching past. "They're all slaves. On their arms. All of them wear a metal band. All of them. They're all slaves."

"Aye. Maybees we have Sulalian kings and thir families usin' no' but slaves tae capture yet more slaves. An' they trust thir slaves tae carry weapons."

As Jasper and Liddie moved further toward the inner wall, Jasper saw what appeared to be the exhibiting and selling of people of various ages. He alerted Liddie.

A loud gong sounded, followed by the blaring of ear-splitting reed instruments. Every one in this inner courtyard turned immediately to face the colossal, closed gates that led through the innermost wall. The deep red, wooden doors slowly swung open. As a drum began to thump, four files of mounted soldiers emerged from the gate, then split into two files to either side of a long pathway spontaneously created by those standing in the vicinity.

Twelve brightly clothed men stepped in unison through the gate, carrying an ornately carved pallet, upon which a man pompously sat within a nest of huge cushions. His massive, white turban had been fashioned in such a way that it appeared to have the wings of a flying bird protruding from it.

Those standing about dropped to one knee, as the man on the pallet was carried past. Jasper and Liddie followed their example.

"Who is that?" Jasper whispered to Liddie.

A stranger immediately in front of them partly turned his head, and whispered, "The High King, Kalish ibn Sulal. Now be still."

The king's pallet was preceded out of the gate in the second wall by four files of foot soldiers, then followed out by all the horsemen. Behind all this, an unarmed, though finely dressed man walked, while carrying a tall basket. Two or three of the bystanders stepped toward him as he passed, and tossed a tied scroll into the basket.

By now, all the observers were back on their feet. The stranger who had whispered to Jasper turned to examine him. He frowned. "If you speak aloud in the king's presence, without his leave to speak..." He shook his head.

"What do they do?" Jasper asked.

"If you are young and healthy, they make you a slave."

"An if yer neither so young nor so healthy?" Liddie prodded.

He pursed his lips, glancing at Liddie. With the lift of one eyebrow, he swiped a finger across his neck. Without further niceties, he merged into the crowd.

Liddie harrumphed. "I can see they tak thir manners serious."

Finally approaching the apparent slave market, Jasper could clearly see that all of those being offered for sale seemed to be nearly his own age or older. None very young, none very old. But they were of every race of man.

Liddie asked an observer if he knew if there had been or would be any younger boys for sale.

"If enough young to make eunuch, and not taken by army, sell at Dire."

"What does 'make eunuch' mean?" Jasper labored at the stern sweep of their dinghy, working his way through the harbor, toward the Kiriati.

"They unsex him. Like ye do wi' cattle or goats."

Jasper's ears rang, as he felt color rushing to his face. "Why..." He swallowed. "Why would they do that?"

"It maks them grow taller. An' they huv nae worries abou' them dallying wi' thir women."

He recalled that all the soldiers and horsemen were unusually tall.

The port city of Dire turned out to be a hub of manufacturing, with busy docks loading and unloading materials and goods. The military presence there was considerably less imposing than that of Almirant.

In one open-air factory, enslaved Dwarfs served as slave masters for hundreds of enslaved Sulalian children–fair-skinned, local Albians–who worked at huge rug looms, tying little bits of wool into knots, to create the intricate patterns of their spectacular carpets. In another open factory, children hammered at thin pieces of metal, making common kitchen utensils.

Upon their finally reaching the slave market of Dire, Jasper was thrilled and relieved to see Bahsa sitting silently in the pen, apparently unharmed–a length of rope dangling freely from the knot, where it had been tied around his neck. He wore a soiled, tunic of homespun.

By the time Liddie had inquired of a nearby stranger about the mechanics of purchasing a slave, Bahsa had spotted them. His eyes brightened, but of course he remained silent, as he had remained since witnessing the death of his mother during the Battle of the Great Pyramid of Shouda.

The interest of buyers seemed to be slow for each of the slaves offered, so Liddie placed the only bid for Bahsa, once his turn had come to stand in the center and be subjected to the humiliating examinations by indifferent purchasers. In her subsequent mannerisms, she revealed no hint of any previous familiarity with her newly purchased slave. She directed Jasper to grasp the end of the rope that was tied about Bahsa's neck, and casually walked toward the gate of the low wall that surrounded Dire, heading for their dinghy, beached at the edge of the harbor.

As they neared the gate, the soldiers standing to either side hustled other pedestrians out of the way, and closed its doors. Hoofbeats approached from behind them, and stopped. Jasper turned around to see a dozen Sulalian horsemen, led by a man whom he recognized. It was unmistakably one of the same Sulalians from whom they had rescued Kozhdu's young daughter, Yava. "They recognize us," he said to Liddie.

To be cast out is to be set free.

Gumushtigin: Meditations

Minkar Jarad could offer up no fear, no dread, not even a gasp. He turned and faced the gray bearded dragon, ready to be consumed by its fire, or torn limb from limb within its lethal maw. His own people had cast him out of their city—had cast him out of their minds. He had been erased form their histories. What could be more fitting, he thought, than for his lingering flesh to be dismembered, and left for the insects.

"I surrender myself to you, Elloh, praise to your name." Minkar bowed to the dragon in the Shouda fashion, and awaited his end.

"I greet you," a deep, airy voice replied. Its pitch was so low that Minkar not only heard the words, but felt them in his bones.

Minkar looked up to the sky, awed by the voice of Elloh.

"You are not afraid of me," the voice said. "Mortal creatures always run away and never speak to me."

Minkar's eyes widened. He lowered his gaze to the immense dragon. His mind groped at conflicting assumptions, then settled on a tentative conclusion. It was not the voice of Elloh, but rather, the voice of the dragon. The dragon was speaking to him. *What does one say to a dragon?* "I am called Minkar Jarad."

"It pleases me to speak with you," the dragon replied.

"By what name should I call you?" Minkar asked.

"I have no name. No one ever speaks to me. My brothers have no need to speak to me."

This presented Minkar with a dilemma. The courtesies of Shouda conversation depended on some means of addressing the listener.

"In ancient times, men called me Drago, but they called my brothers by that name as well. Perhaps you could do me the honor of giving me a name."

Minkar studied the congenial beast. Its golden head was punctuated by two reptilian eyes the size of a man's head. Golden scales overlapped in sparkling rows from its nostrils to the tip of its tail. Short, golden horns crowned its brow. A tangle of long silver tendrils drooped from its yard-long chin. "Sometimes, men of great age and wisdom are called Graybeard. Would you like to be known as Graybeard?"

"It is true that I am of great age," the dragon said thoughtfully, "however each of my brothers is far wiser than I can hope to be. But I am honored by your name. I shall be known, then, as Graybeard, Minkar Jarad."

Graybeard's mouth remained almost closed when he spoke. Only the tip of his lips moved to shape the words. He clearly enunciated his words in perfect, though somewhat elaborate Valish. Judging from the size of Graybeard's head and neck, Minkar suspected that the dragon exerted a great deal of effort in order to raise the pitch of his voice. Nevertheless, as the pitch rose and fell with appropriate Valish inflection, the bottom sounds fell below Minkar's ability to hear them. Those last sounds rumbled, instead, into his feet and throughout his skeleton.

"Where are you going?" Graybeard asked.

"I do not know." His anguish returned. "I do not know where I *was* going."

"That is difficult for me to understand. You were walking this way," the dragon said, pointing with one claw, "so you must have been going somewhere, unless you were just wandering aimlessly."

"I was saddened by recent events, so I was just wandering."

"I do understand that, Minkar Jarad. I too have been saddened by recent events, so I have been wandering. But I never expected to speak with a man."

"Nor I with a dragon."

"We should share our sadnesses so they might be lighter to bear," Graybeard suggested. There was a spark of anticipation in his eye.

"My difficulties would probably be meaningless to you."

"Not at all," Graybeard insisted. "It would be the most meaningful discussion I have ever had. We could visit new places while we talked."

"I suspect that we would travel at very different speeds."

"Not if you ride on my back."

Minkar had always assumed that the frigid lands of the Nether Reaches were devoid of habitation. That was clearly not the case. Below him, villages dotted the vibrant green landscape, enjoying their brief glimpse of summer. They usually flew high enough to avoid frightening people and caribou herds below. Minkar guessed that the villages were separated by about a day's journey from one another.

Vast herds of wild caribou had just begun their southward movement, streaming like a river from their mating grounds. From high above, the flow could be seen to split around obstacles, then merge again farther south.

In villages, Minkar could identify two varieties of domesticated caribou. A smaller variety, kept in much greater numbers, were ranged like cattle. The larger caribou seemed to be treated rather like fine horses, and in fact were seen to be ridden by the local inhabitants. While the common caribou bore coats of mixed gray and white, in various patterns, the taller, more streamlined beasts, those used as mounts, were covered in pure, shaggy white.

As they flew on their aimless tour, Minkar and Graybeard shared the stories of their lives. Graybeard easily raised his voice to be heard over the wind. And even Minkar's softest whispers could be captured by the dragon's acute hearing.

Graybeard explained that he could fly low over a village and hear all the conversations of all the villagers simultaneously. His draconic mind was capable of sorting and comprehending all that was said. In that manner, he and his brothers had acquired knowledge of many dozens of languages and studied scores of cultures.

"My brother who is angry uses that knowledge to identify weaknesses in those he would attack and injure."

"Why would he attack people?"

"He harbors anger over his long imprisonment. He kills to sate his anger. In addition to his anger, he carries now a hatred within his heart. This is a new thing. Since our release from the prison, he has changed, as though he has drawn within himself the hatred so common among humans."

"And your other brothers, do they also kill?"

"They sometimes hunt animals for sport. While we may eat, if we choose, we have no need to eat. We are magical beings."

"I was told that you are ancient creatures of flesh and blood."

"We bear their shape, but we are entirely magical."

"If you do not eat, then from what sustenance do you maintain your life? Even magic requires a source of fuel."

"We draw it, unhindered, from the wellspring of the universe. In every instant, from each transaction of living, mortal existence we exact an imperceptible toll."

"So living things pay a kind of tax to support magical things?"

"In a sense. But it is dispersed over so great a number of living things, that it is a mere suggestion of a tax. You might, rather, consider it an insignificant leakage."

"How long does a dragon live?"

"That is a difficult question to answer. A dragon does not age as mortal creatures, whose days are more or less numbered. But we can suffer injury, and if injured grievously, will die. My brother who covets, is scarred about the neck from being trapped at the opening of the black pyramid. My brother who seeks understanding carries a crushed foot, caused by the collapse of that great pyramid. So while we may live indefinitely, we carry each of our wounds day after day."

"Sadness and burdens do seem to accumulate as we get older." Minkar thought of his son, Bahsa, lost somewhere in the East. "Could we look for my son, Graybeard?"

"If, as you have been told, he is in the Eastern Kingdoms, it would be dangerous for me to accompany you. The people there are learning to hate and fear dragons. My brother who is angry has killed many people there without cause. On one occasion, his left eye was destroyed by a weapon. This has stoked his anger to a frightful pitch. He now harbors a hatred that must be fed continually with human blood."

"Do the other dragons kill people?"

"My brother who is covetous will kill without passion, if a man attempts to hide his riches. But it is not from hatred. It is a cost of acquisition."

"We should land near a town," Minkar said. "The weather gets colder as we move north. I need a warmer cloak." He wondered if Bahsa was warm enough...wherever he was.

"The town is Yavejik," a white haired young man answered.

"Is there a shop where I might find something warm?" Minkar asked. He had left Graybeard to watch the caribou migrations, and had walked an hour along a stony river to reach the small town. Here, it seemed, everyone was as tall as the Shouda, but extraordinarily pale skinned, with white or light yellow hair. Judging from their stares, most had never before seen a man with brown skin.

"If warmth it is that you look for, you have three choices in Yavejik." The stranger ticked off the choices on his fingers. "The trading post, the tavern or the brothel."

"The trading post would be helpful."

"Not my first choice," the young man said, winking a sparkling, blue eye. "That short building is the trading post."

"I thank you."

"If you picked the brothel, you would thank me more."

Minkar's eyes briefly scanned the endless flat, white, apparently barren landscape. "Perhaps."

He headed toward the single story, stone building crowded between two taller structures. White caribou were hitched to posts outside all the buildings. These unusually tall caribou bore saddles with stirrups, and bridles like those worn by horses elsewhere. The males, all geldings, carried antlers which had been sculpted into two forward pointing lances. The mares had no antlers at all.

From the first building, a towering, burly man stepped out. A fur-clad woman of indeterminate age clung to each of his thick arms, kissing them from elbow to shoulder. The man, dressed in white fur skins, shook off the fawning women and walked up to Minkar.

"You have come a long, long way, if I may judge by the color of your skin."

"I am from Shouda. All Shouda people are of this same color."

The man looked up and down the muddy road. "You are on foot?"

Minkar avoided mention of the dragon. "Yes, I have come into Yavejik seeking a warm cloak."

"A beautiful spear you carry, brown man from Shouda."

"It serves its purpose."

"The trading post is that pile of rocks. Have you a name?"

"Forgive me," Minkar said, bowing in the Shouda fashion, "I am called Minkar Jarad."

"I am Kevi. Tell that thief in the trading post to sell to you what you want at Kevi's price." Kevi unhitched a stately caribou, mounted it, and rode north.

Within the cluttered trading post, Minkar explained to the proprietor what he needed.

"I see that you are not Nanish. The Nanes want always their furs white, so they hide while hunting. I have a fur that will suit someone like yourself perfectly." The wrinkled old man dumped a stack of white furs onto the floor, in order to reach a fur at the bottom of the stack. He held it up and slapped it, freeing a cloud of dust. The fur was of a deep brown color that nearly matched Minkar's skin. "Valand bear. This is a rare color, but it's worth the extra cost. For a guest, one gold, six."

"I was told to ask that you sell it at Kevi's price."

"You know the king?" The proprietor's shoulders sagged with disappointment.

"I spoke with a large man who called himself Kevi. He seemed concerned that you might ask too dear a price."

"Alright. It is not often I see a stranger here. I can only hope to earn a living. The brown fur has remained unsold for three years. None of the Nanes want it, not even for a caribou blanket. King Kevlinoor has made many jokes about it. You can have it for twelve coppers."

Minkar covered himself with the heavy fur cape. Its brown fur hung from his neck to his feet. "I will buy it."

Graybeard lifted from the soggy tundra and circled to gain altitude. Minkar looked down in time to see three men in white furs struggling to control their caribou mounts. The man in the center he recognized as Kevi. Minkar spread his brown fur cloak and waved his spear in salutation to Kevlinoor, King of the Nanes. Kevi simply stared back in amazement.

Two days later, they passed over a partially frozen sea and landed between the rocky crags of a small island. There, they entered a huge cavern that branched in many directions. Within the cave, the rock and the air were much warmer than outside, warm enough so that he did not see his breath. Graybeard had explained that this was now his home. Minkar selected a small alcove that ventilated to the outside and made it his own temporary home.

Minkar lived on fish, which Graybeard could snatch from the waters with his claws. The smoke from his cooking fire wafted out the roof. Water trickled continuously from the rock warmed melt of the snow pack above the cave, and formed a small creek within the cavern.

Minkar spent most of his time talking with Graybeard, who, in turn, spoke of his six brothers.

"Would you meet with my brother who wishes seclusion?"

"Where does he live?"

"He lives here. He wishes to speak with you."

Minkar looked about him. "Will I be safe?"

"You have been safe. He knew of your arrival here. I have shared with him my experience with you."

"You have talked with him since we arrived?"

"We have no need of talking amongst ourselves. I have shared my thoughts with him."

They moved through the warren of intersecting caverns for a half hour, Minkar carrying a small torch.

"My brother is there. I will wait here."

Minkar stepped into a grotto. A dragon filled much of the space. It lay curled in nearly a circle, with its chin rested on its front feet. It was similar to Graybeard, with two exceptions. The tendrils beneath its chin were as gold as its scales. Its horns formed a towering crown across its brow.

"You are Minkar Jarad. My brother who is simple tells me that you call him Graybeard. What name will you call me?"

"May I call you Highcrown?"

"You may call me Highcrown if it pleases you."

Minkar bowed in the Shouda fashion. "Graybeard has said that you are leader of the dragons."

"I do not lead. I attempt to constrain the others in a manner that may allow us to maintain our freedom."

"He said that you wished to speak with me. Of what do you wish to speak?"

"Tell me what it is that binds an ancient flying creature to an evanescent human in friendship?"

"I do not understand the word *evanescent*, Highcrown."

"Fleeting. You come beyond the Nether Reaches to be taught your native language?"

"You have experienced my language for more than can be fit into one lifetime of man."

"One chooses to experience to a greater or lesser degree. But we digress. Tell me of friendship."

"I have never considered the nature of friendship. I have experienced friendship, and can identify degrees of friendship. But I am a simple Shouda farmer. You ask a difficult question."

"You are far more than a simple Shouda farmer, Minkar Jarad. You have distinguished yourself in combat. You have flown giant fowl and ridden both a river demon and a dragon. You have seen that magic is part of the nature of things. So, tell me of friendship."

Minkar thought of his Shouda friends. They had abandoned him, because of his willingness to speak the truth. He thought of Ereben Leaf and of Graybeard. "Friendship is the acceptance of another without judgment."

"Regardless of the desires or actions of another?"

"There must be a common...a shared direction to judgment and action."

"Yet you have come here alone. Does that end your earlier friendships?"

"It has been the beginning of my friendship with Graybeard, but my other friends will still be friends when I return to them."

"Then if your actions are made without regard to your earlier friends, you need not share common actions."

"Friendship is within the soul of man."

"Can there be friendship without the acts of friendship?"

He again thought of Otah Kadeef, whom he considered a friend, but who had not acted as a friend. "A friendship within the soul that is not confined by the acts of friendship causes sadness, but the friendship remains." A wave of sorrow and loss swept over Minkar.

"Must both feel that sadness for the friendship to remain, or can it persist as a friendship only in the soul of one?"

Minkar fell to his knees and wept, his hands over his face. "I do not know, Highcrown," he sobbed. "A part of the soul clings to that friendship, while another part mourns its loss."

"I have caused you sadness?"

"No, Highcrown, my words have caused me to think of friends who have not acted as friends. It is that which has made me sad."

"Can there be friendship by acts of friendship, without a friendship of the soul?"

"It is the acts of friendship that plant the seed of friendship within the soul."

"Then it seems that no friendship can be born without the acts of friendship."

"I suppose that is true."

"And no friendship exists beyond a well of sadness without the acts of friendship."

"Yes."

"So I may conclude that there is no friendship apart from the acts of friendship."

"But it lives within," Minkar corrected, unsure of himself.

"I disagree," a dragon voice said from behind Minkar.

Minkar turned to see an unfamiliar dragon crouched behind him. The dragon's right front foot was twisted inward.

"Since you seem to dwell on the superficial," the new dragon said, "you might as well call me *Clubfoot* and be done with it. Friendship is a potentiality that may or may not be manifest. It is the potentiality we must weigh, not the acts."

Both dragons fell silent, occasionally tipping a head or raising an eyebrow. Minkar could only assume that they were continuing the strange debate in a manner that he could not share.

Clubfoot sighed deeply. "My brother who wishes seclusion, Highcrown if you will, would rather be by himself, but wishes to carry his brothers' companionship within him when he goes. I have assured him that this is possible, but you have suggested otherwise. That is just as well, since his presence here is all that prevents my brother who is angry from becoming prime. As long as Highcrown is prime, there is a chance for peace."

"Clubfoot is wiser than me," Highcrown rumbled, "but places that burden upon me because of his injury. The others respect only the claw. They thus regard Clubfoot as unsuitable to be prime."

"Who was prime before you were injured?" Minkar asked Clubfoot.

"For two thousand years we had no need of one to be prime. Beneath the black pyramid there were few decisions."

"And before that?"

"My brother who is simple was then prime."

"Graybeard?"

"Yes, Graybeard. Our incarceration came about from his decisions. His failure caused his mind to eschew complexities. He now lives only for the small joys of each day, never looking beyond that close horizon."

"He seems kind and generous," Minkar offered in his friend's defense.

"Graybeard believes that dragons can be at peace with man. The rest of us have serious doubts as to its possibility."

"Surely peace is possible," Minkar insisted. "Peace is always possible."

"Even as we speak," Highcrown intoned, "men fight against one another. Some kill. Some enslave. Some engage their purile hands in magic aimed at controlling us."

"If dragons harmed no one, if they lived apart from men, there could be peace." Minkar's conviction wavered within his mind. He knew that the blind priest, Crotus, would stop at nothing to destroy the dragons.

Minkar spoke with Highcrown and Clubfoot on two other occasions during the ensuing days, but as with their first conversation, nothing was clarified. It simply intensified his own sense of loneliness. Once, he passed yet another dragon in the cavern. Distinguishing it by silver scales on all four of its feet, Minkar named it *Boots*, though they exchanged no words.

His ease in the presence of dragons increased. He sometimes wandered through the caverns, always careful to mark his route using a stone of contrasting color against the limestone walls. He discovered a cathedral of stalagmites and stalactites and, on another occasion, a high domed chamber which amplified even the sound of two fingers rubbing together.

The cavern smelled only of damp stone, rather than an animal's nest. The dragons were fastidious in their cleanliness, often bathing by diving from a great height into the icy waters of the sea. Then, in an explosion of surf, they emerged from the depths and soared again into the sky.

One day, he continued for an hour along a nearly straight passageway, traversing, he assumed, most of the island. Toward its end, the passage ascended gradually, opening onto the eastern flank of the island's single mountain. The spot offered a panorama of endless sea and ice. He gazed into the frigid expanse until he shivered from the cold.

Entering the cavern again, he wandered into a long side chamber. Heaped in the center were all manner of riches. Golden and silver goblets, necklaces of jewels, crowns, tiaras, coins and scepters lay gathered in a single pile. Scattered within the pile were swords and daggers sheathed in jewel encrusted scabbards. It reminded him of the lavishness of the underground city of Lamblar. The Lamblari Shouda had no notion of wealth, but simply used the materials at hand. Their endless excavations yielded gold and silver, which they used to make practical things.

Minkar remembered Graybeard's brother who covets, who was scarred about the neck. Lord Corban, on being surprised by more than a single dragon emerging from the magic portal of the black pyramid had withdrawn one of the three daggers, causing it to close about the neck of a dragon. It was the dragon's presence within the portal that had caused the pyramid to shatter.

Reaching the intersection with the main cavern, Minkar was startled by the presence of a dragon crouching its way in. The claws of one of its front feet clasped four long swords with green pommel stones—swords of the now banished Protectors of Dragomin. A ring of scales about its neck had been replaced by livid scar. The dragon cocked its head and examined Minkar.

"I am Minkar Jarad," he said with a trembling voice.

"I know who you are. My brother who is simple brought you here. What I do not know is why you have seen fit to inspect my belongings."

"I was only wandering about and came in, not realizing what was here."

"You wear gold about your hips, Minkar Jarad."

"Yes. It was a gift from a friend. May I select a name by which I might address you?"

"You may do that if you wish."

"May I call you Ringneck?"

The dragon raised its brows, then advanced into the chamber of treasures, forcing Minkar to back in as well. The dragon circled the heap of treasure, then plunged its head beneath it all. A massive head rose from the center of the heap. The sparkling of gold and silver and jewels obscured the scar about its neck.

"Now, Minkar Jarad, how would you name me?" The dragon's golden scales merged seamlessly with chalices and bangles, creating the image of two adjoining heaps of treasure, one with a head, the other with a tail.

"I must call you Splendor."

"You must agree that it is preferable to honor one's strengths rather than one's shortcomings."

"Then I may call you Splendor?"

"You may call me Splendor. Now tell me why I should not demand that you give me the gold you wear about your hips."

Minkar strode up to the partially buried dragon. "Because it is not pure gold. Feel it." Minkar lifted one of the golden plates so that Splendor could feel it with his claws. "Steel. It is only covered by gold. Gold makes poor armor. Gold is too heavy and too soft."

"It is indeed steel," Splendor agreed, after scratching the plate. "Had you given it to me, I would have seen that it was mere steel, and returned it to you."

"Where do you find all those treasures?"

"Much is from a place I inhabited in ancient times. These swords I collected near your home. They were left after the great battle there."

"They are steel."

"Ah, but the Protectors used their magical power to control beasts and birds. They are safer with me."

"Would you at least return me to Shouda?" Minkar asked Graybeard.

His friend was hesitant for two reasons which he explained. First was the danger of heading south, toward the conflicts brewing among men there. More importantly, Graybeard did not want his new friend to go away.

Dragons, Minkar had been told, do not cry. But sadness caused their horns to droop slightly, this being possible, he was told, because, unlike a cows' horns, a dragon's horns are boneless, and actually composed of only the skin of his head. Minkar could clearly see Graybeard's sadness. But on account of his friendship, Graybeard agreed to fly him as far as Shouda.

On the morning they planned to depart, Minkar and Graybeard walked together out of the cavern. Minkar considered how much he would miss the place. At least the dragons, who had no need of speech among themselves, spoke with him willingly. His fellow Shouda, however, would never again speak with him. He knew that he needed to talk with Ereben concerning what he had learned from the dragons. And he needed to find his son.

Two dragons appeared in the sky. One had a distinct fork in his tail. The other swayed his head from side to side as he approached, apparently adjusting for his blindness in one eye. When they landed, Graybeard interposed himself between One-eye and Minkar. The dragons did not speak, but the look in One-eye's only eye, and the occasional puff of yellow flame from his mouth quieted any desire on Minkar's part to speak with the newly arrived brothers of Graybeard. As One-eye walked on toward the cavern entrance, Graybeard repositioned himself so that One-eye was offered no opportunity for mischief.

When they were alone again, Graybeard said, "I will not be able to fly you to Shouda, Minkar Jarad. My brother who is angry has seen an army of men, not like yourself, who carry a magical device capable of capturing a dragon. They had captured my brother who wishes to be worshiped, until my brother who is angry caused them to flee. Both were then able to escape. So I will fly you only as far south as I dare go."

In the beauty of nature, we see only the beauty, and not the constant struggle that lies beneath it.
Ereben Leaf: Chronicle of the Counterspell

A thunderous buzz grew louder. Ereben looked up in alarm. He recognized the bumblebee with a green band of fuzz about its abdomen. Its size horrified him. He and Chrysanthus dashed into a crevice in the limestone slab. He had understood the delicate alterations of nature's attunement that would reduce his size and that of his grandfather. He had made the transition without difficulty. What he had not considered in his haste was the vulnerability he would accept in that otherwise simple change.

The bumblebee circled twice, then landed nearby. Huge clumps of yellow pollen decorated its articulated legs, filling the air with the melded fragrance of a thousand flowers. Its multifaceted eyes looked nowhere and everywhere. Palpebrae and mandibles flexed ominously beneath its massive head. Sunlight glistened through the membranous windows of its dark, stationary wings.

"Leg, Yesil," a soft feminine voice commanded. The bumblebee raised one front leg. A beautiful woman stepped onto it and was lowered to the ground.

"I've never seen a human do that before," she said. Her black eyes sparkled beneath long, delicate eyelashes. Short cropped, white hair revealed a little pip of an ear on either side. A bright green tunic, still wet, clung to youthful breasts, and was cinched about her slender hips with a strip of fresh, green grass. "Why did you do that?"

"Uh...so you could take us to Gelith's castle," Ereben replied.

"I never said I would take you there."

Chrysanthus approached the bumblebee and scratched it beneath its neck.

"She likes your friend," the Faerie noted.

"Can you guide the bumblebee when you're flying?"

"She's a bombus. Her name is Yesil. And yes. Why else would I get up there?"

Ereben was flustered. "Would you at least tell us where we can find Gelith?"

"I don't even know you." She folded her arms.

The flower fragrance made him giddy. "I'm Ereben Leaf. This is my grandfather, Chrysanthus."

"That's a little better. I'm Keri."

"I helped you out of that moss stuff. And I helped you wash it off." He smiled.

"But you peeked!"

He sighed.

"Oh, alright. And thank you."

"How did you stumble into it?"

"What?"

"The moss."

"I fell. Yesil was surprised when you swung your hand at her. She turned suddenly. I fell off. So it was kind of your fault."

"I'm sorry."

"We're even. Yesil, leg." The bombus extended its front leg. "Climb on."

Chrysanthus stepped onto the shiny, spiked leg and was lifted up to the thorax.

"Now you, Ereben Leaf. Yesil, leg."

Ereben mounted the leg and steadied himself by holding one of the spikes, avoiding a clump of fragrant pollen. He stepped onto the fuzz-covered thorax. Chrysanthus had seated himself just in front of Yesil's abdomen. Ereben situated himself slightly nearer the head. Keri followed, and sat immediately behind Yesil's head. She placed her delicate hands at the base of Yesil's antennae.

"Hang on."

Wings thrummed into a deep, vibrating hum. Yesil lifted from the ground vertically, hovered a moment, then soared into the flower-filled glade. Keri seemed to steer the bombus with slight pressure on the antennae. Unlike the raw force of wind Ereben fought while riding Titus, the breeze was softened by the fuzz and hair protruding from Yesil's thorax. He looked back at the green fuzz stripe around the abdomen of the bombus. Behind, the limestone ledge where the daggers lay unattended, faded in the distance.

He knew that only these daggers would allow him and his grandfather to return to their previous size. And something was not right. He couldn't be sure what had happened, but he was certain that the life force he had dissipated had not flowed into the stone slab. The rock had not welcomed it. It had gone elsewhere, but he had no idea where. Ailantha had warned him of the counterspell. He had thought he understood its control, but now he knew otherwise.

Maha Neruti had spoken of the chaos that reigned in Ternaria. The Warden of the March had said that his people could not go to Ternaria. *This must be Ternaria.* The paths of attunement were misaligned, were deceptive. And he had not seen it. Perhaps it was a distortion unique to Ternaria.

The bombus carried them through a forest of mushrooms, sometimes flying below the canopy of their immense caps. Bulky stems blurred past. Far above the mushrooms, great sprays of wildflowers cast their shade. Yesil gave wide berth to a towering thistle in their path, then continued on.

So many wonders appeared over Keri's shoulders and zoomed past, that it was a quarter hour before he noticed a small pair of filmy wings folded over Keri's back. He attempted to ask the beautiful Faerie about them, but she could not hear him above the deep droning of Yesil's far more expansive wings. He could only contemplate the marvels yet to be seen in this wondrous place.

They landed and dismounted at the base of a ponderous, conical mushroom, its crenated face pocked by deep compartments. Keri led them through an opening at the base of its stem, and up an internal stairway that spiraled past an occasional window. An earthy aroma of raw mushroom filled the air. Once inside the voluminous, conical cap, chambers and stairways radiated in all directions. They climbed another shorter stairway to the opening of a chamber.

"Oooaah, Brennith," the beautiful Faerie sang softly.

"Oooaah, love," a crisper voice returned.

They entered the chamber. Keri introduced her guests. "This is my mate, Brennith. This is Ereben Leaf and Chrysanthus"

Brennith placed a firm hand on Ereben's shoulder. "Oooaah, Ereben Leaf." He repeated the gesture to Chrysanthus, with no indication of curiosity over the leopard-man's appearance.

"They're humans. They made themselves small while I watched!" Keri clarified.

Brennith's face was more angular at the cheekbones, but his slanted eyes were, like Keri's, black marbles. Also like Keri, he dressed in green and bore small, filmy wings high on his back.

"Really?" Brennith replied.

"We need to speak with Gelith about an important matter."

Brennith leaned out the open face of the chamber and called down toward the ground. "Valcris, have you seen Gelith?"

"He's checking the new site," a voice answered. "He'll be back before long."

"You can wait here for his return," Keri offered. "Brennith, could you get something for our guests to drink? Make yourselves comfortable."

The chamber was furnished with chairs and tables and benches carved of the same material as the walls. A bed was carved into one wall. Using a fleck of snail shell, Brennith split open a melon-sized brown seed and chopped its contents into small chunks. He placed the split seed onto the table, and served a mildly sweet nectar in chitinous cups.

"We will be moving to a new site in a few days." Keri munched a sliver of seed, washed it down with nectar, then held her cup for Brennith to refill it. "The morchellas only last about a month now, then we have to move to new ones."

"Morchellas?" Ereben asked.

"These castles are morchella mushrooms. They're very comfortable. We paint them with dandelion sap to preserve them, but once the maggots get into them, there's nothing to do but move to new ones. It's a tedious process, but the only danger is while were actually moving."

"All of this only lasts a month?" Ereben was incredulous.

"It makes a nice home, and it's easy to work with," Keri said.

"But for just a month?"

"They used to last much longer, but for the past year, ladybugs have been hard to find, so the maggots have gotten worse."

"Why don't you live in something else?"

"It only takes a few hours to move, and about a day to do the work," Brennith added.

"So, Gelith's castle is a mushroom," Ereben said with amusement.

"The next one over," Keri explained, "in Mavi." At Ereben's puzzlement, she added, "This is Yesil. That one's Mavi. Each morchella shares one bombus. A morchella is known by its bombus."

"How many morchella castles are there?"

"We have five," Brennith said, "Kirmizi, Mavi, Beyaz, Yesil and Siyah. The bombi have different colors."

"How many Faeries live in each castle?"

"Between thirty and forty." Keri noticed that Ereben had not eaten, though Chrysanthus had consumed his share and now sat with his hands folded on the table. "Have some."

Ereben crunched a fragment of the nutty material. "Hmm. It's good." He rinsed it down with nectar. "You mentioned a danger while you're moving."

"The Thistlepix watch us," Keri said with lowered brows, "and sometimes cause problems when we're all outside. Since the morchellas have been going soft more often, they've had more opportunities."

"And what exactly are Thistlepix?"

"Pfhh," Brennith muttered. "They're a vile race of thieves who infest the thistle towers and eat flesh. They have no morals, and are promiscuous in their mating habits."

Keri nodded in agreement. "They kill and eat our mice. They even eat Faeries when given the chance."

It was becoming apparent to Ereben that Ternaria was not exactly what it seemed. "You have mice, and the Thistlepix eat them?"

"We keep dairy mice—for their milk," Keri elaborated. "We can't keep them tied up or the Pix'll kill them for food. So we let them wander, and call them in at milking time."

"Brennith," a voice called from outside the morchella. "Mavi is coming with Gelith."

Ereben joined Brennith at the open face of the chamber. A Faerie stood below, pointing. From the indicated direction, a bombus approached and circled, finally settling on the ground beside a nearby morchella castle. This bombus sported a blue band of fuzz about its abdomen. Two Faeries in blue tunics dismounted. Below Ereben, a Faerie in green, whom Brennith had called Valcris, resumed his chore of painting a small toadstool with a bristly seed-stem brush.

"Oooaah, Gelith," Brennith called out. You have two visitors. I'll bring them down."

Gelith looked up at Ereben, then nodded.

Outside morchella Mavi, they sat comfortably beneath toadstools and sipped nectar. Gelith seemed surprised by nothing. He listened patiently as Ereben explained recent events, and their need for sarcite for Moss Abbey and his fear that the Knights of the Redeemer would find the Warded Mines.

Gelith's appearance was like that of the other Faeries, seeming no older, but possessed of a more sober affect. His blue tunic displayed no symbol of rank, and appeared in every way to be similar to the blue tunics of all those who lived in morchella Mavi.

"The journey to the Warded Mines," Gelith eventually explained, "requires two months, by the time our longhaulers go there, mine the sarcite, journey to Moss Abbey, then return. But now that the ladybugs have gone into hiding, we are plagued with maggots. We simply don't have two months to make the trip. There are not enough tortoises to both move our homes and make the trips to the mines. If we send the tortoises on the trip, then moving to new morchellas would be fatal. I don't see any way around it." A sadness came over Gelith's face. "It does not look hopeful."

"Can you tell us how to find the Warded Mines?" Ereben asked.

"If you are human, you can not enter the mines. The ward prevents it. But if you could enter, you are far too small to carry the sarcite without the aid of tortoises. Can you return to your previous size—to human size?"

"I believe we can, but our knives are used to bring it about," Ereben explained. "They are unchanged at the edge of Oldwood."

Gelith scratched his pointed chin. “If you return there and change yourselves, then you will not be able to cross Ternaria without causing great damage.” His black eyes brightened. “After the move, we will send tortoises to transport your knives to the south boundary of Ternaria. Then you can make the change. You will not be able to go to the mines by our usual path above the Cauldrons, since you will be too large to follow it. But if you travel into the Time Mountains, there is a pointer at the summit of the Tooth of Time that points directly to the entrance of the Warded Mines to the West.”

“How do I recognize the Tooth of Time?”

“It is the tallest peak. Its base is forested with blood locust, a thorny tree that bleeds when cut. It grows nowhere else. But don’t tarry in the Time Mountains. It is said that each day spent there is like a year. And inside the mines, a powerful demon, the Sarcoptis, is entombed. It appears dead, but I believe it is simply bound by yet another ward.”

“So, you will have our daggers—our knives—carried south?”

“After the move. But how will you enter the mines?”

“I guess I’ll have to figure that out when we get there.”

“And you must return north by some other route?”

“Yes, we will find another route.”

“Then we are agreed.”

“I’m curious.” Ereben could not help asking. “I see that you have wings. Can you fly with them?”

“Yes, we can, but only to slow a fall from a height. The exertion is great. Any Faerie that uses wings for more than a moment must recuperate for at least a day. And that is a dangerous a choice.”

As Ereben and Chrysanthus watched, standing at the top of the spiral stairway within morchella Yesil, Valcris created a passage to an unused chamber within the giant, conical cap of the mushroom. Valcris wielded a sword-like tool, made from the wing of a small beetle. With deft movements, he sliced easily through the firm, friable mass of mushroom. On entering the new, open faced chamber, he grumbled loudly, then stabbed the blade into a dog-sized maggot, splitting its body just behind the mouth end.

"They've been really bad this year." He kicked the writhing white mass out the exterior opening and shook his head at the damp smear left on the floor. With several more swipes of his blade, he excavated a bed platform into each wall, and two benches. "It's not much, but Gelith says we'll be moving tomorrow."

Ereben tried one of the beds. Though it appeared to be beige stone, its surface was resilient and delightfully comfortable, molding itself under pressure. "It's perfect."

After Valcris departed, Ereben removed a tattered, stitched parchment from a pouch. It illustrated the strangely shaped ax. He struggled to read its Shadae annotations. "Grandpa, you wrote here that the handle is made of blood locust. Maybe we should get a piece of it when we get to the Tooth of Time." Chrysanthus, of course, said nothing.

Five bombi returned from scouting the path to the new site. Each of their riders dismounted at their respective morchellas and declared it as safe as could be expected. Scores of Faeries and Faerie children scurried about in the sunshine, loading belongings onto ten massive tortoises. Behind each, a dairy mouse was tethered. The mice, each larger than any of Liddie Burn's cows, munched on seeds that had been placed there to keep them content during the loading process.

"These morchellas still look pretty good," Ereben commented to Valcris.

"See those stripes of Siyah?" Valcris pointed to black streaks at the base of morchella Yesil. "The roots are gone. It will melt in a day or two."

Ereben examined one of the ropes being used to lash containers to a nearby tortoise. It was slightly translucent. "What do you make these out of?"

"We twist it from spider silk, then dust it."

When all was ready, Gelith gave a signal from the back of bombus Mavi. The five bombi lifted into the air, each carrying two or three Faeries. Drivers on the tortoises snapped the reins. Ten tortoises began to plod forward in a line, towing one dairy mouse behind each. Bombi circled overhead. Faeries, grouped by the color of their tunics, walked beside the tortoises. Ereben and Chrysanthus brought up the rear.

For three hours, the Faerie caravan snaked through the mushroom forest of Ternaria amid bobbing blossoms of wildflowers and the drone of circling bombi. They passed grazing beetles and meandering millipedes. Aboard the last tortoise a domed cage held a pet gnat. Beside it were skeins of spider silk rope and an acorn cap coracle, apparently hauled from the border of Oldwood. Children squealed at the appearance of a stray ant, before it was shoved away by one of their parents. Ereben marveled at it all.

On reaching the new site, Ereben counted seven bright white morchellas that had sprouted beneath a stand of daffodils. Gelith designated which clan was to occupy which morchella, then men set to work carving internal passages while the women and children unloaded the tortoises. The dairy mice were let loose to graze. Since the castles would not be ready until sometime the next day, everyone camped that night on the ground beneath their immense, conical caps.

It was in the wee hours of that moonless night that the alarm sounded. One cicada wing bowed stridently against another. Mothers gathered their youngsters and hurried into the newly carved stairwells at the bases of the morchella castles. The men took up raspberry pikes and stationed themselves beneath nearby toadstools. Ereben crouched with Chrysanthus within the tight stalks of a daffodil.

A keening sound descended from the blackness of the night. A dozen wasps swooped below the daffodil blooms, weaving among the morchellas. The Faeries remained silent and hidden. On each wasp, a rider, slightly larger than a Faerie, carried a crossbow and a quiver of projectiles. One wasp landed near Ereben. Its rider raised a small container and lifted its cover. A yellow-green glow shined out. The rider looked about, then spotted one of the Faeries beneath a toadstool. The rider dismounted, leveled his crossbow and fired. The Faerie fell backwards onto the ground. Two more wasps landed, these closer to a morchella. Raspberry pikes flew from the lowest level of the morchella's cap openings. One wasp thrashed in agony, throwing its rider, who then fell to the ground, impaled by more pikes. The last of the two riders fired his crossbow at the castle, then lifted off. By the toadstool, the first rider to attack grasped the fallen Faerie and carried him toward his wasp.

Chrysanthus leaped from his hiding place toward the black silhouette of the wasp. The insect immediately responded to the movement by lifting into the air and diving into Chrysanthus, its stinger held forward. With one swipe of his steel-clawed hand, the leopard-man amputated the tip of the wasp's abdomen, dropping its stinger amid a gush of dark fluid. The maimed wasp grappled Chrysanthus onto the ground. Its rider dropped the fallen Faerie and loaded his crossbow.

Ereben flung himself into the shadows and retrieved the Faerie's raspberry pike. By the time the attacker had turned toward Chrysanthus, Ereben was upon him, driving the pike into the back of the crossbowman's chest. The victim arched his back and fell, coughing blood onto the ground. Looking up at Ereben, he gurgled through the blood, reaching unsuccessfully for the thorn in his back.

Chrysanthus stood. The wasp that had attacked him lay curled, many of its legs strewn about in fragments. Chrysanthus appeared to be uninjured. Above, the sounds of the other wasps receded into the darkness.

The funeral for the dead Faerie was a simple though reverent ceremony. Time could not be easily spared from the work of preparing the morchella castles. It was also their practice to bury the enemy dead, but without ceremony.

"They hadn't expected us to move so soon," Keri explained. "And they must have thought they'd catch us unprepared last night. It's unusual that we can take down any of the wasps. You and your grandfather were brave."

"It's the least we could do for your help," Ereben responded. "Well, goodbye for now. We should be gone for about two weeks."

"Didn't Gelith tell you? I'll be going with you to get your knives. And Brennith too." Keri smiled. Otherwise you'll get lost. Besides, its tricky when you harness two tortoises together."

Ereben had estimated the actual size of the tortoises and determined that it would require two tortoises to haul each dagger. He had no idea how he would actually move the daggers, so he took along several long coils of spider silk rope. Keri and Brennith carried raspberry pikes. Ereben had taken a crossbow for himself, along with four quivers of thistle bolts.

Their route north brought them past the morchellas that had been vacated only two days earlier. In place of the stately beige cones stood decayed brown mounds covered with slurping maggots. The nearby toadstools had transformed into viscid muck.

Four days brought them to the limestone slab at the northern boundary of Ternaria. Ereben considered the various ways of attaching the daggers, deciding on rigging two tortoises in tandem to haul each dagger. In the end, he elected to pull the daggers handle first. Despite the strength of two tortoises pulling each dagger, their progress was painfully slow, moving at less than half the speed of their outward journey. Brennith and Keri rode the lead tortoises, in order to guide them, while Chrysanthus and Ereben rode the rear tortoises, alert for any danger. At night, while the tortoises slept, they traded shifts on guard.

The proximity of the daggers was comforting to Ereben. Even though he could not hold one, he knew that touching one would allow him to focus magic, should that be necessary.

On the twelfth day, Valcris appeared on bombus Yesil. He had been sent by Gelith to hurry them. "The maggots have gotten completely out of hand. The morchellas are falling apart already. He plans to move as soon as you can get back."

If we ride through the night, the tortoises will be in no shape for the move," Keri pointed out. "I would guess it'll take us about two more days."

"That's too long." Valcris shook his head. "The morchellas won't last that long."

Ereben considered how vulnerable the Faeries were, out in the open. "Let's leave the knives here, then come back after the move."

"That would get us there some time tomorrow," Keri said enthusiastically.

"If you want," Ereben added, "you and Brennith can go back on Yesil, so you can help ready things for the move. Chrysanthus and I can find our way back from here. Then you'll just have to load the tortoises when we get there."

"Are you sure?" Keri asked.

"I'm sure. I peeked on the way out."

"That would be just like you," she laughed. Brennith seemed to miss the humor.

Keri and Brennith joined Valcris on the back of bombus Yesil. "See you tomorrow," Keri called. The bombus thrummed into the air, circled once, then flew off to the South.

The Faeries were in a state of panic when Ereben and Chrysanthus arrived the following afternoon. Six tortoises were loaded and ready to depart with dairy mice in tow. Raspberry pikes were in evidence everywhere. Even the older children carried them. Since mid-day, single wasps had been seen high above. The morchellas, so pristine two weeks earlier, had already begun to slump. maggots, both dead and alive, covered the mushrooms.

"Pack up and let's get moving," Gelith shouted.

"What's happened?" Ereben inquired, feeling responsible for delaying their departure.

"The maggots are more numerous and more voracious than I have ever seen," Gelith answered. "And the Thistlepix are ready for us."

When all was ready, they set out. Each of the five bombi carried only two riders, both armed with raspberry pikes. On Yesil, riding in the second position, Valcris was armed with a captured crossbow. Ereben had given him a second quiver of thistle bolts. He now walked beside Chrysanthus at the rear.

An hour later, the attack came. Ereben counted at least twenty wasps. Each carried a single Thistlepix warrior, armed with a crossbow. The Faeries on foot scattered into the surrounding brush. Those on the tortoises crouched among the parcels. The bombi circled to gain altitude. They could dive faster than the wasps, but appeared to be far less maneuverable.

Ereben crouched against a toadstool, steadied his crossbow and fired. The bolt glanced off a descending wasp. In the distance, a Faerie fell from a tortoise. Bombus Mavi dove into the rear of a wasp, dismounting its rider, who fell to the ground and was promptly dispatched by two Faeries. These two, in turn, toppled under a hail of thistle bolts.

Ereben was struck from behind. All went black.

⁂

In war, each side to a conflict holds the earnest belief that it is the aggrieved party, reluctantly called to arms by its unwavering adherence to what is good and proper.

Ereben Leaf: Chronicle of the Counterspell

Ereben's head pounded. His ribs ached. He opened his eyes. He seemed to be inside a round chamber. Its walls glowed green. A patch of sunlight pierced the chamber from overhead. He felt slightly sick, as though the chamber were swaying back and forth. His hands were tied behind him. He tried to stand, but his head pounded. He sat down.

As his head slowly cleared, he realized that the chamber was indeed swaying. The walls appeared to be some sort of fibrous plant assembled in vertical petals, barely open at the top. It all had an acrid smell about it. Standing now against the wall, he attempted to spread the tough petals apart with his chin. At an angle, he could see the ground far below. No matter how hard he leaned, he could only open a narrow gap.

Smoke drifted by, with the sweet smell of cooked meat. He moved around the wall, pressing against it until he found a spot that provided a view of the source of the smoke, down on the ground. Each sliver of view revealed, when assembled in his mind, that he was trapped atop a frighteningly tall thistle. But his view of the fire sickened him.

About the fire stood a group of Thistlepix. Above the fire, skewered on a spit, the gutted and skinned body of a Faerie roasted. Not far from the fire lay a crumpled, green tunic and a crushed thistle bolt quiver. He guessed that it was Valcris that they had killed, and were now roasting. When he had been told that Thistlepix roasted and ate Faeries, he had assumed it to be hyperbole. Now he knew otherwise. He had never learned if Valcris had a mate, but he knew that the unfortunate Faerie had friends who would mourn him, though never bury him. He slumped to the floor of his cell and wept. *I guess I'll be for dinner tomorrow.* He wondered about Chrysanthus and all the Faeries he had jeopardized by coming here.

The keening of a wasp approached, then stopped as his cell jarred slightly. One petal of the cell hinged downward, admitting dazzling sunlight. A figure entered, while another remained outside the opening.

Ereben's eyes adjusted to the light. A slender man stood quietly, observing him. He was slightly taller than the Faeries he had met. The first striking difference he noted was that this man, whom he assumed was a Thistlepix, had green irises, rather than the black eyes of the Faeries. The lines of his eyes were equally slanted upward to the sides of his face, but somehow far more expressive. Instead of little nubs for ears, his were generous, pointed affairs, distinctly more pointed than the ears of the brown-skinned Shouda. His light complexion was gently freckled, and surmounted by a mop of red hair. He wore a fine silk blouse in black, ballooned at the cuffs, and tightly fitted black trousers, ending in knee high, black boots collapsed into horizontal pleats above his ankles.

"I am Somek," the Thistlepix said in a soft, kindly voice, a little higher in pitch than that of the Faeries. His expression was almost tender. "Would you like some water? You have been here nearly a day."

Ereben realized that his mouth was dry. "Yes," he croaked.

"Unimesh," he said to a man at the door, "would you get some water, please."

Unimesh removed a container from the wasp resting on a nearby leaf, and brought it to Somek. Opening the bottle, Somek extended it to Ereben's lips, but Ereben averted his face.

"Oh, come now, it's perfectly good water. It's my own bottle, for goodness sake." Somek took a drink. "What is your name?"

"Ereben Leaf."

"I like that. It has a...noble quality. They have told me that you are a human, and that you and your companion changed your size. Here, do have some water, Ereben Leaf." Somek held the bottle to Ereben's lips, allowing him to drink. "You see. Perfectly good."

Somek returned the bottle to Unimesh, then squatted in front of Ereben, so that they were face to face. Placing one slender, lavender scented hand under Ereben's chin, Somek used the middle finger of his other hand to wipe away water that had dripped from Ereben's lips. "Something that you did when you changed size has caused the few remaining ladybugs to hibernate, and the maggots have become more active. Did you know that, Ereben Leaf?"

Ereben pulled his chin away. He was conscious of Somek's sweet breath. "I don't know what you mean."

Somek ran his fingers into Ereben's hair and firmly, but gently turned Ereben's face back toward his own. "But you know that something happened there. King Dobar felt it." He released Ereben's hair, then straightened the mussed hair with his fingernails. The Thistlepix rocked backwards and sat on the floor of the cell, wrapping his arms about his knees. "I would like to untie your hands, but I'm afraid that you would pry open the walls and hurt yourself. This thistle is about as tall as they grow, and if you were to fall...well... It would kill you. That is, if you didn't impale yourself on the thistle on your way down."

Somek stood. "We know that you came here from Oldwood. The humans there are having some difficulty with their magic. Perhaps we could assist you in some way." He stepped out the door. "You think about it, Ereben Leaf. May I call you Ereben?"

"Call me whatever you want."

"Just *Ereben* seems more comfortable. I'll visit again. Meanwhile, you should consider how we might assist one another." The door closed. The sound of a wasp departed.

Ereben's eyes slowly adapted to the dim surroundings once again. He desperately wanted to hate Somek. They had killed Valcris, and others almost certainly. But Somek had touched on a troublesome truth.

Something had happened when he and his grandfather changed size. He had felt it at the time. The counterspell had gotten away from him. His dissipated life force, and that of Chrysanthus, had not gone into the limestone slab as he had intended. It had, instead, followed a different path, many different paths. It had echoed from the limestone and resonated —propagated, like ripples on a pond, into the life of Ternaria. And like ripples on a pond meeting ripples from a different source, their intersections caused some to be made stronger, others weaker. But why, he wondered, would it have affected only maggots and ladybugs?

The reality became clearer the more he thought about it. He had affected more than just maggots and ladybugs. His carelessness had touched every living thing in Ternaria, and possibly beyond. And, he decided, he would never learn the true extent of change he had caused. *How can magic ever be safe enough to live with?* The connectedness of all things made the universe an infinite web. Touch it here, and it is felt everywhere, by everything. Cut one strand and tensions change on every other strand, no matter how remote.

Somek visited again the following day, this time dressed in deep indigo. "Come and look out the door," he invited.

Ereben stepped to the opening, then drew himself back. The height appeared to be about a hundred yards off the ground, though he knew it to be only a yard or two.

"If you look carefully, Ereben, you will notice that there is no way to climb down. On our homes we modify the thistle towers so they can be climbed, if need be. But for this...particular tower, we have left it in its natural state. Now that you see the way it is, can I untie your hands?"

"Yes." Ereben faced away from Somek.

"Unimesh, cut his bindings, please."

"Thank you," Ereben said, actually grateful to be able to stretch his arms.

"That is much better." Somek sat on the floor and wrapped his arms about his knees. "Have you given some thought to our discussion?"

Ereben paced nervously. He was not sure of the extent of Somek's knowledge of magic, nor of his intentions. "Why do you fight with the Faeries?"

"We have always fought. They intrude on our land. Their mice eat our gardens and kill the crickets. The Faeries eat all the thistle seeds they come across. Then, once they've spoiled an area, they abandon it and invade another."

"There aren't that many of them," Ereben pointed out.

"You have seen only one tribe. There are dozens of Faerie tribes in Ternaria and they swarm over the kingdom. They multiply without restraint. If we ignored them, we would soon be homeless. We are one tenth their number. The future is bleak if we can't find a way to keep them out of our kingdom. For every Faerie we kill, a dozen more appear."

"I hadn't thought of it in that way."

"Do sit down, Ereben. You're making me dizzy."

Ereben sat across the cell from Somek. Somek sighed, stood, and walked over to Ereben, seating himself beside him. "I don't bite, Ereben."

The scent of lavender emanating from Somek's clothing was so much more pleasant than the bitter, sappy odor of the thistle cell. "You eat Faeries."

"You eat deer and other creatures. We observed you eating squirrel in Oldwood, where the humans eat no meat of any kind. What's the difference?"

"I didn't get to know the squirrels before I ate them."

"The discussion does become a bit cloudy, doesn't it."

"Would you eat me, if I were dead?"

Somek grimaced. "I don't think so. It never occurred to me. What an awful thing to ask."

"If you got to know the Faeries, maybe you could come to some agreement, and end the fighting."

"Maybe. But they're not very bright, and there are so many of them. Besides, the different Faerie tribes are not even friendly with each other. Oh! I nearly forgot. Unimesh, bring Ereben the treat I brought."

Unimesh entered with a gooey square of food."

"It's crushed daisy seeds and soaked with honey. I saved it from last night. You eat it with your fingers. The white part is from a daisy petal, so you can eat that too. It's very good."

Ereben took a small bite. The sweet, nutty taste reminded him of a walnut pastry his mother used to make. He ate the rest, including the disc of flower petal, then licked his fingers. "Thank you, Somek. It's delicious."

Somek smiled, showing smooth, white teeth from ear to ear. "I told you."

"You seem to know quite a bit about what's happening outside of Ternaria."

"We send out scouts. It helps to avoid unpleasant surprises."

"What do you know about magic?" Ereben asked.

"Not very much." He placed his hand on Ereben's knee. "But King Dobar knows much more. Will you speak with him?"

"Alright."

King Dobar smiled cordially when Ereben entered, accompanied by Somek. The king's short gray hair bristled beneath a simple gold ringlet about his head. A black silk robe reached from Dobar's shoulders to the floor of the royal thistle. Like Somek and the other Thistlepix Ereben had met, King Dobar wore a loose blouse and tightly fitted trousers, though in Dobar's case, both were of a glossy canary yellow.

"What a wonder," Dobar uttered half to himself.

"Ereben," Somek intoned formally, "This is Dobar, King of The Pix. My king," he stated to Dobar, "may I present Ereben Leaf."

The thistle chamber was furnished with chairs surrounding a round table. Decorative fabrics hung about the walls. A scent of wisteria filled the air.

With a slight limp, Dobar approached Ereben and softly kissed him on the lips. "I am so glad that you agreed to speak with me," the king said. Taking Ereben's hand, Dobar led Ereben to a chair and seated him, then seated himself beside him, still holding his hand. He held out his other hand for Somek, and seated him on his opposite side.

"Now," Dobar said, squeezing Ereben's hand, then releasing it, "help me make some sense of all of this."

"I'm not sure I can be very helpful," Ereben began. "But I would like to help find a way to stop the fighting between the Faeries and the Thistlepix."

"Pix," King Dobar corrected. "We are Pix. The Faeries call us Thistlepix."

"Oh! Pardon me, your majesty, I didn't know."

"Just Dobar. We don't do 'your majesties' and such. We all know who to credit for wise decisions, and blame for mistakes." The king smiled. "The whole kingdom hardly numbers more than the Dwarfs of Zink."

"You know of Zink?" Ereben asked, amazed at the breadth of their geographical familiarity.

"Oh yes. I have traveled as far as the Broken Mountains to the North, the Three Kingdoms of the Banu Sulal, to the East, and the Legion Dunes and beyond, to the West."

"The wasps fly you that far?"

"Wasps and hornets have only a limited range, but we have a strain of mantis and a locust that are able to fly great distances."

"Can you tell me of things to the South?"

"We never venture into the Time Mountains or the sulfurous Caldrons. At least, those who have, never returned."

"I need to travel there."

"That would be unwise. The mountains cause living things to grow old prematurely, and the Caldrons belch poisonous vapors. Why would you choose to go there?"

Ereben, sensing an honesty in the words of King Dobar, explained recent events, as he understood them. Dobar and Somek listened quietly. He spoke of the Protectors of Dragomin, the battles and the dragons. He revealed many things, but not everything. Since the Pix already knew that he had used magic in the transformation of his size, and that of Chrysanthus, he explained that the act of magic had altered some things in ways that he neither expected nor understood fully.

"Ailantha once spoke to me of the counterspell," Dobar commented. Seeing the shock on Ereben's face, he continued. "Pix, and for that matter, Faeries, are the result of the counterspell. We trace our history back to ancient times. Before that, there is nothing."

"How did you learn of Ailantha?"

"She came to the borders of Ternaria many years ago, before my time. She and a companion planted magical acorns. She said that they would grow nowhere else, but that perhaps they would grow in Ternaria. She marked them with circles of stone. None ever sprouted until this year. This Spring, a strange sapling emerged from one of the stone circles. Instead of leaves it grew green feathers." Dobar shook his head.

"My ancestors had spoken with her then, and I have visited her at her home in the mountains. When we discovered the feather tree, I traveled there to tell her, but found that she had died."

Feeling more comfortable still about Dobar's motives, Ereben explained his need to reach the Warded Mines to obtain sarcite and prevent the Knights from reaching it. Dobar had no knowledge of the location of the mine, and again expressed his doubt that Ereben would survive a journey there.

"Dobar, is there any way that I could help bring peace between Pix and Faeries?"

"In my youth, I counted one Faerie as a friend. He saved my life. I could never speak of it to my people, nor could he with his." The king shook his head. "If we could mark a boundary that all the squabbling Faerie tribes would respect, then there would no longer be a reason to fight. But we have tried to establish such a boundary for centuries, without success."

"They won't even meet with us," Somek added, "so I doubt we would get very far."

"If I could arrange a meeting, would you agree to it?"

"I would consider it," the king answered.

"Can you guarantee their safety?" Ereben asked.

"If they bring no arms to the meeting, we will do likewise. But they must be willing to come to an agreement."

"All I can hope for is that they would be willing to meet."

"Then we will take you close to their fungus houses, and wait for a reply."

The following day, Ereben rode on a wasp guided by Unimesh. Unlike a bombus, this wasp was best suited for a single rider, since there was room for only one to sit comfortably. Ereben had squeezed behind Unimesh, into the same seat. Like all the Pix he had met, Unimesh smelled of flowers. He had learned that they slept on beds of shredded flower petals, permeating each Pix with the scent of his choice.

The wasp landed at a safe distance from the new Faerie site, and waited there with Unimesh. Ereben greeted his friends, who had assumed he was dead, and spoke with Gelith about the proposed meeting. Gelith agreed to send messengers to the other tribes with the proposal, but was not optimistic about their likely response.

"We should hear in about a week."

"Will it really take that long?" Ereben asked, concerned about the need for haste in reaching the Warded Mines.

"There are many tribes. Some are at the far edges of Ternaria."

"Then I will tell King Dobar that we will know something in a week." None of the other Faeries had been able to tell him anything about Chrysanthus, other than that he had been alive after the battle, but had disappeared. "Do you know where Chrysanthus might have gone?"

"Since he saw the Thistlepix carry you away on a wasp, we have not seen Chrysanthus."

Late that afternoon, Somek, wearing dark green today, showed Ereben to his dormitory thistle, not nearly as high as the cell in which he had spent several nights. It was hung with colorful fabrics around the walls, which held compartments full of folded clothing. Three other Pix men were there discussing a recent hunting expedition in which they had tracked and eventually subdued a shrew. One half of the floor was carpeted. The other half was strewn with shredded lavender. The Pix sat on the floor with their arms about each other, slapping backs and pulling ears, reminding Ereben of his childhood with his brother Caris. The Pix laughed and bragged and playfully tormented one another.

"Where do the girls stay?" Ereben asked Somek. The chamber fell silent. "I haven't seen any of them since I got here."

Somek took him aside, placing his arm over Ereben's shoulder. "It's not a topic that you should talk about," he whispered.

The banter gradually resumed, but with less spontaneity than before. Ereben wondered why they were so sensitive about the subject of girls. He had seen neither girls nor women here. The children he had seen were all boys. He knew now that asking about them would not be well received.

"Dobar has assigned you to this dormitory while you are here," Somek announced with a smile. "You'll find it much more comfortable than the high cell."

Ereben felt uneasy about it. "You don't have to make special arrangements for me."

"That's why you'll be staying here. We won't have to send up food, and you'll be able to come and go as you like."

"No, really."

"It's already decided."

That night, Ereben realized that the Pix, like herd animals, sought comfort in closeness to others. A dozen of them slept together in the shredded flower petals as a tangle of arms and legs, sometimes in one heap, other times as several clumps, but never alone. Twice during the night he awoke to find Pix arms and legs draped over him. Since there was nowhere else to go, he rolled over as best he could and drifted back to sleep, once dreaming of sharing his brother's bed. In the morning, he awoke with a sense of well-being and safety.

Ereben rose and put on his shirt, having slept, like the Pix, in his trousers. He exited the dormitory and descended the swaying thistle by way of steps, some down the exterior, others expertly cut within the thistle stem, eventually opening at ground level.

He counted thirty thistle towers before he gave up. Their wasps nested beneath the ground. The cavernous openings to their nests were large enough for a wasp to crawl out with a Pix riding its back. Pix entered the nests on foot and emerged mounted upon wasps.

One particular hive opening remained unused, at least while he observed it. Unlike the others, the earth around the opening was not compacted by foot traffic. Curious, Ereben walked to its opening. Its tunnel appeared to angle parallel to the ground. The laughter of many small children echoed from within. It made sense to Ereben that toddlers would be safer in a cave than atop a thistle tower.

The girls and women stay with the babies. Do they ever come out? Ereben stepped into the tunnel. The passage immediately divided. To the right was the source of the playful laughter, though he could see nothing but the tunnel wall from where he stood. The left, however, seemed to draw him. From it emanated a humming music, soft and soothing. The walls were decorated in gentle, swirling colors that seemed almost to move as he watched. And a fragrance—he could not place it. Something alluring and sensual, with an undercurrent of honey.

From a side passage, a delicate face peered shyly around the corner. It was a Pix face, but one framed by shoulder length red hair. *A Pix woman!*

"Hello," he said awkwardly, aware that he should not be here.

The Pix woman bit her lower lip. "I don't know you," she said in a vulnerable, inviting way. Only her head was visible from the side passage.

"I'm Ereben. What's your name?"

She blushed and blinked. "You're not supposed to be here."

"Tell me your name and I'll leave." Her green eyes held him captive.

"It's Lethia. Now go," she commanded coyly.

"Step out so I can see you, Lethia."

"No." She was clearly enjoying the encounter.

"Why not?"

"Because I'm not dressed for company."

"So?"

Lethia pursed her lips. With a glint of devilishness in her eyes, she leaned a little further into the opening, revealing a smooth, bare shoulder.

Ereben smiled. "I won't bite," he said, quoting Somek.

With a sassy smirk, Lethia leaned a little more, exposing a firm and totally bare left breast.

Ereben consciously closed his mouth and, after a long moment of immobility, averted his eyes. He felt color rising in his cheeks and ears. "I didn't know that's what you meant."

"Was I bad?" she asked, now showing only her face, filled with an irresistible grin.

Ereben glanced up cautiously. "When do you get to come out of here?"

"I'm not allowed. But you can visit if you want."

"Yes, I want. Maybe this afternoon, so you won't be caught...well, you'll have a chance to...know I'll be coming."

She smiled, then vanished. "I'll be here." Her disembodied voice echoed in the tunnel and in his mind.

Ereben exited the hive, looking first in all directions to be certain that he would not be seen. He had gone only twenty paces when he heard Somek's voice.

"You're up early this morning. Did you sleep well?"

"Actually, I slept very well," Ereben replied. He couldn't remember the last time he had felt so full of energy. Puffy clouds drifted lazily across a powdery blue sky. The thistle towers above him swayed in unison to the rhythm of the flower scented breeze. He leaned against a blade of grass and waited for Somek to join him.

"Would you like to see the wasp hives?" Somek asked, pointing toward the huge openings in the ground twenty yards away.

"Maybe later."

"You should have someone with you if you decide to have a look."

"Is it dangerous?"

"Not most of them. The drones are harmless, unless you surprise them, or threaten them. Well, if you go over there, just stay away from that one." Somek pointed unmistakably at the hive in which Ereben had met Lethia.

"What's in that one?" He already knew, but wondered why Somek would want him to avoid it.

"The queen wasp. Anyone who goes in there never comes out. So don't even go near that one. Trust me."

"Right. I won't go near it." *Until this afternoon!*

The day had passed so slowly. He had spent the morning wondering what a Pix girl would enjoy receiving. He couldn't very well take Lethia flowers, since most flowers here in Ternaria were the size of houses. The smallest he had seen were as big as a cow's head. The Pix ate seeds and roots and small animals, but he wasn't much of a cook. He lacked Jasper's ability to whittle something beautiful from a simple twig.

In the back of his mind, he wondered if he and a Pix could produce a child. He knew that some domestic animals, when mated outside their proper strain, produced no young, or made sterile offspring, like a mule. Perhaps it would simply produce a normal child with pointed ears. With his dagger, he might not only restore himself to his previous size, but could make Lethia large as well. Hobart had done it. But these thoughts remained only incipient notions, never quite allowed to fully germinate within his mind.

Ereben had finally torn a thin blade of grass into short strips, curled each one and gathered them into a bouquet with a single strand of translucent spider silk tied in a bow. He had taken care to hide it as he ducked into Lethia's cave.

He turned left at the first intersection, again noting the cacophony of small children off to the right. Standing at the entrance to the passageway from which Lethia had appeared, he whispered, "Lethia?" The same alluring fragrance tugged at him.

His heart pounded with anticipation. The walls swirled with pastel hues—a feminine softness that felt just right. As Ereben stepped in farther, the honeyed scent became more intense, almost dizzying. He drew in a deep breath through his nostrils. Nothing had ever felt so perfect. "Lethia?" he whispered, somewhat louder than before. "It's Ereben."

"I'm in here, Ereben," a soothing, inviting voice beckoned.

Ereben entered a chamber of fabric-hung walls and carpeted floor. Colorful, long pillows were strewn about in a perfect pattern, and stacked against the back wall all the way to the ceiling. He held his breath. Within a heap of pillows, Lethia reclined, smiling a soft, inviting smile, just barely turned up at the corners. Her green eyes sparkled in the warm light from a hidden source. Her lavender blouse hung loosely from her slender neck, leaving her smooth shoulders and delicate arms bare.

"You brought me something?" she asked.

"Oh!" He had forgotten the bouquet in his hand. He held it out to her. "I didn't know what you would like, so I..."

"That's so sweet of you." She rustled the curled shreds of grass against her tiny chin. "You can sit down if you like."

He chose a long, firm cushion about a yard from Lethia. "You never get to go outside?"

"I'm not allowed." Her smile wavered momentarily, then returned.

"Does anyone ever come and visit?"

She saddened again. "Not very often."

"What do you do with all your time?"

"Oh, I make things, like things to hang on the walls, and I make these." She pointed to the neatly stacked pillows that rose to the ceiling behind her.

"They're nice."

"Where are you from, Ereben?"

"Valand. It's a long way from here." He was afraid to mention that normally he was a hundred times larger than at present."

As the conversation become more relaxed, Ereben and Lethia spoke endlessly of trivial things. He had no notion of the passing of time. He was, however fully aware of how wonderful he felt to be here.

"Your hands look so strong and sensitive," she said.

"What do you mean, sensitive?"

"Come here."

"What?"

"Let me see your hand."

He moved to a closer pillow and held out his hand.

"See these little lines over your knuckles?" She held his hand and touched the back of his knuckles with her fingertips.

Ereben breathed more deeply. The words he said simply came out of his mouth in response to the words he heard, none of them fully reaching his consciousness. He watched Pix fingers moving with their feather touch over his hand. Lethia lifted his hand to her perfect lips and kissed the palm. Her breath caressed his fingers.

She released his hand, leaving it hovering unguarded below her chin. Lethia traced his lips with her fingertips, then drew his head closer. Her intoxicating scent blurred his mind. He kissed her lips, tasting her arousal. Ereben pressed himself against her, feeling her heart beating against his own.

Lethia abruptly drew back. A powerful blow struck the side of Ereben's head, knocking him to the floor. Dazed, he turned to see his attacker. Standing above him loomed his grandfather, his leopard teeth bared. Chrysanthus aimed his threat of violence not at Ereben, but at Lethia.

"Grandpa..."

Before Ereben could continue, Chrysanthus grasped the back of his grandson's shirt in his powerful hand and twisted the stunned teenager to face Lethia. Ereben gasped.

"Ereben," she sighed pleadingly. With the enchantment broken, Ereben now saw the truth of what was before him. The beautiful Pix girl was only half a girl. Below her waist were six articulated legs. Beyond, the black, segmented abdomen of a wasp extended. The abdomen pulsated repeatedly. It was twice the length and girth of those he had ridden.

Behind her, the stack of pillows had been replaced by the hexagonal cells of a wasp nest. Inside each cell, within a thick liquid, a Pix fetus could be seen moving. On the floor, between Ereben and Lethia, were the blackened, desiccated bodies of five Pix men. The walls were hung with the same gray paper from which the cells were constructed. The intoxicating honey scent was revealed as honey scented attar.

Chrysanthus placed Ereben behind him as he backed out of the hive, into the dark of night.

ூ

To be powerless is to be chained, with silent hatred as your only response. Making an enemy powerless strengthens his will.

Jasper of Nilwid: The Art of Power

Through the total darkness within the hold of the slave ship, Jasper watched a thick silhouette of a man descend the steep wooden steps from the hatch. Since nightfall two hours earlier, the flickering candle lantern held by this slaver was the first sight to reach his eyes. Vile odors and groans of the hold had assaulted his other senses with an unrelenting testament of his desperate situation. Now, in the lantern light, he could finally see the two dozen other slaves who, like himself—and like Bahsa as well—were on their final voyage into lifelong slavery in Almirant. Liddie had been locked in the galley to cook for the crew.

Jasper's hands had been chained to the bench on which he sat. His ankles throbbed against the tight irons that held his feet to the sloping floor—the damp hull of the ship. Although he could shift his position enough to prevent his butt from becoming numb, he could find no way to move his arms or legs far enough to stretch them. And his right upper arm felt bruised beneath the brass band that had been hammered around it, before they were put on the ship. It would slide a bit, if he tried, but would not fit over his elbow. He was now marked as a slave.

The slaver's lantern moved slowly, stopping at each captive for a moment. All of the captives appeared to be young and male, none much older than Jasper. Some of them were Dwarf boys; several were Orkahti boys. Bahsa, now in the lamplight, was the only Shouda. The rest, over half, were fair-skinned Albians, with a thick braid of dark hair down their backs. The slaver stroked the cheek of one fair-skin boy with his finger, then moved on, working his way toward where Jasper was chained.

The hold had been utterly black when they had brought Jasper down from the sunny glare of the docks of Dire. At least now he could attach faces to a few of the moans he had heard in the darkness.

When he stood before Jasper, he held his lamp close to Jasper's face, then smiled. Within a frame of dark whiskers and thick lips, several teeth were missing. The rest were long and discolored. "Ah, the pretty one," he said softly, with a gush of foul breath. A loosely tied, dark turban crowned his head. He looked quickly about him, then returned his attention to Jasper, glancing first at the irons that held him to the bench. The back of a hand smelling of tar and sweat stroked Jasper's cheek. Jasper jerked his head away, striking it on the coarse wood of the inner hull behind him.

"Heh, playful," the slaver chuckled. "I like that. You are pretty boy, but you never be man. In Almirant, they make you soldier." He chuckled again, then lifted the hem of Jasper's tunic. "They cut these off. Heh. Make eunuch. You..."

The hand trembled momentarily, then went to the slaver's neck. When Jasper looked up to the bearded face, he saw wide eyes and a protruding tongue. A yellow hand, with only three fingers and a thumb, reached from behind the Sulalian and gently took possession of the candle lantern. The slaver's legs thrashed. Once his limp body was supine on the floor, Kozhdu removed a garrote from his neck and relieved the slaver of the key to the shackles. He held a finger to his lips as he unlocked Jasper's manacles and leg irons.

"I get Orkahti boys too," Kozhdu whispered.

A slender, manacled hand touched Jasper's thigh. He turned to see the wide, pleading brown eyes of an Albian who sat beside him. The freckle-faced boy would have been the next object of the slaver's attentions. "What about the rest?" Jasper asked.

Kozhdu held up the lantern and looked at the other captives. "Twenty four." He shook his head. "Okay, Jasper. If we take all, we must take ship. Where they put Liddie Burn?"

"She's in the galley."

"You go there...quiet. You can find in dark?" He freed Bahsa from the chains.

"It's the other hatch."

"You go do. You can swim? Da?"

"Yes."

"If problem here, you go into water with Bahsa and Liddie. Swim to Kiriati. Off back of this boat. Kipik and Muldu up top here, waiting."

Jasper glanced back at the freckled Albian boy, whose smiling eyes sparkled as they followed him in the lantern light. He took Bahsa's hand and led him up the steep wooden steps, onto the quiet deck of the Sulalian slave ship. In the misty moonlight, he recognized the shapes of Kipik and Muldu hiding near the stern. "Stay low," he whispered into Bahsa's ear. Walking in a crouch, he made his way, with Bahsa, to the Orkahti men and told them that Kozhdu was going to free all the captives and take the ship.

"Ten crew," Muldu whispered back. "Too many."

"Nine," Jasper corrected.

"Eight sleep there." Kipik pointed to recumbent bodies near the bow. One more in the food place, down there. We go make them sleep a long, long sleep."

"Wait here," he said to Bahsa. I'm going to get Liddie."

Jasper and the two Orkahtis crept forward. He stopped at the forward hatch, while the Orkahtis continued on, to encourage the sleeping slavers to have a *long, long sleep*. Peeking over the verge of the open, forward hatch, he saw a Sulalian seated at a long table. A scimitar rested on the table in front of him, while he scooped rice and vegetables into his mouth with his fingers.

"You make good food, Dwarf lady," he said in a soft voice. "You have easy life here. Just make food for people. Is good luck for you. No work in cinnabar mines, no work in field. Just make food. We keep you here. You have good life. Yes?"

Liddie came into view. In one hand, she held an iron cooking pan steaming with chunks of fragrant lamb. Her other hand held a long, metal cooking fork. Jasper caught her attention with a wave.

"Ye like my vegetable, do ye?" she asked, with a cheerful smile.

The slaver nodded. Through the food in his mouth, he mumbled, "Is good."

"She approached him with the lamb. "We'll see how ye like these vittle." As the slaver's left hand reached down to Liddie's buttocks, the flat of the iron pan, along with its chunks of lamb, struck the slaver in the face with a thud. Before the stunned Sulalian could regain his senses, Liddie Burn plunged the metal cooking fork into his chest and twisted it until he slumped, face down. "That's what ye can do with yer 'easy life' and yer gropey hands." She passed the scimitar to Jasper, handle first, and climbed out the hatch.

Jasper could not help but admire Liddie's unflinching readiness to do whatever needed to be done. At a deeper level, though, he resented that the Dwarf woman had been granted the opportunity to strike back, while he, in his chains, had been rendered completely powerless. He looked at the scimitar he now held. Plunging it into the belly of the dead slaver lying below deck just couldn't even the score. He swore to himself that he *would* keep score, and that he *would* settle it in due course.

Forward, only the last of the eight sleeping Sulalians awakened enough to struggle, before being dispatched to his "long, long sleep" by an Orkahti blade to his throat. Kozhdu peeked his head above the aft hatch.

"The ship is ours," Jasper shouted, hefting the scimitar high over his head.

"We must take away dead from here," Kozhdu said, pointing to the bodies of the slavers.

"That wed be our pleasure," an older Dwarf boy said. There, emerging onto the misty deck, was Finny Burnewin, son of Mither Burnewin and nephew to the Baillie of Cinnabar.

"Feed 'em to the fish," Jasper commanded, as twenty-three former captives, all children, emerged onto the deck to see Jasper, scimitar in hand, give the order.

"I must admit, Jasper," Liddie said, as the former slave ship approached what passed for a dock at Paradise City, "the bein' here falls a bit short o' my expectation." She stood on her tiptoes to gaze over the bow rail of the Sulalian ship.

For Jasper, the decision to sail for Paradise City—it felt like his decision alone—seemed the obvious choice. Fully half of those rescued claimed to be native to the coastal lands now controlled by their Banu Sulal overlords. All of them had heard of the "free" Paradise City, created by escaped captives and situated on the coast south of the Three Kingdoms of Sulalia. "They said they wanted to come here."

"I hope they hed a notion o' what they wer beggin' fer." Liddie wrinkled her nose. "And a pestilential air wafts about."

From what Jasper could see, Paradise City consisted of hundreds of tottering shanties, many raised on jumbled, crooked stilts above an expansive mudflat, bounded on the north by a sluggish river, on the south by swamp.

"Livin' in a swamp," Finny said, "hes more appeal, I suspect, than the prospect o' bein' turnt intae one o' thir eunuch sodgers, don't ye think?"

"Hmm." Liddie Burn nodded. "Treatin' lads like they wer coos or common animals. Those slavers deservt what they got.

Well, Finny Burnewin, efterin we drop off the two lads what say they come from Malagaro..."

Ten small boats, each holding four men armed with spears, set off together from the docks and rowed toward the Sulalian ship.

"They don't look very friendly," Jasper said.

"We're ridin' in on a slaver ship," Finny clarified. "You know, Jasper, all the lads on board believe yer in command. A prophet o' some sort once said somethin' about a boy leadin' slaves tae freedom. They think yer the one. 'Yes, indeed,' I telt them. 'Jasper o' Nilwid is the one.'"

"Really?" Jasper asked.

"Some even sweart they watched ye break the chains that helt ye, and kill yon slaver with yer bare hand. I saw nae reason tae say itherwise."

"Give 'em the ship, Jasper," Liddie said. "Tell 'em ye brought it as a gift."

"But it's our ship," Jasper protested.

"Would ye rather own a ship fer an hour," Liddie added, "or be a hero and live tae tell the tale?"

Jasper turned to the three Orkahti men who worked the rudder and the sails. "Bring her about," he shouted. "Lower the sail and drop the rope ladders. Allow them to board!"

"Very impressive," Liddie grumbled.

""Come to the rail, lads," Finny shouted to the boys sitting about the deck. "Welcome yer countrymen and give them a shout!"

Nearly two dozen boys of four races of man, short and tall, dark skin and light, rushed to the rail and cheered the approaching boats.

"Now, Jasper," Finny said over the roar of the boys, "don't be makin' any claims about yersel. Let the starry-eyed lads do the claimin'. Ye just offer the ship and maybees that fancy scimitar, what's too big fer ye anyway." The Dwarf boy winked. "And mak sure ye give 'em to the one what's in charge."

Jasper grasped Finny's shoulder. "I'm glad you're here, Finny Burnewin."

"Be careful at yer games, lads," Liddie remarked in a sober tone.

"We will speak the captain," a fair-skin man shouted from one of the small boats that now surrounded the Sulalian slave ship.

"The captain is dead," three boys shouted simultaneously.

"Jasper killed him and the crew," another called out. "He freed all the slaves."

"Then I will speak with Jasper."

"Who wants to speak with Jasper?" Finny asked.

"I am Shirkuh. This is my city. We are no friend to the slavers, but we make no welcome to pirates."

"Shirkuh," Jasper replied, as he stepped to the rail, "I am Jasper of Nilwid. I bring you a new ship. We freed twelve Albians. They asked us to bring them here. The rest of us will leave on the Orkahti ship, Kiriati. It waits in the road stead for your permission to dock."

Shirkuh looked at his companions and smiled with a shrug. "Where is the man who commands?" The muscular, middle-age Albian wore a loose, white blouse, tucked into baggy black trousers. A thick braid of brown hair fell down his back to his waist.

"He is the boy who frees the slaves!" one of the former captives shouted from the rail.

"He's the one," many other boys added, excitedly.

After a brief discussion with those in his small boat, Shirkuh made some hand signals. Two men from each of two different boats ascended the two rope ladders. When they reached the top and peered over the rail, the three Orkahti men offered friendly salutes. The Albians stepped onto the deck and glanced into both hatches before waving to their leader.

Shirkuh ascended a ladder and came aboard. He looked at the Kiriati, standing a hundred yards out. "Have them come," he said to one of his men.

Jasper waited amid ship, holding the grip of his newly acquired scimitar, its sharp tip on the ship's deck. Finny stood beside him. As Shirkuh approached him, Jasper lifted the scimitar and held it horizontally, resting on two open hands. "Welcome to your new ship. This is the captain's scimitar. I'm sure he would have surrendered it himself, if he was still alive."

The ruler of Paradise City accepted the scimitar with a quizzical look. He observed the gleeful faces of the boys who had now closed in around him. He laughed a deep laugh. "Very good, Jasper of Nilwid. You do this well. They say you are 'the one.' All that I can be certain of is that you are the one who brings me a ship." He turned to the circle of boys. "Who wants to live in Paradise?"

Eleven hands lifted into the air. Jasper noticed that only a single Albian boy, one with a squarish, finely-chiseled, freckled face—who stood slightly taller than all the boys but Bahsa—failed to raise his hand.

"You," Shirkuh said, pointing at the freckled boy. "What is your name?"

"Yaqut," the boy replied in a timid, pubescent croak.

"You are Albian?"

"Yes."

"You don't want to stay. Where will you go?"

With a pleading expression, he looked toward Jasper. "Wherever he's going." His long fingers clutched at the full length sleeves of his loose yellow tunic, which mostly covered baggy, red Sulalian culottes.

Shirkuh looked at Jasper with raised eyebrows.

Jasper nodded. "The rest will go with us."

Yaqut's freckled face relaxed. He smiled at Jasper, then bit his lip and averted his gaze.

“Everyone is our guest tonight,” Shirkuh announced. “Tomorrow we will resupply your Orc boat.” He took Jasper’s hand and drew him close. “There are thousands of slaves in the Three Kingdoms,” he whispered. “If you take up the legend, the slavers would hunt you.”

“They hunt us already.”

Shirkuh studied his face. “Then I will tell you about ‘the one.’”

“I guess we’re the lot,” Finny Burnewin stated.

“I think so,” Jasper replied, scanning the faces of the thirteen former captives who would be departing with him on the Kiriati, once it was resupplied. The fourteen of them had been relegated to a one-room, elevated shack for the night. It’s dense wicker floor was a more comfortable sleeping place than any of them had found reason to hope for only two days ago. Though enough air drifted through a wide window opening to cause the single candle to flicker, the heat and humidity were not much better than in the stifling hold of the slave ship.

Finny poked at the brass band on Jasper’s right arm. “Ye know they cut those off all the rest of us?”

“I told them to leave mine. And when it gets too tight, I’ll have a larger one put on.”

“Ye may be loony. Everybody will think yer yet a slave.”

“I want to always remember that I *was* a slave.”

“Well then, you’ve picked a proper remembrance. An’ yer loony.”

“So...I’m Jasper, from Nilwid...and freedom is hot and sweaty!” He pulled his tunic over his head and rolled it into a ball for a pillow, leaving him in just his sweat-soaked shorts.

“I’m Finny, from Cinnabar.” He pulled off his own tunic. Laughter skittered through the room.

“And I’m Pinkie Sweep. For yer information, I’m a Dwarf...” More laughter. “...from Cinnabar. I only knew Finny as a passin' face..." He removed his tunic. "...ootside the whorehouse!"

By now, the laughter was generalized and the pattern set. Next to introduce themselves and undress were the twin Chance brothers from Easlan Brae, Slim and Lucky. "I'm a Dwarf," Lucky added, "but my poor brither is just short fer his age." Slim slapped the back of Lucky's head.

Around the room it went: Dace and Cal, both from Zink, then the two natives of Malagaro. When Khumartakin, the first of the three Orkahti boys to speak, removed his tunic to reveal his deep yellow skin, the room fell silent.

"We have...little teats..." He flicked one tiny, dark nipple with one of his three fingers. "...but big teeths." He flashed a toothy smile. The laughter resumed. "I say right, or I mix up?" More laughter.

Gemel and Masuh, the other two Orkahtis, introduced themselves. Their yellow skin did nothing to diminish to jovial atmosphere.

Bahsa had no tunic. He stood and motioned as though he were about to remove his shorts, then stopped with a broad smile. "That's Bahsa," Jasper said. "He doesn't talk. He's all the way from Shouda City. He's the youngest here, but taller than any of us."

Last came the thin, freckle-faced Albian. "I'm Yaqut. I'm from Jakar," he croaked. "Albians never sleep unclothed, because of all the mosquitoes." He remained in his yellow tunic and baggy, red culottes.

The other boys looked at one another, then quickly pulled their tunics back over their heads. Yaqut whispered something to Bahsa. The Shouda boy's look of concern changed to a conspiratorial smile.

Finny stood. "I am certain that nae body in this room believes that silliness about Jasper bein' 'the One.' Am I correct?" He looked directly at Yaqut.

Yaqut's freckled face took on a smirk. "I was sitting beside Jasper when Kozhdu killed the slaver and unlocked the chains. I think they would have left you and the rest of us, if Jasper hadn't said something. He may not be the one in the legend, but I owe him my freedom."

"Well put," Finny replied with little conviction. "Until each of us gets home—or wherever ye're goin'—we all act like he is 'the One.' Agreed?"

As they settled in for the night, Jasper found himself lying between Khumartakin, the Orkahti boy, and Finny Burnewin. Before the candle was blown out, he scanned the room for Bahsa. On the far side of the cramped room, the Shouda boy was already asleep, curled in a ball against Yaqut. Brown eyes stared back at Jasper from a squarish, freckled face.

A bright, tropical sun cleared the mountain ridge above Malagaro's village of North Port, as the Kiriati eased into the small harbor and dropped its anchor. Since there was no dock, one of the Kiriati's small boats was lowered to transport the two Malagari boys to shore. Kozhdu, Muldu and Jasper accompanied them. Liddie remained with the crew and the boisterous group of eleven boys who swarmed over the crowded deck and up into the rigging.

"No people here," Muldu said, as Kozhdu worked the stern sweep.

"They're afraid of raiders," one of the Malagari boys explained. "The slavers came from around the point and surprised us. That's how they got us."

"Will they come out when they see you?" Jasper asked.

"They better," the other Malagari said.

Though the Malagaris appeared to be of Albian blood, they wore their brown hair cropped short, rather than in the thick braid of the other Albians. Jasper had also noted that each of them bore a small, diagonal scar below each cheekbone.

As the small boat slid onto the sand, and the two Malagari boys jumped out, scores of people emerged from low houses that were set back into the vegetation. Two women, running more energetically than the rest, each grappled one of the boys and smothered him with hugs and kisses.

Most of the Malagaris wore short tunics printed with varying patterns of red, black and orange. The only one who wore a longer garment of solid orange approached the boat, where Jasper waited with the two Orkahtis. "I am Nambam." He shook the hands of all three of them, then took Kozhdu and Muldu by the hand and said, "We should go up to the temple and give thanks. Then we will bless your journey on. Come now."

Kozhdu looked at his countryman and shrugged. "Blessing is good."

Jasper followed at the end of what he guessed were a hundred people, as they slowly wound their way through the simple village and up the slope of the mountain. Religious celebrations were not among his favorite activities, especially after the ordeal with the Dryads.

After a quarter hour, they reached a broad hollow about a third of the way to the summit. Within a carefully groomed clearing, surrounded by luxuriant tropical growth, stood four huge statues of a dove, each carved from a single, translucent green stone that Jasper immediately recognized as the same stone used for a handle on Ereben Leaf's dagger, and that of the other Guardians of the Ruins. Three of the statues, each two yards high, were arranged in a triangle at ground level, ten yards to a side. The fourth dove stood on a central pedestal. Together, they formed the points of a triangular pyramid.

He looked at his quiescent, carved staff, and decided to remain outside the bounds of the triangle. Even so, the milky red pommel stone of his sword, Rat Slayer, emitted a soft hum.

All of the Malagaris entered the triangle. Nambam placed one hand on the side of one of the dove statues. His eyes rolled back as he began to chant in a language that Jasper could not understand. The chanting continued for nearly a half hour, while people stood with eyes closed, rocking gently.

Nambam's facial expression changed suddenly from ecstasy to terror. "Dragoma!" he shouted.

The Malagaris pressed closer to the central pedestal within the triangle of green stone doves and looked skyward. Jasper followed their gaze. High above them, a solitary golden dragon spiraled downward, occasionally rocking its head from side to side.

Jasper dashed within the bounds of the triangle and tripped. When he had caught himself against one of the dove statues, his vision was instantly overwhelmed by fine, bright strands connecting everything with everything. Far to the west, he saw surprised expressions on the faces of men tending a large sphere tipped with milky red stones. They wore brown robes with deep, cowled hoods. He realized that they could see him, and he understood they would help him. The green stone clawed at his strength. He saw the knot of filaments that swirled about the magical being of the dragon, and the magic of his own carved staff. He pulled his hand from the hungry statue and returned to his present surroundings. In his left hand, all of the menagerie of animals and reptiles and fish he had carved into his staff thrashed against their woody attachments, and screamed into the air.

A blossom of yellow-white flame sprouted from the mouth of the rapidly approaching dragon. Flame engulfed them, then abruptly stopped as the dragon passed and circled back. All of the vegetation surrounding the clearing for the statues steamed and smoldered, but the area within the pyramid of triangles was untouched. The spot outside the triangle where Jasper had stood only moments earlier was blackened and smoking.

"It is one-eye dragon," Kozhdu said. "I strike out dragon's eye in Angelsk."

Again and again, the dragon circled and descended, spewing its flames at the stone doves and the people sheltered beneath them. With each attack, the green stone of the statues seemed to darken a bit more, though their protection stood firm. Jasper's staff had ceased its riotous noise. He knew that if he touched the stone again, he would be able to see if the Kiriati was safe, but the frightening stone had sucked at his being.

The dragon descended once more, this time with a boulder in its claw. At precisely the right moment, it released the stone, allowing it to strike the upper dove statue—the top of the pyramid. The green stone of the statue cracked diagonally. The top of the dove slid to the ground and shattered, narrowly missing the two boys they had just returned to their home.

To the gasps of all the Malagaris, a huge dove, larger than the statues, landed atop the green fragment remaining on the pillar. Everyone but the three outsiders fell to their knees and bowed their faces to the ground. Soon, a second enormous dove landed on the head of one of the intact statues.

"Fantas and Pneuma!" Jasper shouted. "My staff called them." The pair had been mates even before Hobart had transformed them to their present size.

As the dragon circled back, the two giant doves took to the air in a terrific flutter. They outmaneuvered the dragon and nipped at its wings, diving, swooping, circling. The Malagaris watched with mouths agape, as their dove goddess and her consort fought to preserve them from the golden dragon.

With a wing injured, the one-eyed dragon turned away. In a last act of spite, it turned its head and sent a gout of flame into Pneuma, destroying her feathers instantly. The injured dove plummeted to the mountain ridge.

Fantas landed nearby. When his mate failed to exhibit any signs of life, Fantas flew to the broken fragment of the central dove and hovered above it. Apparently by the strength of his own will, the giant dove summoned the power to return to his original size. As he shrank and hovered, the remainder of the broken statue melted and dripped, like a candle of green wax, down the sides of its pedestal. Now the size of a natural dove once more, Fantas circled twice over the motionless body of Pneuma, his lifelong mate, then flew away to the west.

❧

Man works to gain what he believes he needs. His beliefs may kill him. He will never know whether they have killed him, or if the true needs which he failed to gain might have saved him.

Ereben Leaf: Chronicle of the Counterspell

Ereben could, of course, get no answers from Chrysanthus, so he could only guess how his grandfather had found him in Lethia's lair. He felt gratitude for having been rescued. Aside from that, he worried over unfinished business. The Pix and Faeries had yet to meet over their differences. He had said no farewells to Somek, who would assume that Ereben had abandoned the anticipated peace discussions. Nor had he arranged for the Faeries to transport their daggers to the southern boundary between Ternaria and the Time Mountains. But despite his protests, Chrysanthus drove him through the night. By morning, Ereben could verify that they were moving south through Ternaria.

Mid-morning, they reached the bank of a river which tumbled down from cataracts to the north-east. They would be swept away if they attempted a crossing here. Chrysanthus turned westward and followed the riverbank. Within an hour they came to a section of deep, relatively calm water. A spider silk rope stretched across the water, and was anchored on this end to a rock pile. On the far side, what appeared to be a boat was attached to the crossing rope with loops. Chrysanthus looked about, eventually locating a thinner rope submerged in the water and attached to several small rocks. Pulling on this thin rope enabled him to draw the boat toward them along the crossing rope.

As the boat neared, Ereben could see that it was nothing more than the cap of an acorn, fitted with rowlocks and a pair of oars. The coracle was large enough to hold a half dozen Faeries.

"This is not your first trip into Ternaria, is it Grandpa? And you made yourself small, otherwise, you never would have known about this ferry."

They crossed the river with Chrysanthus rowing, and Ereben assisting by pulling them along on the crossing rope. Ereben judged that a full sized man would hardly even notice this rivulet as he crossed it in a single step. But then, all Ternaria was like that. The whole of it, north to south, would require only a day or so, rather than many weeks to traverse.

South of the river, they eventually came upon the tracks of tortoises dragging heavy objects. He assumed that these were created by the transporting of their daggers. In fact, he could imagine nothing else that could make such marks in the soft soil. From there, Chrysanthus accelerated his pace. That night, they slept during the moonless portion of the night, then continued by moonlight.

By the following afternoon they reached the southern boundary of Ternaria. Awaiting them were Keri and Brennith beside four tortoises and the two immense daggers.

"Oooaah, Ereben Leaf," Keri called. "Oooaah, Chrysanthus."

"Oooaah, Keri," he responded. "Oooaah, Brennith."

"We were afraid that we'd have to leave before you got here," the beautiful Faerie woman said, running up to Chrysanthus and hugging him. She then hugged Ereben, her Faerie breasts pressing softly against his chest. She took him by the hand and sat him down alongside Brennith.

Brennith smiled. "We thought you were dead."

"Why?" This revelation startled him.

"Somek came alone to us. That took more courage than I could have mustered. He told us that you had gone into the lair of the Queen Wasp. None of the Thistlepix would go in after you.

We didn't trust them, and besides, we were afraid to go there. Only Chrysanthus would get onto Somek's wasp. We told him that we would meet him here with your knives, whatever the outcome."

"What will happen with the peace discussions?" Ereben asked.

"They'll happen," Keri stated emphatically. "We all agree that Somek is sincere. At least some of the Thistlepix want peace. But you took the first step."

They talked about important and unimportant matters until Ereben ran out of reasons to delay their transition back to their original size. They cut down several munu mushrooms, each about ten yards high and, using the tortoises, dragged them to the daggers, which lay parallel to one another in the soft dirt.

"It's probably not safe for you to be very close, "Ereben said. "You might want to be a long way from here."

"How long a way?" Brennith asked, concern on his brow.

"I don't know. I've never done this before. I think it could affect a lot of things nearby." Ereben was almost certain that the transformation of both him and his grandfather would draw life force from their surroundings. The act would increase the chaos of Ternaria. He would have to draw life from wherever he could find it.

They said their farewells, then the two Faeries mounted the lead tortoises in each tandem team and headed back toward their current home. Ereben waited a half hour, then arranged Chrysanthus so that he could place one hand on the pommel of his own dagger and the other on the trunk of a munu, the praying hands mushroom. Ereben stood so that he could do the same with Hobart's dagger. He recognized that if he increased their size, but failed to draw in sufficient life force, both he and his grandfather would die.

Ereben took one last look at Ternaria from a Faerie's point of view. A sadness pierced him as he remembered Lethia's tenderness and beauty. What he had seen after Chrysanthus disrupted the enchantment seemed devoid of reality. He could hardly associate the one with the other. He drew in the musty scent of earth and mushroom and the riot of flowers extending to the North. He closed his eyes and envisioned their delicate relationships.

As he focused his being on gossamer threads that emanated from everything to everything, tension ebbed and flowed in all directions. Rather than beginning immediately to bring about change, he studied the panorama of relationships and dependencies. To the South, stresses were profound. Although the physical imbalances were great, greater than in Ternaria, the most dramatic difference lay in the contortion of time. The density of evanescent strands roiled ominously into the Time Mountains. Events stacked upon themselves, crowding out any hint of respite. He shuddered at the prospect of continuing their journey into that nest of distortion.

Ereben wondered why he had not done this before—to observe rather than disturb. He looked at his grandfather, who floated passively in the soup of existence. Chrysanthus, he could see, was not unaware. The leopard-man acknowledged his grandson with an inaudible purr.

To Ereben's surprise, he recognized that his own observations modified relationships. Even the act of not acting had its ramifications. His own ability to inspect the hidden aspects of nature exemplified a corruption of that same nature.

His unfettered sight assayed the titer of life force required to restore his grandfather and himself. The price to be paid would be drawn from every living thing in an expanding radius until the increased substance of their bodies was precisely attuned with its enclosed life force. His vision blurred, then cleared. Hobart's dagger was in his left hand. His right hand held the hand of Chrysanthus. Chrysanthus held his own dagger. He had succeeded.

This time, he had controlled the counterspell more closely. The result was evident in a circle about them. For thirty yards in every direction all living things: shrub, fungus, grass, insect, flower. Everything was lifeless. Like the first frost of winter, he had halted the life of these things without altering their appearance appreciably. Within a day, it would all wilt and shrivel. It was not so much a zone of death as a sculpture garden of mineral and lignin and chitin.

Turning to the dark mountains rising to the South, Ereben identified their immediate goal, the highest peak, the Tooth of Time. From this distance it stood as a purple prominence on the far horizon, slightly irregular at the peak. In the haze between Ereben and the Tooth, several days of steep mountains were interposed.

From the very first steps he took into the Time Mountains, Ereben felt a deep malaise. His bones ached. His skin ached. His fingernails and toenails ached. Something about the place waged war with the rhythms of his body.

He was puzzled to see the leaves of deciduous trees yellow so early in the season. Where they stopped for the night, oaks and chestnuts were already shedding leaves. Before settling down to sleep, he noticed that his toenails were painfully impinging against the inside of his boots. Using the razor edge of his dagger, he trimmed them neatly, and trimmed his fingernails as well, since they were quite long. He opened his shirt and inspected the smooth skin of his chest. It itched, but showed no sign of rash or insect bites.

A nearby apple tree provided him with supper. Chrysanthus had wandered off for a half hour, presumably to find his own victuals. Sleep that night came in fits, interrupted by pains in his joints, and by the stark silence of the forest.

When he awoke at dawn, he was amazed to see that his fingernails and toenails had grown considerably during the night. He trimmed them again, this time cutting them quite close in the full daylight. While he sat, flowers emerged from the ground.

Conifers appeared as he had remembered them the previous evening, but all the deciduous trees and shrubs had not only lost all their leaves, but were now showing springtime buds. Within an hour of starting off, blossoms were seen on some trees. The landscape glowed vibrant green. Light sprigs of new growth appeared on pines and spruce and fir. By noon, the blossoms were all gone, replaced by luxuriant foliage. The ground flowers had passed their bloom, and stood only as healthy green stalks. In cadence with the trees, young birds had hatched in the morning and were exploring beyond their nests before mid-day.

Ereben established the habit of trimming his nails three or four times a day. By the second evening, his red hair reached below his shoulders, requiring him to tie it back. He discovered a dense fuzz on his upper lip. He began to understand what Gelith meant when he had warned that each day seemed like a year in the Time Mountains. So far as he could tell, he was aging about a year each day. And the plants about him cycled through all four seasons each day, starting afresh each morning.

He saw no distinct changes in Chrysanthus, but wondered what impact this aging would have on him. Since emerging from the dagger, he had appeared considerably more youthful than his years, but how much could he spare?

On the second morning, Ereben witnessed a circle of mushrooms erupt from the ground surrounding a tree stump and, within a few moments, discolor and dissolve. Grasses grew visibly as he watched. A few curly hairs appeared on his chin.

Eight days passed before they reached the slopes of the Tooth of Time. By then, Ereben's hair reached well down his back. A curly red beard hung from his face. His chest had developed its own crop of curly red hair, and his arms were noticeably hairier. His bones continued to ache. He guessed that he was now about twenty five years old. Another month like this, he thought, would make him an old man.

As they ascended the lower slopes of the Tooth, they passed through a stand of bizarre thorn trees twenty to thirty yards tall. The trunks and branches sprouted threatening rosettes of thorns as long as the blade of a dagger. The lower branches were as thick as his thigh. He assumed that this was blood locust. Since Chrysanthus' drawing of the strange ax indicated a handle made of blood locust, he decided to climb one of the frightening trees and select a high branch of suitable thickness. He would use it as a walking staff until he was ready to attempt a forging of the ax.

Ereben trimmed his nails in preparation for the climb. He stuffed the long, braided rope of his hair down the back of his shirt to keep it clear of the thorns, then began the hazardous ascent, branch by branch. Aside from the effort of climbing, he discovered that contorting his movements so as to avoid impaling his arms or legs or torso on the thorns required an even greater exertion.

A half hour of climbing brought him to the upper third of the blood locust, where branches the thickness of his now-hairy forearm sprouted from the main trunk. Standing on one branch, with his buttocks planted against another provided enough stability for him to cut an ideal branch at shoulder height. The branch on which he stood seemed thin enough to give under his weight, but its rigidity was more like steel than wood.

Ereben drew Hobart's dagger and scored the corrugated bark. Deep red sap, oozed like blood from the cut. Since the blade held an extraordinarily sharp edge, he found that drawing its edge cut the wood more effectively than using its minimal weight as an ax. The cutting was slow and exhausting. As he labored, the small, oval leaves of the tree and its neighbors turned to yellow, then floated away in the wind, as a yellow blizzard. By the time the branch finally separated from the tree, both of Ereben's arms quivered from exhaustion.

The severed branch dropped several yards below him, catching in the thorn-clad branches. After allowing the muscles of his arms to recuperate for a quarter hour, he carefully descended to his cut branch. In this relatively short descent, he realized that going down presented a greater challenge than going up, since the thorn rosettes tended to be oriented upward more than downward. He continually snagged his clothing and occasionally his beard or hair. The sun was setting on another year of his life.

Rather than attempt an impossible descent in the dark, he located a suitable crotch in the tree, from which he removed the thorns. By placing his cut branch across three other branches, he was able to create a rude perch upon which he could sit and lean against the deeply furrowed trunk. There he spent the night, mostly awake in the chill air, but occasionally dozing.

Dawn was heralded by the re-growth of the thorn rosettes he had previously removed. Their slowly moving dagger thrust vied for his attention with the pain of his re-grown toenails. With some effort, he extricated his clothing from the thorns and cut them from the bark. Balancing awkwardly, Ereben removed first one boot, then the other, enabling him to trim away his toenails. The second boot fell to the ground.

Poked and scratched and exhausted, he made his way to the ground, dragging his cut branch through one snag after another. Chrysanthus met him at the bottom. With Hobart's dagger, together with the leopard-man's steel claws, they made quick work of trimming the blood locust branch into a sturdy, well balanced staff, a little taller than Ereben. Once stripped of its bark, the staff was left with a dried, glassy hard finish the color of fresh blood. Its odor was similar to the sweet scent of cottonwood. Although as light as cottonwood, its rigidity was more like that of ash or hickory.

"We need to get to the summit and get out of here. It's killing us just being here, Grandpa."

Chrysanthus took Ereben's long, red beard in his hands and, with a few deft strokes of his claws, trimmed most of it away.

"Can you do my hair while you're at it?"

His grandfather lifted the yard-long braid and cut it off in one swipe. Chrysanthus tied both ends and stowed it in his belt. Chrysanthus' own hair behaved more like that of an animal. It shed slightly in the mid-mornings, then grew denser in the evenings.

They climbed the steep slope of the Tooth of Time in a combination of direct ascents interspersed with sometimes lengthy traverses to bypass nearly vertical barriers. About two thirds of the way up, they crossed the tree line into sloping fields of angular black boulders. The wind cut through Ereben's ice leopard cape.

The summit turned out to be the shallow crater of an extinct volcano. Although its wall offered some protection from the wind, nothing protected them from the piercing cold. He examined the twenty yard-wide crater for the expected pointer to the Warded Mines, but found nothing. The barren summit offered little shelter and no food or water. Ereben walked around the rim, looking out at the spectacle in despair. To the South and East the ocean spread, a large, mist-shrouded island rising to the East.

Ereben could not identify Ternaria, but recognized the deep green of Oldwood to the North. The Vermilion Cliffs above Ciboney rested at the horizon. To the West, to his surprise, the mountains of the Time Range dropped off abruptly into a fog-filled basin that stretched for perhaps thirty miles, beyond which a single, isolated mountain rose above its neighbors, its top truncated like the Tooth of Time, on which he now stood. *Another volcano.* Within the crater of the Tooth, the wall stood taller to the East, at one point revealing a small natural window that looked out to ocean. The western wall of the crater was broken into notches at several points.

Ereben climbed outside the eastern window and looked west across the crater. Over a dozen widely divergent pointers could be imagined, none appearing any more prominent than the others. He climbed back into the crater and sat beside his grandfather, who had made no effort to find the pointer to the Warded Mines.

"I can't find it, Grandpa. We'll have to leave in the morning, and I don't know which way to go."

Chrysanthus patted him on the knee.

As the sun set, the temperature fell. The air became still. Chrysanthus and Ereben huddled against one another, their hoods drawn over their heads. As Ereben shivered in the cold, he noticed that Chrysanthus did not. Ereben slept despite the cold, having slept little on his perch in the blood locust the previous night.

When he awoke in the morning, he undertook the laborious task of trimming all his nails, then prepared to leave. The western slope seemed to be the shortest path to exiting the cursed mountains. He walked to the western rim and looked down into the fog-filled basin. "We need to go, Grandpa."

Chrysanthus joined his grandson, sitting beside him.

"We need to go," Ereben repeated. They had failed. But he knew they would both die if they stayed on the mountain much longer.

Chrysanthus remained seated. Reaching up to grasp Ereben's hand, the leopard-man pulled Ereben down to sit beside him.

"I don't know what to do, Grandpa. We're both growing older as we sit here."

All that Ereben could be certain of was that Chrysanthus was waiting for something.

They sat for two hours, facing the light mist that rose from within the crater of the Tooth. As the sun rose higher in the East a beam of sunlight shot through the stone window in the eastern wall, illuminating a ray of mist above Ereben's head. With the upward movement of the sun, the ray of light from the window angled downward toward the western wall. Chrysanthus stood and looked over the broken western rim. Ereben slapped himself on the forehead for having missed the nature of the pointer. He joined his grandfather in looking to the West. When the beam of light from the window angled into a notch on the western rim, it illuminated a line through the fog above the basin and pointed directly to the base of the tallest extinct volcano that rose from the basin's western limit. Chrysanthus patted Ereben solidly on the shoulder. He realized that, without his grandfather's patience, he would have never seen the pointer. Ereben started down the western slope of the Tooth of Time with renewed hope.

By evening, they had put the mountains behind them, and with them, nine years of their lives.

At ground level, the fog that hung perpetually above the Cauldrons could be recognized as vapors belching from an expansive morass of boiling, gray mud. As the mud boiled, hand-sized bubbles rose to the surface, lingered momentarily, then ruptured to release gouts of sulfurous fumes. Dykes of dull brown travertine, decorated with a reticulum of sulfur, wound a serpentine route through the boiling mud. Here and there, rivulets of cold water entered the mud pools from rocky fingers that descended from the surrounding hills.

Ereben and Chrysanthus stepped carefully along the slippery surface of a narrow dyke that headed in a westerly direction, though it was hard to be sure of the direction, given the twists and turns, and the poor visibility afforded by the clinging vapors. Ereben's lungs burned from breathing the sulfurous air.

Occasionally a creature the size of a dog would emerge from the mud, skitter across the surface for a few yards, then plunge below the boiling surface. The creature's tail seemed to be that of a fish, but it walked or dragged along the surface using flat, fingerless forelimbs. It would sometimes bark like a young fox, and in doing so, would open its mouth to as large a dimension as the girth of its body, showing a double row of tiny hooked teeth above and below. Ereben decided to call it a mudpuppy. Although the antics of a mudpuppy were amusing, he recognized that its bite might be formidable.

After the days of urgency in passing through the Time Mountains, it seemed a luxury to walk at a reasonable pace, knowing that, in walking for a day, he would consume only a single day of his life. No longer needing to trim his nails several times a day added a sense of leisure. He also appreciated that his body and that of Phaena were once again aging at the same pace.

A mudpuppy surfaced and barked at Ereben and Chrysanthus. It swayed its head from side to side, seeming to scan its bleak surroundings with bulging fish eyes. The mudpuppy padded its way along the edge of a travertine dike. A broad red streak lashed out from a small alcove, slapped against the mudpuppy and yanked it up from the sucking mud, pulling the creature, screaming, into the alcove. The mudpuppy fell silent.

When Ereben passed near the alcove, stepping around and above it, he found a huge toad lazing in the filtered sunlight. It ignored his presence. Its globose body, larger than one of Liddie Burn's cows, sagged over its legs. Like other toads Ereben had seen elsewhere, the skin of this enormous *mudtoad* displayed a subtly mottled blend of mud colors, matching it to its bizarre surroundings.

He located a slightly raised area of the dyke that would have to suffice for a stopping place. It was barely wide enough for the two of them, but it was the widest spot he had seen. The sun was setting. A small rivulet passed nearby and spilled into the boiling mud. He and Chrysanthus filled their water bottles. They had no food. At least tonight they would not be cold.

As the sun went down, an eerie chorus of chirps and barks arose from the Cauldrons. In the vaporous glow of moonlight, hundreds of mudpuppies could be seen climbing out of the mud and onto the dykes all about. Those that climbed directly onto the dyke upon which Chrysanthus and Ereben had camped found themselves kicked unceremoniously back into the mud. Ereben held his dagger ready.

In the distance, a mudtoad leaped away from an onslaught of mudpuppies, landing in the midst of still others. These mudpuppies fell on the hapless toad, tearing it to pieces and fighting among themselves over the bounty.

Before long, dozens of howling mudpuppies converged on Ereben's clearing. He swung his blood staff again and again. As he kicked one, it bit his boot, not releasing it until Ereben had eviscerated it on the point of a dagger. Chrysanthus dispatched one after another with his deadly claws. The commotion seemed to attract the attention of more mudpuppies. Mudpuppy eyes glistened in the moonlight as far as he could see. He knew if he slipped or hesitated, they would be on him.

From the adjacent rivulet, a parade of crabs poured forth. About half the size of a mudpuppy, each crab wielded one large claw, a little larger than a human hand, and a smaller, narrow claw of about half that size. The first three crabs to reach the mudpuppies clamped onto the moist body of one opponent using their smaller claws. With the large claws they promptly amputated both of the mudpuppy's flipper feet. Countless crabs joined battle with the mudpuppies. Those mudpuppies that anticipated the crab onslaught were often able to dodge the side-stepping crabs and toss them into the boiling mud with the swipe of a tail. Any crab falling into the mud appeared to be cooked immediately. These were then consumed by any mudpuppies that found them.

After an hour of battle, the fighting ceased as quickly as it had started. The mudpuppies returned to the boiling mud. The crabs headed back to the rivulet.

Ereben took that opportunity to fling a crab into the mud, then, after it had cooked, retrieve it. Using the handle of his dagger, he cracked open the claws, sharing the tasty, though slightly sulfurous crab meat with Chrysanthus. Afterwards, they slept in shifts.

About two hours after daybreak, a solitary shaft of sunlight briefly pointed to the base of the extinct volcano, now only a few hours away. They had been walking since first light. Now they could verify their direction. Another hour brought them out of the Cauldrons, into fresh air, and a wasteland of dark gravel. Crossing a few miles of gravel plains, they arrived at the base of the unnamed volcano.

A short way up the steep talus, a mine entrance could be seen. Ereben climbed up to it, noting no sign of recent visitation. The opening itself was unimpressive, appearing to be a squared off entrance to a natural cave. There were no markings or indication of a barrier. Ereben peeked his head into the entrance and was immediately overcome with dread. He lurched back, falling at the entrance and sliding painfully down the talus.

He climbed back up, this time with Chrysanthus. Both of them carefully examined the entryway, again seeing nothing unnatural. Ereben placed his hand on the stone, allowing it to become one with the rock. His hand sank into the stone slightly while he shared its sense of now. He felt the agony of pent up stress. The stone was not at rest. It was being constrained by an intrusive presence. He could see five sarcite pegs at the apices of a pentagon, establishing a field of power inside the entryway. He removed his hand from the stone.

"Grandpa, there are five sarcites just inside the entrance: two near the floor on either side, two partway up the sides and one overhead."

Chrysanthus seemed to ignore him.

"And there are great stresses within the rock."

His grandfather stepped through the entryway.

"Grandpa!" Ereben's surprise was immediately replaced by understanding. *Grandpa is not human.* The Faeries could enter because they were not human.

With a subterranean groan of the mountain, Chrysanthus removed a single sarcite peg, the size of a small loaf of bread, and placed it by the entrance. The pentagon alignment was now broken. The Warded Mines were no longer warded.

Ereben joined Chrysanthus in the tunnel. He had expended a great deal of effort to reach the Warded Mines ahead of the Knights of the Redeemer. Now that he had accomplished that, he realized that he had given little thought as to what action he should take. He knew that sarcite needed to be supplied to Maha Neruti at Moss Abbey. A quantity the size of his fist would probably last the monks two years.

He considered what need he himself might have for sarcite. Sarcite apparently could be configured at five points, as a pentagon, as had been done by the ancients at Ephesia and as a gate ward here. It addition, sarcite could be placed at the apices of a pentalphic sphere to exercise much greater control, like the Sphere of Order used by the monks to hold back the chaos of Ternaria. He decided abruptly that they would obtain all that they could carry, then restore the ward which had protected the mines for millennia. The Knights would be unable to pass the entrance.

As they moved farther into the mine, far enough to preclude sunlight, the walls of the tunnel seemed to emit their own light. A soft, yellow luminance resolved into countless vermicular spots, each in gradual, undulating motion. On close inspection, Ereben realized that these were glowworms, millions of them, that lit the way for him and his grandfather.

They walked into the heat of the mountain for over a mile. The tunnel tended slightly downward, though it was mostly level, and without branches, side tunnels or intersections. When the low ceiling finally opened to a large chamber, the yellow glowworms ended abruptly, replaced by a discomforting red radiance, seeming to come from within the milky red stone of the domed cavity. They were surrounded by sarcite. The green jadeite handles of Hobart's dagger and Chrysanthus' dagger emitted a continuous hum, reminding Ereben of the bombi of Ternaria. The hum was palpable when he placed his hand against his dagger. But these curious findings were quickly forgotten when he looked to the center of the chamber.

A statue, twice the height of a man, stood on a slightly raised, pentagonal platform. It appeared to be carved from pure, milky red sarcite. The figure was somewhat man-like, though with six articulated arms emerging from its segmented chest, each ending in three clawed digits, as did its two feet. Its head extended directly from massive shoulders, with little but a muscular web intervening as a neck. Sharpened teeth showed within its partially open mouth. Its face had a flattened nose, two widely spaced, protruding eyes, and one tiny horn above the center of its forehead. The platform on which the statue was mounted was decorated with a two-yard-high, slender column of sarcite at each of its five corners.

On the far side of the sarcite chamber, another tunnel opened. Ereben assumed it to be either another entrance, perhaps on the western side of the mountain, or possibly the location of the beast of which Gelith had spoken, the Sarcoptis.

"This must be a statue of the Sarcoptis, Grandpa."

The mountain trembled briefly. Ereben remembered the stress within the stone, and the audible groan when Chrysanthus had broken the ward.

"I think we need to get the sarcite quickly, Grandpa. That was a small earthquake."

Chrysanthus drew his dagger and plunged it into the sarcite wall at a corner with the tunnel. The blade sank in to the hilt. He then cut out a cube of sarcite about the size of a man's head. Ereben followed his example, using Hobart's still humming dagger. He felt the cube of the rare stone to be light enough to easily carry under one arm.

"Do you think we'll need more, Grandpa?"

Again the mountain trembled, but with enough force to make it difficult for Ereben to stand. A large crack appeared in one of the sarcite columns surrounding the statue, causing the top corner of the pillar to fall to the floor, where it shattered, its sound lost in the pervasive rumble of the mountain. The eyes of the statue stared at Ereben. He did not remember that penetrating stare. Then the eyes turned to the side.

"Grandpa! That statue is not a statue. It *is* the Sarcoptis." He now understood what should have been obvious before. The monster stood imprisoned by power from the pentagonal field of the sarcite columns. The Sarcoptis itself was made of sarcite.

A slab fell from the roof of the entrance tunnel. Ereben and Chrysanthus climbed over it and ran down the tunnel, holding their sarcite cubes. When they reached about half the distance to the surface, the way was completely blocked by a collapse of the roof. Chrysanthus climbed the heap of rubble, then climbed back down and shoved Ereben back toward the chamber of the Sarcoptis. At the entry to the chamber, the roof of the tunnel had collapsed further, requiring them to crawl through the remaining opening.

The Sarcoptis stood on the low, pentagonal platform, still held by the field of the sarcite columns. They ran around the beast and into the opposite opening. The earthquake shook them again, this time throwing Ereben to the floor. He looked back at the Sarcoptis. Its six clawed arms now moved, as more of the restraining columns began to crumble. Ereben jumped to his feet, helped by his grandfather, then joined him in sprinting into the intact tunnel. The glowworms glowed brighter in proportion to the trembling of the mountain. A crack opened in the floor before them, releasing sulfurous vapors and heat. Ereben held his breath and jumped across, followed by Chrysanthus. He thought for a moment about the possibility that this tunnel might not lead to the surface, but it was their only option. They ran on, occasionally bracing against the tremor. As the air become more and more contaminated with dust and fumes, breathing grew more difficult. On they ran, for nearly a half hour. Hope appeared in the form of a dot of bright light ahead—daylight.

Rushing out into the blinding sunlight, Ereben turned to look at the fitful mountain. Jets of gray fumes sprayed from numerous places high on the slopes. Ereben and Chrysanthus had emerged on the north flank of the mountain at a higher elevation than the first entrance. Heavy fumes now gushed from the tunnel through which they had escaped. Chrysanthus tugged on Ereben's arm. They sprinted away from the mountain.

In the basin to the east of the mountain, Ereben now saw a group of mounted men heading toward the mountain's eastern slope. The horses seemed to be spooked by the tremors and fumes, but their riders wrestled to rein them forward.

Now a mile north of the mountain, Ereben watched as the top third of the mountain exploded to the East. He felt the tremendous jolt in the earth before the cloud appeared. The sound, when it arrived, was deafening. A swelling, swirling cloud of ash raced down the broken eastern face of the mountain. Horsemen in the basin below turned and fled until they were swept away in the voracious cloud. A vast gout of ash shot straight from the top of the mountain, climbing into the sky as an angry black storm, soaring to unimaginable height.

The basin containing the Cauldrons, with its mudpuppies, sulfur crabs and giant toads, vanished beneath the fatal ash cloud, which continued eastward until it had swept up the western flank of the Tooth of Time. The entire intervening valley was filled with opaque cloud.

Ereben and Chrysanthus had found shelter behind a low ridge, recognizing that a cloud such as that filling the valley to the East would snuff out their lives in a heartbeat, if it were to come their way. Despite that bit of luck, chunks of flaming rock rained down about them. Most were small, but a few were the size of a house. Wherever they landed, whatever their size, they ignited the surrounding brush. A thousand small fires sprouted everywhere, some merging to form larger fires.

The mountain exploded again, now spewing flame and black smoke from its devastated summit. Ereben had heard stories of volcanoes, but all were about the distant past. He had never imagined that earthquakes and volcanic eruptions could occur in his day.

"Grandpa, Sister Zaratha said that the Legion Dunes were north of here. Maybe we should head that way."

Chrysanthus stood, facing the ongoing devastation. His feline pupils widened. Ereben stood to see what could be more shocking than what they had already witnessed. There, below the low ridge, standing only a few yards from him, the Sarcoptis fixed its eyes on them. The red creature extended all six arms outward, lifted its thick head skyward and screamed a deafening challenge.

ๆ

One must know how one differs from a rock. This is the first step at the start of life. Then one must climb the strata of enlightenment. The final and most difficult step is to not only know what it is like to be a rock, but to once again become rock.

Ereben Leaf: Chronicle of the Counterspell

Ereben was frozen in place by the bellowing shriek of the Sarcoptis. Escape was impossible, and, even though they had both drawn their daggers, fighting the beast could have only one outcome. Even Chrysanthus, with his deadly steel claws, would be no match for the monster. A flaming boulder landed between Ereben and the Sarcoptis, but neither moved.

The Sarcoptis appeared to be made of the same material as the stone cube which Ereben held. It was true that the jadeite handled dagger cut sarcite as though it were flesh, but the material seemed otherwise as solid as stone. Yet the Sarcoptis moved and lived and threatened. But it did not attack. With a forlorn howl of apparent frustration, the fearsome creature leaped over Ereben and Chrysanthus, and continued to the North in a bounding gate punctuated by occasional leaps of prodigious height and distance.

Dendritic fingers of bright red magma crept their way from the summit of the awakened volcano. Fine, gray ash drifted down from a tormented sky and settle everywhere. Ereben took a quick bearing, then headed north, hopefully to the Legion Dunes.

Within minutes, the sky darkened to the point that Ereben found himself, as in their midnight flight from the Mohani in Whitewood, navigating by dead reckoning. This uncertainty was rendered more ominous by the knowledge that the Sarcoptis had fled in roughly the same direction.

The beast avoids our jadeite handled daggers. Or the sarcite we carry. Maybe it only appears to be dangerous, but does no harm. But someone went to a lot of trouble to prevent it from escaping. He pondered the fact that Crotus and the Knights of the Redeemer would never gain access to the sarcite mine. Nor would anyone else for a long, long time. The large cubes of sarcite that he and Chrysanthus carried had become more valuable and perhaps a target for the Knights, if they became aware of anyone possessing it.

By nightfall, they reached a wooded area that was free of ash. The westerly wind carried most of the ash over the Time Mountains, and probably out to sea. With any luck, Ereben thought, they would reach the Legion Dunes by tomorrow evening.

The transition from young pine forest to desert occurred over a zone of about a mile. Trees became sparser and more stunted. Beyond this, nothing grew. Fine, red sand extended in an undulating plane to the northern and western horizon. It was at this margin of the desert that they found the mangled remains of an animal. On closer inspection, it could be identified as a small woman. There were shreds of blood soaked, purple clothing scattered about. The flesh had been partly stripped from the bones. Some of the bones had been crushed by sharp teeth and the marrow consumed. Ereben detected no odor of decay.

"This is a fresh kill, Grandpa, but I don't see any tracks in the sand." He noticed that his own tracks quickly disappeared from the surface.

A hundred yards away, still at the margin of the red sands, they found an odd, stone dish—a basin large enough to hold several people inside. It contained two light, metal paddles. The stone barc seemed all the more bizarre resting at the edge of a desert. But it gave no indication of having been there very long.

A quarter moon rose in the East. With only a few hours of daylight remaining, Ereben was not comfortable about starting out into the desert. He walked onto the sand to judge how difficult it might be to walk upon. The surface tended to yield beneath his feet, allowing them to sink in a bit.

"This is going to be pretty exhausting, Grandpa."

Chrysanthus remained at the margin, examining the stone barc.

"If you stand still, your feet sink in." He trudged his way back. "Let's wait until morning." He looked out at the desert. "There do seem to be some dunes out there."

As he watched, the nearest dune appeared to move closer. About twenty yards from the edge, it rose into a low crest, then broke like a wave, scattering a spray of red sand. Waves of sand became more frequent and broke in higher waves. The margin of the desert crept slowly toward the forest. Chrysanthus ran to the stone barc and pulled it closer to the trees. The leopard-man looked up at the rising moon then back at the flowing red sand. Ereben understood.

"The tide of sand is rising with the moon."

A few hours after sunset, with the moon now overhead, the tide encroached about forty yards toward the forest. At its peak, yard high waves were common. As the night wore on, the tide ebbed and the dunes diminished.

When morning came, the desert lay quiet—a flat plain of red sand. The fragments of body had been swept away during the night. He assumed that it was the body of a Rock Gnome. It had seemed about the same size as Sister Zaratha and Brother Eretz Mor. The Sarcoptis was, of course, the most likely cause of the Gnome's death. Ereben could only wonder if the Sarcoptis was able to traverse the sea of dunes. *Maybe it sank.* He immediately dismissed the thought as overly optimistic.

Ereben and his grandfather pushed the stone barc into deeper sand, then hopped in with their precious load of sarcite. Ereben shoved them off with his blood locust staff. With one of them paddling on each side, the elongated craft handled easily, and glided silently over ripples of sand. They headed north, hoping to find some sign of the homes of Rock Gnomes. If not, Ereben knew they would eventually reach the grass plains of West Graze.

Several hours of paddling brought them no closer to a landmark of any kind. The monotony was almost unbearable. Ereben amused himself by counting how many little swells passed the barc between the larger, double-size swells. He was surprised at how regular that was. For every fifteen to eighteen small swells there was one double-size swell. He assumed the sand was very deep, though all he knew for certain was that the metal paddle in his hand cut deeply and easily into it, leaving a little swirl at the end of each stroke.

At mid-day, they reached a stone mesa. Its light brown strata stood only a few yards out of the red sand, but its width reached about a hundred yards. Its only distinctive feature was the partially eaten hand of a Rock Gnome. Ereben knew that this was a different Gnome from the first one they found, since both hands had been present. Somehow he and Chrysanthus were following the route taken by the Sarcoptis. He worried that if the beast reached a village of Rock Gnomes first, there would be no one left living when they arrived.

The prospect of being caught out on the open sand when the tide rose worried Ereben. He guessed that wind contributed little to the might of the sand swells, but that the lunar tide always resulted in high sands and greater danger to a small vessel on its surface. He wanted to be on something solid when the next tide came this evening.

A stiff wind came up suddenly, as a single dark cloud passed rapidly overhead. Several hundred yards out, it dumped an opaque sheet of rain. From the turbulent underbelly of the cloud, a twirling, gray finger dipped down into the sand and plucked up a dancing sand spout. The spout wandered about briefly, then dissipated into the rain.

It was late afternoon when he sighted another mesa. By then, the moon had lifted on the horizon. The sands had begun to raise a chop, and with it, a flinty, frictional scent. They hurried to the land, located a docking point, and tied up to a stone post. Ereben expected this mesa to be a simple flat table of stone. This one, however, hid in its center a pit, forty yards deep and nearly eighty yards across. The pit was clearly not a natural occurrence. Its edges were angular and cleanly dressed. On exploring its margin, Ereben located a stone stairway that descended to progressively deeper levels of carved stone chambers, all opening to the center. Some were workshops, others residence chambers, but every one was recently abandoned. He saw no blood nor sign of conflict.

Altogether, seven levels of chambers and open verandas had been sculpted out of the rock strata that comprised the mesa. Some balconies hung with carefully tended grape vines, but most of the cultivation had been accomplished in the flattened floor of the pit. In addition to fig and citron trees, there were fields of squash and beets, beans and cabbage, herbs and onions. Water trickled down a channel in one wall and was directed through a system of open canals to each part of the garden.

Ereben sensed that this village's inhabitants had hidden themselves, rather than fled. He placed his hands against the limestone wall, but before he could commune with the rock, Gnomes began to appear all about him, coming directly out of the rock.

The women were dressed like Sister Zaratha, in purple robes and each carrying a sickle under the cinch. The men wore brown robes. Children wore raggedy tan tunics. All of them seemed to already know the identities of Ereben and Chrysanthus.

"Come on into my office." A Gnome woman rushed Ereben and Chrysanthus up the steps and into a chamber that opened onto a balcony at the level below the uppermost ring of carved apartments. Along the way, others stepped aside deferentially. "I'm Sister Jenearla. I'm superintendent of the pot. Well, you've probably never heard that term. I'm like a commander of the town, except it's carved into the shape of a pot, so we don't call it a town, but a pot."

Ereben opened his mouth to speak, but Sister Jenearla continued. "It was a little hard for us to follow exactly what went on south of here, but we know a volcano came back to life. A red beast appeared right about then, and has been chasing our sandbarcs. It was here not long before you arrived. That's why you found us in the rock when you arrived."

"We've seen two bodies," Ereben interrupted, "two Gnome bodies to the South."

"They must be from a different pot. We'll let the others know." Sister Jenearla placed her hand against the stone wall by her seat. "We don't know much about the beast."

Ereben explained what he knew concerning the Sarcoptis, and what he had guessed. When he attempted to elaborate on other subjects, such as the Knights of the Redeemer and Holnick Firth, he was cut off by a peremptory, "We're aware of that."

Another sister entered. All the sisters bore a striking resemblance to one another, at least, he admitted to himself, he had difficulty telling them apart.

"Sister Lynfra," Jenearla said, "you can get the work details going again."

"Yes ma'am," the slightly stocky Gnome answered. She stepped out to the balcony and shouted, "Brother Jonath Win, your men can get back to the garden." She leaned her head back in. "Will you be here for supper?"

"Of course they will," Sister Jenearla replied irritably. She returned her attention to Ereben. "So, you think a little sarcite charm will scare away that beast?"

"I really don't know, but it might."

"Well, we'll see what our engineer can come up with."

A heavy set Gnome man entered, puffing the stub of a smoldering bundle of foul smelling, dried leaves. "Yeah?"

"Brother Ronal Leet, we do have guests," the superintendent said pointedly.

"Oh," he replied, looking at Ereben and Chrysanthus, then puffing out a cloud of white smoke. "You called me, Sister Jenearla?" He clearly found the formality a burden.

"Notify all the pots that two dead have been found to the South. One was definitely a woman. Also have them send couriers here to pick up something that can help defend against the red beast. Oh, and the beast is called the Sarcoptis.

"All of them?"

"All of them what?"

"You want me to notify *all* the pots?"

Sister Jenearla's reply consisted of an intensely impatient stare.

Brother Ronal Leet smacked his lips, rolled his eyes upward, puffed his smoldering leaves once more, then left. "All of them," he grumbled, shaking his head.

"He does good work," Sister Jenearla said apologetically. She touched the wall again.

So far as Ereben could determine, Sister Jenearla was able to communicate with, or at least summon, specific members of the pot by placing her hand on the stone wall beside her.

"It resonates throughout the pot," she said, as if reading his mind. "A different technique is used to read messages and stuff over really big distances."

Shortly, another sister, somewhat older, entered, at which Sister Jenearla stood. "Thank you for coming. This is Sister Diporta," she said of the older woman. She is acting Pot

Mother, during Mother Franearla's illness." Introduction of Ereben and Chrysanthus was unnecessary, since all the Gnomes seemed to already be familiar with them.

"Please come with me," Sister Diporta said, "to the meditation dome. We can attempt to understand what is happening elsewhere. With your presence, we should obtain a clearer picture."

They descended to the lowest level of the pot, then entered a domed chamber carved deeper into the hollowed mesa than the other chambers Ereben had seen.

"Sister Cherya," the interim matriarch said to a young woman at the entrance, "we'll need your help."

As they approached the central area of the chamber, enclosed by a circle of stone benches, Ereben became aware of the footfalls of all those present. The center of the floor resonated with the slightest impact, like the tightly stretched head of a drum, only this drum head was made of an exposed layer of slate. The five of them sat on the benches. When the three sisters removed their sandals and placed them on their benches, Sister Diporta indicated to Ereben that he should do the same with his boots.

"Chrysanthus," Diporta said, "you must not touch your claws to the stone." At her signal, they all held hands, forming a circle. "Close your eyes."

A light vibration carried through the slate floor to Ereben's feet. He could tell that it came from Sister Diporta's drumming her bare toes against the floor. Soon a counterpoint arose from his opposite side. *Sister Jenearla.* A third set of toes joined from the other side of the circle. *Sister Cherya.* The vibrations moved across the slate like ripples in a pond from three separate sources. Waves crossed each other, some amplifying, some canceling. The propagated waves and their patterns of reinforcement and interference then echoed from the edges back to the center, gaining in magnitude. An audible sound, a three part harmony of humming emanated from the stone floor and echoed within the dome. As its intensity rose, Ereben's eyes began to vibrate within his head, generating random phosphenes of sparkling light against his close eyelids. He realized that his toes as well were joining in the symphonic image.

He recognized patterns that appeared in his eyes. He was seeing the gossamer strands of connectedness ranging out into greater distance than he had imagined possible. But the perspective differed from what he could see with his dagger. Rather then being in the center looking outward, as had always been his experience, he saw from the view of stone, the simultaneous experience of all the continuous layers of bedrock and mountain crags, of river bottoms and stone temples, of islands and canyons. The common origin of all strands was stone. He saw hundreds of towering stone mesas of the Legion Dunes nearly drowned in an opaque sea of red sand.

Sister Zaratha sat within a hidden stone chamber at the bottom of the Great Canyon. Ice leopards yawned in the afternoon sun along the stone walls of a blind alcove high in the Broken Mountains. A golden dragon slept amid a huge pile of treasure within a stone cave far to the North. Beneath the pyramids of Shouda, in a subterranean city, he watched as tall, brown-skinned men solemnly placed the dead body of Ibrah Kadeef, Mufta Gebir of the Shouda, into a newly carved crypt. The images far beyond the touch of stone were too confined for him to interpret. But they were there. The Kasazi could be seen clearly in their cliff city, but the thick loam of the forests to the South and of Ternaria obscured it from him.

He could sense that the Rock Gnomes with whom he shared this vision were able to use his knowledge and recognition of places and people, and that of Chrysanthus, to fill out their own interpretation of what they saw. Within their more distant vision, he synthesized his own understanding of that which he was unable to see.

The blind priest, Crotus, had been assassinated by Holnick Firth. Firth now controlled a dragon, using a Sphere of Order, a pentalphic sphere. Its apices held sarcite stones.

The armies of the Three Kingdoms had conquered and enslaved the Dwarfs of Cinnabar, Zink and Easlan Brae. They moved against the Knights of the Redeemer in the hills of Knurlan.

But nowhere did he see a sign of Phaena or those who had vanished with her. Nor did he see Minkar Jarad or Barrow. "They are too far from stone," a voice said within his mind.

Ereben became aware that the sound had ceased. The vibrations of the slate floor had subsided. The strands of connectedness were no longer visible. But still he shared an afterglow of thoughts with those in the circle. Eventually, even that quieted to an imperceptible stillness. His hands dropped to his side.

After a quarter hour of exhausted silence and solitude, Ereben opened his eyes. Chrysanthus and the three sisters were there, seated, motionless. He drew in a deep breath and savored its coolness.

Supper was served communally, but divided into one dining hall for each of the four purely residential levels of the pot. Ereben and Chrysanthus thus dined on the level below Sister Jenearla's office. Two long, stone tables paralleled the curvature of the inner pot wall. Men were all seated facing the balcony, women with their backs to the balcony. Other than that, there seemed to be little formality. Men waited on the tables and apparently had prepared the meal of fresh and cooked vegetables and a smoked meat that Ereben was told came from a variety of sand serpent.

Conversation centered about the progressively more violent tides of the sands. Some present believed that it was not at all unusual, while others were certain that a dangerous trend could be detected. At the far end of Ereben's table, Sister Jenearla sat beside an empty head chair. The empty chair, Ereben was told, belonged to Mother Franearla, who had not been well for the past several months.

"If too much sand washes into the pot," brother Jonath Win was explaining to Ereben, "we just absorb it into the rock and it's gone."

"Easy for you to say," Sister Lynfra muttered in reply. "*We* have to do the work to get rid of it."

"Then show me how to do it," Jonath Win snapped.

"Huhh. You hardly get done what you're supposed to do."

The meaningless conversation droned on. No one asked Ereben about his journey or his past, since all the Rock Gnomes seemed to know most of it already. Chrysanthus sat at the table farthest from the balcony. Knowing that Chrysanthus could not reply, the Gnomes seated about him never stopped talking. Glancing back to his grandfather, who was seated only a couple of yards away, Ereben thought he detected a primal, animal expression of social agony. Ereben replied with a smile.

Chrysanthus and Ereben were invited to speak with Mother Franearla later that evening. When Ereben entered the bed chamber, accompanied by Sisters Jenearla and Diporta, he immediately sensed an acrid air of failing flesh. Mother Franearla lay propped on her bed amid cushions and quilts. Most of her hair was gone, and her tallowy skin, bruised in many placed, hung limply from her arms and skull. Despite her obvious state of deterioration, the Pot Mother smiled cheerfully. One of her yellowed and cracked teeth stood askew as a prelude to being shed, but she displayed considerably more teeth than one would expect for someone so old.

"You saw a pentalphic sphere in Holnick Firth's hands," the old woman said in a soft, hoarse voice. "We've discovered a drawing of one in the archives. Until now, we didn't know what it was for or what kind of stones went on it. Well, now we know.

It's not the sort of thing we would want to dabble with, but it might be important for you if you go up against Firth."

"What we see happening," Sister Jenearla added, "is that the Knights will have to fight the armies of the Three Kingdoms. Who knows which side will win, but either way, the winner's going to conquer as much territory as he can. You're going to have to fight one of them or both of them."

"The Banu Sulal enslave with irons and the whip," Mother Franearla croaked. "The Knights will enslave with magic. And we don't know what to think about the dragons. So we come to the question of how you wish to use the sarcite you have brought from the mines."

"Well, Mother Franearla, we need to send a portion to Maha Neruti at Moss Abbey—enough for two or three years. I think that would be a quarter of one of the two blocks of sarcite. That would allow enough time to find another source, or maybe mine it from the original mine."

"It might be years before that volcano calms down," Sister Jenearla commented.

"If we set aside the remainder of that block," Ereben asked, "would that be enough to make charms for all the pots?"

"I think so," Sister Diporta replied. "They would have to be small."

A stately, gray-haired Gnomish man entered. "Sorry I'm late, Mother. I just finished the new drawings." He held a broad sheet of paper covered with diagrams.

"This is Brother Richit Mor," Sister Diporta said with a smile. "He's our engineer."

"The two versions in the archive drawings," Richit Mor continued, "are of different size spheres. The diameter of the apex stones vary in direct proportion to the length of the structural legs. The best I can determine, the radius of a pentalphic sphere cancels out."

Mother Franearla sighed. "What would that mean if you said it in Valish?"

"The radius doesn't matter!" Richit Mor exclaimed. On seeing blank expressions on all the others present, he clarified, "I can make a pentalphic sphere of any convenient size. It doesn't have to be any particular size."

Ereben recalled the large, hungry sphere in the Sanctum of Moss Abbey. "I think its power is in proportion to its size."

"But the smaller it is," Richit Mor added, "the more mobile it is."

Ereben considered this, then positioned his hands as if holding a ball about a quarter yard in diameter. "This would be a good size."

Brother Richit Mor looked to Mother Franearla. She nodded. "Make it," she ordered.

"Yeah, it's only when they're away from stone that they get caught." Brother Ronal Leet continued to prepare the parcels containing tiny sarcite stones and written instructions for mounting them in a necklace. He lifted his smoldering leaf roll from its resting dish and drew out a puff of pungent smoke. Then, holding it with his teeth, he carefully tied another parcel. Speaking to Ereben around the leafy log between his teeth, he continued. "If there's any rock large enough, then they can just go into it. That Sarcoptis can pound on it with all six arms forever. They just wait 'til it goes away, then come out and do whatever they were doing before."

"So the Sarcoptis is north of here?"

"Yeah, quite a ways north. It's been to ten different pots that we know of, all north of here."

"Will someone from the other pots come here to pick these up?"

"Only from Katai and Muavi, since they're close. I'll have to carry the rest of these to Homigi. That's more central. The others'll pick 'em up from there."

"I don't even know the name of this pot." Ereben thought it odd that the subject had never come up.

"This is Katcha Pot."

"So, when do you leave?"

"Oh, maybe an hour. One of the other brothers has already left with that big chunk for Moss Abbey." A ragamuffin Gnomish boy in a tan tunic ran in, unannounced.

"What?" Brother Ronal Leet asked around his smoldering leaf log.

"Brother Richit Mor told me to find Ereben Leaf and bring him." The boy stood slightly taller than Ereben's knee. His eyes glowed with self-importance above an engaging smile. The boy took hold of Ereben's hand and tugged.

When Ereben stood, he found it rather uncomfortable to stoop low enough to be led by the hand, so he lifted the boy overhead, to screams of glee, and sat the giggling Gnome on his shoulders. "You just tell me which way to go."

Rather than telling Ereben which way to go, the almost weightless boy steered Ereben by the ears. "What's your name?"

"Palmer. I'm seven."

"Seven. That's pretty old."

"Yeah. I'm in first stratum."

"What is that?"

"In school."

"Hmmm. Why aren't you in school today?"

"Because its Silverday, silly. Nobody goes to school on Silverday."

"I guess I don't know about Silverday."

"You don't? Zincday, Tinday, Ironday, Golday, Copperday, Bronzeday, Brassday, Silverday, Steelday, Leadday."

"That's very good, Palmer."

"I can count to a hundred, almost."

"Do you have any brothers and sisters?"

"What do you mean?"

"You know, in your family."

"I don't know."

Ereben thought this odd. "Where do you live?"

"I live here, in Katcha Pot."

"Do you stay with your mother and father?"

"I stay with all the kids." He pointed to an area on the lowest level of the Pot. "Right there. You wanna see?"

"Isn't Brother Richit Mor waiting?"

"It's on the way."

Ereben was steered into a large chamber filled with children of all ages. They screamed and played and ran in every direction. Four adults patiently kept the dozens of children one step below pandemonium. Bunks three layers high were carved into the walls. When the Gnome children saw Palmer riding atop the tallest person they could imagine, they swarmed around Ereben's feet, begging to be given a ride.

"Maybe later," Ereben said. "I have to do something right now."

Palmer steered him out the door. "See. That's where I live. This is the school," he pointed out, as they passed an adjacent set of empty chambers. "And this is Brother Richit Mor's lab."

Ereben lifted the waif from his shoulders and lowered him to the ground. "Thank you for the tour, Palmer. Maybe some day I can show you some of the places I've lived." *The ones that haven't been destroyed.* He watched Palmer skip his way back to his home, dragging his fingertips along the classroom walls.

Entering the lab, Ereben found five men, whom he vaguely recognized from the dining hall, hunched over various projects at work benches. Some nodded in recognition, but all continued with their work. Through the doorway to a deeper chamber, he spotted Brother Richit Mor at a bench. He was surrounded by drawing tools and measuring rods and unidentifiable instruments. Before him on the bench sat a pentalphic sphere sculpted of filigreed silver metal. At many of its apices it held small, pentagonal-cut sarcites. From the inside angle of each apex, a single rod extended to a point in the center of the sphere where they all joined in a complex, twenty point star.

"Ah, Ereben," Richit Mor said. "I think I've worked out all the problems. It's made of a new metal that I call bauxium. It looks like silver, but will never tarnish, and is much stronger. It's also light." He handed it to Ereben.

The oddly decorative sphere felt much lighter than its appearance suggested. The filigree made it easy to hold with one hand. The back struts at each apex prevented even the slightest flexing. The apex stones were set so as to not protrude from the surrounding bauxium mountings. "What are these?" Ereben asked, pointing to peculiar hinges attached to only some of the back struts.

Richit Mor took the sphere and manipulated one of the hinges. "Each of these allows one of the apex stones to be swung into the interior of the sphere, breaking the attunement of its pentagon. Since each apex is shared by three pentagons, we only need five hinged stones to disable all twelve pentagonal fields. And this..." He held up a fine chain of bauxium links. "...will go around your neck and attach to the..." He inserted one finger to the center star. "...center of the sphere. And if you touch...here, all the hinged stones will spring into place."

"That is remarkable work," Ereben said, impressed by the intricacy of the design and the precision of the moving parts.

"It should be finished by tomorrow."

"Is there any way to test it to see if it works?" Ereben asked.

Brother Richit Mor rested the sphere on the work bench and turned to Ereben with a grave expression. "I am no worker of magic, Ereben Leaf. I am an engineer. I can tell you that a pentagon of sarcite establishes an attunement. I assume that the pentalphic solid will attune yet another dimension of nature, whatever that might be. And I have no desire to sample its power. It may be quite dangerous. It is sure to have capabilities that can only be discovered with time. The sisters may be willing to explore it."

"I have seen the power of the great sphere within the Sanctum of Moss Abbey," Ereben whispered, remembering its fearsome hunger. "It killed one of the monks, and nearly killed a second."

"Then you understand why I've designed this so you can disable it, and why I will test only the mechanics of its moving parts."

By the time Ereben and Chrysanthus, whom Ereben had insisted join him, had given at least two rides to each Gnomish child old enough to care, he could barely lift his arms. He wandered out to the garden and plopped onto a bench to rest and allow the ringing in his ears to subside. Brother Jonath Win leaned his scuffle hoe against the bench and sat beside him.

"They say there might be a war up north," Jonath Win said.

"I think it's already started. The army of the slavers has taken half of Knurlan, and the Knights of the Redeemer are trying to push them back."

"Which side are you going to fight on?"

"I'm afraid that we might have to fight against them both."

"Doesn't sound promising."

"I don't know. We've sent word to anybody that might help. With enough allies, we might have a chance."

"Hmmm."

Ereben laughed uncomfortably. "Whatever happens, there's going to be a lot of killing."

"What ever happened to diplomacy?"

"It's gone. Between religious zeal and greed and lust for power, there's no room any more for diplomacy."

"They say that magic is coming back."

"Magic has always been a part of the way things are. It's just that, once again, people who don't understand its effects are trying to use it."

"Do you understand its effects, Ereben Leaf?"

Ereben hesitated. "Each day I understand more, but not nearly enough. What will you do here? For protection, I mean."

"We don't get many visitors. Most people and animals can't cross the dune sea, except that Sarcoptis thing. Birds don't usually venture very far from the solid land. They saw a dragon over one of the pots a couple of decs ago."

"Decs?"

"A ten-day. Three decs in a month."

"What do you do if danger does show up at your pot?"

"We just hide in the stone. That Sarcoptis looked everywhere. You could tell that it could smell us—that we had been here moments before. But it got tired of looking and just gave up and went away." Brother Jonath Win pointed up to the pot rim. "They're ready, I think."

Ereben collected his belongings from the chamber in which he and Chrysanthus had stayed. He had divided the remaining sarcite with Chrysanthus. They each carried it in a pack. Ereben lifted Richit Mor's Gnomish Sphere and tethered it about his neck. The sphere itself was enclosed in a brown fabric purse, its drawstring pulled tight. Hobart's dagger was, of course, at his side. With the blood locust staff in hand, he climbed the stairs to the rim.

He had decided not to activate the Gnomish Sphere within the crowded pot. When he was alone in an open place, he would explore its power.

At the top of the mesa, by the outer rim, Sister Jenearla organized a party of nineteen other sisters, armed as always with sickles. Each carried a rolled, fabric pack draped diagonally across one shoulder. A stack of metal paddles stood nearby. Ereben saw none of the sandbarcs.

"We'll put one of you each in a sandbarc," Sister Jenearla said. "Those sandbarcs will have four sisters each." She indicated four sisters assigned to Ereben and four to Chrysanthus. "The six of you will take the third sandbarc, and the rest will be with me in the lead."

A sister emerged from the pot and ran to Sister Jenearla. She whispered a message.

"Gather everything and bring it back into the pot. Mother Franearla is dying."

In Mother Franearla's bed chamber, Sister Diporta sat on one side of the bed, holding the hand of the dying Rock Gnome Pot Mother. On the opposite side of the bed, sisters lined up to speak, one by one, to Mother Franearla. None of the brothers was present. When the Mother saw Ereben, she motioned weakly for him to come near. He approached.

Holding his hand, she drew him close and whispered in a breath of decay. "You must defeat the slavers of the Banu Sulal, and you must defeat the Knights of the Redeemer. Beyond, the danger will be greater. You alone have the ability to see it through." She weakly squeezed his hand, then waved him away, to continue her farewells to the sisters.

Ereben left the chamber and sought out Chrysanthus. He found him alone in a dining hall. Chrysanthus sat at a table, holding his dagger, his eyes closed. Ereben could sense that his grandfather was attempting to focus his awareness using the dagger. Although Ereben could not know the degree to which Chrysanthus could control his awareness, it was clear to him that the leopard-man's ability was greatly diminished. Chrysanthus lowered the dagger and turned to Ereben with an audible sigh.

Chrysanthus was attentive as Ereben recounted the words of Mother Franearla. "I'm not ready for this, Grandpa. I've studied what I could. But every time I touch magic in any way, I learn something, but I also disturb things that I failed to consider. I can't learn fast enough. If only there were someone who could teach me. Like arithmetic, there must be a proper sequence to learning magic. There must be rules to anticipate the counterspell."

Chrysanthus tugged open a pouch on Ereben's belt and extracted the tracing of the Glaive of Brenden. He unfolded it on the table.

"This is the order for learning magic?"

Chrysanthus then turned the drawing face down on the table.

"The other side is important!"

The Rock Gnomes were fairly pragmatic about their ritual transitions. Some simple words were said over Mother Franearla's body, then it was sealed within the stone of Katcha Pot. Following the funeral, Sister Diporta assumed the role of matriarch, with the new title of Mother Diporta and the responsibilities of Pot Mother. Sister Cherya assumed Diporta's former duties in meditation and intelligence.

Two hours after first assembling on the mesa, they once again prepared to leave. Sister Cherya, who had been among the original party, was now replaced, due to her important new duties. Sister Jenearla commanded the expedition.

When the party of six sisters assembled for the first sandbarc, they lined up parallel to the edge. In response to softly spoken words, the six sisters sank downward until they were just above the sand level. Then the stone under their feet shaped itself into a sandbarc with Sister Lynfra in charge. Within minutes, all four sandbarcs were under way, carrying Ereben, Chrysanthus and twenty armed Rock Gnomes, toward the northern border of the Legion Dunes.

The hand of death often chooses out of turn.

Malagari Proverb

"How dragon can find me?" Kozhdu asked, as Muldu worked the stern sweep of the dinghy, taking it back to the Kiriati, her two masts bare against the brilliant blue sky.

"Maybe it didn't even know you were there," Jasper replied. He had felt it. The one-eyed dragon had sought out someone at the shrine of the dove–maybe Kozhdu, maybe someone else. He couldn't tell.

"Nye, nye, Jasper. I poke out dragon eye at Angelsk. Is not luck dragon come to Malagaro. I am there only one time in my life. Dragon come. Is not luck. Is looking. One-eye dragon look for me. How he see me and I can not see him? He is much bigger."

"I don't know." Jasper had never seen the Orkahti chief so shaken. Muldu, on the other hand, had not said a word.

"What we do if dragon come to Kiriati? We have long way to be home."

"Jasper!" Pinkie Sweep called from the deck of the ship, as the small boat approached. "Did ye see that dragon an' the giant birds fightin' oop in the sky?"

"Yes," he replied. Jasper turned to Kuzhdu. "Should we tell them what happened?"

"Drago may come to Kiriati. Muldu, we tell them?"

The Master of the Kiriati nodded. "Everybody should know, Natiq."

"Da. Hard to tell lie," Kozhdu agreed. "Easy to tell truth. You tell them truth, Jasper."

"If the dragon looks for you, Natiq," Muldu added, "he finds the Kiriati. If he finds us at sea, we are dead. The big birds that chase him are no more. We are dead."

Jasper cast a bow rope to Kipik, who leaned over the rail. A rope ladder dropped.

"It flew o'er the ship three time!" Pinkie continued. "We thought wed all be roastet."

Kozhdu carried the stern rope with him, as he followed the others to the deck. "We sail now," he said to Muldu, "then we talk to everybody."

"Weigh anchor, and full sail," Muldu stated softly to Kipik, who then bellowed the orders to the crew.

Jasper, Cal and Dace shuffled along the deck, untying the main sail as they went. They then joined in hoisting the yard high on the mainmast, allowing the ribbed sail to fill in the wind. The Kiriati's crew had been delighted to encourage them.

As her sails began to catch wind, the Kiriati eased her way northward from Malagaro, toward Sulalian waters, but also toward its home port of Angelsk, on the north coast of Orkahtsk. The strait west of Malagaro carried a strong southward current that wished to send them further down the coast of the island, but the prevailing south wind easily overcame the stubborn current.

It was the clap of lightning that awakened Jasper. The Kiriati rolled and pitched violently. He stumbled his way to the ladder, and climbed to the deck. Muldu's crew were hastily trying to furl the sail on the mainmast, holding on for dear life with each wave that crashed over the deck and poured down the ladder way. Jasper tipped his head into the hatch, and shouted, "Everybody stay below!", then quickly covered the hatch with its cover, holding it in place with a tethered wedge of wood passed into a slot in its frame. He tugged his way toward the foremast along safety ropes that had been tied the length of the deck. Each time rushing water swept him off his feet, he held desperately to the rope, then stood, and continued forward.

Before the crew had brought down the main sail, a sickening snap of the mast brought it down on top of them. Jasper moved toward the foremast with more urgency, but had only come within a yard of it when it too snapped.

Daylight streamed into the hatch. Jasper, in his bunk, his clothes damp, pried open his eyes. *Just a dream!* He sat up. His head pounded; his body cried out with aches. Even his fingers hurt. He lay back down immediately, now confused.

"I begged the crew to not toss yer limp carcass o'er the rail." Finny Burnewin stood alongside the bunk, Pinky Sweep behind him.

"What happened?" Jasper asked.

Pinky smirked. "Ye yelled fer everybody to stay below, then they brought ye doon here, all loopy."

"A yard arm whacked yer head, my friend, but the sail kept ye from washin' away." Finny added.

"The storm?"

"O' course the storm." Pinky shook his head. "Loopy. You been senseless fer most o' the day."

Jasper slowly sat up again. A lump throbbed on the very top of his head. "Is the ship alright?"

"If havin' ne'er a mast is alright, then, yes." Finny looked more serious. "At least she's still afloat, as ye can see."

"Muldu say we're just adriftin' south in the current." Pinky mumbled. "He dinna know jus' where we are. So they put oot the small boat to tow us west, toward land. They got two crew with planks o' lumber to use fer paddles. I dunna see tha' wee boat helpin' much, to be honest."

"We huv to head back oop an' help wi' riggin' a jury mast." Finny leaned closer. "Ye ought to stay in yer bunk a bit langer, Jasper. I wudna wish to jump into tha' water to hoist ye oot, efterin ye topple o'er the rail."

Jasper accepted Finny's advice. As he slept, he was awakened by body aches each time he attempted to roll over. When bright light finally shone through the hatch again, after a fitful night, he went above deck.

The crew had rigged one downed yard arm as a jury foremast, which supported a partially unfurled sail close to the deck. The dinghy had been brought back on board. From the position of the morning sun, it was clear to Jasper that the Kiriati was heading southwest. Those not occupied seemed to be scanning a distant shore.

"Yer lookin' sturdier, young man." Liddie approached from aft. "Bless yer heart. Ye hed me worried."

"Where are we headed?"

"The'r lookin' for a forest wha' can supply two mast. The coast look mighty flat and mighty barren, bu' Kozhdu think yon blue mountain maybees is close enough to haul oot two well-trimmed trees."

"Does anyone know where we are?"

"Jes tha' we drifted well south o' Sulalia. Maister Muldu hes ne'er sailed so far south. All the ither boys seem eager to set foot on some solid earth. I suppose they've hed thir share o' sea life fer a while. I can say I've hed my share o' twelve raucous boys runnin' loose on a tiny ship."

Jasper placed his hands on Liddie's shoulders, and touched his forehead down to hers. He smiled, as he wept. She hugged him, and silently patted his back.

Thin, dark brown arms surrounded them both. Jasper looked up into the face of Bahsa Jarad. Bahsa's mouth twitched, then his lips parted.

In a hoarse whisper, he croaked, "Thank you Liddie. Thank you Jasper."

"Ye both may need some o' yer belongin' when ye go ashore." Liddie had ushered the two of them to her quarters. "No tellin' what danger lurks, or who may be waitin'. She untied a long bundle resting on her bunk, and lifted a golden, chain mail hood. "Bend yersel doon," she instructed Bahsa, "yer gettin' way too tall fer me arm." The hood fit him better than the last time Jasper had seen him wear it.

"The Chamberlain's armor," Bahsa rasped.

"An yer Bat Slayer." She strapped the dagger at his waist, its translucent red pommel stone dancing with light. "Ye remember this?" Liddie handed him a yard-long staff.

"Hobart's alderwood staff," he replied.

Jasper smiled at the details that Bahsa could recall. "My armor." He slipped into his steel chainmail shirt, now closer to a proper size, though still with room to spare. A wave of comfort surged over him, as he donned his golden helmet, and moved his short sword, Rat Slayer, over the chain mail. Finally, he draped his silver wolf cape on his shoulders, and tied it.

Liddie's iron mace remained on the bunk. "E'en a fool would think twice afore messin' wi' ye. Now go. An' Bahsa, dunna cut yersel wi' yer blade!"

Their first chore, after the small dinghy ferried everyone except a single crew member to the sandy beach—four people at a time—was to draw the bow rope of the Kiriati up the slope, until the ship was securely on the sand. This required over an hour of exertion, falling and slipping by the Orkahti horsemen, the other crew of the Kiriati, Liddie, and an assemblage of a dozen boys of various maturity.

"Back in the water, lads," a mud and sand-covered Liddie Burn commanded, when the task was done. Her filthy hair stood out in several directions. "Wash yer clothes and yersels, 'till ye sparkle. Sparkle! An' yer not tae come oot afore ye pass my inspection. Now!" She placed both hands on her generous hips, and lifted her chin.

The men present seemed equally intimidated by her command as the boys, and all immediately plunged into the surf. As they all scrubbed away the grime, beneath Liddie's unflinching gaze, a loud flapping of wings caused everyone to look up.

A giant peregrine falcon descended toward the beach, in wide circles. Liddie held her hand out at the men in the water, indicating that they were not to come out to retrieve their weapons. When the falcon landed in a flutter, at the crest of the beach, Barrow hopped down to the muddy sand. The Dwarf strode over to Liddie, leaving his golden battle-ax strapped to the bird.

"Yer a sight fer sore eyes, Liddie Burn."

"As are you, Whittig Trench." She absently tidied the mud and sand in her hair.

With a burst of deep laughter, Barrow snatched her in his arms, mud and all, and spun her around. The two of them then walked back up the slope of the beach, out of ear shot of Jasper, who was also overjoyed to see him. Now, he realized, Ereben and the others may finally learn where they are. And about losing Phaena to the Dryads. He knew not to intrude on their reunion.

By the time most had trudged, soaking wet, from the surf, Barrow and Liddie reappeared. Barrow briefly waved to Jasper and Bahsa, mounted the giant falcon, Pelegri, and lifted away to the west.

Liddie's facial expression indicated that there was bad news, and perhaps disappointment. "Yuv all done well wi' scrubbin'. Sparklin' e'ery one o' ye." She then ignored those who asked questions about the Dwarf visitor on the giant bird, and walked forlornly into the water to bathe.

Kozhdu dispatched his two fellow horsemen, Chigu and Kuyuk, to accompany Muldu and his crew in their trek to the distant forest, just barely visible in the west. The Kiriati would remained beached, until her new masts were installed.

When Liddie, now much cleaner, rejoined Kozhdu and the twelve boys, she located a suitable place for everyone to sit, then explained the current situation, as relayed by Barrow.

"The blind priest, Crotus, wi' his Kights o' the Redeemer, hes grown much stronger, an' has conquert much o' the west. The Sulalian forces huv mostly left the coast, and travelt into the Dwarf lands of Knurlan. The slavers have captured Cinnabar, Easlan Brae and Zink. Only thir slave sodgers an' a few officers now guard thir own cities o' Bur Nor, Almirant an' Dire.

"Barrow hed to fly away to recruit support from smaller tribes, fer a fearsome confrontation wi' both Crotus an' the slavers as well. Barrow feels it will be a close thing."

Finny Burnewin looked at Pinky Sweep, then asked, "What happent wi' the folks in Cinnabar?"

"No one knows, love," Liddie replied, a sadness sweeping over her. "I know both yer families are there... an' in Zink..." she glanced at Cal and Dace. "...an' in Easlan Brae." Her tender eyes settled on the twins, Slim and Lucky Chance. "We jes dunna know."

Bahsa, who alone had remained standing, pointed a lean, brown arm to the west. "Horsemen," he said audibly.

Everyone immediately stood to look. Approaching them from a half-mile away were three huge horses, each carrying an armored rider. As they neared, Jasper realized that the riders were not human, but instead were much larger, and with very small heads. Even closer, the beasts upon the giant horses seemed to have gray skin, and frightening facial features.

"Trolls," the freckle-faced Albian boy, Yaqut, said in a trembling voice.

ൟ

Even the weight of a gnat may sometimes tip the balance beam.

Phaena Cervona: Legacy of Man

Phaena listened silently and attentively to the grim news that Drusa brought. A great war was raging. Her home in Valand was now in the hands of the Knights of the Redeemer, while much of Knurlan had been conquered by the Sulalians.

She had no idea if Ereben was still alive, or where he might be. And her travel companions had vanished into Sulalian lands, with no word of their situation.

"What will we do?" Phaena now regarded herself as Dryad. Her tree, though injured, still lived.

"Most agree that it would be unwise to interfere." Drusa's shoulders shrank a bit. "There are so few of us, compared to the vast numbers in the warring armies. How could we make the slightest difference?"

"So we do nothing?"

"We observe. And we consider possible actions."

Phaena thought of her companions, all far away now, but all willing to commit themselves to what they believe is just. "I feel that I should help in some way."

"You are carrying a child. What could you do?"

"May I speak to the council regarding the war?"

Drusa lowered her head. "I will ask that they convene." With that, she stood and departed.

It was obvious to Phaena that her notions about the conflict differed from those of the other Dryads. She pressed her tunic against her belly, sensing a slight swelling with her fingertips. "Are you the child of an Orkahti sailor or the child of a kelpie? Will you have five fingers or three fingers? Or no fingers at all? I will try to love you."

Ellea Stentor sat on a higher step of the palaistra. Now Prime Dryad, following the death of Aldebith Gai, she presided over the council, gathered to hear Phaena address them regarding the current wars.

"I cannot speak of whom you love, beyond the bounds of our own land." Phaena drew a deep breath, to calm herself. "Nor can I speak of what things or events in the wider world are of importance to all Dryads. What I do know is that many of my friends and the people I love are scattered to the far corners, and a war that reaches so widely may endanger them. It eventually may directly endanger us here."

Ellea Stentor, visibly annoyed, interrupted her. "Thank you for your insights on...love. We have assembled here to decide. We all know of the present events, as well as their likely risk to Dryads. What is it that you wish us to decide, Phaena...Corban?" The Prime Dryad flashed an awkward smile.

Phaena hesitated at the implied attack. "I ask that the council dispatch a force of Dryads to aid in this struggle against evil. 'You must stand up.'"

Beneath the desiccated twigs of her shriveled brow, Ellea Stentor's face showed unrestrained contempt. "How facile a suggestion, while you yourself are pregnant with...perhaps a child. Would you propose risk to other Dryads, when you are exempt?"

"I, Phaena Cervona, pledge that I will join such a party, regardless of my personal limitations. I will train, and render myself worthy of your trust. 'Strength hides within weakness.'"

"I see." The Prime Dryad engaged in a whispered discussion with three of the oldest council members seated immediately below her on the steps within the palaistra. "I propose the council authorize, if there are no objections, that such a force of Dryads be formed, but with the following conditions. You must personally lead the force. It shall be comprised only those whom you are able to persuade to join. This will be your personal...project. Should you succeed in recruiting and training any willing Dryads, succeed in traveling to war...and should you return alive, then you will be expected to present a clear and detailed account of your endeavor to the council."

As Phaena sprinted around the running track, fine limestone crunching beneath her sandals, she became aware of another runner catching up to her. Phaena sprinted with renewed energy, motivated by the competition, but the other runner easily drew alongside her.

Drusa panted through a smile, then gasped, "I'll join your army." Drusa cruised ahead.

Phaena stopped abruptly, and stepped off the track. Drusa was now her first recruit. "Thank you!" She shouted across the palaistra infield.

For the past week, Phaena had spoken with nearly every Dryad old enough to fight, yet young enough to endure the rigors. Most had been kind enough to listen, but she had sensed only minimal interest from her sister Dryads. Drusa had seemed to be the least convinced of a need for Dryads to intervene in the war.

Now, some notion of a plan for what they were capable of achieving, and how they might train for it, slowly formed in her mind. They could never hope to present strength against greater strength. Her Dryad force, likely quite small, must turn their apparent weakness into its greatest strength. She needed to clarify in her own mind the ways in which their enemies' strengths of weapon and armor, and their superior numbers could be transformed into unexpected vulnerabilities.

ঌ৵

The framework within which we view the world will determine what aspects of reality we see and what aspects we fail to see.
Gumushtigin: Fundamentals of Conjecture (5th revision)

Jasper studied the three great trolls mounted upon colossal, white stallions. Despite their brutish physiques, they seemed to present a picture of calm reason and restrained curiosity. Their bronze helmets, each plumed with a white horsetail, covered a small, blockish head that seemed to rest directly on massive, armored shoulders. Gleaming bronze reflected the mid-morning sun from each torso. These warrior beasts carried spears longer than the Shouda spears, their bronze points held toward the sky. The horses too were armored, with drapes of white padding studded with bronze discs, and a sculpted bronze plate between the eyes and up over the top of the head. Each great hoof was obscured by a skirt of long, white, natural hair. The nearest beast prodded a sandaled foot into the flank of its horse. The horse stepped closer to Jasper and his companions. The bare legs of the beast glistened with sweat, rendering a marble-like appearance to the slate gray skin. Jasper shifted his golden helmet toward the back of his head so that it would not fall off, then bowed in the fashion of the Shouda. Beside him, Bahsa, as well as the ten other boys who had escaped the slavers, did the same.

"I am Jasper of Nilwid. Our ship lost its masts in a storm."

The mounted beasts looked silently from Jasper to his friends.

"I Kozhdu, of Orkahtsk," Kozhdu stated, moving to the front of the group. He pointed a yellow finger to each of the others, naming Liddie and each of the boys as he went. We look food and cover. We find two trees for ship mast." He gestured with his arms above his head. "Not know where this." He indicated the ground on which they stood.

"Timbul," the lead beast stated flatly.

"Not understand," Kozhdu replied.

The beast glanced toward its two companions, then shook its head. "You have come into the lands of the city of Timbul. Do you understand?"

"Yes," Kozhdu answered. "Good. We find food?"

"Four orcs, a Shouda, a Valander, an Albian, a Dwarfish woman and six Dwarfs. All the boys with Shouda manners, two of whom are fitted as warriors. What a strange party. As you might guess, we are Timbulians. Never has it been said that Timbul refused aid to those in distress."

"What sort o' distance might yer city be?" Liddie asked.

"The distance is less than a day." The Timbulian tossed a liquid-filled skin to Jasper. "Spring water. We will find food only in Timbul. We have tall pine trees, suitable for ship masts, to the west of Timbul."

Toward late afternoon, the rolling grasslands of Timbul gradually rose in elevation. Jasper walked carefully to avoid the occasional, chalky rocks that seemed to be spread randomly over the landscape. During their day of walking, Jasper had learned that the leader of this Timbulian patrol was named Timur, and that the patrols were composed of Timbul's citizens, who took turns of ten days as a warrior, once every year.

At the top of a rise, Timur halted his horse alongside his two fellow citizen guards, and waited for all of their guests to catch up. When Jasper reached them, he gasped with surprise at their first view of Timbul, still several miles away. On the highest ground this side of the haze of distant hills stood a collection of white buildings, each a different shape, but all similar in their peaked stone roofs and tall columns. Some were rectangular, some circular, but all spectacular. Jasper concluded that they were either deserted or very large, since he could discern no movement near them. Of the many buildings, three were distinctly larger than the others. Unlike the pyramids and spires of the Shouda shrine, these buildings seemed to have at least window openings. In the center of it all stood a bronze-armored, white statue of what, even from this distance, was obviously a Timbulian woman holding a bronze shield and a spear taller than the statue itself.

"Timbul," Timur stated with some pride.

"What is that big statue?" Jasper asked.

"That is Athimba, the city's goddess."

"Some of these brave souls put aside their safety, and risked their very lives, entering into the Three Kingdoms without the strength of military force, disadvantaged by their obvious appearance as outsiders, suspect and carefully watched by those who would bring their endeavor to an unhappy end, in order to free one young Shouda boy from the unconscionable slavery of the Banu Sulal." The crowd remained hushed. Gumushtigin paused to adjust his toga and, Jasper suspected, for dramatic effect after nearly a half-hour of oration. Jasper had met with the crafty general almost daily during the twenty days that they had resided in Timbul, awaiting the democratic decision as to whether or not they would be officially welcomed in this city of trolls. Gumushtigin surveyed the faces of the mass of Timbulian citizens gathered in the arena. "Allow me, citizens of Timbul, to tell you the remarkable tales of their lives, and how they came to confront our enemies."

"I call the vote!" a citizen shouted.

"I will temporarily relinquish the rod for a vote, only if I may continue my argument, should the vote be unfavorable." Gumushtigin turned his head toward Jasper and winked. He wore no armor here. No citizen, Jasper was informed, could enter the arena with weapon or armor during such a civic gathering. The general's only mark of office was the crimson border of his toga.

"Agreed," the citizen said, with a dismissive wave of his hand.

Gumushtigin turned to Jasper and his companions. "By the rules of the city, you must leave the arena before the citizens cast their vote."

Jasper followed his thirteen companions off the speaker's platform and out the open end of the arena. "What do you think will happen if they don't welcome us?"

"Bad not have only one man decide," Kozhdu mumbled. "One man make choice. Many men make no choice."

"I kinna imagine," Liddie said, "yon civil folk would do us harm, efterin nearly a month o' hospitable behavin'." She reclaimed her iron flail from the niche into which they had all placed their armor and weapons prior to entering the arena. "And we hed best be movin' homewart soon, what with all that stirrins tae the north."

"We wait for ship repair," Kozhdu said, "or pass into Sulalia," He pointed east. "...or walk long way around." He tossed his head toward the west.

"But Gumushtigin said they might send some cataphracts to come with us," Jasper reminded them. He had learned that the Timbulians called the armed, mounted trolls cataphracts. "I don't think we should wait for the ship. Muldu said another three or four weeks. Look at those mountains. He pointed at the misty blue peaks to the West. "I think we have to go through Sulalia."

The sound of thousands of voices rumbled from the direction of the arena. Soon, Timbulian men began to stream out, with Gumushtigin at their head.

"Good news," the general said with a toothy smile. He grasped Kozhdu's right hand between both of his massive paws.

"You are now honorary citizens of Timbul. You may stay as long as you like, and return whenever you wish. He grasped the hand and nodded to each of them. When he finally came to Liddie, though, he folded his hands. Squatting to look her in the eye, he said with equal cheer, "And you, Liddie, are now the guest of these honorary citizens."

"That is quite the honor," she replied.

General Nasrola, whom Jasper had met once before, walked past them without acknowledgment. He seemed to intentionally look the other way.

"Now the issue of an escort through the Three Kingdoms is still opposed by general Nasrola," Gumushtigin continued, gesturing to the older general, now beyond ear shot. "If, as you have reported, the armies of the Banu Sulal are in the Dwarfish lands, then there would be little risk in taking a small escort through their territory. It will come to a final vote in a week. In the mean time, Jasper, you must continue to attend the lectures of the Sippers. I'll see you there this afternoon." The general walked on into the city, lost in the rest of the citizenry.

"Sippers?" Liddie asked.

"Well, the Physicalists. That's what they call their school. It's kind of a nickname. They say it's because they take a sip of wine every now and then."

"Aye, I can imagine," Liddie said. "Perhaps if I should brew oop a batch o' barley-brei, they might consider makin' me an honorary citizen, in the stead o' just a friend o' a friend."

"No woman citizen," Kozhdu pointed out.

"Aye, I might huv guessed."

Jasper entered between the towering, fluted columns of the portico. The Physicalist school met within the rooms of a circular, marble edifice. Its entry split immediately into a circle of hallway that surrounded the spacious, domed central space. Small chambers branched regularly from the outer wall of the hallway. He had come to the Sipper's meeting early, mostly to get away from Liddie Burn's grumbling.

The school seemed to be deserted. Somewhere far down the hallway he heard voices. As he approached, he could sense a conspiratorial tone, despite being unable to make out the words. Jasper slipped into the chamber closest to the one from which the voices came. Only when the volume rose could he make out what was being said by two distinct voices, one male and one female.

"...my fill...Nasrola...." the male voice said.

"...drastic...." the female voice replied.

"...must be done...tolerate that..."

"...timing..."

"...time is up...before...meeting."

"Yes, general."

With the last comment, Jasper recognized one of the two voices as that of general Gumushtigin. *A plot!* The troll city of Timbul seemed to hold more intrigue beneath its civilized surface than he had realized.

Jasper waited alone in the chamber until he could hear that dozens of members had arrived for the afternoon meeting. He slipped into the crowd.

Gumushtigin's insistence and attention were all that brought Jasper to these philosophical discussions. He usually understood little of the fine points that were being argued. Today they spoke of the senses, and whether anything really existed if one could not sense that it existed. Their consensus seemed to be that if you couldn't sense something, then it might exist or it might not exist, but you couldn't say which. But if you could sense it, then it must exist.

"Jasper of Nilwid," the lecturer said, bringing Jasper to full attentiveness, "can you give an example of something that might exist but nonetheless can not be sensed?"

The first thing that popped into Jasper's mind was, *a plot!* After a moment, he replied, "Magic."

Laughter rumbled through the domed, central space. Perfumed trolls in wrinkled togas elbowed each other and whispered to one another. Jasper felt warmth rising in his cheeks.

The lecturer tapped his speaker's rod against the stone arm of the speaker's chair. "Would you acknowledge a difference between what is imagined and what is real?" More laughter. The lecturer smiled indulgently. "We are currently focused on what may actually exists though can not be sensed."

Jasper carefully assembled a response in the style of the Sippers' debates. "Are you saying that magic can't exist just because you think it's imaginary?"

All faces in the audience turned to the lecturer. "Well put," he heard a nearby troll whisper.

"Indeed," the lecturer replied. "If magic is not imaginary, then it is at least thoroughly overlooked."

"What about the legend of the Sarcoptis?" one of the members asked.

"That is presumed to be merely legend." The lecturer pointed to Jasper and said to the audience, "I suspect from his expression that young Jasper is not familiar with that legend. Perhaps one of you could explain it...briefly."

General Gumushtigin, seated as a member of the audience, stood and cleared his throat. Other members rolled their eyes. "On occasion, I too can be brief." When the laughter died down, he began.

"Other than the mythology of the city goddess, Athimba, which is generally accepted to be purely myth, the legend of the Sarcoptis is the only instance of magic that appears in our so-called histories. In ancient times, according to the legend, a Timbulian resident named Sarcos—this is before the time of citizens and democracy—was caught stealing from the temple treasury. The punishment for theft from a temple was, in those days, to cut off one hand, in order to subject the offender to life-long humiliation. But the high-priestess of Athimba reported that in a vision, the goddess herself had come to her and forbidden amputation for any crime.

"So the rulers of the city employed a conjurer to solve the dilemma. The conjurer's solution was to use magic to cause Sarcos to grow more hands, and to thus be forced to live out his days unable to hide his humiliation. When the conjury was complete, Sarcos indeed had more hands. In fact, Sarcos now bore six arms and six hands, which he promptly used to kill his guards as well as the rulers of Timbul."

"What happened then?" Jasper asked.

"The conjurer somehow trapped Sarcos inside the center of a distant mountain—the Mountain Beyond Time. And there he remains, awaiting his freedom." Gumushtigin took his seat.

"So, everyone thinks this is imaginary?" Jasper asked.

The membership chuckled again. "Do you believe otherwise, Jasper?" the lecturer asked.

"I've seen dragons that were locked away beneath the Shouda shrine, and they were very real."

At this, the lecturer was unable to end the laughter and comments of the membership, despite his raps of the rod on the arm of his chair, so he dismissed the meeting with a smile and a shrug.

Jasper sat beside Kozhdu in the arena. As honorary citizens, they were permitted to attend, hear the discussions, and even participate if they chose, but were not able to vote. As the citizens gathered, a whisper spread through the crowd of trolls, punctuated by gasps and sidelong glances.

"Something happens," Kozhdu said to Jasper. "People not happy."

Jasper leaned to the nearest citizen and asked, "Has something happened?"

The troll looked at him silently, then whispered, "General Nasrola has died this morning. They say he died of age, but no one believes that. His serving woman has been taken to be questioned."

A shiver passed through Jasper. He knew exactly what happened. "General Nasrola has died," he whispered to Kozhdu.

After the citizenry had settled, general Gumushtigin rose and explained the need for a military escort to accompany Jasper and his companions back to Knurlan. He stated that the number of citizens needed for the escort would be reasonable, but that he had not yet determined the exact number, given the current uncertainties. Gumushtigin asked that they agree to this, and to allow him to determine the size of the force as he saw fit. He proposed the mission begin in five days. To Jasper's surprise, the citizens remained silent, rather than engaging in any sort of debate. The vote passed unanimously, if unenthusiastically.

"But you can't walk all that way," Jasper repeated. "It's just like a pony, only taller."

Liddie had said nothing during the quarter hour since being presented with the prospect of riding an immense Timbulian horse back to Knurlan. She stood motionless, her arms crossed beneath her bosom, while her companions encouraged and cajoled her.

"They're not much taller than the kelpies." Jasper was at the point of just letting her walk. "Are you ready to get up there, Bahsa?"

Just then, the ten other boys approached on ten nimble, Sulalian horses. Each boy carried a freshly made spear or lance. Some boys expertly guided their mounts by the reins, while the others simply clung to the mane. Jasper had been aware of the captured, Sulalian horses, but had decided on the far larger, Timbulian stallion.

The Shouda boy approached the head of the Timbulian horse beside Liddie. Leaning back, he reached up and scratched between its nostrils, while whispering at its ear. The horse whinnied, then awkwardly lowered itself to its knees. Bahsa offered a smug smile to Liddie, then pulled himself onto the saddle cloth.

"Ah, the weenies are wonders," Liddie mumbled as she mounted the kneeling horse. Bahsa slid back to the bags draped over its rump, to provide room for her leg to swing over.

Jasper and Kozhdu had each been provided with their own huge, Timbulian stallions, which had already been packed with their meager belongings. "Gumushtigin said our escort would come by here to get us." Jasper wore his armor and sword, and carried his carved staff.

"How many troll come with us?" Kozhdu asked.

"I don't know." Jasper was about to elaborate on his last conversation with the general when he was interrupted by a thunderous rumble from within the city. It sounded to Jasper like a thousand hooves striking the paving stones.

From around the nearest stone house, fully equipped cataphracts began to emerge in two columns. At their head rode general Gumushtigin in full panoply. Behind him, two standard bearers led their respective columns. As the general neared, the columns grew longer.

Jasper counted them by twos. Near the rear of one column rode Timur, the Timbulian who had first met them nearly a month earlier. He recalled that Timur should not be serving as a warrior for another year. *This is an army.* He sensed that Gumushtigin had more on his mind than simply escorting them to Knurlan. He wondered if this Timbulian campaign might be at the root of general Nasrola's assassination. He had heard nothing more of the interrogation of Nasrola's servant. "Eighty!" he called to Kozhdu over the rising noise. "He's brought eighty cataphracts." *More plotting!*

Gumushtigin surged ahead of his columns of cataphracts, and brought his massive stallion alongside Jasper. "Our cataphracts will remain behind your people, so you don't have to breathe the dust from their hooves. But I would be honored to ride alongside 'the One'."

"Do you believe that?" Jasper asked, as they all began to move eastward as a group.

"No. But the slaves of Sulalia will believe it when they see you, armed and armored, astride a Timbulian stallion, and leading the cataphracts. Their senses will tell them that it must be real."

Shouting arose from the columns of cataphracts. Some pointed to the sky. Far overhead, Jasper identified a dragon traveling to the northeast.

"The Sippers," Gumushtigin mumbled softly, "may need to...adjust...their assumptions."

ം

To defeat a great army, a leader must inspire its opponents one by one.

Ereben Leaf: Chronicle of the Counterspell

The four sandbarcs were merged into a single boulder at the northern margin of the dune sea. Grasslands of West Graze now separated Ereben from Valand to the North and Knurlan to the Northeast.

"We should try to avoid the Beddu," Sister Jenearla suggested. "They're ignorant and dangerous."

"Where do they live?" Ereben asked.

"They're nomads. They wander the grasses with their cattle."

"In what way are they dangerous?"

"Their minds are simple, and their tempers are short."

"Maybe they could help us."

"That's not likely," Jenearla answered. "They usually keep to themselves and are not very friendly to strangers."

Chrysanthus and Ereben, accompanied by their guard of twenty Rock Gnomes moved northward through the rolling hills of West Graze. Here, waves of grass seemed more like a sea than the red sands of the Legion Dunes. The swishing of knee-high grass lulled Ereben into a dreamy detachment, interrupted only occasionally by the complaints of the Gnomes. For them, the waist-high grass was as tedious as deep snow. On the rises, Ereben could see ten miles in every direction. Grass spread to the horizons.

When they stopped for the day, Ereben wandered far enough from the group so that he could be alone to explore the capabilities of the Gnomish Sphere. He removed the sphere from its bag. Late sun sparkled from hundreds of facets in the filigree.

Fire glinted within its sarcite apex stones. Carefully, he clicked the five hinged mounts into place. With the final stone in position, he held the sphere by its bauxium flourishes.

One thumb pressed against a single apex stone. The scene about him remained unchanged, but superimposed in his mind, he saw the now-familiar connecting strands. But they were unique. There were only a small number of these strands, and they appeared to be red, rather than the colorless strands he had experienced at other times. A single braided cord of strands reached from the sphere to a point far to the Southeast. Three other such braided cords reached out to the Northeast. One of these was much more intense than the others.

Ereben turned to face the southeast cord and focused his attention. In his mind he drew it toward him. With it, the landscape swept past his awareness. His vision moved across the Legion Dunes, over a great forest of pine and on into what he recognized as the ancient trees of Oldwood. At its terminus, Ereben looked into the surprised faces of the monks of Moss Abbey, as they ministered to the Sphere of Order in Moss Sanctum. Slowly, the monks registered recognition of the new presence and acknowledged Ereben. In his mind, he greeted them and shared knowledge of his success in obtaining sarcite for their use, and passed on his encounter with Gelith, the events at the Warded Mines, and the escape of the Sarcoptis. Somehow, the monks were already aware of the Sarcoptis. He bid them well and returned his awareness to West Graze.

Next, he explored the longest, weakest of the braided, gossamer cords. He passed the western mouth of the Great Canyon, across the Barrens of Knurlan and, after a great distance, crossed into an unfamiliar range of mountains, beyond anywhere he had ever been. There he sensed the broad face of a single old man in a black turban. The old man seemed stunned, as he held a wildly vibrating sphere. The sphere seemed to cause pain to the old man. Ereben sensed that he was overloading its resonance. Ereben backed away.

By now, Ereben guessed that he was seeing, in the braided cords, the nexus of power created by other pentalphic spheres. If that was true, he thought then the strongest cord might be the one Holnick Firth possessed. He avoided that cord for the moment and sought out the remaining one. It was the shortest of them, and the least structured. Its pattern of braiding underwent continuous change. Following it to the bank of Iron River, near the mouth of the Great Canyon, Ereben found himself witnessing the death of a deer, being disemboweled by the savage slashes of the Sarcoptis. The beast seemed to have no awareness of Ereben's presence. It tore apart its victim and consumed its flesh in great, bloody chunks. Ereben's presence retreated.

Seeing the Sarcoptis frightened him. But the knowledge of its location brought with it a measure of relief. He did not want to know where it was. He was comforted to know where it was not.

The location of Holnick Firth would be invaluable in the weeks to come. He considered the unfollowed cord. If he pursued it, then Firth would learn of Ereben's own location, and further, would discover the existence of the new Gnomish Sphere. Perhaps, he thought, it would be best to leave that last path for another time. Ereben removed his thumb from its apex stone. The paths vanished. Tension in his shoulders relaxed. His finger groped within the filigree sphere for the lever that would release the hinged mounts and disable the sphere. As his finger located the small cam, Ereben became aware of a presence. After a moment of confusion, he recognized the clean-shaven visage of Holnick Firth, unmistakably perplexed. Ereben pressed the cam. With a sharp click, Firth vanished.

Ereben replaced the cloth sack and tightened its drawstring. His hands trembled. In this brief period of activating the sphere, Firth had been able to locate him. It seemed to Ereben that Firth had not recognized him. *I'm nine years older!* He had hardly touched upon the abilities of the Gnomish Sphere, yet its dangers were already becoming obvious.

If, while it was activated, Firth held his own Valish Sphere, it would announce his location and possibly more.

Traveling with the Rock Gnomes, Ereben noted that they became progressively more irritable and argumentative the farther they strayed from solid rock. The grasslands of West Graze were nearly free of exposed rock. Only when they reached the Legion River, with its rocky cut into the rolling landscape, did they regain their familiar self-assured attitude. The crossing required a descent of a five yard cliff on the near side and a wade through shallow brown water where it spread over a granite shelf. On the far side, a stone alcove offered shade from the sun and a perfectly laid out spot to break for lunch and a short nap. As usual, when resting within reach of stone, the Gnomes posted no guard.

Once Ereben had eaten his lunch of smoked meat of some sort, he and Chrysanthus climbed the small cliff of the north bank. At the top, two yards from the river, stood a solitary girl, half again Ereben's height. Large eyes looked with curiosity on Ereben and Chrysanthus. Her broad forehead tapered to a square chin. Though her head was covered in a shoulder length beige scarf, her cleanly sculpted cheekbones and long, slightly hooked nose reflected youthful beauty. A full-length, beige robe fluttered gently in the afternoon breeze. Her left hand held a bundle of clothing. Her right hand steadied the tapered end of a massive club, which rested on the ground.

Chrysanthus lifted his right hand to his face with his thumb almost touching his nose and tipped his head downward. The girl leaned her cudgel against her left hand and returned Chrysanthus' gesture with her right hand. Ereben repeated the gesture. The girl acknowledged him as well.

"My name is Ereben Leaf and this is..."

The girl's face expressed discomfort. She took up her massive club, turned and walked away.

Chrysanthus followed her. Ereben went along. Again he wished that his grandfather could speak, that he could share his vast knowledge of places and customs. They followed the girl over a rise. Below stood a cluster of black tents, and beyond, a herd of very large, grazing cattle. About two dozen people moved about the encampment and among the cattle. As they neared the camp, the size of its inhabitants became clearer. The adults towered over Ereben at more than twice his height and more than twice his width at the shoulders.

A man in a dark brown robe stepped forward to meet them, his head covered in a brocaded, white keffiyeh, held in place with a black rope about the crown of his cask-shaped head. His generous, leathery face had been shaved smooth. Ereben saluted him in what he assumed was the Beddu manner.

The man laughed thunderously. "That is for women!" He pressed his palms together at his face and nodded. "This is for men." He turned to the girl. "Go."

Ereben blushed as he repeated the two handed gesture. "I am Ereben Leaf and this is my grandfather, Chrysanthus."

The giant studied Chrysanthus. "You have been a guest of the Beddu a long time ago. You have changed much, my friend."

"He can't speak," Ereben said.

"You are Chrysanthus grandson, Ereben Leaf?"

"Yes."

"I am Thom Na. You are welcome here."

"Thank you, Thom Na. We have come with a group of Rock Gnomes from the Legion Dunes." On seeing the giant's surprise, he added, "We left them by the river."

"The Tiny Ones seldom come into the Beddu lands. I will go to the river with you and greet them." Thom Na returned to his tent and came back holding a cudgel the size of Ereben. To Ereben's questioning look, he clarified that the Beddu always carry a weapon when leaving camp.

As they walked to the river, Ereben explained recent events, and expressed his hope that the Beddu might help in their confrontation with the Knights of the Redeemer.

"Two months ago these Knights entered Beddu lands. We had decided to let them pass through, until they slew two of our cattle. We killed one of the Knights and drove the others away. I do not know if these Knights sent a demon here as punishment, or if the demon came of its own. But it recently came into our camp."

"What happened?" Ereben knew he spoke of the Sarcoptis.

"We drove it out."

Ereben could believe that, given the great size and strength of the Beddu. "Was anyone hurt?"

"Ja No was terribly frightened. She is the girl who brought you to our camp. The demon came upon her by the river."

"How did she escape?" He wondered if she might be wearing a sarcite.

"She did not escape," Thom Na chuckled. "She drove it off with her weapon. It fled to our camp, where we gave it chase so that it would not attack our herd."

Ereben's respect for the martial prowess of the Beddu, even Beddu children, grew. "She did seem fearless."

"Fear is natural, but a proper response is only the result of training."

When they reached the river, the Gnomes were not there. Ereben looked up and down the river. "Sister Jenearla!" he called. He looked again into the alcove below where he stood.

The diminutive shape of the Gnomish military commander stepped smoothly out of the rock face. "You really could have said you were going somewhere."

"Sorry. We didn't know we were going to find the Beddu."

Sister Jenearla became alarmed. "Where are they?"

Thom Na stepped to the cliff edge. "They are here," he said in his sonorous voice. Sister Jenearla gave a perfunctory salute. Thom Na returned it courteously. "How many of you have come?"

"Come on out."

Nineteen more Rock Gnomes stepped into the alcove. None seemed happy to see the giant standing on the cliff above them. Only Sister Lynfra expressed her sentiment about them with a sarcastic, "Great!"

Walking back to the camp, Sister Jenearla spoke candidly with the giant. "It's no secret that we haven't gotten along in the past, Prince Thom Na, but we really have a situation here."

"Yes, sister, Ereben spoke of it."

"So we'll be passing right through, and will try to be no bother to you."

"I've asked Thom Na for their help," Ereben interjected.

Sister Jenearla frowned. "In what way?"

"I will discuss it with my people," Thom Na answered. "You will eat with us tonight. We will decide in the morning."

Ereben waited until midnight to sneak out of the camp with the Gnomish Sphere. He reasoned that Holnick Firth was unlikely to be using the Valish Sphere at that hour. West Graze offered him clear sky and a breezy chill. He walked through the tall grass until he was well beyond the sight of those Beddu watching the cattle. Seating himself on the ground, Ereben removed the sphere from its cover and activated it.

He placed his thumb on the same stone as before. Immediately, connections appeared to Moss Abbey, the unknown weak sphere to the far northeast, the Sarcoptis and the strong cord to Firth's Valish Sphere. His mind traveled the latter route to a location just west of Zink. He sensed no presence at that sphere. *Firth is not watching.*

He placed the same thumb on a different apex stone. This made no difference. Ereben expected that outcome, since the pentalphic sphere was completely symmetrical. Any single stone would hold the same attunement, regardless of which stone.

His next step was to touch both thumbs to different combinations of stones. This configuration resulted in a dramatic increase in the number of visible connections. Which connections appeared depended on the geometry between the two stones selected. One showed him the relationships between massive objects. Another, those of living organisms. Yet another, the balance of interactions among the tissues of nearby living things. One arrangement revealed magical objects. The number of unique geometries was large and impossible for him to remember. With each view of the connectedness of the way things are, Ereben recognized that the proper tensions and pressures within his mind could, if he chose, alter those relationships. He could envision the Dark Path, the Light Path and the Path of the Horizon. For now, he only observed.

Ereben added a finger. The connections multiplied in their number and complexity. Each arrangement of these three digits presented a significantly different image of existence, each so rich in subtle detail that he could not interpret what he saw with his mind. The multiplying complexity did not require Ereben to increase the intensity of his concentration. Rather, the sphere drew the concentration from him without his consent. He recalled the sphere at Moss Abbey sucking the life force from the monks. The Gnomish Sphere, with its sarcites intact, did not draw life force from him, but it did draw at his mind. He deactivated the sphere

“We will spare thirty Beddu to join your campaign against the Knights,” Prince Thom Na declared.

The sun had risen. The sisters were preparing to depart. Ereben was pleased and surprised at the number of Beddu giants who were joining them. He had quieted Sister Jenearla's concerns by relating how a single Beddu child had driven off the Sarcoptis with her cudgel.

"It just feels awkward, she admitted, "to have the Beddu men coming to fight while the women remain behind to tend their homes and cattle."

The giants emerged from their tents wearing brown robes, but with their white keffiyehs replaced by grass green. The Beddu wore no armor. Each carried a leather bag of provisions over the left shoulder and a man-sized cudgel in the right hand. Unlike the Rock Gnomes, who tended to walk in a column, by twos, the Beddu walked as a herd, with Prince Thom Na in the lead. Ereben suspected that the giants would not fare well against arrows and the like, but in melee, nothing could stand against them. They moved in long, weighty steps, holding their massive cudgels just off the ground—an unstoppable moving wall four yards high.

As the war party marched northeast through the grasslands of West Graze, the Beddu broke into song from time to time. Low, somber melodies drifted above still lower harmonies, accompanied by the rhythmic stomping of their bare feet, occasional banging together of cudgels, and the thumping of fists against resonant chests.

At night, the Beddu slept in the open, in a tight circle, head to toe, completely surrounding Ereben, Chrysanthus and the contingent of Rock Gnomes. The Gnomes, if judged by the snoring, seemed to sleep more soundly than on previous nights beyond the safety of rock. Ereben found the close quarters uncomfortable after traveling in the silence of Chrysanthus' company for so long a time. Now, unable to wander off at night to experiment with the Gnomish Sphere, Ereben discovered that he was glad to find an excuse for leaving it alone.

On the third day since being joined by the Beddu, they forded the Death River a mile above its mouth, and moved into Knurlan. All that Ereben knew for sure was that two large armies, the Knights and the Slavers, were at war, and that Holnick Firth had been near Zink when he had seen him through the Gnomish Sphere.

Keeping to the east bank of the Iron River, they marched north, so that they might approach Ironhole from the hills to its west. Ereben had discussed his strategy with Sisters Jenearla and Lynfra and with Prince Thom Na. They agreed that, with the war currently active in eastern Knurlan, Firth would not be prepared for an attack in his rear. It would be critical to prevent any news of their presence from reaching the main body of the Knights, so Ironhole would have to be taken by surprise and taken quickly. Then a small party would be dispatched north to Siller Hole to determine the strength of the Knights there.

When they reached the hills above Ironhole, Ereben found that the wooden tower had been replaced by a stone tower of about the same height. The town's wooden picket wall was as he remembered it. An hour of observation indicated that Ironhole was garrisoned by about fifty Knights. The single entrance, facing east, had been fortified with a substantial wooden gate manned by four guards armed with pikes. Guards that walked along the walls showed no sign of a heightened state of alert.

"We need to take care of a number of things," Ereben explained. "Most important, we need to seal the town so no one can get out. We have to get inside somehow, and before the Knights can respond. We have to take the tower. And we have to locate all the Knights and either kill or capture them."

"This will be difficult to do without being seen," Thom Na added.

"It looks like we could move in directly behind the tower," Ereben observed, "and maybe move along outside the wall to reach the gate."

"The Sisters could do that," Sister Jenearla said to Thom Na, "but it would be nice if some of your people were there to hold the gate."

Prince Thom Na's face brightened. "We will help some Sisters over the wall near the tower and wait for a distraction. Then the Beddu can move to the gate."

"Should we wait for dark?" Ereben asked.

"We can move about more easily in the dark," Thom Na answered, "but the Knights can escape more easily."

After more discussion, it was decided that twenty Beddu would watch the wall for any attempted escape, four would hold the gate and the remaining six Beddu would enter the town. All of the Rock Gnomes would be lifted over the wall near the tower, along with Ereben and Chrysanthus. Half the Gnomes would take the tower, the others would subdue the Knights. They would begin with three hours of daylight remaining.

Ereben walked out of the hills, the sun at his back directly toward the stone tower at the western edge of Ironhole. Sister Jenearla, nearly stepping on his heels, walked behind him. Even though the stone tower was new, the town was not. Ereben's memory of his last visit festered beneath his consciousness. He had come within a blink of being burned as a heretic.

Why, he wondered, if Firth wanted to acquire magic, hadn't the ambitious Knight pressed Ereben and Barrow for knowledge of spells and the location of artifacts. Was Holnick Firth ignorant of the existence of the Guardians of the Ruins? After all, he had held the last of the Guardians as well as the Grand Master of the Observers, and had intended to execute them as mere rebels. Or perhaps he knew, but believed that his own acquisitions of magic rendered them irrelevant.

Sister Jenearla and Ereben reached the wall, apparently without being noticed. He lifted the wiry little Gnome to his shoulders. She stood and hauled herself upward with a loop of twine, to where she could peer through a notch formed by the pointed tops of two adjacent pickets.

"Whoever is in charge here," Sister Jenearla said, after returning to the ground, "isn't very good at it. Must be some junior officer. All the guards on the wall are watching the people inside."

"They're probably more concerned about the Dwarfs inside the town," Ereben suggested.

Sister Jenearla signaled to the waiting Sisters, who then sprinted in a single line toward them. Ereben held his breath while the nineteen Gnomes made their way across one hundred yards of open grass. Anyone who bothered to look could not have missed it. When they had finally huddled against the picket wall, Sister Jenearla made her dispositions.

"Sister Lynfra, I want six of you hidden near the gate. Send three around that way..." She pointed north. "...and you take the other two this way. Get as close as you can to the gate without being seen. Don't let anybody get out while the giants get into position. Once they hold the gate, you'll have to decide whether or not to go inside. Go now."

Sister Lynfra selected five other sisters. Half went one way around the town, the others circled in the opposite direction. They held close to the picket wall.

"Ereben, you and I are going to hoist everybody else over the wall. Are you going to come in?"

"I don't think I can do much good out here."

Sister Jenearla climbed again onto Ereben's shoulders. One by one the sisters climbed over both of them and over the picket wall.

"I don't think we can pull you up here," Jenearla said.

"Go on over. I'll just go in with the giants."

Sister Jenearla pulled herself over the wall. "Wait 'til you hear a commotion, then signal the giants," she whispered.

Ereben had no idea what the Gnomes had in mind. A scratching sound caught his attention. Above him, half way up the outer face of the stone tower, he saw Chrysanthus slowly scaling the stones. The leopard-man passed between two openings and clawed his way over the top. His grandfather had listened to their planning, but could not, of course, explain his own intentions.

After a quarter hour of waiting patiently for some sign of a distraction, Ereben had no difficulty recognizing the moment when it arrived.

"The barracks is on fire!" a voice shouted.

Ereben signaled to the giant Beddu. A mob of giants, brown robes fluttering, stomped down from the hills. Ereben hoped that, amid the growing chaos in the town, no one would look their way. The Beddu covered the distance to the wall with amazing speed and a thunderous rumble of their bare feet against the turf. As they spread around the picket wall, Ereben followed a group of them to the gate.

The gate guards were the first to recognize the attack. They swung the solid gate closed, but before they could bar it, a giant lifted one hand and pushed the gate with such force that it broke away from its upper hinge and flew open, crushing one guard. The other guard plunged a pike into the giant's leg before a massive cudgel crushed the guard's chest. The giant entered, followed by five more giants, Ereben and the six hidden Gnomes. Four giants remained just outside the gate.

An officer shouted orders. One archer on the wall drew an arrow in his bow, but was snatched over the picket by a huge hand. From the plaza Ereben saw the heads of giants peering over the wall. About twenty black-uniformed guards assembled into a phalanx of pikemen thirty yards from the tower. Another, smaller group to their left formed into a body of archers. Behind them, the barracks burned. Men wielding long swords emerged individually and in pairs from the side streets. Some fell, screaming, as concealed Gnomes slashed at leg tendons with their sickles.

A giant toppled backwards, an arrow protruding from his eye. Seeing this, Thom Na became enraged. "Kill them all!"

Arrows flew at them like angry hornets. Most of the arrows that struck their easy targets were ignored by the raging

Beddu. No guards remained alive on the walls. When most of the disorganized guards had been crushed, strangled or slashed, the two formed bodies of men were ordered to retreat into the tower. They found their refuge barred from the inside.

Dwarfs began to gather at the edge of the plaza as the mayhem, directed exclusively at the Knights of the Redeemer, reached a crescendo. Archers were slain from behind by blood spattered Rock Gnomes. The Beddu plowed into the phalanx, enduring the defensive stabs of the horrified pikemen. One of these pikemen managed to escape the slaughter and flee to the town gate.

A frantic officer pounded on the tower door, demanding to be let in. His persistence was rewarded by the door opening only long enough to let him in, then latching behind him.

Ereben turned to the Dwarfs at the periphery. "Look for any soldiers that are hiding."

"Tha' wed be a pleasure," a dust-smudged miner replied. "Find the bastarts!" he shouted to his fellow townspeople.

Dwarfs ran through the streets, passing the word along and growing in number. The one guard that Ereben saw evicted from his hiding place had already been beaten to death by the time he was tossed into the street.

Ereben buckled his golden breastplate. It seemed better contoured to his chest than he remembered. Now that he wore his own dagger at his right hip, he had moved Hobart's dagger to the left hip. They had learned, from the officer, the only survivor of the battle, that Firth had killed the imprisoned monk, once his Valish Sphere was complete. Most of the magic library that Ereben had seen in the old wooden tower remained in the new stone tower.

The laird of the Goat's Teat Drinkerie was happy to be rid of the Knights, but nothing could convince her that the bearded man who had liberated Ironhole was the same teenage boy she had saved from the fire just a few months before.

With all the captured weapons, the Dwarfs of Ironhole were more than happy to arm themselves against anyone who would threaten their freedom. The town elders met and appointed a new baillie, a store keeper named Verik Dunn, who promptly took charge of his new troops.

The Rock Gnomes had wanted to burn the bodies of the dead soldiers. The Dwarfs suggested a mass burial pit. But Thom Na had insisted that each fallen soldier be buried individually and with respect. The giants had dug all the graves south of the town wall in less than an hour. With great sorrow, he buried the one dead Beddu alongside them.

Not a single Sister had sustained any injury during the fray. The giants, however, had presented much larger targets. Each of them had sustained at least two wounds, most more than that, though none were mortal, with the exception of the giant struck in the eye by an arrow. Sister Lynfra coordinated the healing work of the Sisters.

Once the town was secure and the fires dowsed, Ereben had sent Prince Thom Na and fourteen more of the Beddu with Sister Jenearla and half the Rock Gnomes north to Siller Hole. Chrysanthus, for reasons which he kept to himself, accompanied them. The captured officer had said that a bridge had been built across the Iron River west of Siller Hole. Thom Na and Jenearla were to go there as well. According to the prisoner, there was no regular garrison at Siller Hole.

The Sisters who remained in Ironhole passed the time by reshaping the inner and outer surfaces of the stone tower. They began by merging the separate stones, one by one, into a single piece of rock. Then they smoothed the surface to eliminate any trace of the seams between stones. As a final touch, they chamfered all of the edges of the openings, as well as the perimeter of the parapet. At night, they slept inside the tower, preferring the proximity of stone. In the five days before the return of the Siller Hole expedition, they succeeded in transforming a rather ordinary stone tower into a wondrous, sculpted monolith.

Each night, Ereben climbed to the open parapet to experiment with the Gnomish Sphere. One of the captured scrolls discussed the nature and use of a pentalphic sphere. Ereben had been able to translate only portions of its ancient Shadae script, but he understood enough of it to make substantial progress in controlling the Gnomish Sphere. Most importantly, he had learned how to block his presence from the view of other spheres, though doing so diminished its focus.

On the fifth day after the taking of Ironhole, the expedition to Siller Hole returned. With them came Yarnish Blen on horseback.

"Where's my grandfather?" Ereben asked.

Thom Na shrugged his thick shoulders. "He continued alone into the mountains, and did not return."

"You should have seen it, Ereben," Blen exclaimed. "I was being chased by a dozen Knights from Rippleton. When I reached the new bridge across the river, Chrysanthus was standing at its western end. After I passed him he made fearsome sounds that spooked the horses of the Knights, then sprinted back across the bridge. By the time the Knights had regained control of their horses and started onto the bridge, six giants lifted the eastern end from its pilings and tossed the entire bridge into the river, Knights and all. None of the Knights and none of their horses survived the frenzy of garfish that set upon them. After that, Chrysanthus ran off into the high mountains."

"And Siller Hole?"

"It's been deserted for some time," Sister Jenearla replied. "We found one Dwarf who said the silver had played out a few months ago."

"There's more news," Blen said. "Crotus has been assassinated by the Knights. Holnick Firth is now in control."

"Yes," Ereben replied. "I had heard that."

"Did you know that he commands ten thousand men against the Banu Sulal?"

"Ten thousand?" Ereben was shocked.

"And somehow he has trapped one of the dragons, and controls it. They say that it flies at the head of his army and spits fire at his enemies. The last I heard, he was moving against King Kalish near Cinnabar."

"We don't have a chance against ten thousand men," Ereben moaned.

"Minkar is rumored to be heading here from the Nether Reaches with a large force under the Nanish King."

"Minkar?"

"I was surprised to hear that myself. He went to Shouda to ask for their help, but I haven't heard what came of that."

"That still leaves us outnumbered ten to one," Sister Jenearla observed.

The sun stood several hours above the western horizon when Ereben ascended to the parapet. With four fingers touching apices in a masking configuration, he activated the Gnomish Sphere. By now, he had recognized that every additional apex stone that he touched simultaneously increased the sphere's demands on his physical and mental resources. Another consideration became apparent as well. Even though a larger sphere could focus more power along its selected paths, the number of simultaneous contacts that were possible with human hands decreased the larger the radius of the sphere. By his arbitrary choice of a size sphere that would be convenient to carry, he had instructed Brother Richit Mor to build the most powerful sphere that could be fully utilized by human hands. The masking configuration alone required him to spread the fingers of his left hand to their limit. Based on this, he doubted that it would be practical with a sphere much larger than his

Gnomish Sphere. He had sensed the greater power of Holnick Firth's Valish Sphere. *He probably can't mask it.*

Today, Ereben would test the limits of his ability. Eight stones had left him exhausted after his previous excursion. He placed an entire munu mushroom into his mouth and held it there with his teeth. Fingertip by fingertip, he increased the stone contacts to eight, flashing throbbing layers of attunement into his mind with each new stone that he touched. The munu sustained him. He touched a ninth apex. All became silent, without connections, without space. His mind explored the nothingness, finding no landmarks, no guideposts, only himself. Ereben's thought drifted to his lost gyre falcon, Titus. "I am coming," echoed in his awareness. The words came from a direction, but not a place. *Titus is alive!* It came from the North, without distance. A wave of exultation swept over him. He chose to think of Phaena, now only a slowly fading ache within his breast.

"I am trying," she replied from the East.

Phaena! He needed more. He needed to know where she was at that moment. He needed to see her, to touch her presence. Extending his remaining digit, Ereben made contact with a tenth apex stone.

A tide of thoughts engulfed him. Unfiltered, untuned and varying wildly in intensity, the thoughts of thousands, of millions of creatures flooded through him, of humans, faeries, animals, insects, fowl. The cognitions of every living thing. All overlapped and merged into an irresistible chaos, beyond hope of understanding.

The munu in his mouth melted to nothing. As the sphere tugged at his life, Ereben forced one finger from its stone and moved it to the hidden cam, deactivating the sphere.

What is a master, if his slaves reject enslavement?
Gumushtigin: The Liberation of Sulalia

Jasper felt uncomfortable thinking of the Timbulian cataphracts as *his* army, though he did regard his friends and the other boys as perhaps *his* army. Some of them, at least, actually believed the myth of 'the One.' Of course, Liddie and Kozhdu did not and would never consider him their leader. But they seemed content to allow him to symbolize that role. And Gumushtigin appeared to weigh that subterfuge as an advantage in possible encounters with forces of the Three Kingdoms of Sulalia.

For the first time in his life, Jasper sensed his own growing appreciation of the subtleties and complexities of social interactions, and the webs of myth by which leaders lead. He knew himself to be a novice at this. His exposure to the philosophical debates of the Sippers seemed to trigger a cascade of curiosity and insight within him.

Paradise City, their first destination, chosen by the Timbulian general, lay on the coast, to the northeast. The intervening swamp of the Muck River required them to travel instead directly east, until they reached the shallow hills near the sea. By the late afternoon, they had come within sight of that somewhat squalid community of freed slaves.

"Jasper, perhaps you and your young warriors should approach them directly, while Kozhdu and the cataphracts hold back, out of sight. If what you have told me about them is true, then we may be able to recruit a hundred willing soldiers to accompany us."

"Don't hold back too far away. They may be freed slaves, but they're also a pack of robbers and thieves."

Liddie volunteered to return to solid ground, and walk the remainder of the distance to Paradise City, in order, she claimed, to allow Bahsa to ride solo, alongside Jasper, on their Timbulian stallions.

Jasper and Bahsa, both in their armor, both with blades strapped at their hips, rode toward the western edge of the unfortified city. On a massive, white stallion, alongside Bahsa, and at the head of ten armed boys, mounted on twin columns of Sulalian horses, Jasper chose to be both a leader and a fraud.

He halted a distance from the westernmost structures, and waited for someone to notice them. Fifty men and women, armed with farm implements and some weapons emerged on foot. Running out after them, their leader, with a wagging brown braid swishing from his head, pushed through to the front of them. He carried a scimitar.

"Who comes?" the leader asked.

Jasper walked his stallion closer, while asking Finny Burnewin and Pinky Sweep, oldest of the other boys, and by right of seniority, the leaders of their respective columns, to wait. "Shirkuh, it's Jasper," he shouted. "Remember?"

Shirkuh, still winded from running, dropped his head briefly, handed his scimitar to someone, and walked forward. "I see you and your friends didn't get back home."

"That's a tale, alright, but we're planning to pass up through all of Sulalia, and free slaves."

"A noble cause. Your armor and weapon seem suitable, but your...troops are a little light on intimidation." He turned to go. "Best of luck to you, Jasper," he said over his shoulder.

Jasper drew Rat Slayer, and held it directly over his head. Thunder rumbled from behind him. Eighty Timbulian cataphracts appeared over the rise, and walked forward, toward Jasper.

Shirkuh spun around. “What is this?” he asked, his eyes wide.

“They are my allies. King Kalish took most of the Sulalian army to invade the Dwarf Lands.” He swung an arm toward Gumushtigin. “The general plans to move up through the Three Kingdoms, and free the cities.”

“The trolls?”

“Yes. Can you add a hundred fighters to our group?”

“The Sulalians are weak, and the trolls are helping you.” Shirkuh seemed dumbfounded. “So you really believe you’re ‘the One.’”

“I’ve never said that.”

“Camp here for the night, Jasper...what is your whole name again?”

“Jasper of Nilwid.”

“Your people camp here, and I will see who in the city is interested. You will know if anyone will go, in the morning. They won’t follow the boy named Jasper of Nilwid, but some just might follow ‘the One.’” As Shirkuh turned to leave, he stopped, placed both hands on his hips, and spun back around. He peered into Jasper’s face for a long moment, then returned to the city.

Gumushtigin and his cataphracts had been ready to depart for the swampy ride to Dire shortly after sunrise. Now, two hours later, even the boy soldiers were impatient to depart.

“Nae a hint o’ courage in the lot,” Finny grumbled, as he hoisted himself onto his Sulalian horse, at the head of his column of five.

Kozhdu sat silently on his Timbulian stallion. Jasper gestured to Liddie and Bahsa to go ahead and mount. He mounted his stallion beside them.

"It was a tenuous hope," General Gumushtigin said, coming alongside Jasper. "We should depart now, to make it beyond the swamp before darkness raises the pestilential insects."

Reluctantly, Jasper agreed. He motioned to his boys that they should follow, and turned his stallion northwest, heading for the trade road.

"Why the haste?" Shirkuh shouted, walking slowly and alone from the Paradise City. His scimitar was strapped to his back. He wore a padded helmet and padded armor, all quite tattered.

Jasper said the others should continue, while he wheeled his stallion, and approached Shirkuh. "One man on foot will slow everyone else."

"What does it matter? One man or a thousand?"

Before Jasper could reply, a single line of both men and women, all armed with a variety of implements, emerged from the ramshackle, western edge of Paradise City. The line continued, with no end in sight. By now the other boys, as well as the cataphracts had halted to watch the stream of volunteer foot soldiers.

After a quarter hour, Shirkuh had assembled five companies of soldiers into ranks and files. Each company numbered nearly two hundred souls, Jasper guessed. *What does it matter? One man or a thousand.* Four wagons, filled with supplies, were drawn out with a pair of donkeys each. Shirkuh turned toward Jasper, Kozhdu and Gumushtigin, spread his arms wide, and bowed. In response, the cataphracts clacked their gauntlets against their breast plates, and the boys simply cheered aloud.

Shirkuh placed his five companies, one after another, followed by the supply wagons, between the leading boys and the trailing cataphracts. The growing army now marched on, toward the unsuspecting—and recently diminished —defenders of Dire.

Jasper awoke confused. In a cloudless sky, the sun had risen a fist above the horizon. He found himself sprawled on the prickly stubble of prairie grass, nearly a yard from the silver wolf cape that he had spread beneath him when he first went to sleep. The night had been miserable, alternating between jabs from the uneven sod, and bites from swarming flies. At least the breeze had shifted to a westerly, finally situating him upwind from a sickening stench that wafted from the swamp surrounding the Muck River, only a hundred yards to the east. He felt that he had hardly slept, but forced himself to sit up. Most of the others nearby were busily packing their gear and readying their mounts. To the south, where a thousand foot soldiers from Paradise City had made camp, tendrils of smoke rose from a hundred small campfires.

"When thae flies wished tae bite me while I lay," Pinky Sweep said, squatting beside Jasper, "I points o'er toward yer carcass, an' tells 'em, 'Yon lad there be 'the One''. I hopes they werna much bother."

Jasper examined the bites on his arms and legs, then glanced at Pinky's. "It looks like they weren't too choosy."

"Aye." When the muscular Dwarf boy stood again, he reached an arm to Jasper, and hoisted him to his feet.

Within a quarter hour, the army was once again assembled, and following the trade road toward Dire. Dust from feet and hooves conveniently drifted eastward as they headed north. General Gumushtigin, now riding alongside Jasper, estimated that they would reach the city by late afternoon —too late in the day to consider initiating any military action.

The General raised an arm, a signal to halt the march. He pointed up the road. "I see people moving this way. Two miles."

Jasper saw nothing, but his eyes did not ride as high above the horseback as those of General Gumushtigin. "Are they soldiers?"

"Despite their distance, I see no glint of armor or weapons. They all appear to be on foot, several abreast. Perhaps you should move your army off the road. Perhaps to the west side." After a pause, Gumushtigin said softly, "Raise both of your arms, and swing them toward the west. They will follow."

Jasper turned partway around, then gave the signal that the general had suggested. He found it gratifying to see an entire army immediately follow his silent signal.

"You lead well, Jasper of Nilwid. Soon, you will not need the guidance of an aging general."

When those walking toward the army noticed the soldiers and cataphracts, the group slowly came to a stop, a quarter mile from Jasper. After what appeared to be a chaotic discussion, a single man slowly walked toward them, showing his hands empty of weapons.

"We are seeking shelter in Paradise City." The man briefly bowed his balding head, then turned pleading eyes to Gumushtigin. "Most are women and children. A few old men, like myself."

"How many of you are there?" Jasper asked.

"I don't know. We all left late in the day from Dire. We walked all night."

"Why did you leave your city?" Gumushtigin offered the old man a water skin.

The man drank greedily, then returned the skin. "A great, winged serpent came to Dire. It spewed flame. It burned parts of the city. Killed many people."

"And your soldiers?" the General asked.

"Ha. The officers hid in fear. From disgust, the slave soldiers slew all but one of them, who escaped north toward Almirant."

"Are the soldiers still there?" A swirl of ideas carried Jasper's imagination in several directions.

"They remain. But they are slaves with no master."

Jasper lifted the right sleeve of his steel chainmail shirt, revealing a brass band about his arm. "This is my army." He swept that arm toward the rear.

Tears came to the rheumy eyes of the old man, as he hesitantly slid up the right sleeve of his tunic, revealing his own mark of enslavement. "You are 'the One!'" He wept.

Smoke still rose from within the single, stone wall that surrounded the city of Dire, in the Kingdom of Jakar. From the slight rise to the south of the city, Jasper conferred with General Gumushtigin, Kozhdu, Liddie Burn, Shirkuh, who led the volunteer foot soldiers from Paradise City, as well as the two boy leaders, Finny Burnewin and Pinky Sweep. The hope of all of them was that, without officers, the slave soldiers would willingly join their campaign.

"Can we trust them to bring their weapons among us?" Gumushtigin asked. "And we know very little about the make-up of their forces. Do they have horse? Are there archers? Who should be left behind to garrison the city, should they all wish to depart or join us? He paused. "Should we allow armed men to depart as they might wish, possibly posing a threat to other areas of the kingdom, or even to the citizens and residents of Timbul?"

"I never thought of those things," Jasper admitted.

"When I wes a wee one," Finny Burnewin said, "Mither wed always allow her hazel switch tae be visible—aff in the distance o' course—whilst she spoke me in reasonable tone." "Tha' hed a way o' focusin' the mind."

"A fine tactic, I say." Liddie added.

Shirkuh burst out in laughter. "Mother's know!"

"I think, from a military standpoint," Gumushtigin clarified, "that would suggest that Jasper, Bahsa and perhaps Finny and Pinky's horsemen should go forward to speak before the city gate, while all the rest of us wait conspicuously on the rise." The general turned to look at each of the others in the conference, one by one, waiting for a nod of agreement.

"We should do this now," Jasper said, "and allow the soldiers in the town to think about it overnight."

The late afternoon sun cast long shadows of the riders on their horses, as they slowly approached the closed city gate. Looking back, Jasper was surprised at the ominous silhouettes of a thousand foot soldiers and eighty cataphracts assembled along the near horizon. *That's quite a hazel switch!*

"Who will speak with us?" Jasper called out toward the city gate. Smoke still rose from beyond the wall. He was certain that their arrival had been shouted throughout the city, even before his leaders' council. He hoped that the youth and small size of his lightly armed group would allay their fears.

One side of the huge wooden gate creaked open, allowing a single, uniformed soldier to exit, before immediately closing behind him. The man carried a bare scimitar in his left hand. As he neared, smudges of soot became visible on his face and hands and uniform, though his white turban appeared to be freshly wrapped from clean fabric.

He walked directly to Jasper, and held up the weapon with one hand at either end. He lowered his head.

"I am Jasper of Nilwid. I do not accept your surrender. I and my allies are freeing the slaves of the Banu Sulal. I want you and your fellow soldiers to join us." Jasper placed his hand in the middle of the scimitar blade, and lowered it. When the soldier looked up in surprise, Jasper lifted the right sleeve of his chainmail shirt, exposing the brass band.

"How can this be?"

Jasper pointed toward his small group of boys. "All of us were slaves. We now have one thousand men and women who have joined us from Paradise City, and eighty Timbulian cataphracts as our allies. We plan to march on Almirant. We heard about the dragon attacking yesterday. If you join us, you can keep your weapons. If anybody wants to leave Dire, but not join us, then they have to give up their weapon. And somebody has to stay to protect Dire."

The man was speechless. He looked about him, then back toward the town. Finally, he thanked Jasper for his mercy. "We will try to decide tonight. I know many will want to stay, and some will accept your offer." He bowed once, then walked back to the gate, now carrying his scimitar in his right hand.

The Timbulians had raised a small, fabric pavilion beneath which to meet with the leaders of Dire. Five of them came out, two hours after sunrise. The group consisted of one woman, who spoke for those residents of the city who wished to remain, one senior sergeant now in command of city defenses, and a sergeant each for archers, infantry and cavalry. All of them had been slaves.

The woman supported the slave military that would remain to protect them. Eight hundred soldiers would stay to man the walls against a return of the Sulalians. That number would barely staff the perimeter wall for three shifts. They would keep all their weapons.

Apparently all the inhabitants who had wished simply to leave the city had marched past Jasper's forces the previous morning, on their way to Paradise City. While there was no accounting for old men, skilled craftsmen or common laborers, the remainder of the military members, all slaves, were agreeable to joining the campaign against Almirant. These consisted of one hundred cavalry, with their Sulalian horses, six hundred well-drilled infantry, with their weapons, and three hundred archers. They also planned to bring a substantial baggage train, drawn by donkeys.

When the meeting ended, and the guests had returned to the city, Gumushtigin turned to Jasper. "That was not a negotiation of terms. It was a celebration. And your army grows."

During the two days they moved northward, sometimes along the coast, sometimes over the narrow strip of vegetation adjacent to long stretches of sand dunes, Jasper pondered the words of Muldu, in describing Almirant. *Almirant has never fallen in war. A thousand years.*

He recalled the colossal walls—three rings of them, and the uncountable towers. Even the vaguest idea of how they might approach such a challenge eluded his imagination. General Gumushtigin had so far mentioned nothing about it, but the Troll seemed as relaxed as he had been at the start of the campaign.

As the green sparkle of Almirant's rooftops in the afternoon sun became visible on the northern horizon, still many miles distant, Jasper addressed the issue with Gumushtigin, who had been riding alongside Jasper's stallion. "General, I've seen the three walls and the battlements of Almirant. Liddie and I wandered within two of the inner yards. Our ship's Master said that the city had never fallen in war for a thousand years. How can we conquer it with two thousand, half of them untrained?"

"Ah, Jasper. You don't understand what has already occurred." Gumushtigin rubbed his massive, gray chin. "I find no hope in myth or prophecy. But on occasion they imply a set of conditions which, if met, might allow the fruition of their fantasy."

"I'm not sure I understand what you just said. A prophecy or a legend might be a kind of 'if?'"

"Exactly! Very good, Jasper. Your time was well spent with the Sippers."

Jasper gave rein to his insight. "So *if* the ocean swelled up around a mountain, a fish might climb the summit. But the legend would just say a fish will climb a mountain." Jasper laughed at his own example.

"Indeed." The general laughed with him. "The legend here says a boy shall lead the slaves to freedom. But the *if*, the missing *if*, requires that Kalish ibn Sulal remove most of his army from the Three Kingdoms; that a suitable youth appear at the right time and place, and with the credibility of having been enslaved, yet is now free; that a convincing military force ally itself with that youth, and that political opposition to the use of that force be...absent."

"So, we're *making* the prophecy come true?"

"We are *encouraging* the prophecy to *be* true. The prophecy of 'the One' is our tool, to wield or to cast aside. If we allow the soldiers of Almirant—the *slave* soldiers of Almirant—to invoke their own myth, then Almirant will fall." He laughed again. "To you! After a thousand years."

Jasper still worried. The slave soldiers of Dire had attacked and killed their officers, following the destruction caused by the dragon. But one officer had escaped to Almirant. Having been warned, the city's military would be expecting an attack by rebellious slaves in Sulalian military uniforms. They would be prepared.

All of Jasper's forces revealed themselves at the crest of the elevation just south of the city, and halted in sight, still five hundred yards away from the outer wall and its southern gate. Jasper and his Guard, which is how he now referred to Bahsa and the ten other boys, separated from them, and moved closer to the wall. General Gumushtigin had advised that Jasper advance only another one hundred yards beyond the main force, in order to remain outside the range of the city's archers.

When Jasper reached his stopping point, he realized that he could never hope to be heard by anyone in the city, much less be seen clearly. After the other eleven boys agreed to venture closer, they moved to within about one hundred yards of the wall.

"Hallo the city!" Jasper shouted. After a moment, the clamor of voices inside the wall subsided. "Hallo the city of Almirant! I am Jasper of Nilwid. I and my companions..." He gestured to his Guard. "...were all enslaved. We are now free. We bring allies with us. The cataphracts of Timbul, the freed slaves of Paradise City, and the freed slave soldiers of Dire." The murmur of a thousand whispers echoed from the battlements. "If you wish to be free, then come and join..."

"Archers take aim!" The commanding voice was out of Jasper's sight.

"If you wish to be free, then come and join us now."

"Release!" the hidden voice ordered.

From the top of the outer wall, arrows arched toward Jasper and his Guard. He imagined a thousand arrows, yet only twenty or thirty were in the air, and those coming only from the most distant portions of the wall east and west of him. They all appeared to miss or fall short, as they thudded into the dry ground about his group.

Khumartakin, one of the three Orkahti boys, riding last in Pinky Sweep's column shouted, "Yaqut is hit!"

Jasper turned his head to see Yaqut, the freckle-faced Albian boy, who had vowed to follow Jasper anywhere, firmly gripping his home-made spear at the ready, face unflinching, as he slowly toppled sideways from his horse. A long arrow protruded from the center of his chest.

Jasper was about to order his party to retreat, but hesitated when a loud roar of voices rose from the outer wall of Almirant. No further arrows had been launched. A thrashing, uniformed man was then flung from the central parapet, dropping a dozens of yards to the well trodden earth outside the wall. Five others were tossed from the wall at dispersed locations. Then nothing but shouting and chaos could be heard coming from the city.

When Jasper looked back to Yaqut, he had not moved. Khumartakin knelt beside him, crying.

When the western gate of Almirant swung open, a single soldier walked out. The gate remained open, revealing a general confusion within. The soldier, unarmed, slowly walked to where Jasper sat on his stallion. Beneath his white turban, deep brown eyes rode above a thick, black mustache that reached to either side, ending in a broad, upward curl just beyond each angular cheekbone.

Without a gesture of deference or submission, the soldier began. "The officers of the Banu Sulal have been slain or are being hunted. Many of their administrators have been taken to the prison." There seemed to be no joy or pride in his demeanor. "It is an ugly thing to watch, when well disciplined soldiers overthrow their masters, Jasper of Nilwid. Many believe you are the boy of the legend."

"I've never claimed that." Jasper felt directly responsible for the deaths and the disruption within Almirant, as well as for the death of Yakut, who had blindly trusted him. "I'm sorry."

"I too am sorry. Freedom is a good thing," the soldier added, "but it brings its own horror in the making of it. Our leaders will meet tonight, to decide our destiny."

"What is your name."

"I am just one of five thousand disobedient soldiers." After glancing at the dead, freckle-faced boy nearby, he lowered his head, and returned to the city. He merged into the chaotic crowd within the wall, the gate remaining open for anyone to come or go.

"Of three kings of ibn Sulal dynasty, King Mustah, in Bur Nor, is more weak, no competent. That is reason King Kalish and King Fahnu leave King Mustah behind. For maintain order in all kingdoms, because they go out, wage war on Dwarfs."

A committee of formerly enslaved soldiers and some low-ranking civil administrators had come out from Almirant in the morning, to explain the current situation. They now sat in

General Gumushtigin's small, fabric pavilion, speaking with the General, Liddie, Kozhdu, Shirkuh, Jasper, and the new commanders of archers, cavalry and infantry from Dire.

"Will you send forces with us to liberate Bur Nor?" Gumushtigin asked.

The committee members looked toward the most senior soldier among their group. The middle-age sergeant thought for a moment. "King Mustah did not wish to feed the military from his own purse, so he deployed much of it to Dire and Almirant. Bur Nor is weak from its poor engineering, and now holds no more than six hundred infantry, archers and cavalry. Your present force might easily induce them to submit, even without besieging the city.

"A thousand infantry and archers can hold Almirant against any force. Most of us would choose to join an army of free men, to prevent King Kalish and King Fahnu from ever returning. Perhaps two hundred archers, hmmm...three hundred cavalry and two thousand infantry may join with you."

"The families of the slain officers have begged for them to be interred within the military graveyard to the west of Almirant." A petty administrator from the city had approached the General and Jasper.

Gumushtigin clenched his massive jaw, while considering the matter for a moment. "They have indeed fallen in battle." He looked at Jasper. "One other has fallen in the same battle."

"Yakut told me that he had no family," Jasper said, shrugging his shoulders.

"We will permit them to be buried there, and with suitable military honors. But before I will allow that, some of us will honor the death of a member of Jasper's Guard, an Albian boy, and bury him within the bounds of Almirant's military graveyard."

After Gumushtigin, Jasper and several of the other boys had offered their all too brief memories of Yakut to those at the graveside ceremony, his simply wrapped body was placed into the grave. Jasper leaned down, and positioned Yakut's home-made spear at the ready, over his right arm.

Eighty mounted Timbulian cataphracts opposite the grave banged a bronze gauntlet once against their bronze breastplates, holding the salute in a frozen pose. The others in attendance, nearly a thousand of them, both civilians and soldiers, spontaneously sang a song of mourning, a Sulalian dirge apparently known to them all.

While the cataphracts maintained their rigid salutes, each other individual in attendance approached the grave, and tossed in a handful of dirt, then departed.

"Last evening, I sent two women to Bur Nor," Shirkuh said to General Gumushtigin, as their massive military body began to assemble north of Almirant. "They would be allowed into the city without suspicion. I asked them to report the recent events privately to the most senior sergeant."

"Now they may have knowledge of our movement," Gumushtigin complained.

"No preparations can save Bur Nor, but perhaps a quiet insurrection may save lives, and prevent King Mustah from fleeing at our approach."

Jasper remembered clearly the narrow road through the mountain pass, down to Cinnabar. "If King Mustah made it to the road to Cinnabar, we wouldn't be able to catch him."

The matter weighed on Jasper's mind throughout the two tiring days to Bur Nor. He was surprised when the city first came into view. He could see, assembled outside the walls of Bur

Nor, much if not most of their military. Well to the front of that body rode a single, mounted soldier, waiting to talk with leaders of Jasper's oncoming forces. He guessed from the soldier's clothing that he was not an officer.

Jasper and his Guard rode to meet this lone soldier. None of the military from Bur Nor made any preparations for battle. They simply waited.

"My congratulations, Jasper of Nilwid. I must speak with you and your other leaders."

The soldier returned with Jasper and his Guard to Gumushtigin and the other leaders. There, he announced, "It is over. Bur Nor, and so all of the Three Kingdoms of Sulalia are free."

"And King Mustah?" Kozhdu asked.

"He learned of our plans, and attempted to escape, disguised as a woman. But he was captured, and brought back to the city. The few officers in Bur Nor have all been retained. As far as we have knowledge, no one made it to the road up Cinnabar Pass.

"Our own leaders prevailed upon the King to affix his royal mark to a Great Charter of Freedom. A new Council will rule, while the King serves only as the symbol of the new *Free* Kingdoms of Sulalia. He has assumed the new title of King Mustah Jubaili. His only hope is that his cousins will return from Knurlan, and restore him to power."

"That is still possible," Gumushtigin pointed out.

"It will not happen. *If* you will move your forces into Knurlan to confront King Kalish and King Fahnu, we will join you with one hundred archers, one hundred cavalry and three hundred infantry.

Jasper nodded to Gumushtigin. "That has been our plan," the general said, with relish.

Kozhdu turned to Gumushtigin. "General, I now return to Orkahtsk. This strong stallion?" He patted his huge Timbulian stallion on its flank.

"Consider it a gift, Kozhdu."

The Orkahti immediately mounted, and galloped off to the north.

Shirkuh, leader of the rebel slaves of Paradise City, smiled broadly, jumped up, and with his long braid of brown hair wagging from shoulder to shoulder, sprinted back to where all of Jasper's forces had been waiting. "We have won! King Mustah has been overthrown! You now stand in the *Free* Kingdoms of Sulalia!"

In retrospect, it was our grand alliance, our coming together against a common foe, that became the first steps of the mass migration, the beginning of a period now called the Great Wandering.

Ereben Leaf: Chronicle of the Counterspell

Morning came to Ironhole with the frightened screams of panicked Dwarfs running for the protection of any building available. Ereben looked out the window of his room above the Goat's Teat. Several giants stood motionless, looking up to the clear morning sky, their cudgels held ready.

"What's happened," Ereben called to one of the Beddu.

"A great bird was seen over the rooftops."

Titus! Ereben dressed quickly and ran into the dusty street. Seeing nothing in the sky, he ran toward the plaza. The stone tower would allow him to see to the horizon. Turning out of the side street, his heart filled with joy at the sight of Titus descending into the center of the plaza in a rush of air and dust. Chrysanthus rode on his shoulders. The Beddu were awed by the size of the bird, but approached Titus without hesitation.

"How did you find him, Grandpa?" He hugged Chrysanthus as soon as the leopard-man had dismounted.

Titus lowered his feathered head for Ereben to scratch it, then looked at an approaching giant with suspicion.

"It's alright, Titus," Ereben reassured the gyre falcon. "They're friends."

Thom Na greeted Chrysanthus with a two handed nod in the Beddu fashion. "You always amaze me, old friend."

Ereben sent Titus to wait atop the parapet. "We need to decide on some plans."

Sisters Jenearla and Lynfra had joined Thom Na in the plaza. "Sister Lynfra, find Yarnish Blen and have him meet us in the Baillie's office," Jenearla said.

Sister Lynfra smirked and grumbled a bit as she went to locate Blen. The rest of the leadership headed toward the stone tower, the ground level of which the newly appointed Baillie of Ironhole had selected as the perfect spot for the seat of his administration. Since the Gnomes had refashioned the stone into a monolith, the baillie had renamed it Ironhole Keep. The keep suited municipal purposes, with its jail cell on the second level, complete with a prisoner, the captured lieutenant of the Knights. In as much as the coming plans would affect the safety of Ironhole, Ereben wanted the baillie in on the discussion.

Thom Na, though able to squeeze through the door, could only fit below the ceiling by sitting on the floor with his knees in his chest. Once situated, his eyes dared anyone to comment on how absurd it appeared.

"Firth is moving east from Zink," Blen explained to those gathered within the Keep, "to catch the army of King Kalish before they reach Cinnabar Pass in their retreat. We want to engage Firth's forces from the rear while they're busy with the slavers."

"We don't have the strength yet," Ereben complained, "even if Minkar arrives with Nanish forces."

"I have some news that may interest you," Sister Jenearla interrupted. "We have learned that a rebel army has formed in the Three Kingdoms and has overthrown the government. There is one report, not yet confirmed, that this rebel army is pressing toward Cinnabar to confront the Sulalian King."

"Would they support us against the Knights?" Thom Na asked, "or would they join with the Knights to destroy the army of King Kalish?"

"We don't know," Jenearla said bluntly. "But we also have word that the Dwarf, Whittig Trench, has had some success in gaining an alliance with tribes to the South. We do know that both Kasazi and Mohani forces have crossed the Death River and are ascending the Great Canyon."

"How many of them?" Ereben asked.

"Well over two hundred," Jenearla replied. "And there is rumor that the Orcs are active as well, with a substantial army just across the mountains from Easlan Brae. That information is sketchy."

"If they all came together at once," Ereben said hopefully, "we might have a chance. We'd need to raise all the Dwarfs from Siller Hole to Zink."

"We might raise a hundert Dwarf," Verik Dunn added. The baillie seemed excited about the possibility of dealing a serious blow to the invaders.

Voices were raised in alarm from outside the Keep. Ereben opened the door to see what was happening. A great peregrine falcon had landed within the plaza. Down from its back hopped Barrow, smiling and waiving to the astonished Dwarfs of Ironhole.

"Barrow!" Ereben called, running out to greet him.

"Ereben Leaf?" the Dwarf asked, somewhat confused.

"Who else?" Ereben answered.

"Yer a wee bit aulder than ye have a right tae be." He grasped Ereben's arms. "Mither o' the gods, lad. What happent?"

"It's a long story. Come on in the Keep. We're making plans right now."

Barrow approached the stone Keep and studied it from base to parapet. "That's quite the rock."

"That's another long story."

They entered the Keep. Introductions were made. When Barrow was told of a hundred Dwarfs to be recruited, he seemed stunned.

"I would need tae raise a tax," Verik explained, "but I think that wed work."

"Hundert? Tax?" Barrow interrupted. "Nae disrespect, Baillie Dunn, but those Dwarfs have been kilt and burnt and what's worse, insultet by Redeemer Knights." He twirled the blade of his golden battle ax. "I swear tae round oop six hundert angry Dwarfs willin' tae be unpleasant fer free. I would need ten day, and nae tax."

"That appears a bit o' a stretch," the Baillie replied. In the subsequent, awkward silence, Verik Dunn eventually yielded to Barrow's unflinching stare. "Perhaps that could be done."

"Have you seen any dragons, Barrow?" Ereben asked.

"Aye. A number o' time. I present mysel as evidence that Pelegri can oot fly a dragon."

"Can we move on Zink in ten days?" Sister Jenearla asked. "We can't exactly go after Firth if we leave the Knights holding Zink."

Thom Na nodded, careful not to bang his head on the ceiling. "How many Knights in Zink?"

"Word came," the baillie explained, "that all those Knights have gone oot o' Zink tae fight yon slavers, with only about seventy sodgers remainin' fer garrison."

"How about if Zink retaks itsel?" Barrow proposed. "We can sneak weapons intae the city. If the Dwarfs o' Zink know that we're ootside, they'll tak the sodgers where they stand."

Before the meeting broke up, plans were made over the Baillie's map for troop movements and coordination. Barrow would inform the tribes coming from the South, then coordinate the assembling of the Dwarf army. Blen and Dunn would arrange the smuggling of arms into Zink. Ereben would fly north to rendezvous with Minkar and the Nanish force. With luck, all would converge at Zink in ten days.

After the meeting, Chrysanthus, Ereben, Yarnish and Barrow took their lunch at the Goat's Teat. Over a rich stew, served with the usual, vile barley-brei, they shared adventures and observations.

"She hes grown oop," Barrow said of Phaena. "She spent time with those Dryad witches from the island o' Parnoth. Her will is firm."

"Did she ask about me?" Ereben asked. His heart pounded as he attempted to sound casual.

"Aye, she did, lad." Barrow Grimaced. "Ye can hardly be calt *lad* now, can ye?"

The subject of Phaena slipped from the conversation. They commented on the lack of information about the Shouda, and the scant details about what the dragons were doing. After Barrow courteously handled a bit of outrageous flirting by the fat, young laird of the drinkerie, they all said their farewells and wished each other good fortune in the upcoming days.

Barrow departed on Pelegri. Chrysanthus and Ereben flew north on Titus.

From high above, Shouda City appeared deserted. Titus circled twice, spiraling downward. Ereben saw motion near one of the white stone guard houses.

"Silim!" he called out.

A Shouda guard, preparing to flee into the underground labyrinth, waited to watch the great bird land thirty yards away. Ereben hopped down from Titus and bowed in the Shouda fashion. The guard hesitantly returned the bow.

"Do you speak Valish?" Ereben asked.

"I speak small Valish," the Shouda man replied.

"Can you take this message to Otah Kadeef?" Ereben held out a folded note he had written before leaving Ironhole.

"I take Otah Kadeef. You stay?"

"No. I must go. Thank you, my friend." Ereben bowed again, then returned to Titus. Chrysanthus was no longer seated on the great gyre falcon. "Grandpa," he called, looking about.

In the distance, running rapidly up the trail into the Broken Mountains, Chrysanthus slowed, looked back at Ereben, then continued up the trail. Ereben watched his grandfather sprint upward until he could no longer distinguish his gray cloak from the shadows of the rocky trail.

Mounting Titus, Ereben took to the air. He decided to search for Minkar and the Nanish forces, then find Chrysanthus when he crossed the Broken Mountains on his return toward Knurlan. As he gained altitude, a great gray owl lifted from the western hills to join Titus in flight. Krey was easy enough to recognize, but only when the owl came closer was he certain that she bore no rider. Ereben recalled that Minkar had departed Liddie Burn's coo farm on Krey's shoulders, heading for the subterranean city of the Shouda, Lamblar. Krey accompanied him, just behind Titus' left wingtip.

Along the northeastern shore of Shouda Lake, movement caught Ereben's attention. It appeared to be a substantial, though surprisingly orderly herd of white animals. After studying the herd for while, he convinced himself that the animals carried riders. His only explanation was that this must be the Nanes.

Rather than fly to them directly, and risk frightening the animals, Ereben took the great birds to the ground south of the lake and waited a half hour for the riders to reach him. As they approached, the animals appeared to be some sort of antlered cow, though taller and leaner, and with short, snow-white fur. They rode ten abreast in groups roughly ten rows deep. Ereben guessed that there were about two hundred of them. *Only an army from a treeless, roadless wilderness would ride ten abreast.*

"Minkar!" Ereben shouted, when he recognized the only rider wearing brown fur.

Minkar Jarad looked curiously at Ereben, then at the two great birds stationed fifty yards away. Minkar spoke to a rider beside him who then ordered a rest. Both of them dismounted and approached Ereben.

Minkar bowed, then recognition flashed over his face. He laughed aloud and hugged Ereben. "I did not know you, Ereben Leaf."

"It's me," Ereben said. He seldom remembered how different he now appeared from when his friends had last seen him.

"You look much older. And the red beard!"

"Yes. I'll tell you about it when we have a chance."

"Have you found Bhasa?"

"Barrow has seen him and he is safe."

Minkar hesitated, apparently wanting more details. "Ereben Leaf, I present you Kevlinoor, King of the Nanes. This is my companion, Ereben Leaf."

The King extended a thick arm, clad in white fur. "Call me Kevi."

"I see you found Krey," Minkar said with a smile.

"She was somewhere nearby, and just joined me."

"The dragon frightened her, and I have not seen her for a long time."

"I saw the gyre falcon," Kevi said to Ereben, "but I didn't realize how huge it was until I saw it standing there." He pointed to Titus. "Gyre falcons live only in the northern reaches, but none that size. Do you ride it like Minkar rides the golden dragon?"

Ereben looked inquiringly at his Shouda friend. Minkar simply raised his eyebrows in response. "I guess we both have a lot to talk about, Minkar Jarad. Barrow said that you came up here to ask the Mufta Gebir for help."

Minkar frowned. "They are not interested."

"What did he say?"

"Minkar told me about it," Kevi interrupted. "They have a problem with magical stuff."

"The truth," Minkar clarified, "is that they can't accept that a Shouda would approve of magic. They feel that it violates their belief in Elloh, blessed be his name."

"Is it hard to ride one of those big birds?" Kevi seemed to be intentionally changing the subject.

"It's probably easier than riding your...whatever it is."

"They are caribou," Kevi laughed. "We breed them and train them."

"Well, Minkar, I sent a note to Otah Kadeef about our plans. I thought they would be helping."

"They will not," Minkar said emphatically. "Tell us what is happening."

Ereben summarized the current situation and recent events. "We hope to converge at Zink in nine days."

"How far is that?" Kevi asked.

Ereben drew a map in the dirt, pointing out the landmarks and mountains and difficult areas. "We're hoping not to have to take Zink. We're smuggling weapons into the city so the Dwarfs inside can take care of that."

"How strong is Crotus' army?" Kevi inquired.

"First of all," Ereben explained, "Crotus has been killed by Knights loyal to Holnick Firth. His army is about ten thousand..." He held up his hand to stave off their exclamations. "But he's moving against the army of the Three Kingdoms, to drive them out of Knurlan. We're hoping to attack his rear while he is engaged with the slavers. With all our allies, we should have a pretty good chance."

"It doesn't sound pretty good," Kevi commented.

"There's one other problem," Ereben continued. "Firth is controlling a dragon with a magical device."

"Which dragon?" Minkar asked with sudden concern on his face.

"No one's even thought about it. Can you tell them apart?"

"Oh, yes. They are each very different. Some would be our allies. Most would ignore us. Some are hateful and would see us all destroyed."

"I don't think we'll find out until we confront Firth." Ereben touched the bagged Gnomish Sphere that hung above his waist. "I have a...tool that may help us divert Firth's dragon." He knew that he had only used the sphere to see, never to control or alter, but he also knew that he would have to attempt to use its power if they were to win.

"We should start now," Kevi said, "if we're going to make it in nine days."

"If you choose to send your force ahead without you," Minkar suggested to the Nanish King, "you and I could ride the great owl together."

"Hmm," Kevi muttered, scratching his blond beard. "It's not a dragon, but it will do." He walked back to his men, gave some orders, then returned with his spear.

The Nanish force moved southward toward Shouda City under the leadership of one of its tribal chiefs. King Kevlinoor rode behind Minkar on the shoulders of Krey, while Ereben took to the air on Titus. Even though Titus and Krey were separated by fifty yards, Ereben could clearly hear Kevi's laughter and exclamations as the king experienced his first flight.

They left the Nanes behind as they flew toward Shouda City. Ereben could see Minkar pointing out the destroyed central pyramid, apparently recounting the great battle that had taken place below them. Minkar shouted at Ereben, then pointed toward the southernmost guard house, part way up the slope of the foothills from the city. A stream of Shouda warriors emerged in battle armor, all armed with spears. Ereben brought Titus down nearby.

He recognized Otah Kadeef and ran toward him. Otah's battle dress included the golden epaulets of the Chamberlain's armor, from the ruins of ancient Ephesia. Otah softened his stern expression and bowed courteously. Beside him, Menash and Amal Hidad bowed as well. Menash carried the Chamberlains golden shield and Amal wore the golden gauntlets. Ereben returned the courtesy of bowing. Otah Kadeef's eyebrows shot up, as the clarity of recognition seemed to sweep over him.

"Are you coming to fight alongside us?" Ereben asked, gesturing to the Nanish forces approaching from the plain of the city.

Otah Kadeef turned to see the two hundred mounted Nanes passing beyond the northern pinnacles. "Your message has shamed us. If all those about us are willing to fight against a tyranny that we dread as well, we *should* be at their side."

"I didn't intend to shame you," Ereben replied. "I didn't know 'till later, when I spoke with Minkar, that the Mufta Gebir had decided against it." The three Shouda warriors averted their eyes to the ground. Ereben turned to speak to Minkar and, only then, realized that Minkar had remained with Krey and, in fact was looking away from them.

"Ibrah Kadeef now dwells in the arms of Elloh," Amal Hidad said, gesturing upward with his arms. "Otah Kadeef is now Mufta Gebir of the Shouda."

"Forgive me," Ereben said spontaneously, though he vaguely recalled knowing that already. "I don't believe Minkar knows."

Otah looked uncomfortably at Amal Hidad, then said to Ereben, "Please tell your companion that I am glad to see him, and that when we return here, I will work to reverse the decision regarding him. For now, it must stand."

"I don't understand," Ereben said. He again looked back to Minkar.

"Yes," Otah added. "He will understand."

"I am Kevi," Kevlinoor said to Otah Kadeef, extending an arm.

"Oh," Ereben said, now aware that Kevi had been there all along. "This is Kevlinoor, King of the Nanes." He pointed a finger at Otah. "Otah Kadeef, Mufta Gebir of the Shouda, Amal

Hidad, Weapons Master, and Menash." They exchanged greetings.

"Ereben's friend," Kevi said, "has spoken fondly of Shouda, and has mentioned each of you with affection."

Otah nodded silently.

"I'm going to fly ahead and look for my grandfather." Ereben pointed to the ragged mountains. "He ran into the mountains this morning."

"It is good to see you, Ereben Leaf." Otah touched Ereben's shoulder. "We also will look for a lost grandfather as we march."

"How many warriors do you bring, Otah Kadeef?" Kevi asked.

"We have two thousand Shouda with us," Amal Hidad answered.

Ereben flew Titus in a zigzag up and down the northern face of the Broken Mountains. He was approaching the end of his second day of searching for Chrysanthus. Minkar flew Krey in a parallel pattern farther east. The head of the column of Shouda warriors would stop for the night below the Ledge of Leopards. Ereben would sleep with them tonight, as he had the previous night. He and Minkar had spent some time alone, discussing matters at length. At night, however, Minkar returned to camp with Kevi and the Nanes.

With a motion of his arm, Ereben signaled to Minkar that he was done searching for the day. Krey pulled away and descended the slope toward the Nanish column. Below Ereben, the Shouda were breaking into encampments.

As Ereben put Titus into a gradual spiral, he noticed movement to the West, on the northern extent of the Ledge. He swung toward it to investigate. From his current altitude, the movement seemed to be a heard of small animals moving toward the Shouda camp. A taste of bile rose in his throat at the thought of ice leopards attacking the unsuspecting Shouda. *There are so many of them!* He descended closer. The reality was more shocking. Scores of silver wolves, perhaps a hundred, were rushing toward the Shouda encampment.

Ereben dropped Titus into a steep dive toward the head of the wolf pack, hoping to turn their course. Jasper had spoken of the silver wolves. When Corban's Protectors had attacked Shouda City, they had controlled a great pack of silver wolves. No one had ever learned where the wolves had gone after the battle. Now he knew that they had not gone very far. Titus swooped into the leading edge of wolves. The wolves, in response, parted for the gyre falcon, then continued as before.

He considered trying to use the Gnomish Sphere to control the wolves, but was certain that he would not have enough time to figure it out. He pushed against Titus' neck and dove toward the Shouda. As he passed close overhead, he pointed behind and yelled, "Wolves!"

By the time the Shouda recognized the danger, the wolves were upon them. Several men fell to the wolves. Others, quicker with their spears, turned away the tide, killing many of the wolves in the process. Amal Hidad quickly formed up a defensive line to the West. The wolves circled above and attacked again, this time from the East. Three more Shouda fell.

As the light was fading, word propagated down the long, drawn-out column of Shouda to watch for the wolves. The weakest point, however, was the very head of the column. Only three or four warriors could stand abreast on the rocky trail. The deepening darkness was accompanied by a cacophony of howls and snarls on the Ledge of Leopards above them.

The sound changed. Amid terrific growls and roars and howls of pain, chaos had broken out within the ranks of the silver wolves. Wolves fled past the Shouda column on either side, where some fell to Shouda spears. The mayhem continued in the darkness for a quarter hour, then all fell silent.

Few Shouda slept that night, for fear of another attack, but none came. Some fires were started, lending a sense of greater security. From time to time throughout the night, a small cheer would erupt far down the column. Ereben assumed that an occasional stray wolf had been killed.

When morning came to the frosty slope, Ereben saw dead wolves scattered along both sides of the Shouda column. He and Otah Kadeef, together with Amal Hidad and Menash, cautiously climbed the trail up to the Ledge of Leopards. There, spread across the terrace, were the mangled bodies of wolves—dozens and dozens of them. The rocky soil was splashed with blood and entrails.

Otah Kadeef whispered one word. "Leopards."

Only two more Shouda had been killed the previous night, though about thirty had been injured. Six were not fit to continue, so Otah dispatched a group to return them, with the six bodies of the dead, to the subterranean city of Lamblar. The rest, still nearly two thousand, assembled and marched south onto the Ledge.

Amal stood just below the Ledge, instructing each twenty-one man squad to form up a wedge as soon as the trail widened, then to cross the width of the Ledge in that formation. Ereben offered to fly overhead, to provide a warning if leopards were sighted.

With enough altitude, Ereben gained a more accurate assessment of the wolf pack's size and the devastation wrought by the leopards—if leopards indeed were the cause. Wolf carcasses spread nearly a quarter mile in either direction on the Ledge. He found himself searching for his grandfather's body among those of the wolves.

Then leopards came, just before the leading squad reached the southern boundary of the Ledge, where the trail continues up to Punishment Pass. He spotted them springing through a rock defile. Ereben remembered climbing up that same defile. He had drawn a leopard into his dagger there. He and Minkar had continued into the blind canyon that served as the leopard's den. Now leopards, he counted over thirty, streamed down toward a wedge shaped phalanx of Shouda leading the crossing.

Ereben dove Titus toward the Shouda column. He would have time to reach them before the leopards arrived. He landed the gyre falcon in front of Menash, who held the tip of the first phalanx. Without dismounting, Ereben pointed with his dagger. "Thirty leopards!"

Otah Kadeef stepped from the back of the wedge and, using a hand signal, brought up the next phalanx just to their east. The third phalanx would not reach them in time to help deflect the initial assault. Each phalanx presented spears from each of its three sides—four points from the outer row and three from behind.

Before the leopards reached the Shouda, Ereben lifted Titus from the ground. What he saw shocked him more than if the leopards had attacked. At their lead, Chrysanthus sprinted. His grandfather had doffed his cloak. He wore only his baggy, gray trousers, his tail thrashing behind. Chrysanthus brought the leopards up short of the Shouda phalanx, turned them toward the South, and formed them into a column by twos, slowing them to a walk. Now thirty three ice leopards, led by the leopard-man, marched in the lead of the army.

After a moment of stunned silence, Otah Kadeef ordered his two thousand warriors to follow the leopards toward Punishment Pass. Two hundred white robed Nanish cavalry, mounted on white caribou, brought up the rear, with Minkar Jarad flying Krey in a broad circle above them.

❧

Seeking fulfillment of one's dearest dream may be a path to ruin.

Gumushtigin: Philosophical Meanderings

Thousands of freed slaves, both soldier and civilian, gathered in the morning sun, on a slope to the west of Bur Nor. Shirkuh had said their hope was to name a supreme leader of the Sulalian Free Army. It would be the first time that many of them had a voice in selecting any kind of leader.

From a distance, Jasper could sense an occasionally raucous debate during the two hours that the meeting continued, though he could not make out what was being said or argued. He had meanwhile been occupied with Gumushtigin in clarifying their military plans for the next few days, now that it had become clear that they would go on to confront High King Kalish ibn Sulal's forces, and those of his cousin, King Fahnu ibn Sulal, in Knurlan.

Although the meeting of freed slaves had apparently not yet concluded, Shirkuh approached the general's fabric pavilion.

"Tired o' the argy-bargy?" Liddie asked.

"It has been tedious," he admitted, "but I've come out to pose a proposition to the general and to Jasper. A majority of the soldiers feel that Jasper should be elected as their leader."

A cold fear came over Jasper, the very same feeling as years ago, when he had been caught stealing a neighbor's carrots.

"But," Shirkuh continued, "even though Jasper is an inspiring and clever young man, he lacks a notion of military tactics and strategy—legend aside."

"What is it that you propose," Gumushtigin asked.

"Soon, we hope to assemble a small, military council to consider such issues, but that may take weeks or even months to function well. There are no rules to guide us yet." After a long pause, he asked, "Would you, General, agree to advise Jasper and assist us in forming our council, until this war is finished?"

Jasper still was not sure that he felt comfortable about the matter. "I'm Valish, and not old enough to actually lead a whole army of Sulalians."

"We are in the Kingdoms of Sulalia, but many of the soldiers are Valanders as well as Albians and others, enslaved as boys."

Gumushtigin, resting his massive, gray head against his bronze breastplate, settled the matter with a single word, "Yes."

Liddie's weathered hand went to her mouth, her eyes wide.

The Free Sulalian Army had made camp in late afternoon on the small, grassy plateau just east of Cinnabar Pass, in the very spot at which Jasper and his companions had once been caught between the slavers and the Orkahti horsemen, while fleeing with Kozhdu's young daughter, Yava. Beneath a fabric pavilion, General Jasper sat with Liddie, his nine new captains, which included Shirkuh, and with his chief adviser, General Gumushtigin.

Lieutenants Pinky Sweep and Finny Burnewin finally returned with their seven other Guard troops from a reconnaissance down the western slope of the pass. They had spread from either side of the road on foot, to covertly examine the dispositions of King Kalish's army units about Cinnabar.

"We wudna stand a chance goin' doon Cinnabar Road," Finny announced. "Far too narrow, an' well protectet. None o' our group could mak it inside the walls o' Cinnabar, bu' around the cinnabar mine an' slaver camp, nae sentry seems tae be postet. Most o' King Kalish's sodgers be situated southwest o' town, an' ootside the walls."

"North o' the Pass road," Pinky chimed in, "all the land is too rough tae march doon. An nothin' tae look at there but the bare wall o' Knurlton. The Kings mustna see a risk from tha' direction."

Gumushtigin scratched his hairless, gray chin. "Do you believe that cavalry can descend through the hills above the mine?"

"Aye," Finny replied. "That be the only way in."

"Archers could mak it doon tae the north o' the road, an' assemble in good order tae support yer horse coming in at the mine," Pinky added. "But mind ye, all thae moth-riddlt tents oop close aside the mine, they harbor nae but poor slaves what work in the mine—half dead already. Dunna send yer arrows that way. Aim fer thae fancy, bright color tents, an' ye maybees could poke a hole in a officer or two."

"The King's forces must not be allowed to retreat into the city gate," Gumushtigin said, "or we will have a siege of many, many months."

With a full view of the slope of the cinnabar mine, and the Sulalian Quarter of the City of Cinnabar below him, Jasper studied the dispositions of King Kalish's units beyond to the west. The forces of King Fahnu appeared to be mixed among them, rather than a separate force. His silver wolf-skin cape over his shoulders, and the warmth of his Timbulian stallion against his legs, were just beginning to drive off the chill of having descended the mountains during the night.

"After the first arrows, our cavalry must drive directly through the Sulalian Quarter, to attain the city gate, before the King can move his forces." Gumushtigin's animated hands and arms duplicated his advice as he spoke. "As soon as our archers east of the city have spent their first batch of arrows on the Quarter, they must rush toward the gate in anticipation of our cavalry. Infantry will then sweep across the Quarter to a position southwest of the cavalry at the gate. Meanwhile, Shirkuh's force will have taken the King's force that flees from the Pass road."

Jasper clearly understood what Gumushtigin was saying, but was awed by the complexity of actual battle tactics. And the thought of the inevitable blood and death that it implied left him queasy. He had never felt more like a fraud. *General Jasper of Nilwid.* He realized that he was a mere symbol, of myth and of the reality of freedom achieved. But he now felt the crushing weight of being responsible, in a way, for the mass killing that was now about to begin.

"Signal the archers," Gumushtigin said softly.

Jasper raised his right arm high toward the north in a circling motion, ending with a closed fist drawn sharply to his side. As in a dream, the arrows of 600 archers lifted silently, like a flock of starlings, from just east of the city. Before they reached the height of their arch, more arrows, now more randomly released, rose to follow them. It was still the early hour after dawn.

As the initial volley began to drop into a wide portion of the tents and booths and barely awakening market streets of the Sulalian Quarter, avoiding the slave tents to their east, the screams began, soon intermixed with shouting and chaos.

After what felt to Jasper like an hour of horror, though in reality only a long moment, Gumushtigin said, "Signal the cavalry."

Rosie Burnewin stomped about the fallen benches and upturned tables on the blood-smeared ground floor of Mither's Corner, her inn in Knurlton. Her mood and her words alternated between horror and anger.

"Bless ye, dear," Liddie Burn said, encouraging her to calm down. Liddie handed her a mug of barley-brie. "Tak a sip o' this."

Mither Burnewin snatched the mug and gulped it down. “Anither, please, Liddie.” Finally she sat at a table with her son, Finny, Jasper, Bahsa and Pinky Sweep. She propped her elbows on the table, and covered here face with her hands. Without looking up, she said, “Ye look like a slaver, Finny, with tha’ hefty slaver sword an’ a crookt dagger at yer waist. Pinky as well.”

Abruptly, she placed her hands flat on the table, and looked directly at Pinky Sweep. Sadness shaped her face. “Pinky, lad, yer family...Yer mither an’ yer father huv both been kilt by thae slavers. An’ they stole away yer two weenie sisters. All are gone. Consider Finny yer brither, an’ this yer home.” More tears came to her eyes. She turned to Liddie. “My brither, Baillie o’ Cinnabar, an’ his wife, also huv perisht. Ther’ be nae need fer all such killin’ an’ destruction.”

A pair of free Sulalians clomped down the stairs with the dead body of yet another of King Kalish’s officers. Mither Burnewin paid them no attention.

Pinky Sweep surged to his feet, and ran out the door, immediately slamming into a huge, armored Troll. Without a word, Pinky turned and sprinted away.

General Gumushtigin dipped his head, as he entered the doorway from the courtyard. Rosie Burnewin, though much calmer than at their first meeting, still seemed to view the Troll with some alarm.

With a single hand, Gumushtigin pulled an empty bench toward where Jasper was seated. “The body of King Fahnu has been found among the tents, with an arrow in his back. Scouts report that King Kalish has halted his retreat at Easlan Brae, and formed his units about the city. Tomorrow we will march against them, depending on the reports of scouts sent out to the west.”

“Is ther’ somethin’ happenin’ west?” Finny asked.

“There is rumor from refugees that Holnick Firth may be moving this way with a large force.”

From the backs of their Timbulian stallions, Generals Gumushtigin and Jasper met with all of their nine captains, as well as Lieutenant Finny Burnewin, who was now in sole command of Jasper's Guard. Pinky Sweep had not been seen since he ran out of Mither's Corner. The Guard positioned itself close around the meeting.

They were gathered on a rise just south of Easlan Brae, while the body of the Free Sulalian Army remained hidden from eyes in the city by the contours of the land. The task that lay ahead would require thoughtful planning. Although King Kalish had suffered substantial losses at the Battle of Cinnabar, and the Free Army few, the High King was now aware of the threat, and appeared to be in a strong defensive position.

The moated and walled city of Easlan Brae stood snugly against the rugged range of mountain to its west, limiting any maneuver from that approach. To its east lay the rising end of the Easlan plain, closed at its northern and eastern margin by the mountains that separated it from the grassland plateau of Orkahtsk. Any units that Jasper placed to the east or north of Easlan Brae would have no reasonable path of retreat, should that be necessary.

"The city's moat and wall are well suited for defending against marauders," Gumushtigin explained, "but the outer, earthen wall is too high, compared to the inner wall, and too close. Fire could be cast into the city, along with a rain of arrows."

"Have we heard more about Holnick Firth's movements?" Jasper asked.

"The scouts never returned," Shirkuh stated. "I've sent two more toward Zink this morning."

"What dispositions do you propose, Jasper?" Gumushtigin asked.

Jasper felt cornered. He took a deep breath. "It's too late in the day today, so at dawn, we will move our units into position."

Gumushtigin smiled, gently nodded his massive head.

"We have to use archers near the top of the outer wall to begin," Jasper continued, feeling encouraged, "so they will need to be supported by infantry in key positions. Archers should occupy maybe half the circle of the wall, mostly to the southeast. That would mean infantry units to the southwest, south and southeast, with cavalry positioned behind them. Archers will attempt to burn the wooden door, then infantry will force the gate and go into the city. This afternoon, we will need to cut two or three trees to use to knock down the burned door.

"Since a lot of the infantry will have nothing to do, we should keep a quarter or more of it in reserve, behind the cavalry."

Gumushtigin's eyes brightened.

"We need to avoid damaging the city and the people trapped there by King Kalish." Jasper glanced at Slim and Lucky Chance as he said this. He knew they would worry for their family and friends. Jasper then turned to his captains, asking their opinions, one by one.

High peaks to the west reflected a brilliant light onto the dry grass of the plain—still sparkling with dew and the tiny, delicate webs of uncountable spiders stretched between blades. The sun had yet to clear the eastern range. Beneath a cloudless sky, all of the units of the Free Army of Sulalia marched through the chill to their designated positions.

Gumushtigin remained with Jasper and his Guard on a slight rise, in order to observe and control the movement playing out before them. Bahsa, now mounted alone on his stallion, since Liddie had remained in Cinnabar with Rosie Burnewin, was alongside. Eighty Timbulian cataphracts stood in reserve nearby. Jasper noticed for the first time that the visible colors of the turbans and other headgear worn by the various units were distinct from one another, creating the appearance of a stitched, homemade quilt spread over the space that separated him from the main gate of Easlan Brae.

"General!" a frantic voice called from behind them. When Jasper looked about, he saw an Albian man dressed in peasant clothes running desperately toward them. He was followed by a fantastical, six-armed beast that ran on two powerful legs. The beast easily overtook the Albian, and immediately tore the man's head from his shoulders. There the beast paused to allow blood from the man's severed head to drip onto its tongue, while the limp body crumpled to the grass. After casting the head aside, it lifted its face to the sky. At the moment the sun cleared the eastern mountains, and shone upon the beast's glowing red face, it spread all six arms widely, and bellowed a horrid shriek—revealing dozens of long, pointed teeth.

It was then that thousands of mounted Knights of the Redeemer, and uncountable ranks of pikemen first came into view on a distant rise. Gumushtigin readied his pike. The menagerie of animals carved around Jasper's staff began to stir. He drew Rat Slayer, its sarcite pommel stone sparkling in the dawn. Bahsa took Hobart's alderwood staff in his left hand, and drew his Bat Slayer, a smaller twin of Jasper's blade.

"We will be trapped between Kalish at Easlan Brae," Gumushtigin said, "and the advancing Knights. Signal all units to pass to the east of the city."

"But it's a blind valley." The gravity of their situation frightened Jasper.

"I am afraid it is the least worrisome of the two choices we have. We can regroup there and make further decisions."

Jasper waved his arms in the complex message.

"We should join my cataphracts."

All the units of the Free Sulalians began to slowly move in order, toward the east side of the city. The hideous beast then sprinted toward Jasper and his small group. They turned about to face it, their weapons ready, when it drew up short, hesitated for a moment, then ran away toward the rising slopes of the mountains to the west.

The Knights seemed to be advancing toward them rapidly, still several hundred yards from Jasper. And the Knights were now surely visible to the defenders of Easlan Brae as well. Jasper and his party turned away, quickly joining the cataphracts.

It was then that archers began to stream out through a port in the eastern walls of Easlan Brae. The numbers of them grew to well over a thousand. They slowly assembled along the northern bank of a dry creek bed.

Gumushtigin grumbled. "Kalish has seen the Knights, and will block us from the eastern valley. Clever move. Signal the units to halt, and form up where they now stand. Then have them turn about to face the Knights. We have been trapped."

Jasper gave the signals. When he looked again at the oncoming mass of Knights to the south, a huge dragon swooped low over them from the south, and close over Jasper's head, flying directly toward the city of Easlan Brae.

ঌ৹ও

The tip of a sword is only a prelude to what may follow.

Phaena Cervona: Legacy of Man

Phaena, with eleven sister Dryads, stood beside Kozhdu, who, with nearly three hundred Orkahti horsemen, watched a stream of archers pouring from a sally port in the eastern walls of Easlan Brae. Phaena's position at the edge of the plain east of the city could easily be seen from the walls of Easlan Brae, if anyone had gazed in that unlikely direction.

She had encountered the Orkahti chieftain unexpectedly, while passing through the mountains that separated Orkahtsk from the plain of Easlan Brae. Her now quite visible pregnancy did not concern her, although the occasionally steep descents had been, at times, trying. Kozhdu had urged her to be more considerate of her situation. But she and her sisters had continued to accompany the horsemen down the slopes and ravines.

To the south of them now, a large army in the field stood facing an oncoming enemy of knights and pikemen, and with the city and its archers apparently preventing their retreat. She was unable to identify the force south of the city's main gate, but it seemed to have been attacking the city, and its obviously Sulalian occupying force.

Before their departure from the islands, Phaena had heard news of the overthrow of the cities in the Three Kingdoms. She decided now that King Kalish must be within Easlan Brae, and the Sulalian rebel army had pursued him there. The knights and pikemen were, of course, the forces of Holnick Firth.

Between the two armies facing one another to the south, she spotted a group of huge horses carrying equally huge, armored riders. Among them were a dozen smaller horses with unusually small riders.

But as Phaena looked on, a dragon swooped low from the south, and over Easlan Brae, spewing gouts of flame into the city. Again and again it circled and dove, setting much of Easlan Brae ablaze.

The Dryads immediately descended into a dry creek bed nearby, and moved silently down its weed and brush-filled course. Its path took them directly in front of the lines of distracted Sulalian archers—some facing their enemy, while many seemed transfixed by the dragon.

When she heard a command shouted in Sulalian dialect, and at least some of the archers proceeded to nock their arrows, she gave a silent signal to her sisters. The nearest dozen archers collapsed to the dry grass, with necks broken. Phaena stabbed the archer in the next row with the point of her javelin, then threw it into an archer in the third rank. After lifting the bow and quiver of arrows from her initial victim, she saw that all of her sisters had done the same.

The ranks of archers scrambled in chaos, as more of them fell to arrows from the Dryads. By the time commanders had recognized the threat, and began to reorganize the archers to take aim at them, a thunderous roar of hoof beats from the east generated yet more chaos.

Hundreds of Orkahti horsemen swept across them, dropping swaths of unarmored and startled archers to the ground. The archers broke their ranks again, and fled toward the city's sally port, but were cut off by still more Orkahti horsemen.

As the archers of Kalish were being destroyed, nearly all of the units of the rebel army turned, and marched to the east of the city to take their place. The knights and pikemen continued to advance toward the main gait. At the same time, disorganized fragments of Sulalian cavalry and infantry began to flee from the city's main gate.

The knights and pikemen, as well as the dragon, fell upon them. In their panic, they were killed by the hundreds.

Phaena watched as the dragon suddenly lapsed into erratic flight and apparent confusion, ultimately landing at the far western edge of the plain, beneath low cliffs of the western mountains.

Somehow, she sensed within herself that Ereben was near, as well as Jasper and Bahsa. It was then that she first saw yet another massive army surging from the south toward the black-caped Knights of the Redeemer at the gate of the city.

Phaena pressed her robe against her swollen belly, and looked down. Tears welled up. She walked alone to sit on the bank of the dry creek bed, while the battle raged. "I know that you are a boy," she whispered to her womb. "I will name you Kehl Corban, for my father, and for Kehlibar, your kelpie father." She swallowed the bile that rose in her throat. "Will you be a good person? Will you even be a person at all?"

So it is true that the mass migrations of people from numerous races and unique nations, which later became known euphemistically as the Great Wandering, and which resulted in such widespread, sometimes catastrophic alterations in what we all had assumed to be the natural order of things, began not as emigration from adversity, but rather as an unprecedented alliance, united against a common foe.

Ereben Leaf: Chronicle of the Counterspell

Ereben watched as the dragon and Firth's Pikemen killed the Sulalians and civilian Dwarfs who were fleeing the flames of Easlan Brae. To his east, he identified other Sulalian forces that appeared to oppose those of Kalish as well as the Knights, but he did not fully understand who they might be. South of these "friendly" Sulalians, and separated from them by a hundred yards, stood a group of bronze-armored horsemen atop massive horses. A much smaller group of horsemen, numbering less than a dozen, accompanied them on horses of a more usual size.

He vaguely sensed that Jasper was there. Taking out his Gnomish sphere, he considered the impact of activating it while Firth himself, less than a few hundred yards away, appeared to be actively using his larger sphere, perhaps controlling the dragon or the Sarcoptis—maybe both. After deciding that at this stage of the encounter between their two armies, it could not make much of a difference, he activated his sphere.

With the click of the actuating link, he immediately saw Phaena, to the East of the "friendly" Sulalians. He had not expected her to be there at all. The evanescent filaments of connectedness seemed convoluted about her. They felt wrong—

unnatural. She seemed to be surrounded by Orc horsemen who paid her no attention.

In almost the same line of sight, in his strange vision of diaphanous connectedness, he located both Jasper and Bahsa much closer—among the nearer, bronze-armored horsemen. He forced the connections, to join those of the two boys with that of Phaena. *They should know the whereabouts of their companions.* He quickly disabled the sphere with the tip of his finger. He would need a safer and less chaotic moment to understand what he had sensed surrounding Phaena.

Firth's Knights surged northward to join with the right flank of his pikemen. This move left Jasper's group unable to safely move toward the "friendly" Sulalians. Soon, Jasper's horsemen cut southward, then swung toward the west of Easlan Brae.

The dragon! He placed a munu mushroom between his teeth, then re-activated his sphere. With all the power that he could muster, he attempted to wrest control of the dragon from Holnick Firth. Firth, startled by the conflicting commands to the dragon, redoubled his effort.

The dragon, disoriented and exhausted, winged away from the battle, and eventually settled on the ground below a cliff at the base of the western mountains, not far from Jasper's group.

Firth, still struggling against Ereben's interference, ordered his substantial body guard to accompany him closer to where the dragon had landed, and toward Jasper's group of horsemen. Ereben, with his own body of horsemen, followed.

Thirty Beddu Giants, armed only with their cudgels, bounded toward the dragon. Their robes fluttered wildly behind them. Ereben saw no sign of the twenty Rock Gnomes who had been beside them just moments before.

Archers of the "friendly" Sulalians launched a cloud of arrows into the ranks of Firth's pikemen. From Ereben's right, more than two hundred Kasazi and Mohani warriors, now moving as a single, allied force, plowed into the right flank of the Knights and pikemen, but were easily repulsed, with many of them killed.

Barrow ran toward Firth's increasingly disorganized units, with six hundred armed Dwarfs following close on his heels. As the Knights and pikemen turned about, and began to reassemble their order in proper ranks and files, to defend against the Dwarf onslaught, two hundred Nanes, mounted on their white caribou, together with two thousand Lamblari Shouda warriors on foot, rushed forward against them.

Ereben continued to close on Firth and his guard. On reaching within thirty yards of his adversary, he halted. Thirty three ice leopards, led by Chrysanthus, leaped into Firth's mounted guards, savagely slashing horses as well as guards, and throwing those horses still unharmed into a stampede of panic.

A deep rumble briefly drowned out the noise of battle. From forty yards above where the confused dragon lay, half of the cliff had suddenly sheered away, dropping enormous boulders onto the dragon. Rock Gnomes could now be seen at the fracture point, looking down.

The dragon screeched in agony, belching flame in random directions. A gout of flame surged toward Bahsa, but he raised his alderwood staff, and forced the flame skyward. With a forceful swing of the staff, to point directly at the dragon's head, the beast's fire was quenched.

Minkar Jarad, now alongside Ereben, called out in horror, "It is Graybeard! He is good! He is a victim!"

Graybeard, in a profoundly deep and mournful sob, spoke loud enough for all in the battle to hear. "Please help me!"

With the dragon's final words, Thom Na, Prince of the Beddu, brought his massive cudgel down onto the Graybeard's skull, crushing it.

Minkar touched Ereben's arm. "Our only hope of peace with the dragons has just perished."

Firth, frantic at the loss of his dragon, now used his sphere to force the Sarcoptis to return to the field, and attack Ereben. But when the six-armed beast neared Ereben, it would go no closer. By now, Ereben and Holnick Firth, both still mounted, were within five yards of one another.

The leader of the Knights of the Redeemer, and the source of so much suffering throughout the land, screamed. A group of bumblebees and wasps swarmed about his head, stinging him on the face. Firth released his sphere, while swatting at his face. The sphere dropped to the ground, fracturing one of its essential rods as it rolled away. Ereben immediately felt the absence of the opposing sphere, like the haunting silence following a storm.

The Sarcoptis appeared to sense it as well. It pivoted, and in three steps, knocked Holnick Firth from his terrified horse, pounced upon him, and simultaneously tore off both of his arms.

Ereben, with no munu mushrooms remaining, forced the Sarcoptis into immobility. Bahsa jumped from his Timbulian stallion, ran directly to the Sarcoptis, and struck it with his alderwood staff. The beast was immediately frozen to a solid, red statue, atop the hopelessly exsanguinating body of Firth. Thom Na, with a swing of his cudgel, shattered the Sarcoptis into a thousand shards of sarcite.

Ereben had difficulty focusing his eyes. He carefully disabled the Gnomish Sphere, and returned it to its bag. The world spun.

ꕥ

There is but a single certainty in all of life. It is the assurance that whatever outcome we imagine for any event will always be incorrect.

Ereben Leaf: Chronicle of the Counterspell

Ereben opened his eyes. He lay on a pallet within a small, semi-circular chamber with heavy wood beams above him. Light entered through several small slits partway up the curved wall, and cast a bright glow onto a flat, wooden wall with a closed door. No one else was there. He attempted to sit up, but discovered himself to be too weak to do so.

He tried to call out for someone, but found his feeble voice to be only a hoarse whisper. His tongue felt dry and thick. He drifted into sleep, dreaming of a colossal battle of four great armies, and of a Sarcoptis and a dragon and death. Death all around him. He dreamed of Phaena.

I am in Ironhole Keep! Ereben awakened to discover an unfamiliar Dwarf girl seated on a stool beside him, wiping his brow with a damp rag.

She lurched backwards, nearly falling from her stool. "Maister Ereben hes woke!" she called out, wringing her hands with her rag.

After a noisy ascent of a stairway, Yarnish Blen rushed into the chamber. He appeared to be truly surprised. "You've come back to us, Ereben."

"Blen. The battle is over?", he rasped.

"The battle is over. The war is over."

"What happened?"

"Firth is dead. The remnants of his knights have surrendered their weapons, and dispersed. King Kalish is dead, along with nearly all of his military."

Ereben attempted to grasp what Yarnish Blen had just described. "How long..." He cleared his throat. "Water?" he asked the Dwarf girl. "How long have I been here?"

"We thought you were dead in the field. That was ten days ago. You have not tossed or turned or stirred in any way since Thom Na carried you here in his arms."

"Ten d..." Ereben paused. "The counterspell. I exhausted the munu, but continued to use the sphere. Where is the s..."

Blen pointed to a collection of Ereben's belongings against the round wall. The cloth bag with the Gnomish Sphere rested on the floor, beside a glistening red staff of blood locust.

The Dwarf girl lifted Ereben's head, and allowed him to sip water from a clay bowl.

"It stole life from me. Where is everybody?"

"Many remained here for a week, hoping you might recover. Then they reluctantly returned to their homes."

"Phaena?"

"She remained until yesterday."

"Yesterday!" An ache swelled within his chest. "Where has she gone?" His eyes were too dry to provide tears to match his anguish.

Yarnish Blen lowered his head. "She...needed to return to the Dryads. She lives there now. Phaena wanted you to know the words of the pythia at Parnoth, should you awaken. I recorded them." Blen rummaged through Ereben's belongings, and lifted a single sheet of vellum. He handed it to Ereben.

Ereben's heart raced. He squinted his eyes, but the writing appeared blurred. "Can you read it to me?"

Blen held the vellum into the light from one of the wall slits. "You must stand up. That which has been divided must be rejoined, or all shall be lost. Strength hides within weakness.

Defeat travels the road of death; victory, no road at all. Even the innocent may bear evil."

"That's all? That's all she wanted me to know?"

"That is all she wanted me to record." He returned the vellum to Ereben's shaky hand. "She felt that it would be important for you to know."

Ereben felt crushed. "Is my grandfather here?"

"He returned to the high mountains with his ice leopards."

"Minkar? Bahsa? Barrow? Liddie? Jasper? Where have they all gone?"

"Minkar has taken his son back to Shouda. Barrow is rebuilding Zink. I don't know where Liddie might be. As for Jasper, he has gone back to Timbul with the trolls."

"But..."

"Ereben, they all care about you. They need to carry on with their lives, now that the war is over. None of us had ever seen someone wake from so long a sleep. I will send messages, so they will all know that you have returned to us."

Ereben lay silently for a while. "...victory, no road at all. I know what it is like to be a rock. Can you find me a pipe and some coltsfoot leaf?"

THE END

of volume two

Appendix 1

States of Matter and their Paths of Transformation

(Asserting that there must exist more than four paths of transformation)

Structure by Wilder. Translated by Ailantha.
Ereben Leaf: Chronicle of the Counterspell, Documents

Axiom 1. Every path of transformation is a collection of states of matter.

Axiom 2. There exist at least two states of matter.

Axiom 3. If ***s*** and ***t*** are states of matter, then there exists one and only one path of transformation containing both ***s*** and ***t***.

Axiom 4. If ***P*** is a path of transformation, then there exists a state of matter not on ***P***.

Axiom 5. If ***P*** is a path of transformation, and ***s*** is a state of matter not on ***P***, then there exists one and only one path of transformation containing ***s*** that has no conjunction with ***P***.

Definition: If a state of matter ***s*** is an element of the collection of states of matter which constitute a path of transformation ***P*** (see Axiom 1), then we may say that ***P*** contains ***s***, ***s*** is on ***P***, or ***P*** is a path of transformation containing ***s***.

Definition: Two paths of transformation $\boldsymbol{P_1}$ and $\boldsymbol{P_2}$ are said to have no conjunction if there is no state of matter which is on both $\boldsymbol{P_1}$ and $\boldsymbol{P_2}$.

Theorem 1. Every state of matter is on at least two paths of transformation.

Proof. Let ***s*** denote any state of matter. Since by Axiom 2 there exist at least two states of matter, there must exist a state of matter ***t*** distinct from ***s***. By Axiom 3 there exists a path of transformation ***P*** containing ***s*** and ***t***. By Axiom 4 there exists a state of matter ***u*** not on ***P***, and by Axiom 3 a path of transformation ***Q*** containing ***s*** and ***u***.

By Axiom 1 every path of transformation is a collection of states of matter. For two paths of transformation to be distinct, one of the two collections must contain a state of matter that is not contained by the other collection. The paths of transformation ***P*** and ***Q*** are distinct, then, because ***Q*** contains a state of matter ***u*** which is not contained by ***P***. As ***s*** is contained by both ***P*** and ***Q***, the theorem is proved.

Corollary to Theorem 1. Every path of transformation contains at least one state of matter.

Proof. There exists a state of matter ***s*** by Axiom 2, and by Theorem 1 there exist two distinct paths of transformation P_1 and P_2 containing ***s***. If there exists a path of transformation ***P*** that contains no states of matter, then both P_1 and P_2 have no conjunction. As this would contradict Axiom 5, there can not exist such a path of transformation.

Theorem 2. Every path of transformation contains at least two states of matter.

Proof. Let ***P*** be any path of transformation. By the above corollary, ***P*** contains a state of matter ***s***. Suppose ***s*** is the only state of matter that ***P*** contains. By Theorem 1 there is another path of transformation P_1 containing ***s***. Now P_1 must contain at least one other state of matter, ***t***; otherwise ***P*** and P_1 would each contain only ***s***, hence be the same collection of states of matter and so be the same path of transformation (by Axiom 1). By Axiom 4 there is a state of matter ***u*** which is not on P_1, and by Axiom 5 there is a path of transformation P_2 containing ***u*** and having no conjunction with ***P***. But both ***P*** and P_1 are paths of transformation containing $\boldsymbol{s}$ and not in conjunction with $\boldsymbol{P_2}$, in violation of Axiom 5. We must conclude that the supposition that $\boldsymbol{s}$ is the only state of matter on $\boldsymbol{P}$ can not hold and hence that $\boldsymbol{P}$ contains at least two states of matter.

Corollary to Theorem 2. Every path of transformation is completely determined by any two of its states of matter that are distinct.

Proof. By Axiom 2 there exist at least two distinct states of matter $\boldsymbol{s}$ and $\boldsymbol{t}$. By Axiom 3 there exists a path of transformation $\boldsymbol{P}$ containing $\boldsymbol{s}$ and $\boldsymbol{t}$, and by Axiom 4 there exists a state of matter $\boldsymbol{u}$ not on $\boldsymbol{P}$. By Axiom 5 there exists a path of transformation $\boldsymbol{P_1}$ containing $\boldsymbol{u}$ and not in conjunction with $\boldsymbol{P}$, and by Theorem 2 $\boldsymbol{P_1}$ contains at least two distinct states of matter.

Theorem 4. There exist at least six distinct paths of transformation.

Proof. Given a path of transformation $\boldsymbol{P}$ containing the states of matter $\boldsymbol{s}$ and $\boldsymbol{t}$ and a path of transformation $\boldsymbol{P_1}$ not in conjunction with $\boldsymbol{P}$ and containing two states of matter $\boldsymbol{u}$ and $\boldsymbol{v}$, by Axiom 3 there exist paths of transformation $\boldsymbol{Q}$ and $\boldsymbol{Q_1}$ determined respectively by the pairs of states of matter $(\boldsymbol{s},\boldsymbol{u})$, $(\boldsymbol{t},\boldsymbol{v})$. The state of matter $\boldsymbol{t}$ is not on $\boldsymbol{Q}$, else by Axiom 3 $\boldsymbol{P}$ and $\boldsymbol{Q}$ would be the same path of transformation (which is not true since $\boldsymbol{u}$ is not on $\boldsymbol{P}$). Also, $\boldsymbol{v}$ is not on $\boldsymbol{Q}$, else $\boldsymbol{Q}$ and $\boldsymbol{P_1}$ would be the same path of transformation. Similarly, $\boldsymbol{s}$ is not on $\boldsymbol{Q}$, and $\boldsymbol{u}$ is not on $\boldsymbol{Q_1}$. Now there also exist paths of transformation $\boldsymbol{R}$ and $\boldsymbol{R_1}$, determined respectively by the pairs of states of matter $(\boldsymbol{s},\boldsymbol{v})$, $(\boldsymbol{t},\boldsymbol{u})$; and we can show that $\boldsymbol{t}$ is not on $\boldsymbol{R}$, $\boldsymbol{u}$ is not on $\boldsymbol{R}$, $\boldsymbol{s}$ is not on $\boldsymbol{R_1}$ and $\boldsymbol{v}$ is not on $\boldsymbol{R_1}$. It follows that no two of the paths $\boldsymbol{P}$, $\boldsymbol{P_1}$, $\boldsymbol{Q}$, $\boldsymbol{Q_1}$, $\boldsymbol{R}$, $\boldsymbol{R_1}$ are the same.

The discussion regarding the implications of there being at least six paths of transformation has been lost.

Appendix 2

Anonymous Aphorisms on the Second Law

Collected from various document fragments.

Ereben Leaf: Chronicle of the Counterspell, Documents

Overall, chaos never diminishes.

In general, any spontaneous change in the state of things will lead to an increase in chaos.

The Second Law signifies that everything tends toward a balanced state of most likely arrangement, the one which is most chaotic.

Ordered arrangements tend to degenerate into disordered ones.

The long-term behavior of everything is characterized by a succession of fluctuations in chaos, with an almost certain return upward from any low value that it attains.

The Second Law is an overwhelming tendency for organization to move toward chaos.

Any living thing delays its decay into death with its capacity to maintain itself at a fairly high level of orderliness, by continually discarding its own chaos into its surroundings.

Every local increase in orderliness must come at the expense of an even greater increase in the chaos of its neighbors.

The Second Law represents the gentle sea of chaos that, little by little, wears away the jagged reefs of orderliness.

www.ingramcontent.com/pod-product-compliance
Lightning Source LLC
LaVergne TN
LVHW050923080826
845145LV00001B/185

* 9 7 8 0 9 7 6 1 5 5 9 1 1 *